THE WISHING BRIDGE

AN O'BRIEN TALE

STACEY REYNOLDS

The Wishing Bridge: An O'Brien Tale

July 29, 2018
Published by
Stacey Reynolds

❀ Created with Vellum

AUTHOR'S OTHER WORKS

RAVEN OF THE SEA: AN O'BRIEN TALE

A Lantern in the Dark: An O'Brien Tale
Shadow Guardian: An O'Brien Tale
Fio: An O'Brien Novella
River Angels: An O'Brien Tale
The Irish Midwife: An O'Brien Tale
Dark Irish: An O'Brien Novella
Burning Embers: An O'Brien Tale
His Wild Irish Rose: De Clare Legacy
The Last Sip of Wine: A Novel of Tuscany

This book is dedicated to Vic.

List of Characters from The O'Brien Tales Series

Sean O'Brien- Married to Sorcha (Mullen), father to Aidan, Michael, Brigid, Patrick, Liam, Seany (Sean Jr.), brother of William (deceased) and Maeve, son of Aoife and David. Retired and Reserve Garda officer. Native to Doolin, Co. Clare, Ireland.

Sorcha O'Brien- Maiden name of Mullen. Daughter of Michael and Edith Mullen. Sister of John (deceased). Native to Belfast, Northern Ireland. Married to Sean O'Brien with whom she has six children and eight grandchildren. A nurse midwife for over thirty years.

Michael O'Brien- Son of Sean and Sorcha, married to Branna (O'Mara), three children Brian, Halley, and Ian. Rescue swimmer for the Irish Coast Guard. Twin to Brigid.

Branna (O'Mara) O'Brien- American, married to Michael. Orphaned when her father was killed in the 2nd Battle of Fallujah (Major Brian O'Mara, USMC) and then lost her mother, Meghan (Kelly) O'Mara to breast cancer six years later. Mother to Brian, Halley, and Ian. Real Estate investor.

Capt. Aidan O'Brien, Royal Irish Regiment- Son and eldest child of Sean and Sorcha O'Brien. Married to Alanna (Falk). Father of two children, David (Davey) and Isla. Serves active duty in the Royal Irish Regiment and currently living in Shropshire, England.

Alanna (Falk) O'Brien- American, married to Aidan, daughter of Hans Falk and Felicity Richards (divorced). Stepdaughter of Doctor Mary Flynn of Co. Clare. Mother to Davey and Isla. Best friend to Branna. Clinical Psychologist working with British military families battling PTSD and traumatic brain injuries.

Brigid (O'Brien) Murphy- Daughter of Sean and Sorcha, Michael's twin, married to Finn Murphy. Mother to Cora, Colin, and Declan.

Finn Murphy- Husband to Brigid. Father of Cora, Colin, and Declan. I.T. expert who works in Ennis but does consulting work with the Garda on occasion.

Cora Murphy- Daughter of Brigid and Finn. Has emerging gifts of pre-cognition and other psychic abilities. Oldest grandchild of Sean and Sorcha.

Patrick O'Brien- Son of Sean and Sorcha. Married to Caitlyn (Nagle). Currently residing in Dublin after joining the Garda. Serving on the National Security Surveillance Unit on the Armed Response Team.

Caitlyn (Nagle) O'Brien- Daughter of Ronan and Bernadette Nagle, sister to Madeline and Mary. Married to Patrick. Early education teacher. English as a second language teacher for small children. No children of her own as she has fertility issues. Native to Co. Clare.

Dr. Liam O'Brien- Second youngest child of Sean and Sorcha. Currently abroad and finishing his residency while on a medical mission in Manaus, Brazil. Internal medicine and infectious disease. Recently engaged to Dr. Izzy Collier.

Sean (Seany) O'Brien Jr.- Youngest child of Sean and Sorcha. Serving with the fire services in Dublin. Trained paramedic and fireman. Unmarried and no children.

Tadgh O'Brien- Only son of William (deceased) and Katie (Donoghue) O'Brien. Special Detectives Unit of the Garda. Married to Charlie Ryan.

Charlotte aka Charlie (Ryan) O'Brien- American FBI Agent with the International Human Rights Crime Division. Married to Tadgh. Sister to Josh. Currently working in Europe as the liaison to Interpol.

Josh O'Brien- Formerly Joshua Albert Ryan until he changed his name. Lives in Dublin with his sister Charlie and his brother-in-law Tadgh. Attending junior college for Maritime Studies.

Dr. Mary Flynn-Falk- Retired M.D., wife of Hans Falk. Stepmother to Alanna O'Brien and Captain Erik Falk, USMC.

Sgt. Major Hans Falk, USMC Ret.- American, father of Alanna and Erik. Married to Doc Mary. Retired from the United States Marine Corps.

Daniel McPherson- Son of Molly Price and Jonathan (John) Mullen. Just recently found the Mullen family. Was an unknown offspring of John, who never knew he had a son. Raised in the Scottish borderlands by his English mother. Molly Price married an old friend who claimed Daniel as his son.

Maeve (O'Brien) Carrington- Daughter of David and Aoife. Wife to Nolan, mother to Cian and Cormac. Sister of Sean Sr

Katie (Donoghue) O'Brien- Native to Inis Oirr, Aran Islands. Widow of William O'Brien. Mother of Tadgh O'Brien.

David O'Brien- Husband of Aoife, father of Sean, William, and Maeve. The oldest living patriarch of the O'Brien family.

Aoife (Kerr) O'Brien- Wife of David O'Brien, mother of Sean, William, and Maeve. Originally from Co. Donegal.

Michael Mullen- Native to Belfast, Northern Ireland, married to Edith (Kavanagh). Father of Sorcha and John.

Edith (Kavanagh) Mullen- Married to Michael Mullen, mother of Sorcha and John.

Dr. Isolde (Izzy) Collier- Doctor/Surgeon recently detached from the United States Navy. Originally born in Wilcox, Arizona. Close friend to Alanna O'Brien. Daughter of Rhys and Donna Collier, apricot and apple farmers in eastern Arizona. Engaged to Dr. Liam O'Brien.

Jenny- Daytime barmaid at Gus O'Connor's Pub

St. Clare's Charity Mission

The Sisters

Reverend Mother Faith- From Co. Sligo, Ireland. Abbess and boss lady at the mission. Seventy years old.

Sister Maria- Native to Brazil. The sister who is in charge of the orfanato and school.

Sister Catherine- Native to Ireland. Works in the hospital as a nurse midwife.

Sister Agatha- Native to Ireland. A novice nun who helps with the technology and administrative aspects of the abbey and mission, as well as helping with the children.

***Other sisters occupy the abbey, but these sisters have played a key role in the stories.

The Local Staff of St. Clare

Paolo- Groundskeeper and handyman of the mission.

Gabriela- The cook for the entire mission and in charge of the cantina.

Raphael- Brazilian military and the full-time security for the mission. Also acts as an interpreter for the volunteers.

The Médicos of St. Clare

Dr. Seamus O'Keefe- Native to Ireland. OB-GYN.

Dr. Antonio Rinalto- Native to Italy. Lives and works in Manaus at a private hospital, but volunteers once a month at St. Clare's Hospital as a general surgeon.

Dr. Quinn Maguire- Native to Ireland. Pediatrician.

Pedro- The laboratory technician for the hospital.

***There are other local staff that work at the hospital who are not listed, as they play no key role in the story.

Orphaned children in residence at St. Clare's Charity Mission

Genoveva- 15 yrs.

Emilio- 17 yrs.

Henrico- 16 yrs.

Luca- 14 yrs.

Rosalis- 14 yrs.

Cristiano- 12 yrs.

Estela- 3 yrs.

***There are currently over twenty children in the orphanage. The listed children are those most featured in the storyline.

PROLOGUE

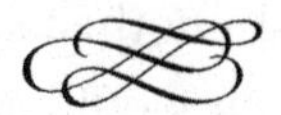

DOOLIN, CO. CLARE, IRELAND

But to see her was to love her, love but her, and love forever—
Robert Burns

Caitlyn stirred in the soft sheets and old mattress as the morning light touched her face. She could hear the surf; the window opened for fresh air. She turned and had to suppress a giggle. The guest room at her parents' home was lovely. It had the best view in the house, but the bed she currently shared left not a spare inch of space when she occupied it with her husband. He'd fallen asleep on his side, which wasn't usual. He normally slept on his stomach; his face always turned toward her. As if even in his sleep, she commanded his undivided attention. Now he had his arms pulled in, his knees up toward his chest, trying to fit (both in length and width) into the tiny iron bed. They'd taken to throwing blankets and pillows on the floor when they made love. The bed squeaked its protest with the slightest movement and would never withstand the power that the two generated when they came together. She felt an ache in her chest as well as lower, deep in her belly. A stirring that hadn't waned with four years of marriage. When he came to her, the world disappeared. With the desperation of new lovers, the wanting was always there. An under-current in every moment, together or separated.

She'd had the dream again. The one that would take her about a quarter mile to the west. To the craggy shore of the Atlantic. The same beach she'd been to a hundred times. The dream was always the same. She approached the stone beach, Patrick's back to her. He held a child in the crook of his arm, and another stood at his side, holding his hand. Two children. The dream would always end before her view of them could come into focus. All she felt was an overwhelming swell of love. Caitlyn looked over again, away from the window that she'd shifted her gaze to instinctively. Patrick's eyes were open.

"Good morning, love. You're looking wide awake," Patrick said. He had a boyish smile and mischievous eyes. "I must not have worked you out hard enough last night. Maybe I'm losing my touch."

He gave her a rakish smile. She couldn't resist. "Aye, you might be at that," she said with a shrug. She was under him in a flash, his big body pressed into her. She couldn't suppress her squeals. "Take it back, woman, or you won't get a lick of sleep tonight. I'll roger you until you can't move."

She lifted her face, her hands pinned against the mattress. "Promises, promises."

Patrick growled, taking her mouth as he pressed his arousal into her. Squeaking bed be damned. Then they both heard the footsteps. There was no lock on the guest room door. Caitlyn's sister Madeline did a drive-by remark into the crack of the door. "Would you two knock it off! You're corrupting your younger sisters." Caitlyn cursed under her breath as she heard Mary, her other sister, laugh. Then Caitlyn's mother piped in.

Patrick sighed as his mother-in-law's voice carried down the hall. "Stop that, the both of you. Give them some privacy for pity's sake." *Good old Bernadette.* He'd heard tales from his friends and brothers about how small, meddling children could interfere with your sex life and had no respect for the marriage bed. But he was certain that little sisters and mothers-in-law were at the top of the list of cock-blockers in all of humanity.

He rolled off of Caitlyn, taking her with him. She straddled his hips, and he thought again about just going for it. She was so beautiful in the morning. Tousled hair and drowsy eyes sparkling green like emeralds. She pulled him out of his thoughts, surprising him. "Let's go for a walk. After we've had a bit of breakfast, let's walk to the sea."

They dressed and came into the kitchen, the smell of baked goods penetrating the fog of morning. "This bread your mother makes is the best in the county, I swear it." Bernadette, or Bernie to her loved ones, said to Patrick. They'd seen his parents yesterday and had dinner with his family. Branna and Michael had brought the twins, Brian and Halley, and their newest addition to the family, little Ian. Brigid and Finn came as well, with their three children. Cora, who was the oldest, and their two sons Colin and Declan. It had been good to see them all. Dublin wasn't so very far, but he missed them when the weeks ticked by without a visit. His mother had baked the entire day, as well as cooking up a delicious bacon boil. She'd sent her cranberry bread to the Nagle family, as she always did. If not bread, then cookies or hand pies.

"I can make you some eggs and bangers if you like. You can start with that and some tea." Bernie was an amazing woman. Some men complained about their in-laws, but he'd lucked out in that department.

"No thank you. This will do just fine. Caitlyn has a mind to take a walk this morning."

Caitlyn accepted a plate of bread as well and went about putting the butter over it and then some marmalade. "Yes, mammy. It's a grand, fresh morning. I want to see the surf. Then we'll head back to the city." Patrick watched as Caitlyn's mother came around the corner and enveloped Caitlyn in her arms. She was a good mother. She loved her daughters to distraction. She was a retired teacher, which is probably why his Caitlyn had been drawn to the profession. She pushed the hair off Caitlyn's face and kissed her forehead. "My darling girl. I wish you lived closer." That tweaked at Patrick's heart. His mother said the same thing to them.

Ronan, his father-in-law, came in behind them and gave his shoulder a squeeze. "A little more time on the job and maybe you can transfer."

* * *

CAITLYN APPROACHED the rocky shore with Patrick at her side. Even in the time between late summer and early autumn, the breeze was crisp. The sea mist was cold. The grey rocks were solid under her feet, steadying her a little. She was nervous. Patrick was holding her hand, and she looked at him. His eyes were so blue, with just a hint of green that reminded her of the sea. His hair, for the most part, was brown. But he had those auburn highlights that blazed in the morning sun. And his stubble was coppery like the hair on his body. He was beautiful.

"Did I ever tell you that I dream of this spot? Right here on this bit of beach," Caitlyn said. Her voice sounded as if she was between reality and the dreaming.

Patrick raised a brow. "No, ye never did. Is it homesickness, do you think?" Guilt washed over him. The idea of being in the city had excited them, but this western shore was beginning to pull at both of them. The Wild Atlantic Way was a good name for it. The nickname for the western shore of Ireland. It was wild and unruly and ancient. And it's where both of their families were.

"No, I had it when we lived here as well. It's not just the beach. You're in the dream."

He straightened at that. "You never told me."

"Aye, well. It's a bit silly, I suppose, believing in dreams. It's just, it never changes. It's the same every time. It's not terribly clear but..."

"But what?" He turned her now, facing him. The sight of her green eyes took his breath. There were tears. "What, darlin'?"

"You're never alone. You hold a child in your arms, and another is at your side. I used to think they were our children...but then..." She closed her eyes. "Then I lost the two pregnancies and wondered if maybe…" Her breath caught. He pulled her closer. "No, let me get this out. I thought that maybe it was their souls. The two we lost." She was crying now.

"Oh, my love. Don't cry. Please. We're enough, you and I." She shook her head.

"I know you say that, but I also know you want children. We talked about it when we were seeing each other. Before you asked me to marry you, you told me you wanted a big family. I did too. I feel like I've failed." He hugged her tight.

"No! Never. Do you hear me? Never, Caitlyn. You're everything. You're the pulse in my veins. The breath of my body. All I need is you." He took her face and kissed her. Kissed away any protest she might offer. He had the sort of kiss that a woman felt down to her toes. She smiled under his mouth. "That's my girl," he said sweetly.

"No, I'm smiling because I have some news." He backed up enough to see her face. "I'm pregnant Patrick. I really think this time is different. It's why I waited to bring you here. I think this time it will stick." He had a mixed look of joy and puzzlement on his face.

"I'm happy, darling. So happy. But I don't understand. Do you feel differently this time?" She shook her head.

"Then why? I worry for you. You know that. I'd rather not have kids than to keep putting your health at risk."

"I know because this is the longest I've ever made it. The doctor said…" she stopped as his expression changed.

"What do you mean? You've been to the doctor? Caitlyn, how far along are you? How long have you known?"

She smiled, not picking up on his tone. Not letting herself hear it. "I'm twelve weeks." He reared back like she'd slapped him. "What's wrong? I thought you'd be happy."

"You're entering into your second trimester, and you are just now telling me? Jesus Christ, woman. What were you thinking, keeping this from me?"

"I wanted to wait. I didn't want to disappoint you again. I figured…"

"You figured what? That if you lost it, I never needed to know? Like our child is just some stressor, some inconvenience that I never needed to know about?"

She stopped, swallowing. "I thought you'd be happy about the baby."

"Of course I am! I'm ready to split down the middle right now! Half of me is happy, excited, hopeful because you've come this far. And the other half is scared shitless and pissed off. You're my wife, Caitlyn. We are supposed to do this together. The good and the bad. The pain and the joy. Would you have even told me if you'd miscarried? Or would you have kept the whole thing from me?"

She folded into herself. "I don't know. I was just afraid to hope. And I thought if I kept it quiet, only one of us had to face this goddamn crucible over the last two months! I don't know why I did it!" Her volume raised, she was shouting now. Then she shoved him. "You're spoiling this! I had it planned! I planned this weekend to tell you, ye bloody-minded, stubborn, pushy dickhead!"

Her chin was up, and her eyes were sparking. She had her fist coiled like she wanted to punch him, and Patrick only had one thought. The rest of the bullshit drained out of him. As he looked at his beautiful, handful of a mate, he thought…*She's back.* He pulled her to him and kissed her, shutting down her tirade. They were both a little edgy. Both pissed off and happy in equal measure. A confusing and intoxicating sensation that they put full force into their kiss. It was only when some sea kayakers hooted at them that Patrick realized that he could not, in fact, shove his wife's knickers aside and mount her on the closest patch of flat rock. He pulled away just enough to speak as she panted against his mouth. "Welcome back." Then he picked her up and swung her around, delighting in her laughter as it caught on the coastal wind.

CHAPTER 1

DUBLIN, IRELAND—SIX WEEKS LATER

Everyone can master grief by he that has it—William Shakespeare

Patrick ran toward the bus, making it just as the driver began closing the doors. He jumped on as the brakes hissed their release, showing the driver his city bus pass. He stood, taking in the crowd of tourists and commuters. Caitlyn was taking the car today, headed to her doctor's office to give a blood sample. The weight of her condition was a constant stressor. As happy as he was about the child, he couldn't shake the fear that surrounded the whole business. She'd lost two pregnancies already, at the end of the first trimester. She said it was different this time. She felt positive, and he was trying like hell to get on board. He wanted children, yes, but not at the expense of Caitlyn's health.

He thumbed through his phone, finding the text from his mother. It had been a follow-up to the ultrasound photo he'd sent. *Looking good. The hardest part is over.* God, he hoped so. Another text came in from his father. He'd spoken to Liam and Izzy in Brazil. It was incredible news. Last time they'd all seen Izzy, she was headed to the

Brazilian city of Manaus to find Liam. And what a blessing that was. Apparently, she'd gotten through to that thick-headed brother of his, because after months with no word, Liam had finally called home.

The thought of Liam made Patrick's mind wander into dangerous territory. When Liam's girlfriend Eve had been murdered last year, it had devastated the family. Hell, it had rocked the entire city. Dublin had lost one of its bright and shining stars. The life of a local girl had been snuffed out in a senseless act of violence.

The thought of something happening to his beloved Caitlyn caused Patrick's skin to prickle across his back and chest. He looked out the window as the bus came to a stop. He could see the river. One more stop and he'd step off into the street and head to work. Today they were working the Dublin Port. Running training drills.

He loved his job. He'd been promoted a year ago to the National Security Surveillance Unit and been placed on the Armed Response Team. It was exciting, as Garda jobs went. On occasion, his work intersected with his cousin Tadgh's, and on an even rarer occurrence, Tadgh's wife. Charlie was a U.S. FBI agent that was stationed abroad, working as a liaison in Europe for the FBI's International Human Rights Crime Unit. She and Tadgh had fallen in love while working together on a joint task force. Like a lightning strike, Tadgh had been done for. It happened like that with O'Brien men.

It had been the same with Caitlyn. She'd gone to an all-girls school, so Patrick hadn't met her during their younger school years. He'd gone to university in Galway and met her by chance, even though they only lived about ten miles from each other as the crow flies. He'd been struck stupid at the sight of her.

The bus driver yelled out the stop, and he came back to himself, exiting with several other riders. He walked toward his headquarters, ready to distract himself with some door kicking and room clearing.

* * *

PATRICK SAT across from his cousin Tadgh, watching in fascination as his lovely wife wolfed down a double cheeseburger and a platter of chips. Tadgh was smiling as well, and Patrick shook his head. Charlie froze mid-bite. "What?"

"Where do you put it all? Do you run marathons in your spare time?" Patrick said with a smile.

"I have a fast metabolism. I need my strength," she said with a shrug. Tadgh stole one of her chips, and she eyed him aggressively. "You have your own."

Tadgh grinned as he chewed. "I know, but they taste better when they're stolen. Like kisses." She warmed at that.

"All right you two, no honeymoon looks over the table. What's this about? Tadgh never offers to buy me lunch unless he's got some sort of scheme."

"I resent that!" Tadgh said, but he knew Patrick was only teasing.

Charlie nudged him. "We just wanted to touch base. We work such crazy shifts, we've barely seen you two. We've been worried about her. How is she?"

Patrick's brow furrowed. "She's fine. I mean, I think she's fine. Did she say something?"

Charlie put a hand up. "No, no. Not at all. It's just, she looks tired. Josh helped her up with the groceries a couple of days ago and she was complaining about having a stitch in her abdomen. She said it was growing pains, but I just want to make sure she's okay."

"Aye, well Mam says that's normal. Her muscles are stretching. She's just starting to get a little swell in her belly. She's on her feet too much. I told her to quit her job, but she loves the children. And we need the money. Dublin rent is a bit dear. I don't have to tell you that."

"Well, maybe once Seany moves in and starts paying half the rent, she'll reconsider," Tadgh said. "It's good of you, by the way, taking him in like this. He didn't fancy living with a stranger. Since Liam never came back, the last couple months have been tight."

"Yes, well we've got the room. For now anyway. He may transfer out after the baby comes. I think he's disenchanted with the city life," Patrick said. "I can't blame him. I wouldn't mind getting out of the city either. Maybe I could look into a transfer to Shannon and commute from the coast, once the baby comes. Michael does it twice a week."

Tadgh said, "We've talked about it as well. Our work is in Dublin, but it might be worth the commute to get a house somewhere out of the city. Especially if..." Charlie kicked him under the table.

Patrick looked between them. "What's this? Are you pregnant, then?"

"No! God, no. Not yet. It's just, well, I'm twenty-eight. It'll happen eventually. We were just talking. No solid plans."

Patrick leaned back in his chair, a speculative smile as he looked over the two of them. "I think you'd be amazing parents. Good for you."

* * *

CAITLYN WAS SQUATTED down on her haunches, trying to process the problem before her. The tear-stained face looking back at her was enough to break her heart...if the reason for the tears hadn't been what it was.

"Jason, I think we need to go see Nurse Julie. Perhaps she'll have a better idea of what to do."

One of the young boys behind her yelled, "She's going to cut it off!" Which started a fresh batch of tears.

"Jonathon Clancy, I said that's enough!" She used her best school teacher tone. She couldn't be too hard on them. They were only four and five-year-old children. She looked back down at the water bottle, the green felt, plastic eyes, and red stripes glued to it in attempt to make it look like a hungry caterpillar. This one, in particular, had decided to try and gobble up the little four-year-old's manly appendage. She shook her head wondering how in the world he'd managed to get the damned thing stuck in the mouth of the bottle. She had her suspicions that he'd been dared to do it by none other than little Johnny Clancy, the designated class instigator. She gave Jason one of the art smocks to fold in his hands and hold in front of himself, and they walked down to the nurse's office. Her teaching partner kept her eyes diverted, trying with all her might not to burst into laughter.

* * *

PATRICK WAS LAUGHING SO HARD, he dropped his salad fork and started coughing. Caitlyn handed him a glass of water. "It wasn't funny! You should have seen the nurse's face!"

He wiped his mouth, his face flushed with mirth. "So what did you do? Give it a yank?"

"Heavens no! He'd already tried that, which made it worse. I didn't want to damage his little thingy before he ever had a chance to use it!" She was laughing now, despite herself. "No, in the end, it was simple. As a man, I'm sure you're familiar with the phenomenon of shrinkage."

"Oh, you didn't." Patrick's face was aghast.

"No, I didn't. We called the boy's house, told the father the problem. First, he told the nurse to castrate the little fecker because he was obviously too daft to be allowed to breed." One corner of her mouth turned up as Patrick cracked off a laugh. "Then, he told us to go dunk the boy in the cold river. That would sort him out. Which is how she thought of the solution. A big tumbler of ice water and it retreated like a little hermit crab. The bottle popped off without incident."

Caitlyn stood, ready to grab the pot of soup she'd been heating on the stove. The pain in her back stopped her short. "Ach, damn."

Patrick was on his feet in an instant. "Are you okay?"

She nodded, waving him away. "My muscles are all out of whack. You know, stretching. I'm fine."

"How was your appointment?" Patrick's face was strained, even though he was seated again.

Caitlyn stood before him and smoothed a hand over his short hair. "It wasn't an appointment. My doctor is in Tahiti. It was just a blood draw. Different standard tests. A couple more weeks and I'll have my next ultrasound. When he gets back from holiday. He'll be able to tell us whether it's a boy or a girl. You can tell now, but the bloody doctor decided to take a holiday instead of being at my beck and call."

Patrick ran a hand over her belly. It was just barely swollen. A sweet little bump where she carried their child. Caitlyn had just started wearing roomier clothes, excited to hit the maternity shops and feed her fashion jones. Just yesterday, she'd felt it move for the first time. Like a butterfly flapping its wings. That's how she described it. A fluttering. "I don't care about the gender. All I care about is that you're both okay."

Caitlyn smiled, kissing him soundly on the mouth. Her long, blonde hair brushed his shoulder and cheek. "We're both fine." She straightened and grimaced a bit. "I think I'll go have a shower. Maybe the hot water will do me some good."

PATRICK RAN to the phone just before it stopped ringing. It was his mother. "Hello, mam. How's everyone in the west?" Patrick spoke with his mother for a few minutes, catching up about the calls that Liam had made to them from Brazil. Then Sorcha asked to speak to Caitlyn. He was just about to see if she was out of the bath and dressed when she appeared in the bedroom door. She was starkly white, agony showing on her face. Then he saw the blood through her yoga pants. She reached for him, blood on her hand. So much blood. "Patrick," she moaned his name as she started to go down. He dropped the phone and ran to her. His mother forgotten.

"Oh, God. Caitlyn, no!" He fumbled for the phone, "Mam, I need to call an ambulance!" Then he ended the call and dialed 999 for emergency services. Caitlyn was trembling, quiet sobs were all the noises she made.

Caitlyn was dying...at least it felt like she was. Or maybe she just wished she was. She wasn't in pain anymore. Just terribly cold and incredibly sad. *Our baby.* She knew the coldness wasn't from the blood loss. It was due to the fact that her baby was leaving her. The shelter she'd given the child, warm in her body, had failed its most simple function. So the baby was leaving her alone. She felt so empty.

* * *

TADGH RAN THROUGH THE HEADQUARTERS, almost knocking his boss out of his sensible loafers. "What the hell is it, lad?"

Tadgh was pretty close to going apeshit. "It's Caitlyn. Patrick's wife. She's miscarrying. It's bad! I've got to go!"

"Aye, son. Go ahead. I'll find Charlie. Does his da know?" Sullivan asked.

"Yes, his parents know. They've called her parents as well. I just don't want him at the hospital alone. Try calling the fire station. We need Seany!"

* * *

AS SOON AS Sean Jr. heard the address for a paramedic run, he knew what it was. "Caitlyn. Oh, Jesus." He yelled to his Lieutenant, then hopped a ride in the ambulance. He was a trained paramedic, but he was assigned as a firefighter until a position opened up. His boss was a family man, though, and he was willing to let him go. As they ripped through the Dublin streets, he tried Patrick's phone, but it went straight to voicemail. *Female, 28 years of age. 18 weeks pregnant, hemorrhaging, possible miscarriage.* He put his head in his hands and prayed.

* * *

PATRICK WAS SANDWICHED between Sean Jr. and Tadgh, waiting for Caitlyn to be transferred to her own room. That's when he saw his mother. The despair quivered through his body, a wave of pain that landed in the space between his throat and his chest. She came to him gently, like a rider that was approaching a skittish horse. Like she was afraid he would shatter. He was pretty fucking close. She knelt down, taking his face in her palms. All he could think of to say was, "It was a boy." Then he let go. He finally allowed the grief to pour out of him. As if his mother, the one who kissed his cuts and bruises and chased bad dreams away, had drawn forth the anguish from his body. He bled in her arms.

"I'm so sorry, my lad. I'm so very sorry."

The doctor came through the swinging door, and the group stood in unison. "Can I see her?" Patrick croaked, barely able to speak. The doctor's look of compassion almost undid him. "Yes, Mr. O'Brien. She's starting to come around. I think it would be best for you to be there when she wakes up. She may know already, given her condition when she came in, but we'll need to tell her about the fetus."

"Child. It was a child. Our son. Not a fetus." Patrick snapped.

"Of course. I'm sorry. The child. And we have grief counselors. I know her doctor is on holiday. I would be happy to take her case over in the doctor's absence. I'm sorry I couldn't do more. I did manage to take care. The..." he stopped and corrected himself, "I mean your son. He's whole. Some people don't want to, but you can see him if you want. You can say goodbye."

Sorcha felt her son start to tremble in her embrace. She almost answered for him, but he stiffened and sat up. "I would. I need to see Caitlyn first. Then we can do it together if she's up to it."

* * *

SORCHA WATCHED her son leave with the doctor, and she felt herself crack down the middle. Then Seany and Tadgh were on either side of her. Charlie took her hand. She hadn't even noticed her come in. "I don't know how to help them."

Charlie took her in her arms. "You're here, Sorcha. That's all you can do." Charlie looked up as Sean Sr. appeared, and Caitlyn's parents, Katie, and Caitlyn's two sisters were behind him. The evening seemed to continue like that. A steady stream of family showing up, bringing sack dinners and fresh cups of tea. Making phone calls. Ronan and Bernie took turns going in to see their daughter. Then Madeline and Mary, her sisters, took their turns. The whole display was heartbreaking. Josh had been a huge help, taking care to keep the little ones busy after the rest of the O'Briens showed up, but he needed a break. Charlie said, "Josh, honey. I have an idea. Why don't you and Seany take Caitlyn's sisters out to get a real dinner? They need some downtime."

Tadgh heard the exchange. "That's a brilliant idea."

He dug in his wallet, but Seany stopped him. "I've got this brother."

As Madeline and Mary took orders, promising to bring back some take-away, they started toward the main hospital entrance. Madeline, the older of the two, turned to Seany. They'd gone to school together. "Thank you for this. We needed a break. It's all a bit much. The waiting is the hardest. They only let us have a few minutes. She was..." her voice cracked, and Seany put his arm around her. "She's so pale. She didn't really say much. It's like the life has been drained out of her."

Her younger sister spoke then. "Patrick has been wonderful. I know this is hard for him as well. He tries to be strong for her. I hope I have a husband like him someday."

Seany smiled. "Aye, you will. Just learn how to weed out the tossers early on." They walked and chatted, finding the restaurant they were looking for. It was a small Indian place the locals liked. The tourists stuck to the pubs and higher end places. This little shop was mostly takeaway, but there were a handful of tables, and they had great chai. Sean Jr. looked over to speak to Josh, who'd been very quiet. That's when he saw it. It was subtle, but it was there.

Josh was watching Madeline out of the corner of his eye. They were close in age, so it wasn't really a surprise. Both of Caitlyn's sisters were beautiful. Long blonde hair, pale skin, beautiful eyes. Mary, the younger one by a couple of years, had bright green eyes like Caitlyn. But Madeline's were the color of her mother's. They were almost grey, with a mix of deep blue and mossy green. Like the sea during a storm. Seany had never fancied her. Not in a romantic way. They'd been schoolmates and friends. She was more like family. But Josh had stars in his eyes. *Interesting.*

* * *

CAITLYN WOKE IN SLOW DEGREES, hearing unfamiliar sounds and muffled voices. She opened her eyes, and Patrick was there, holding her hand. Still right by her side. She had vague recollections of her parents coming in, and her mother crying. She'd cried herself hoarse as well. Now she just felt empty. His face, so familiar, kept her grounded. "Water," she croaked. He snapped to attention, pouring her some ice water from the plastic pitcher. She drank deeply, feeling the chalkiness in her throat and on her lips subside. She put the cup down and looked at him. "Did you see him? Did you see our son?" The tears started again as if by hydrating that small amount, she'd renewed her ability to cry.

"I wanted to wait for you. If you are ready, we can get you in a chair. I don't think you should walk yet. I just...couldn't do it alone." His voice was hoarse. Thick with emotion. "I wanted us to be together. Listen, if you aren't up to this..." She cut him off with a hand to silence him. She said nothing, her throat working overtime to contain the lump. The sobs that would escape and never stop. She pulled her blanket aside and put her legs over the side of the bed. A silent command. He just nodded and went to get the nurse.

The nurse helped transfer Caitlyn into a wheelchair, and they wheeled her down to the place where the child had been cleaned up and swaddled, ready to be taken down to the morgue. Then he would be taken to the crematorium. The hospital had sent a chaplain who stood by silently, prepared to offer his support. He'd blessed the child, even though his spirit was long gone.

It was so very small. The child could have fit in the palm of one of Patrick's hands. But he was their baby, and he'd be treated as such. At eighteen weeks, he had ten fingers and ten toes. He had a little head about the size of a plum and a mouth and a little nose. He was so much more than a fetus to them. Caitlyn had felt him moving inside her body. He'd been alive.

They wept. Each quietly sobbing as they clung to each other and their son. Patrick cradled the child in his hands, wrapped in a tiny blanket, as he leaned into his wife for support. "I'm sorry," Caitlyn said. "I'm so sorry, my lad. I tried." Her voice caught on a sob. "I love you," she whispered as she laid her hand on her son, saying a final goodbye.

* * *

CAITLYN STIRRED as she heard the door to her bedroom open. She'd been allowed to go home after a day. She was surprised to see who it was. "Hello, lass. I didn't mean to disturb you. Patrick went down to Tadgh's to have some supper."

"It's okay, Katie. I wasn't asleep. I was just kind of lying here." Katie came in with a bowl of soup, bread, and two cups of tea.

"I thought maybe I'd sit and have tea with you for a bit. Keep you company."

"That would be nice." Caitlyn gave her a weak smile. She'd been surprised that Katie had come. She was Patrick's aunt and a kind woman. She wasn't around a lot. She spent a lot of time between Galway and Inis Oirr, going between her parents' home and her rented cottage on the island. But she'd been kind to Caitlyn over the years, especially since she'd begun having health problems.

"I'm sorry, lass. That's all I can say. All of the platitudes that people offer after you lose a baby are seldom comforting. At least, they weren't comforting to me." Katie took a sip of her tea, and Caitlyn's eyes shot to hers.

"You lost a baby? I never knew that."

"Aye, I did. Before Tadgh, and it was many years before I was able to conceive again. It was a difficult time, but I had a good man. The best, just like you do. And I think in hindsight, that's what got me through."

"I'm sorry, Katie. Does it ever go away? Do you stop thinking about it?"

"It gets better. I promise you that it does. But you don't forget. My baby would be thirty-nine years old now." She shook her head. "No, you don't forget the ones you've lost, but you learn to be grateful for what you have. You come to peace with it."

"But you have Tadgh. What if I never have a baby?" She wiped a tear from her cheek and Katie took her hand.

"I'm not just talking about being grateful for Tadgh. I was grateful for the love of my life. My William. For as long as I had him, and for the family he gave me. Sorcha and Sean are like my own blood. I have a lot of things to be grateful for, and so do you. And I truly believe that some way, somehow, you will build the family that you want so desperately. I feel it in my bones, sweet girl."

CHAPTER 2

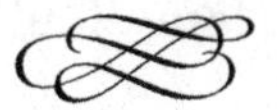

Patrick started the kettle, stretching his shoulders in the early morning dimness of the apartment. He had to work part of the day but would be leaving to pick up Caitlyn and take her for her follow-up appointment. They were at the six week mark, and it had been difficult to wait. For both of them. No sex for six weeks. Caitlyn had tried to weaken him starting at the four-week mark when the bleeding had stopped, but he'd sooner cut his own balls off than put her health at risk.

Besides, he had other talents. He knew plenty of ways to satisfy his woman that didn't involve intercourse. The thought of it, even this early in the morning, made his arousal stir awake. He'd had the day off yesterday. They laid around in their comfortable clothes, shared a light dinner with a little wine. Then he'd shown her just how skillfully he could work around the no sex rule.

He'd started out just trying to make it about her, but she was having none of it. As he leaned over her, his head between her sweet thighs, she'd ferociously fumbled with his fly, hungry for him to join her. *Fuuuuck.* She'd ended up over his face, while she took him in her mouth. He'd cupped her ass and gotten serious, her hips rolling as she arched and climaxed against his mouth.

"And what are you grinning about? Ye look downright devilish, my love." Patrick was startled by Caitlyn's voice. Then he smiled widely.

"Well, if you must know, I was doing a playback in my mind of last night. You were a proper vixen in my bed." Especially when she'd finished him. He shook himself. "I need to go to work. If we keep talking about this, I'm going to be late."

She scooted by him to get a cup from the cabinet, deliberately rubbing her ass against him. "Jesus, Caitlyn. I'm serious." He hissed as he jerked his hips away.

"I know. Very. But it's been six weeks. You know what that means." She gave her own wicked little smile.

"Aye. It means you go back for your follow-up and we let the doctor decide how to proceed."

She waved a hand. "I feel okay. He's going to give me a clean bill of health. Then we can get on with our lives." She turned to him. "We can try again."

Caitlyn saw her husband's body tense. She saw the worry on his face, and his jaw tighten. "I'm fine, Patrick. We'll be fine."

He kept himself from looking at the small urn that was on top of the bookshelf in the sitting room. They hadn't decided where to spread the ashes yet, or maybe they just weren't ready to do it. He didn't look at it, but she sensed his hesitation. Today was not going to be fun. He and the doctor needed to be a united front. They had to be the voice of reason for her sake. She was too fragile and had too much guilt about this whole thing to make a rational decision. They had to make her listen. He would never again sit helplessly in an ambulance and watch his wife bleed out. There were other ways to have children.

THE DOCTOR FINISHED the exam and removed his gloves, looking away as Caitlyn sat up and rearranged her patient gown. Patrick stood next to her, holding her hand. The doctor typed on his computer, then turned to them, giving his full attention. "Everything looks good, Caitlyn. I can't tell you how sorry I am that I wasn't here when this happened." She'd seen the doctor for the last year, switching after her second miscarriage. But it hadn't been the doctor. The problem was with her.

"That's good then. I'm healthy enough to try again." She felt her husband tense and heard him curse under his breath. She shot daggers at him with her eyes. "You heard him, Patrick. I'm okay."

Patrick was so frustrated. How could he make her understand? She'd become obsessed with the idea of having a child. The last three years had taken so much out of her. She was a shadow of the woman she'd been. She took the whole matter on as a personal failure. It was killing him to see her being eaten alive by this.

"Caitlyn, darlin'..." he exhaled, trying to find the words. "This isn't the only way. We can explore other options. I don't want you risking your health. I would rather have no children than to see you go through this again!"

"That's easy for you to say! You're not the problem. You don't have to live with the guilt of knowing..." but he cut her off.

"You think this is easier on me? You think I wouldn't lay down and bleed for you if I could? You think I get a pass on the suffering and heartache? I lost them too! I can't do this anymore!"

The doctor interrupted, standing and taking Caitlyn's other hand. "You need to listen to him. You are partners in this. Perhaps I could bring a counselor in for you to discuss these other options."

"No! I'm healthy. You told me I was. I can do this! Why are you both giving up on me!" She was crying now, and the doctor gave Patrick a compassionate look.

"The problem is, Caitlyn, that you may not be able to do this. You have two different issues working against you. It wouldn't be easy."

"What do you mean, two? The last doctor said I had a hormonal issue. We did the treatments. I got pregnant after that. Three times!"

"Yes, but this was a second-trimester loss, Caitlyn. There's more going on here. I suspected, but this last miscarriage confirmed it. I think we are looking at cervical insufficiency. The other name for it is an incompetent cervix. The miscarriages usually happen later, in the second trimester. The first two losses were at ten and eleven weeks.

That's early, so I wasn't sure. Now I am. Your cervix begins shortening and opening too early and can't sustain the child through the pregnancy, so you miscarry."

Caitlyn was shaking now. Patrick had an arm around her, squeezing her to him. She looked up, tears in her eyes. "But it's not impossible. Surely there's a treatment we can try."

"There are some things we could try. Nothing is absolute. I'm worried about another serious miscarriage, Caitlyn. You've lost weight. You're anemic. You lost a lot of blood this time. I read the emergency room notes. They had to transfuse."

"But it's still possible. It's my body. I can decide whether it's worth the risk." Her chin was raised in defiance.

Patrick cursed. "Jesus, Caitlyn. I don't want to put your body through any more. I'll get a vasectomy. We can look into adoption!"

She reared back like he'd struck her. "You will not get a vasectomy. You will not!"

He threw her words back at her. "It's my body. I can decide."

The doctor put his hands up in surrender. "Okay, both of you need to calm down. We have time. Nothing needs to be decided right now. I can prescribe birth control…"

"No! I will not go on the pill!"

"Caitlyn, it could regulate your cycles again. It can buy you time to decide what you want." The doctor was trying to appease them both, giving them some breathing room and a cool down period.

"I already know what I want. I want to try again."

"Then give me time," Patrick said more calmly. "We'll use condoms for the next couple of months. Give me time," he repeated. "This is too fresh, Caitlyn. You aren't the only one that is hurting. I lost a son, just like you did. I need time." All the fire had gone out of Patrick, and she turned to him just in time to see a tear escape and go down his cheek.

She choked on a sob, pulling him to her. "I'm sorry. Oh, God. I'm so sorry. You're right. I'm out of my head." She whispered in his neck, his body shuddering. "Please, love. Forgive me." He held her then, and the tension in the room eased a bit.

For a time, it eased.

CHAPTER 3

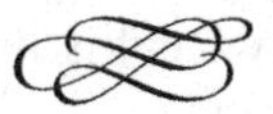

"Patrick, it's been three weeks. I haven't even gotten a period. We don't need to keep using condoms." She cupped his arousal, stroking him. "I want to feel you. All of you." He hissed, then growled.

They were in the kitchen. She'd been innocently chopping a pineapple, licking her sticky fingers. Next thing he knew, he had her spread eagle on the kitchen rug, skirt rucked up around her waist. "Dammit, Caitlyn. You're killing me!" He fumbled in an overhead drawer. He had bloody condoms stashed all over the house. Always somewhere within reach. His appetite for his wife was strong enough that he never knew where they'd end up. Bent over the kitchen counter, in the shower, on the sofa. The only way to stick to the condom rule, and not lose his head, was to have the damn things on hand. He should just get matching candy dishes and put them on every surface of the apartment.

"Yes, found it!" He tore the wrapper as Caitlyn raised her hips, rubbing on him. She was trying to distract him. Damn the woman. It almost worked. He sheathed himself and pulled her to him.

In the aftermath, they lay sprawled on the kitchen floor, panting. She'd taken a minute to get on board, but he was a persistent man. He wasn't going to let her shut him out. *Look at me, Caitlyn. Don't think about anything but what I'm doing to you. Do you hear me? Feel me.* He'd pinned her wrists above her head, lifted her hips, and ridden her hard. Until there were no defenses left. Until she released herself to him. Until she remembered that he wasn't just a goddamn sperm bank. He was her mate. Her personal plaything. That making love was about loving each other and about mind bending pleasure. Not just about getting pregnant. She came twice, his named ripped from her throat, and he reveled in the victory. *Mine.*

* * *

CAITLYN EMPTIED the pockets of Patrick's jeans, wondering why man purses had never caught on. A pocket knife, coins, a dental pick? What the? Now she understood why real men couldn't wear skinny jeans. The pockets were too small. She spread the chattel out on top of the counter as she stuffed the small combo washer/dryer unit with his jeans and a couple of his favorite t-shirts. As she unscrewed the cap from the laundry detergent, she caught sight of a small card among the pile of belongings. An appointment reminder card. *Dr. J. O'Leary, Urologist.* Her blood chilled. The appointment was for two days from now. Patrick was healthy as a horse. There was only one reason he could be seeing a urologist.

As if on cue, he came whistling down the hall. She heard the key go into the lock and he entered the apartment. As he came into the kitchen, he stopped, sensing something was wrong. Then he looked in Caitlyn's hand. She was furious. "What the bloody hell is this?" He sighed, rubbing the bridge of his nose. "Answer me, Patrick!"

"Ye can see fine what it is. It's just a consult, Caitlyn. A fifteen minute consultation."

"When were you going to tell me? Were you just going to do it without asking me?" She was yelling now.

"Of course not. I would never do that to you. I just thought this consult should be on my own. It is, after all, my cock and balls in question. I just wanted to talk to the man. I haven't decided anything.

I wouldn't make this decision alone. Unlike you, I realize this is a partnership!"

"How could you even think of it, Patrick? How could you give up any chance of having a family?"

"You are all that matters to me. I would rather have no kids than to put you through one more miscarriage. I'd be doing this for both of us. I love you."

"Well you shouldn't! You shouldn't love me!" she shouted. "I can't give you children. The O'Brien and Nagle families have been in Doolin for hundreds of years. Huge families with children to spare! Look at your sister and brothers with all of those beautiful children." She closed her eyes, tears escaping. Then she opened them with purpose. "You shouldn't love me!" He was grabbing her, trying to pull her to him. She fought him, but he was stronger.

"No! Don't say that. Don't you ever say that! You're my life. The blood of my body, mo chroí. I love you."

"You deserve someone who can give you children. A big family like you wanted," she croaked.

"You don't understand, Caitlyn. You are it for me. Until I'm dead and buried, my love. You're all I need. I wish that was enough for you. Why can't it be enough?" His eyes bore into hers and his heart broke. Because she didn't have an answer for him. Not the answer he wanted to hear.

SHE WASN'T SLEEPING, she barely ate, and Patrick didn't know how to help her. She'd originally agreed to wait another two months, then discuss things again, but she wouldn't allow herself that break. But she needed it, and so did he. With no other answers in front of him, Patrick knew he needed help. So he took her home for a visit. His mother was good at this type of stuff. And surprisingly, Caitlyn seemed to have taken some comfort from Katie's presence. So he went home, hoping the rooms full of children wouldn't make things worse. It wasn't like he didn't understand. He loved kids. The nieces and nephews that his siblings had given him were the children of his heart. But when he held little Ian in his arms, or had sticky toddler fingers in his hair, or watched his beloved Cora practice her violin, it tore at his soul. The thought that they might never have children of their own made him terribly sad. He couldn't share that with Caitlyn, though. It would do her in as surely as if he'd stuck a knife in her heart. So, he never spoke of it. Not even to his family.

Caitlyn slept on the way to the coast, exhausted because she tossed and turned every night. When he stopped for petrol, he called Michael. They were all headed to Gus's for Sunday lunch. A perfect time to see everyone before he headed to Ma and Da's house. He didn't just want to talk to his mother, he needed his da. He had a way of making sense of everything. Of knowing how to say the right thing. Da said it came with practice. Years of practice butting heads with his feisty Mullen woman, and losing every fight.

Sometimes you just needed your parents, no matter how old you were. He couldn't fathom how Liam had stayed away so long, but at least he was communicating. He'd even called to check on Caitlyn. He missed his brother so much, it was like a deep, buried ache in his chest. As if that particular pain knew better than to rear its ugly head, given the last two months. That one more speck of despair would buckle his knees and he'd never get up again.

He headed down Fisher Street and the sea air was sharp in his nose. The silly pink cottage with the thatched roof acted as a sort of gateway for locals and tourists alike. He parked as close as he could get to Gus's. The tourist season was dying down, but you never knew when a hoard of holiday Yanks were going to come pouring in. "Wake up, Caitlyn. We're here."

Caitlyn shot up in her seat, looking around her. "Oh, love. I'm such an ass. I slept the whole way." He laughed and pulled her in for a kiss. She was so damn sexy when she woke.

"You needed a nap. Let's go have a proper Sunday roast, like the good old days. I can practically smell it already."

She smiled, but it didn't reach her eyes. "It will be nice to see everyone. I've missed the children. They're getting so big." Patrick's heart squeezed.

"Me too." He gave her another quick kiss and they were on their way.

They walked in to Gus's and it was like a sort of homecoming. Dark wood, old photos on the walls, packed full of tables and chairs for locals and tourists alike.It had a long, winding bar full of sparkling bottles and glasses that were ready to be filled. There were offshoots of different rooms, and he sniffed out the area where the musicians played, knowing that was where his family always sat. The smell of meat and potatoes pulled at his stomach.

Patrick saw Branna first, her dark tresses pulled up in a loose bun on her head. He patted the little spikes that stuck out of the sides. She was usually more buttoned down with tightly bound hair and sedate clothing. "Don't mock me, Patrick. I was up every two hours."

He laughed and kissed her on the cheek. The reason was obvious, a cooing little bundle strapped to her chest in one of those wraps. Caitlyn ran a hand over the baby's silky, short hair. "How's our little Ian doing? Wearing your poor mammy out, I'd guess." Then she gave Branna a careful hug, not wanting to squash him. His hands shot out as fast as lightning, grabbing fists full of hair.

"Now you see why my hair is on top of my head like a bird nest. He's in that hair-grabbing phase. Ian, let go of your Auntie Caitlyn." But instead, he put the little fist in his mouth, drooling and sucking on his prize.

Caitlyn giggled. "Is that good? Probably not as good as your mammy's, huh?"

Patrick watched the entire display with a heavy heart. His poor Caitlyn was always able to put on a brave face. After untangling the little fiend, they went further into the room. Cheers came from all around, and he was happy to see that his grandparents and Doc Mary and Hans were here as well. Jenny shouted from the bar. "What will it be, Patrick? Caitlyn? I've got bellinis."

"I'll have a bellini, and get this man a lager," Caitlyn said. "And one

Sunday roast and one chicken salad." Patrick gave her a sideways glance. "What?"

"Ye need to eat more than a salad. You didn't eat breakfast. Get the chicken roast at least. Your trousers are hanging off you, lass." She looked down, and to her surprise, he was right. She crinkled her forehead, trying to remember when the last time was that she'd weighed herself. At the doctor's office, she supposed. She lifted a shoulder in a half shrug.

"Aye, I guess they are." She looked at Jenny who just nodded, changing the order with a grin.

There were two spots left next to Doc Mary and her handsome husband. It was the shock of the town when the self-proclaimed town spinster, known to everyone as Doc Mary, impulsively skipped town on holiday with Alanna's father after Aidan's wedding. Aidan had met the beautiful young woman in America, through Branna. When Hans had come to Ireland for the wedding, sporting his dashing Marine Corps dress blues, Mary hadn't stood a chance.

It was a testament to true love and second chances. They'd maintained a long-distance relationship for six months, him stationed in Spain before his retirement. When they married, she'd traveled back and forth and so had he. For eighteen months they met each other in different parts of Europe, getting an extended honeymoon before they both retired. Now Mary worked part-time, not quite ready to leave medicine completely.

"Hello, Caitlyn. It's good to see you both." Patrick sat down and handed both the women a bellini and Hans another Creans. As they started to catch up, Doc Mary dropped a huge announcement to anyone within earshot. Some already knew, because Alanna had been too excited not to share the news before heading back to England, but many people didn't know.

"Yes, Liam and Izzy video conferenced me and we had a long talk about the doctor shortage at St. Clare's. When a couple of the doctors rotate out in two weeks, I'll be taking their place with a big Marine for a bodyguard." She pointed a thumb in Hans's direction.

Everyone was taken aback. The news of Izzy's brush with the drug cartel, and her heroic trek through the jungle to save her interpreter, had spread through the town. Now Mary was going to the same mission. Saint Clare's Charity Mission in Manaus, Brazil, right on the Amazon River. The hospital and orphanage were run by an abbey full of sisters and a local and volunteer staff. Liam had left for a medical mission and still had not come home.

After the shock and excitement had died down, Caitlyn leaned in to speak to Mary. She had so many questions. Patrick had since started to wander around, talking with his family. Hans was in deep conversation with Sean and David, the two patriarchs of the O'Brien clan.

Mary took her phone out and pulled up a video from YouTube. "It's an amazing place. The sisters have carved this place out of the jungle and kept it going for forty years. But they need doctors, nurses, midwives, dentists, even teachers."

That's when it happened. A spark. Something in Caitlyn's chest that ignited. She watched the video with greedy eyes, looking at the pictures of the modest school and the children. She wasn't sure what the hum was that she heard in her mind, but it was there. And it didn't subside, even after they'd left the small town the next morning.

CHAPTER 4

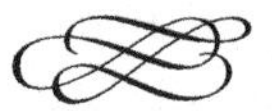

What a strange thing man is; and what a stranger thing woman—
Lord Byron

Caitlyn woke to realize it was after eight, and Patrick had already left for work. She didn't need to get up. Since the miscarriage, she'd taken a leave of absence from her work. She wasn't sure when she'd go back. She loved being an early childhood teacher. She loved her work with the English as a Second Language students as well. She just couldn't face all of those little four and five year olds yet. Couldn't watch the rows of parents waiting open armed at the end of the school day.

She walked into the kitchen, started the kettle, and leaned over the counter. Her heart was so heavy. Today was the day. After all the back and forth between herself and Patrick, he'd never actually cancelled the consultation with the urologist. She couldn't let him do it. No way in hell could he sterilize himself.

Putting aside the fact that they were both Catholics, it was wrong. He was young and virile. She could get hit by a bus tomorrow. She could choke on a chicken bone. She could get eaten by a bear...well maybe not that one. The point was that no one knew what was around the corner. Look at what happened to Eve. Dead at twenty-three. Or...she closed her eyes as a wave of sorrow went through her. Or she could let him go. Give him a chance to find love again. Not weigh him down with this unbearable grief and disappointment. He couldn't do some irreversible action that would forever make him unable to have children. She poured her tea, thinking about these last couple of months. Then she thought about all of those beautiful O'Brien children running around during Sunday lunch.

Out of nowhere, the images of St. Clare's Charity Mission popped in her head. The video Mary had shown her. She envied Mary. A chance to get away to somewhere completely new and foreign. A place to focus on her work, and nothing else. Just like Liam had done. Just like Izzy. Before she knew what she was doing, her laptop was open and she was clicking on the link of the mission's webpage. She navigated the site, marveling at the work that was being done there. The photos of green, twisting vines and exotic birds. Of a modest play yard and a sparsely equipped schoolhouse. Of beautiful, dark-eyed children and solemn-faced Irish nuns.

Then she hovered the mouse over another link. *Volunteers Needed.* As she looked over the list and the contact information, one position popped out at her. *Urgently Needed: Certified Primary School Teacher. Ages 3-10. Portuguese helpful but not necessary. English as a second language instruction, literacy, and basic mathematics for an 8,12, or 24-week commitment. Please contact...*

So, she accessed the email for a Reverend Mother Faith, Abbess of St. Clare's Charity Mission and began to write.

* * *

PATRICK HAD COME HOME every night for the last week and felt a thick cloud of something he couldn't name. Like it had settled over their home. Seany had moved in two days ago, but it wasn't about him. He was dutifully washing the cooking pot while Caitlyn set the table for dinner. She kissed Patrick as he came into the apartment, said all the right things, but he felt the distance.

She hadn't asked about his appointment, and he hadn't spoken of it either. After a fifteen minute chat with the doctor, O'Leary had encouraged him to either get his wife on the same page, or consider an alternative to a vasectomy. It was the type of action that a couple had to agree on. This type of division ended marriages. He'd seen it happen. And in hindsight, Patrick knew he was right. But with the moving day for Seany, his work schedule, and her keeping him at a comfortable distance, he hadn't found a way to really sit down and talk to her about it.

They hadn't made love since that time on the kitchen floor. When it came to sex, they were both voracious. It was almost a daily union. It stung him deep in his chest, the loss of her. Like she was pulling away. He didn't really know what she did during the day. He was glad she'd taken the time off of work. With Seany sharing expenses, they didn't need the money. He wondered if she'd looked into seeing a therapist, like her doctor had suggested. Would she even tell him?

How had this all deteriorated so quickly? She came into the bedroom while he leaned over the sink. She was buzzing around like nothing was amiss. But he was so in tune with her, she couldn't hide anything from him. That's when he looked down into the rubbish bin between the toilet and the sink and saw a fresh bandaid. It had a spot of blood on it, like someone who'd been given a shot or had a blood test. His brow furrowed, he turned to her. "What's this? Have you been back to the doctors? Did you have a blood test?" She froze, following his gaze. "What is it, Caitlyn? Are you keeping something from me?"

He knew she wasn't pregnant. They hadn't had unprotected sex since she'd lost the baby. She stiffened her back, then just sat on the edge of the bed. He approached, but she started talking quickly, stopping him in his tracks. "I received some vaccinations. Some that I needed."

"What vaccinations do you need at twenty-eight that you haven't already had?" The tension should have left his body, given her explanation, but that nagging sensation that she was keeping something from him persisted. "Caitlyn, what's this about? What vaccinations?"

"The ones you need if you're going to travel to South America," she said plainly, and finally met his eyes. "I signed on for an eight week commitment in Brazil as the primary school teacher. They need one badly and…"

"You did what?" His voice cracked through the apartment before he realized Seany was standing in the open doorway of their room. The place was small. He'd obviously heard everything. Sean gave him a look that said, *Don't go apeshit on the poor lass. Rein it in asshole.* Fuck that for a laugh. "There's no feckin' way you are running off half-cocked to Brazil! I won't permit it!"

He heard Seany curse under his breath. Then step out with another look that said, *You're on your own dipshit.* Seany just looked at Caitlyn and said, "I'll have dinner downstairs. Josh could use some company."

Caitlyn raised a brow, like a warning shot across the bow. She stood slowly. "Excuse me? You won't permit it? Who in the hell do you think you're talking to? I am your wife, not your child."

"Then stop acting like one!"

"You didn't say anything when Izzy went, or when Mary said she was going! Why is it different for me?"

"Izzy is not my responsibility and Mary is taking Hans with her. She's got a fucking infantry Marine watching her ass."

"Well, I guess he can watch both our asses, then. It's done. They need a teacher. I'm available. I'm not working right now."

"How could you do this, Caitlyn? How could you just leave me without even discussing it? When the hell were you going to tell me? Jesus, it's right before Christmas!"

"I leave in a week. I wasn't able to get on Mary's flight, so I fly out three days later. You're the only one who knows other than the abbess at St. Clare's. Mary doesn't even know. Neither do Liam or Izzy. This is my business and I don't need anyone interfering or trying to dissuade me. I expect you to keep it that way until I decide when and if to tell them. It goes without saying that if you try to either follow me or stop me, the gap will widen between us. You need to let me do this my own way."

"Wait...back the hell up. Ye bought a bloody plane ticket?" Caitlyn started actually worrying her husband's head was going to explode. His face was red, the veins were popping out in his neck. If she were the sheepish type, she might be intimidated. Screw that. He was not her lord and master.

"Calm down!" she snapped. "Mary said that it's safe. She wouldn't go otherwise. They have full-time security now, and a bonus fucking infantry Marine as you pointed out. I'll be fine. I need to do this!"

"Why? Why now? Is this about that bloody consultation? You didn't ask, but I've decided not to do it. I would never make a major life decision unless we were both on board with it. I wouldn't do that to you. I'm sorry you don't feel the same way."

All the fight drained out of Caitlyn. "Patrick." It was almost a plea. "I need this time to myself and so do you. We need time to decide what we want."

"What the hell does that mean?" His voice was low and quiet. He sounded almost sick. His blue-green eyes burned. He looked like half demon, half angel. Tears pricked her eyes.

"It means that ye need some time away from me to make up your own mind about the future. I wouldn't blame you, Patrick. The church would give you an annulment if we said..."

He swayed. He actually swayed and caught himself on the dresser. "You're leaving me? You want a divorce?"

She snapped. "Of course I don't! You're the love of my life, you bloody-minded eejit! But maybe I don't have to be yours!" She choked on the words. "Maybe with someone else..." Patrick grabbed her before she could finish, pulling her to him with a punishing kiss. She was right with him, tearing his shirt open. He had her down on the bed in a flash. He ripped her pants off and freed himself in under a second. Then he pushed inside her, pulling her face up to him as he did it. He didn't even think about a condom. "Mine," he growled the word. "Ah, fuck." He rolled his hips, his thrusts demanding. "You're mine. Do you hear me? And you fucking own me. You own me! Forever!"

A moan ripped out of her as she came. Then he filled her up, coming hard and deep inside her. She raked her nails across his ass as she continued to orgasm. A never ending wave of pleasure and pain. Pleasures of the flesh and pain from the deep recesses of their hearts.

* * *

MARY WENT over her checklist again, ignoring the string of colorful curses that were currently flowing from her husband's mouth. He was on the phone with the U.S. Embassy, trying to pull strings with the local jarhead in charge. The man was sympathetic and a bit of a kindred spirit. Mary could hear his counter curses, bitching about red tape and bureaucrats and SNAFUs. Marines loved their acronyms, this one she understood as meaning *Situation Normal All Fucked Up.* One of his favorites. Even on the phone, he was speaking with the knife hand pointed at the air, as if he could conjure the eejit that had screwed up his departure timeline. Hans was not, in fact, leaving with her in two days. His visa had been denied. A U.S. citizen, traveling to South America from Europe, with what they described as "ties to terrorist nations." Some idiot had seen the part of the application that asked for travel history, seen Iraq, Afghanistan, and the Horn of Africa, and decided to stop reading and stamp the denial. If they'd looked closely at the employment history, they'd have seen that he was retired military and had been on official orders at the time of all of these trips, but the government and its many hoards of employees didn't always work like that.

Hans ended the call and exhaled like an angry bull. Mary looked at him to see if he was stomping his hoof. They'd agreed that if this marriage was going to work, they had to take turns being stressed and unreasonable. The other had to take the opposing side of calm and clear headed. She guessed it was his turn to stomp. She smiled, putting her pad and pencil aside. "It's okay, love. They'll sort it all out. This is just a bump in the road."

Hands on his hips, head bent low, he finally met her eyes. "You can't go without me, Mary. Not after what happened to Izzy." He shook his head before she could offer a rebuttal. "Don't you get it? I wasn't there for Alanna. She got snatched by some fucking pervert. A pervert who tried to rape her as a teenager. All of this shit went on under my nose and I dropped the ball with my own daughter. Right when she needed me, I wasn't there. Then poor Liam. Jesus Christ. First Eve gets killed, then this whole scene with Izzy." He ran his hands through his shorn hair, his eyes desperate. "You can't ask me to do this. Don't ask me to stay back while you go!"

She approached him and pulled his arms down away from his head. She said calmly, "Be easy, Hans. You aren't being rational. You need to take a breath and calm yerself. This isn't going to delay you all that long. I made an obligation. Ye can't ask me not to go." She emphasized the *me,* making sure she had eye contact. "I would never take unnecessary risks. You know that. You know me, Hans. Better than anyone." She pulled him down, taking his wide shoulders in her arms. "I leave in two days. It's the weekend. This is not going to get settled over a weekend, especially being so close to Christmas. Ye just need to trust me. And I trust you. You'll find a way to come to me. You'll be by my side in no time and we'll do this thing together." Before he could argue anymore, she pulled him to her for a kiss. A distraction that always worked, despite his efforts.

He laughed against her mouth. "That isn't going to work." But even as he said it, he closed the distance between their bodies.

* * *

PATRICK HELD her in the darkness that surrounded them. He held on too tightly, but he was afraid she was going to disappear. Slip away like a spirit. She was still awake. They'd been wild, out of control, and the power between them still hummed too fiercely to let them settle into sleep. He'd taken her three times, feeling like he had to drill the truth into her. She'd responded with every bit of the wild desperation that he felt. She'd marked him. Nail marks in his ass and a pink mark from her teeth on his chest.

Now the coiling panic was back, both because she was still leaving, and because he hadn't used contraception. What if she found out she was pregnant while on this mission? Why hadn't he used a fucking condom? *Because you wanted to mark her as well,* he thought to himself. He'd wanted to leave himself inside her like some sort of raiding barbarian. She'd wanted it too. Demanded it of him. Taken him as hard as he'd taken her.

He pulled her closer. "I'll wait for you, mo shíorghrá." *My eternal love.* "I'll wait for you to come back to me." He whispered. He felt her tremors, as if finding some relief from the tension that had sprung between them. She exhaled wearily, and finally they both slept.

CHAPTER 5

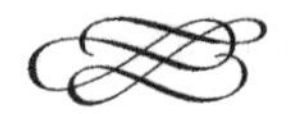

MANAUS, BRAZIL

Caitlyn cleared immigration easily, making her way through the airport. As she claimed her luggage, the balmy air blew in like a warm breath. There were people buzzing around in every direction, but she finally caught sight of a man standing with a sign that said *Caitlyn O'Brien*. She waved to him as she approached. "You must be Raphael." She shook his hand and asked, "Where's your car?" He gave her a chiding look. "Senhora, you should ask for identification. I could be anyone."

"Well, normally I would, but I saw you on the video from the website. Izzy and Liam have talked about you so much, I feel like I know you."

His eyes sharpened. "You know them?" Then he looked at the sign. "Of course. O'Brien. Are you his sister? You've just missed him!"

"Oh, I thought he was leaving next week. I was going to surprise him. Did they both leave early?"

Raphael nodded. "Yes, Senhora. They wanted to…how did you say…surprise? For the Christmas Eve, they wanted it to be a surprise." He looked at his watch and shook his head. "They've likely boarded the plane. Do you want me to try to call Izzy?"

Caitlyn stopped him as he went for his phone. It was probably best. If Liam saw that she was here alone, he'd likely cancel his trip home. O'Brien men protected their women, and that included sisters-in-law. "No, Raphael. His family needs him more than I do. He needs to go home." She teared up. "I'm so glad he's going home."

"Yes, and with a new bride," Raphael said with a smile.

Caitlyn dropped her bag and her eyes shot to his. "You're takin' a piss!" But she could tell by his face he wasn't kidding. "Oh my God! Liam and Izzy?" She squealed and hugged Raphael before he knew what was happening.

He patted her awkwardly. "Yes, it is a very good thing. Izzy is like a sister to me, and he is my brother. They are very good together." He picked up her bags. "Now, let's get you to the mission. The rain is not so heavy today, but we will get more later. Sister Maria will be glad for the help. The children are very excited."

A feeling of excitement fluttered in Caitlyn's belly. She couldn't wait to see the school and the hospital. To meet the children and the sisters and all of the volunteers. And Mary was going to be shocked speechless at the sight of her. At least she got to surprise one person.

* * *

DR. MARY FLYNN had been practicing medicine for decades, but nothing other than hands-on experience could prepare a practitioner for this sort of work. You could read about parasites and strange fevers. You could see slides of what someone looks like after being bitten by an exotic insect or spider. You could also learn how to diagnose malnutrition, but nothing makes such an impression as staring into the soulful eyes of a starving child. Only with your boots on the ground, as Hans would put it, can you really learn the way of it all. And she knew that after all the years of doctoring the villagers of County Clare, this experience would impact her the most. Both as a physician and as a human being.

She'd sent the child away with Sister Agatha. She'd be washed, fed, given new clothes, and then she'd be given a home with the other children in the orfanato. At seven years old, she looked about four. The knot in Mary's throat was choking her. She looked at Seamus, the OB-GYN on staff, and he just gave her a look of understanding. He had his own daughters, she knew. They'd become fast friends as well as colleagues in the few days she'd been here. He'd also filled her in on the many adventures that he'd had with Liam and Izzy. He'd leave in another two weeks or so, after his high risk patient came through a safe delivery.

Mary had already contacted the hospital in Galway, knowing a perfect position for a talented and experienced doctor. They'd be crazy not to hire him. A pediatrician would soon arrive from Dublin, and hopefully another gynecologist, to replace Seamus, would come at some point. Until then, she and the resident midwife, Sister Catherine, would be handling deliveries.

"That was a tough one. They won't all be like that. Most of the people in these parts love their children. They care for them. They may not have much, but their children have a full belly and a loving family. I promise you, they won't all be like this."

She smiled sadly. "One child is too many."

"Aye, I know. But the good news is that she's got the sisters now. She couldn't be in better hands. She'll be safe, she'll fill out on Gabriela's cooking, and she'll go to school. It's a modest school, but a good one. And we have a new teacher coming in just today. It'll all be grand. You'll see." Then Seamus left, giving her a pat on the shoulder as he did. "Supper is in ten minutes, Doctor. Get something in your belly. You'll feel better."

She gave Seamus a sort of clinical assessment. A detached appreciation that a female gives a male that she finds pleasing, but isn't attracted to. He was forty-seven, divorced, a great doctor, and an all around nice man. He was also handsome in that tall, burly type of way. He had the dusty blue eyes, so common to the men of Ireland. Sandy brown hair that had gone silver at the temples. His face was kind.

Then she thought about her husband. He was over ten years Seamus's senior, only a year younger than her. Which meant he was pushing sixty, just like she was. But he was devilishly handsome and fit. His blonde hair was light enough to camouflage any emerging gray. Those delicious Viking genes rewarding him with great height and broad shoulders. He had sharp, lively green eyes and a wide smile when he wasn't growling at someone. She missed him. He'd called her with an update last night. He'd be here soon, and she couldn't wait to show him around. He'd like Seamus and Antonio. He'd really like Raphael. Same ilk and all that. But what he was really going to love was the children, and Gabriela's cheese bread.

She headed out of the hospital and toward the cantina, loving the smells that were wafting out of the building. That's when she heard a ruckus. Clapping and excited children. If she'd had fifty guesses, she'd never have guessed correctly. Nothing had prepared her for walking in and seeing Caitlyn O'Brien standing in the center of a group of small children. "Well, I'll be damned," she whispered.

"Interesting choice of words," the abbess said behind her. Mary jumped. Jesus. She felt twelve years old again, getting a stern look from a surly sister. "Sorry, Reverend Mother. It's just shock. She didn't tell me."

"She didn't tell anyone. Well, she told her husband, but she was rather mysterious about the whole thing. We're just happy to have her. The particular terms don't matter as much as the result. Don't you agree?"

Mary smiled. "Yes, I'd have to agree. I was her doctor from the time she was a small lass. She'll be a wonderful asset, and I think she needs this. Things haven't been easy for her. She's a truly wonderful young woman." That's when Mary caught her eye, and Caitlyn left the children to run into her open arms.

* * *

Doolin, Co. Clare, Ireland

Christmas Eve

Patrick's heart was doing acrobatics. Flipping from one side of the spectrum to the other. His brother was home. Just looking at his little brother, younger by a year, brought fresh tears prickling at the corners of his eyes. He looked so different. His hair was longer. As long as Seany's and Tadgh's had once been. His eyes were older, his jaw leaner. He'd lost any shreds of boyhood in his face and body, but the smile was back. That quick smile and wit that had always served him so well. And he had Izzy by his side. There was a chemistry there that was as old as the O'Brien bloodlines. The hum between two people that would always draw them back to each other. He knew it well. He'd felt it instantly with Caitlyn, and in the absence of her, he felt like an amputee. Not due to the physical separation so much as the emotional one. Like she'd erected a wall with no door through which he could pass.

It was bad enough when Hans had been delayed, but now Liam wasn't with her. It went against his every instinct to let her go. His ugly, barbarian twin fighting to get out. Demanding that he drag her home and keep her there until she submitted. But that wasn't the real him, and Caitlyn wouldn't stand for it. She loved big. She fought hard. She was loyal. But she would not be forced into something, or out of it. It's why he loved her.

He'd spoken to Liam for a bit, and was surprised to find out that he still hadn't known about Caitlyn's departure. Obviously she'd expected to surprise him, and that hadn't worked out. Liam and Izzy had left Brazil early, and they'd missed her by mere hours. The only reason he hadn't gone into full meltdown was because of Izzy. Well, Izzy and Liam. Raphael, the military man that had been hired by Izzy to interpret, was now a full-time, armed guard for the abbey. To hear them talk, the man was like some sort of action hero. Although he suspected that Izzy fit that description as well. Brave and fierce, like all O'Brien women.

He'd often wondered how Liam had been drawn to such a calm, quiet lass like Eve. But she'd shown her mettle in the end. Brave and willing to sacrifice her own safety for another. For a stranger. This wasn't helping. Thinking about Eve's death was definitely not helping him slow his roll.

"You're deep in thought, brother. How can I help?" Brigid's voice was uncharacteristically soft. "I wish I could do something. I feel useless."

He smiled, capping a hand over her auburn hair and smoothing it down to her neck. His only sister by blood, and the beating heart in his chest. She'd seen so little of the world. So happy and blessed. Three beautiful children and a good man. The best. Finn was the perfect mate for Brigid. A cool breeze to her fire storm. He saw her and only her. He was the perfect specimen of two ancient bloodlines. Murphy and O'Donnell. Truth be told, he often wondered if there wasn't some Pict blood in the man. Like he'd been brushed by the Fae, with his black hair and golden skin. His dark, unfathomable eyes.

Patrick looked at his beloved Cora. The first of the O'Brien offspring. Dark curls and those same, all-knowing eyes. It wasn't the Fae, he reflected. It was their Selkie blood. The dark Irish genes that ran alongside the coastal paths. A throwback gene that had given Cora the gift of sight. A sort of precognitive ability that was both a blessing and a curse. What he wouldn't give for a little encouragement from Cora's dreamscape. A happily ever after tale, dreamed just for him.

He turned to his sister. "The best thing you can do for me is to stay put. If one more person I know runs off to the bloody jungle, I'll declare war and raise a feckin' army."

"I won't leave you, brother. But you shouldn't judge our Caitlyn too harshly. I know this is difficult. I can't even imagine. But the losses she's suffered..."

"I suffered them right along with her!" he said, biting back his harsh tone.

"I know that, brother. And we all bleed for you. We do. But as a woman..." She shook her head. "I've carried a child in my body. I've birthed three beautiful children. And the thought of losing one of them before I ever had the chance to know them..." She stifled a sob. "To feel their soul drift out of my body. To suffer the moment when they'd never move inside you again. It's a particular sort of anguish that only a woman can know."

They were both tearing up now. "I don't say that to hurt you, or to make you feel like your pain was less. Your pain is doubled because you grieve for your child and you weep for Caitlyn. All I mean is that she's suffering on a very personal level right now. A grief that isn't just in her heart and mind. It's in her body. She feels empty. And for now, she needs something more than being your wife to fill it. She needs a purpose that goes beyond that safe little school where she teaches, and beyond the walls of your home. She needs something to shake her out of this grief. Maybe by going to such a foreign place, and seeing this different way of life, by giving of herself to God's work. Maybe that is where she'll heal. And she'll come home understanding how blessed she is. To see new opportunities with more open eyes. Does that make sense, brother?"

He pulled her to him. "Yes, it does. Thank you, Brigid. Oh, God. I know you're right. I just feel like my heart has been ripped out of my chest. What if she leaves me for good?"

Brigid pushed him back and met his eyes. "No! She would never leave you. It's her love for you that strangles her the most. The thought that she's hurt you with these losses. She blames herself. But there are more ways to be a mother than to birth a child. And maybe she'll come to understand that during her time in Brazil."

Patrick nodded, wiping his face. "Did I tell you I looked into alternatives? I even read up on surrogacy. It's just so expensive. We couldn't hope to pay for it, even with a loan. The procedure aside, you've got to pay the female's expenses, pay her to do it. Hope that it all takes on the first attempt. And I don't know if Caitlyn could..."

"I would do it." Brigid's voice had an ache to it. He met her eyes, shocked. "I would do it for you and Caitlyn. It would be her fertilized egg, but I would be her vessel, brother." Behind her, another soft voice spoke. "I'd do it, too." He looked up and wondered when Branna had appeared. She knelt down before him. "And we'd pool our finances. All of us would. There is nothing we wouldn't do for you and Caitlyn. Brigid and I discussed it. Whoever was more suitable according to the doctor. We'd carry a child for you. And I know that if Alanna was here instead of England, she'd throw her uterus in the ring." She smiled, knowing that her cheeky humor might lighten the mood. Brigid cracked off a laugh. They bracketed him, his beautiful sisters, and he felt so very loved.

"I don't know what to say. It's nothing I'd ever ask of you. To carry a child and give it up."

Brigid took his face in her hands. "We wouldn't be giving it up. Do you think I look at little Brian or Ian, or wee Davey and love them any less than the sons of my body? Do you think that Branna wouldn't die a thousand times over for my Cora? Do you think Mam loves Tadgh any less than she does her other six children? They're the children of our hearts. All of them. None less precious because we didn't give birth to them. Just think about it, brother. Maybe Caitlyn couldn't bear it, but maybe she could. Maybe she'd give us her precious child for safe keeping, only for a while. And then let us give it back to her."

He squeezed their hands, kissing them each on the head. "I want you to know that whatever path we take, I will be forever indebted to you for offering. I love you both."

CHAPTER 6

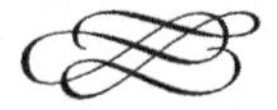

Caitlyn ended the call home. Her parents had been emotional, which was difficult, but hearing her sisters lighthearted giggles and their many questions had lifted her spirits. The Christmas service had been lovely. Father Pietro had come in from the city. From his own parish, he'd left to do another mass just for the occupants of St. Clare's. With so many children, staff, and volunteers, they couldn't hope to get everyone transported into the city at once. Especially during the rainy season.

Her first day of orientation had been exhausting. She'd met the children, the sisters, and some of the doctors. The groundskeeper, Paolo, had been at breakfast, and the full time cook, Gabriela, was always busy, rolling from one meal to the next. Dr. O'Keefe and Dr. Rinalto had been absent most of the day, having taken the floating clinic into the forest. Raphael had accompanied them with Paolo at the helm. She'd only caught a glimpse of the two doctors before they'd headed out. It was the Christmas weekend, and at home they may have not gone to work, but the rhythm of St. Clare's was unique. The practical work, as well as the service related duties, never seemed to let up.

Apparently there had been a few sick children in the village, and an elderly patient, so they'd gone. The infectious disease specialist from Australia didn't arrive until next week, along with a pediatrician and hopefully Mary's husband. A few days later, a surgeon would arrive from England with his anesthesiologist riding shotgun. Until then, Antonio would be on call or they'd transport into the city. The Land Cruiser could be used as a sort of ambulance, if time was critical. Mary had given her a tour of the medical facilities, and she was very impressed. Izzy had done a beautiful job putting together a surgical unit. There would only be a two-week dwell between her departure and the other surgeon's arrival.

Caitlyn was still getting acclimated to the time change, finding herself close to nodding off by teatime yesterday. Last night, she'd been fast asleep by 5:30. The women's shower area was under construction, being renovated with a recent influx of funds. For now, the single locker room was co-ed by two-hour rotations. After hearing the tale of Liam walking in on Izzy, she couldn't help but laugh at the oversized sign, stating which gender was occupying the showers at any given time. So, she'd taken a quick shower to get the bug repellant and travel sweat off of her body, then crashed in the tiny bed she'd been given. It was good that she was so tired. Sleeping in a strange place without Patrick was going to take some getting used to. She missed him with an ache that was deep in her chest, but she knew this had been the right thing to do.

The rain had settled to a fine mist as she made her way to Gabriela's Christmas lunch. The smell of roasting pork and tropical fruit was deliciously hanging in the air. She was hungry for the first time in weeks, and the thought of smoked sausages, cheese bread, sweet cakes, cookies, and fruit pies made her stomach roar to life. She noticed out of the corner of her eye that the young girls were watching her. Varying ages and sizes, they were all lovely. Their dark eyes and innocent faces so curious about her.

A new little girl had come into the orphanage the day she'd arrived. She noticed that the older girl, Genoveva, the tallest and most unique looking out of the group, was holding the child's hand. She had a smaller girl on her hip who must be little Estela. The tales had trickled in during Liam and Izzy's calls home, being retold with excitement as the family called each other after they'd heard from him. And now he was with Izzy. A testament to second chances.

Liam had been convinced he'd never move on from Eve, but he'd done it. And she was so happy for him. So proud of him. And the thought of having Izzy for a sister warmed her heart. Unless she went home in two months and Patrick served her with annulment papers. She'd all but invited him to do just that. What the hell had she been thinking? He was everything to her. The great love of her life. She shook her head, not willing to think about it anymore. She was here to do some good and distract herself. So she'd do just that.

"Hello, girls. Happy Christmas to you." All of the girls giggled shyly and spoke to her in their best English.

"Happy Christmas, Mrs. O'Brien." They spoke in unison, except for the new girl who turned her head into Genoveva's arm. And Estela, who popped her thumb out of her mouth and said, "Feliz Natal, Senhora!" with such exuberance that it made Caitlyn giggle with pleasure. Genoveva whispered to her, and she struggled to say it again in English. "Happy Christmas to you."

She smiled knowingly at Genoveva. "Well, I've heard a lot about you all from my husband's brother and from Dr. Collier. I'm so excited to have you in my classroom." This was directed at the smaller children, but her eyes returned to Genoveva. "I hear from Sister Maria that you are a very good helper with the small children. I would love for you to help me as well, until they get used to me. Would you like that?" Genoveva's back straightened, and she showed her beautiful white teeth and stunning green eyes in full measure.

"Yes, I will be very pleased to help you."

Next time she spoke with Liam or Izzy, she'd have to ask them more about this quiet, beautiful girl. She knelt down next to the new child, so shy and unsure. Mary was right. She was malnourished. Not just because she was small. Her bones jutted out at sharp angles. "And what is your name?" Genoveva asked her again in Portuguese. The girl's big eyes met hers.

"Zantina," she said softly.

"That is a pretty name." Caitlyn spoke slowly and clearly, knowing that this girl would probably have little to no English. "What does it mean?"

Genoveva answered her. "It means, *Little Saint*." Caitlyn's heart squeezed. Estela spoke then, chasing the sadness from the exchange. "She is our new sister." The words were labored, like she was really concentrating so that Caitlyn would be impressed with her English.

"Well, you're lucky to have found each other. I have many sisters, and I love them very much." They walked into the cantina, listening to Caitlyn tell them first about Madeline and Mary. And then about Brigid, Branna, Alanna, Charlie, and soon to be Izzy.

* * *

REVEREND MOTHER FAITH watched as the lovely new teacher walked into the cantina. Every eye was on her. She had the fresh, fair look of a proper Irish lass. Sparkling eyes and a quick smile. But those eyes held sadness. They held loss. She'd read the woman's file, and had Seamus go over it thoroughly. At least the medical part. She'd recently lost a child fairly far along in her pregnancy. She knew this because Liam had grieved the loss deeply during his time here. And it hadn't been her first. She'd been so surprised to see the name on the application. Eager to get another teacher, she hadn't put it together at first. There were a lot of O'Brien's in Ireland. And although she'd assumed that the lass must be a relation, she hadn't put it all together until she'd seen the medical screening and the listed next of kin. Patrick O'Brien. Liam's brother.

She'd corresponded with the young woman with the assistance of Sister Agatha. E-mail was the easiest, as she was a writer by nature. When she'd heard from Liam this morning, she knew that her instincts had been correct. This woman was hurting, and she'd fled to Brazil in order to escape that hurt. She understood, and she'd agreed to the two-month commitment because better for the child to come here than to escape into a less productive direction.

She remembered Liam's words. *Do you remember our agreement,*

Reverend Mother? Do you remember the conditions that you set on my service? I think, perhaps,the weekly teatime meetings you subjected me to would greatly benefit Caitlyn. Do you understand what I'm saying? Mrs. O'Brien was not going to appreciate that arrangement any more than her brother-in-law had, but he was right. She'd given her two days and the holiday to settle in, but it was time they talked.

Caitlyn rubbed a hand over little Estela's head as she saw them to their table with the other students. Then she joined the staff and volunteers on the other side of the room. "Happy Christmas everyone," she said brightly. She was surprised to see Dr. Rinalto was joining them for dinner, because he lived in Brazil long-term, and had a villa in a more affluent part of the city. She said as much and he blushed. "You must call me Antonio. We are not very formal among the staff. And as for why I am here, my villa is beautiful. I am fortunate in that regard. But without loved ones to fill it, I'm afraid Christmas is a bit lonely. I wouldn't miss Christmas lunch with my St. Clare's family for anything."

Caitlyn thought about the fact that she'd left her husband on Christmas and her stomach turned. Hopefully his family was keeping him company. She'd certainly call him after the meal. "I think that's wonderful. I'm sure no one in the city will be served a finer meal. It smells gorgeous altogether."

The platters began to be passed down the tables. Unlike the normal days, when the meals were served cafeteria style, Christmas was family style. Dishes were heaped with roasted pork, fresh fruit, salt cod fritters, cheese bread, beans, crispy bits of fried cassava flour, piles of garlic drenched kale. It was overwhelming. Caitlyn ate more than she had in weeks. She wondered if it was the change of scenery. She'd come to Brazil to try to heal. To find something new with which to feed her soul. Maybe the food was the same. She'd lost weight. Had no appetite since the tragedy that brought her here. But this food was a taste of something new. Something exciting that didn't remind her of home. She suddenly wished Patrick were here. He loved to eat. He would have stuffed himself to bursting. She hadn't run from her husband. Not really. She'd just taken herself away from him. Given him a chance to think clearly without her there. It didn't mean she didn't miss him.

She looked up into Mary's knowing eyes. "Have ye called him?" Mary asked.

"I will in a bit. Hopefully he's still in Doolin. If not, I'll try the flat." She took a bite of the pork and sighed. So good. "What about you? Have ye called that big Marine of yours?" Mary laughed at Seamus's expression.

"I can't wait to meet this man of yours. How in the bloody hell did you end up marrying a Marine from America?"

"Ye know what they call Marine Corps dress blues in the U.S.?" Mary asked with a grin. Seamus shook his head. She leaned in and whispered, "Panty droppers." And that's when Antonio spit his juice out his mouth and nose.

Coughing and laughing, he wiped his mouth and the table in front of him. "This is why I love Irish women. Sweet, innocent faces, but you never know what is going to come out of their mouths."

Seamus clapped him on the back and raised his glass. "Amen to that, brother."

* * *

PATRICK RAN to the computer just in time to catch the call. His heart caught in his throat at the sight of her. "Hello, darlin'. Happy Christmas."

His voice was sad, even though he was trying to muster a smile. Caitlyn's eyes started to tear. "Happy Christmas, love. I'm glad I found you. I thought you'd still be at your ma and da's house. Why are ye in uniform? Did something happen?"

"No, I cancelled my night off. I took a shift so that one of the men could spend the rest of the day at home with his family."

"That was nice of you. How is everyone? How's Liam settling in?"

"Well enough. He seems happy. They both do. And how are you settling in at the mission? Have ye seen your students? How is Mary?"

They spoke for a while, and Patrick was trying like hell to keep it upbeat. Before they ended the call, he said, "If you look in your luggage, I put a small gift in there for you. It's hidden in the green socks in the zipper area. Although, I suppose you've unpacked since you'll be staying a while."

"Do you want me to go get it? I can open it while we're still together."

But we're not together, he thought. *Not really. I can't touch you. I want to touch you.* "Not at all. Open it later. It's just a trifle."

"I left something for you as well. It's hidden in my knickers drawer." She smiled, wiggling her brows.

He laughed. Then he looked at the time. "I'm sorry, love. I've got to go to work. When can you call again? I want to talk more when we aren't rushed."

"Maybe in a few days. I need to start teaching tomorrow and with the time change and all, well...I'll try in a few days."

"I love you, a chuisle. I love you so much." His voice broke and he covered his eyes. "I'm sorry. I swore I wouldn't do this."

She put her hand to the computer. "I love you too, Patrick. With all my heart and soul, I love you. Be careful. Don't work distracted. Promise me."

"I promise."

* * *

PATRICK CAME HOME from work knackered. He hated how empty the apartment was. Seany was at work until tomorrow afternoon. He worked 24 hours on, 48 off. He was going to be glad for the company. After talking to Caitlyn, he'd been wrecked, rattling around in his own head all evening. He hadn't opened her gift yet. So after stripping off his uniform and throwing on a pair of sweats, he went to her bureau. The top drawer was where she kept her knickers and bras. He was such a sap. The sight of it half empty made him want to break down like a pussy and start crying in her panty drawer. He shoved them aside, finding a small wrapped gift. He also saw something he wasn't expecting. "Oh, Jesus." It was a scrap book. A new one that was barely out of the shopping bag. A baby scrapbook. She probably forgot she had it in the same drawer, because he was positive she wouldn't have set him up like this. Caitlyn didn't have a manipulative bone in her body. She'd probably blocked the purchase out of her mind. He took both items and sat on the bed, taking a few deep breaths.

The gift was small. Something wrapped well, but small. He opened it, finding a note attached to a key. *Gotcha. You didn't sniff my knickers, did you?* He barked out a laugh. It was just like her to make it a game. He knew the key. It went to the cedar chest that was currently occupying the living room. It had been in the guest room, but that was Seany's now. He went into the living room where they'd shoved the chest into a corner. They kept a few spare blankets in there, usually, and that was it.

He knelt down and used the key to unlock it. He saw that there was something concealed under the blankets. What on earth had she done? When he pulled the blanket aside, he made a sound deep in his throat. She'd bought him an Irish bouzouki. An eight string, medieval sounding instrument that was every Irish musician's dream. "Jesus, Caitlyn." He picked it up like a newborn. "Ah, you are beautiful now aren't ye?" he crooned to the instrument, as if it were a living, breathing thing.

She undoubtedly had the case hidden somewhere else. He took the red bow off of the neck and rested it on his knee. Strumming a few times, it sang under his touch. She'd really outdone herself. He suddenly found himself doubting the gift he'd bought her. He eyed the other bundle. He shouldn't look at it. No good would come from it, but he wanted to understand his wife. He needed to get in her head and see where she'd been and where she was now. He couldn't lose her. And it was in that moment that he realized she had indeed left this where he could see it. Not to manipulate him, but to make him understand. He had gone through this last pregnancy with fingers crossed, teeth clenched. But she'd really thought this time was different. The child had quickened, letting her feel his movements. She'd been ready to fill this scrap book.

He swallowed, then he opened it. She had notes from her early appointments. Something bulky was between the pages. When he opened the book further, something slid into his lap. It was a homemade Christmas ornament. The kind her students made in class. It was a framed picture, decorated with candy canes and sprigs of holly that were cut out from colored foam. A piece of yarn glued for hanging it on the tree. *Baby's First Christmas.* The ultrasound photo they'd taken at fourteen weeks was framed.

Patrick fell back as the couch caught him. His eyes closed as the tears began. He leaned forward, pain ripping through him as he clutched the ornament. In the silence of the apartment, where Caitlyn wasn't watching, they came. Where his family wasn't watching. Even with them, he'd held back. He knew that seeing one of them suffer split the other ones down the middle. They loved deeply, and when tragedy struck one of them, they all bled.

So in this place, where he didn't have to be strong, he finally wept with the full force of his grief. He cried until he shook. For his baby, for his wife, for his loneliness. After he was done, and his body had settled, he stood and hung the ornament on the tree. He walked past the little urn, kissed his finger, and touched it. "We'll find a place for you, lad. When she returns we will find a place to put you to rest. I promise." Then he went to their empty bedroom and climbed in bed.

CHAPTER 7

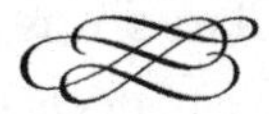

ST. JAMES HOSPITAL, DUBLIN, IRELAND

The life of a good man is a continual warfare with his passions—
Samuel Richardson

Dr. Quinn Maguire sat speechless, looking into the kind brown eyes of his new acquaintance. She was an American doctor, accompanied by her fiancé, an Irishman who had worked at this very hospital as an intern. Izzy Collier and Liam O'Brien had both just come from Brazil. Specifically, they'd come from the St. Clare's Charity Mission in Manaus. A place he knew well. A place he'd tried and failed to forget. *Angela.* He whispered her name in his mind. A silent plea.

"Forgive me. I'm a bit..." He couldn't even put it into words. "Could you start over and say that again? I'm just a bit rattled, and I need to make sure I heard you correctly." But he had heard them. There was a child. Angela had given birth over fifteen years ago to a baby girl. His daughter. And she'd never told him. Never reached out. Had frozen him out of both of their lives. And now she was gone. How was he supposed to be angry with her when she'd fucking died on him? Him and his little girl. *Genoveva.* A beautiful name. A beautiful young girl. She had his eyes, but he saw some of her mother in there as well. The whole meeting was a blur. But the two unlikely new allies were so compassionate. So understanding.

They'd left him after lunch. He barely remembered eating. What in the fuck had he actually consumed? Some sort of curry poured over chips. Yes, one of the few edible dishes at the hospital cafeteria. They'd told him all about what St. Clare's was like now. About the hospital and the orfanato. The only clear decision that had come out of the whole afternoon was that he was headed to Brazil. As soon as he could get to his boss's office and arrange it, he'd be on emergency family leave. He would go to Brazil. He would return to the one patch of earth that he swore he'd never set foot on again. He'd go back for his little girl, while the small remnants of her childhood still remained. He'd failed her mother, but he would not fail her.

* * *

One word frees us of all the weight and pain in life. That word is love—Sophocles

St. Clare's Charity Mission, Manaus, Brazil

Caitlyn sat on the edge of her cot for several minutes, just looking at the little gift that Patrick had wrapped so perfectly. She never asked for anything. The true joy of Christmas presents was the surprise. And her Patrick was a particularly good gift giver. No endcap shopping for O'Brien men. They were as thoughtful as they were decorative. She smiled, thinking about the time, early in their courtship, when Michael had gifted Branna with an antique spinet piano.

Patrick's gestures, despite their small budget, had always been romantic and thoughtful. She laughed out loud, thinking about him rifling through her knicker drawer. She could just picture… She shot up, abruptly standing at attention, flooded with panic. *The scrapbook.* A wave of nausea hit her. She'd left the scrapbook in the deep recesses of her lingerie drawer. She put her hand on her chest, moaning. "Oh, God. Please don't find it."

With her gift still in her hand, she scooped up her laptop and ran to the only place on the grounds that had WiFi. Fumbling, she set up on the library table and was calling the flat within minutes. *Please, God. Don't let him have picked it up.* The ornament, the notes from her office visits. It would be like a knife in his heart. It rang for so long, she was afraid he wouldn't answer. What if he'd been working distracted? What if he was hurt? Before the next *what if* formed in her mind, he answered.

"Oh, God. You're there!" He was startled out of his sleepy state.

"What's happened? Are you okay?"

"Yes, of course. I just…" She wasn't sure how to go about this. If he hadn't found it, she'd have Seany take it out and put it somewhere else. Dammit she was such an eejit. "How was work?"

He cocked his head curiously. "It was quiet. Everyone was behaving, I suppose. Lass, I don't want you to think I'm unhappy you called again so soon, but you seemed very relieved when I picked up. Are you sure you're okay?"

She smiled, holding up her package. "I haven't opened it. Did you like your gift?"

His face warmed. "It's exquisite. She plays beautifully. I named her Roxanne." He wiggled his eyebrows.

"You're making me jealous. I'm glad you like it. Aidan helped me pick it out when they last visited."

"Open yours, then. It's not as fabulous as Roxanne, but I think you'll like it." He gestured to the package she held.

Caitlyn knew her husband. He was trying to be upbeat and playful, but his eyes were swollen. More so than just from sleep. Had he been crying? He leaned in and smiled, "It's okay. Just open it."

She pulled the bow and wrapping, revealing a velvet bag. "What have you done? We were on a budget!"

He cracked off a laugh. "You're one to talk! I suppose that gorgeous bouzouki fell within the budget? Just open it, hen. The suspense is killing me."

She loosened the string on the velvet bag and gasped as she poured the contents into her hand. "Oh, Patrick. Oh, my love. It's perfect!" He let out a sigh of relief that he'd gotten something right in the last two months.

"It's Art Deco, from the twenties is what Granny said. She helped me find it. She knows where to go for an honest dealer. Ye know how she loves her vintage bobbles."

Caitlyn couldn't believe the gorgeous bracelet she held in her hand. White gold filigree with three marquis emeralds. One larger in the middle and one to either side mounted horizontally, about two inches from the center. It was perfection with curling lines, accented by the jutting straight lines and angles that marked the time period. The clasp was enamel coated with the swirling tones you'd find in a peacock feather. It was unique. He must have really looked within the vintage jewelry markets to find something so perfect. She loved vintage jewelry. "I don't know what to say. It's so perfect."

"And they're emeralds, like your eyes." His face took her in, hungry for connection. Like he wished he could touch her. Her throat constricted. Before she could ask him, he said, "I love you. I'm so sorry, Caitlyn. I'm sorry for how you've suffered."

He knew. Jesus, she hated herself right now. She'd gone through the last weeks in a haze. "Oh, love. You found it. Oh, God. I'm such an eejit. I was hoping you hadn't. I remembered, and that's why I called. I was hoping maybe I could have Seany move it before..." She covered her mouth. "I'm so sorry. You're there alone. I left you right before Christmas and I forgot that damn book in my drawer." The tears were flowing.

He looked puzzled. "I thought you wanted me to see it. That maybe that was your way of trying to help me understand."

Her heart sank. "Oh, darlin'. I wouldn't do that to you. You understand me more than anyone. I know it doesn't seem like it, but I do know that. You're my best friend."

"And you should know that trying to hide things from me is pointless. I know your soul, Caitlyn. We share it all."

"How are you, really? If we share it all, then tell me why your eyes are swollen."

He held her gaze for a moment, swallowing hard. *Do it. Tell her, or you're a coward and a hypocrite.* "Because I couldn't be strong anymore, and I cried until I shook with it. I cried for us. For our families. For the children we lost. I cried until I couldn't cry anymore."

Caitlyn put her hand up to the screen, shuddering from her silent tears. "I wish I could hold you. I'm sorry I can't. I'm sorry that I'm so bloody selfish."

He shook his head. "No, mo shíorghrá. You're the most selfless person I know. I'm sick without you. I won't lie. But if you need to do this thing, then do it with my blessing. I'm not goin' anywhere. Just come back to me. Promise me that ye'll come back to me, no matter what."

She ran a finger over his jaw, wishing the hard computer screen was his warm, stubbly skin. "I promise. And I love my bracelet. I'd be afraid to wear it while I'm here, but I love it." She blew him a kiss, and let him go back to sleep, his heart a little less burdened.

* * *

CAITLYN KNOCKED on the abbess's office doorway, ducking her head in with a shy smile. "There you are, my dear. Please, join me for a cup of tea. We've been so busy with the holiday, I feel like I've been neglecting you."

Caitlyn came into the room, taking a seat in the chair opposite of her old desk. The office was simple, efficient. Nothing but a picture of the Pope and a crucifix adorning the walls. The abbess was in her brown linen habit today, as the ground was muddy from the rain. "Not at all, Reverend Mother. It's been a bit overwhelming, and I'm afraid I snuck off for a nap more than once."

"Aye, well it'll get easier. How are you feeling otherwise?" Her look was direct and Caitlyn squirmed like a school girl.

"I'm fine, Reverend Mother. Why do you ask?" But she knew. She'd been given medical clearance, but the box for *Have you been hospital-*

ized for any reason in the last year? Yep. "I'm assuming you're referring to my latest hospital stay. I assure you that I'm fit and ready for duty."

"I don't doubt that you are physically capable of doing your assigned work. My concern is how you are feeling otherwise. Did your brother-in-law happen to mention what my expertise was prior to and during my time as a sister? No? Well then, I was a psychologist. A mental health therapist, more specifically. I spent the last year counseling Dr. O'Brien. It was a term of his extended time here."

Caitlyn knew where this was headed. "Yes, well he suffered a terrible loss."

Reverend Mother Faith cut her off with, "As did you."

She wondered if it was indeed Liam that she could thank for this little meeting. *Damn you, Liam.* But the abbess's shrewd blue eyes gave nothing away.

* * *

SEAMUS AND MARY were consulting on an infant case of influenza. Dangerous even for adults, the parents had been frantic when they arrived at the hospital on foot from the neighboring village. The child was stable now, taking fluids and finally sleeping. The fever was under control. They both looked to the side in sync, and away from the child's chest X-ray that they were looking over. "Hello, Caitlyn. No school today, eh?" Seamus said, smiling.

Mary narrowed her eyes. She knew this young woman like her own daughter. "What's amiss?"

Caitlyn's jaw tightened. Seamus's breath hissed from between his teeth. "She's been to see the abbess, I suspect."

Caitlyn folded her arms, her long braid getting trapped between her arm and her ribs. She flicked it behind her back irritably. "So is it one of you that I have to thank for these little counseling sessions?" Her gaze flicked back and forth between the two doctors.

Seamus put his hands up in defense. "Don't look at me. I mind my own business when it comes to matters of the mind." Both the women chuffed.

"Right. Sure ye do. That's contrary to what Liam tells me. That aside," Mary turned to Caitlyn. "I didn't have anything to do with it. I do know that Liam, despite his protests, took great comfort from his time with the abbess. Does it really matter? She doesn't seem the sort to be easily dissuaded. I think it's a brilliant idea."

"Agreed," Seamus said. "I know you O'Briens think you can handle anything on your own, but sometimes you don't have to. If you had been my patient back in Ireland, I would have suggested counseling. And if the Reverend Mother had asked me, I'd have agreed with her."

"I'm fine."

Seamus snorted. "Famous last words of any woman headed for a meltdown. Save it, lass. I've three daughters, a mother, four sisters, and a crazy ex-wife. I am expert level at deciphering the code of womankind. Just do the damn sessions and enjoy the biscuits and tea." He took the x-ray from the illuminated mount, and went to the desk to put it in the patient file.

"I can't help with matters of the heart, Mrs. O'Brien. I am, however, well versed on childbirth, the physical aspects of a female, and fertility matters. My former partner, who bought the practice, was a fertility specialist. We worked side by side for ten years. If you'll let me, I'd like to help you. When you're ready, I'd like to hear it all and review your case. Once I leave, two weeks from now, I'll most likely be at the main hospital in Galway. I know you live in Dublin, but I'm not so far from Doolin. I'd like to help you."

Mary squeezed his shoulder and excused herself. She'd treated the girl, and maybe through divine providence, Seamus could treat the woman. He was very well respected. He'd get that position in Galway. She wouldn't be surprised if they both heard from the hospital chief tomorrow. Between her introduction, Sorcha's nudge, and Liam's letter of recommendation, they would push them over the edge. Seamus O'Keefe was at the top of his field. Maybe he'd put his head together with Caitlyn and find some resolution to her problem. That second opinion that would give her tools for success, or help her finally accept that she shouldn't have biological children. And she herself would step in not as a doctor, but as a woman and a friend.

Caitlyn stood across from Seamus, blushing for some ridiculous reason. He sensed her hesitation. "Perhaps when ye've been here a little longer. It's no pressure." He backed up, headed for the doorway. Caitlyn closed her eyes, afraid to hope that a third doctor could really help her.

She said the words like rapid fire. "I've lost three children." He stopped, and it was his eyes that undid her. She covered her mouth, trying to rein in the emotion. Swallowing, she composed herself and began to talk.

* * *

GENOVEVA LOVED DAYS OFF. Like any child, the respite from school was welcomed. Unlike regular children, however, it was the downtime that was often the most difficult. In a normal childhood, days off of school were spent away from classmates. The hours of freedom were spent in a private residence. Maybe with siblings watching cartoons, or with parents on a day trip. That wasn't how it worked at St. Clare's. A child in the orfanato lived among her classmates. The shared dorm rooms offering no escape. The dinner table was filled with the same children you'd had your mathematics lessons with that morning.

Right now, she was trying to exercise. She missed Izzy. She'd been a sort of buffer between Genoveva and the prying eyes of her judgmental classmates. With Izzy, she hadn't felt excluded. She'd felt special and valued. Dr. O'Keefe was a nice man. He and Raphael would pull her into a workout on occasion, but it wasn't the same. If Izzy were here, she'd feel strong. She'd ignore her classmates and concentrate. She pulled down on her shirt as she finished with the burpees. Then she noticed the female doctor. The new one with the small frame and the short dark hair, the same length as hers. She smiled shyly. "Hello Dr. Falk."

Mary waved a hand, "Everyone calls me Doc Mary at home. If it's okay with Sister Maria, it's what I prefer."

"Okay, Doc Mary," she said shyly. The woman was pretty. Intense looking, but attractive. "Am I needed?"

"No, I was just watching your workout. You're made of tough stuff, lass. I don't think I could keep up with all that jumping and throwing things around, but when my husband gets here, I think you might have someone to exercise with. Would you mind?"

She shook her head. "No, Doctor. I just wish…"

"You wish Izzy was here," she filled in with a knowing smile. "I understand. Well, he's no Izzy, but he's a good guy. Don't be too hard on him. He's getting old." Genoveva covered her mouth with a giggle.

She looked sideways, and Emilio and Henrico were still watching. Along with the new girl who had come to them a few weeks ago. She'd been living with her grandmother, who died in the hospital, so Rosalis never left. It was similar to how Genoveva had ended up here.

Rosalis was a nice enough girl, but she was quiet. She was pleasant to look at. Like a proper Brazilian girl. Small waist, dark eyes and hair. She was one year younger than Geonoveva and about five inches shorter. Delicate, unlike her. She had a crush on Emilio, but he said she was too young. Emilio was almost seventeen. Henrico was sixteen. Six months older than Genoveva. Soon they would all age out and have to leave. The thought took her breath.

"Have you tried asking the older kids to work out with you? They seem to watch you rather intently," Mary said.

"No. They watch to see if they can find something funny. See if I make a mistake. Talk meanly about…" She pulled on her shirt again.

"Well, maybe they're just jealous. You're very strong. I was watching you. You have a powerful body. That can intimidate some people. Even adults. You are very pretty, which can also intimidate young boys. Sometimes they tease because they're afraid to tell you what they really think."

"I don't think so, but thank you." She wiped her hands on the track pants that Izzy had given her, and then said, "I think I'll go have a shower. Thank you, Doc Mary. I know you try to help, but no one can help me. I'm different, and soon I will have to leave this place. These things will happen to them as well." She gestured to the other teenagers. "Then we will have bigger problems, I think, than how I look when I exercise."

Mary's heart broke as she watched the pretty young girl, with the weight of the world on her shoulders, walk away.

Henrico's heart did a little sink as he watched Genoveva walk to the girl's dormitory. He liked watching her do this CrossFit. She was strong. Her pretty green eyes focused. He'd never known a girl like her. Emilio nudged him. He said in Portuguese, "You are pathetic, brother."

Henrico shrugged him off. "I don't know what you're talking about. Now, are you going to use that football or sit there and lean on it?" He smacked the ball out from under Emilio's elbow and ran for it, with Emilio hot on his tail.

* * *

SEAMUS REACHED a hand across the table where they were seated and put it over Caitlyn's. He squeezed. "I'm so sorry, lass. To lose one is hard enough. I had no idea."

"No one here knows."

"And it will stay that way unless you tell them. You are officially my pro-bono patient. And if it gets too much for you, we can stop and talk another day. You're in charge." He gave her hand another reassuring squeeze and pulled away. "Now, I'm going to ask you some questions. When we're done, I'm going to send you down to Pedro for some blood work. I'm sorry, I have to ask. Could you be pregnant now? When was the last time you had a test?"

"I didn't have one. My paperwork was rushed, and I didn't have any reason, at the time of my physical, to think that I was."

"Past tense? Is there a chance?"

"Well, the last time before I left." She rubbed her upper lip nervously. "We didn't use anything. But there's no chance. I haven't even begun cycling again. We weren't trying."

"Aye, well if you aren't trying to prevent it, then you're trying." He gave her a chiding look. "Then first things first." He pulled a home pregnancy test out of his drawer of supplies. She looked at it and her shoulders slumped. "They're very accurate. We use them in the field."

"It's not that. It's just...I don't have fond memories of sitting and waiting to see if I get the double blue line." She shook herself. "It's okay, though. If I must do it, then best to get it out of the way."

She watched as he put it away. "Pedro needs to draw blood anyway. He can check that way. The key to our relationship is me not causing you any more stress. Now, tell me about each pregnancy. Actually start before that. When did you first start trying?"

So she told him. She told him about their trouble in the beginning, the eventual hormone shots that helped jumpstart her system. Then she told him about the first two miscarriages. She'd almost made it out of the first trimester, but not quite. About her husband's desire to stop trying. Offering to sterilize himself and explore other options. About the severity of her last miscarriage. About her little boy, small enough to put in your palm.

"The third time, I made it a lot longer. I was eighteen weeks, as you read in my file. I felt the baby moving. We thought he was fine, but I was having some stitches in my abdomen and back. I thought it was normal growing pains. I should have gone to the hospital."

"It likely was growing pains if you were starting to show. It would be difficult to know the difference between that pain, and anything else that was going on. That second trimester, your body is overwhelmed with sensations. This wasn't your fault. Now, eighteen-week miscarriages don't happen that often. There could be a few reasons."

"My doctor said something about an incompetent cervix."

Seamus sighed. "I really hate that term. Cervical insufficiency isn't much better, I suppose. He's likely right. I think with your doctor being on holiday, not regularly checking your cervix, means that your cervix could have been changing and you just didn't know. It probably happened in that gap between check ups. Have they checked everything else? Cysts? Endometriosis? A double uterus?"

"Yes, they checked all of that. I'm clear. I had irregular cycles when I was younger, sometimes going four months between. The hormone shots seemed to help. I got pregnant three times. I just couldn't hold them." Caitlyn wiped a tear away.

"Listen, Patrick might be right. There are other ways to have children without putting your health at risk," he said. She stiffened.

He put a hand up, "But you're in charge. With repeat miscarriages, I am going to have to agree on the doctor's diagnosis. However, there are ways around it. There are methods of securing your cervix until we get you to full term. When we're all back in Ireland, if you want to try them, then I'll help you."

Caitlyn hugged him fiercely. "Thank you, Seamus."

"First we need blood. And I'm not promising anything other than I will help you try. I'll explain it all to Patrick when the time comes to put his mind at ease a bit, but you need to involve him in all of these decisions. He's your husband and you're in this together. Ye likely scared him to death. I'd feel the same way on the matter, if I'd watched you bleed out like that. Don't be too hard on him, okay?"

CHAPTER 8

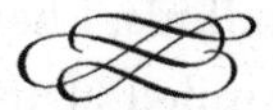

"Be strong, saith my heart; I am a soldier; I have seen worse sights than this."
Homer, The Odyssey

Hans Falk was a retired Sgt. Major in the United States Marine Corps. He'd been to many different places all around the globe. He'd been to several developing countries and areas destroyed by war. Bosnia, Africa, and several areas in the Middle East.

Somehow, he'd never managed to get used to the sight of poverty. He supposed that was a good thing. Some things you shouldn't get numb to, or what the hell were you fighting for?

As he looked out the open side of the Jeep, he took in the sight of the Manaus slums. Tipsy houses on sticks, stacked on top of each other. Streams of raw sewage. Raphael read his thoughts. "It's not all like this. This is the worst of it. It is a very poor area. You saw that parts of the city are very wealthy. But this part of Brazil isn't like the southern part. There is much more poverty, drugs, and poor living conditions."

"Your English is very good, Raphael. I can see why they hired you.

How are you with that knife?" Hans said, gesturing to the large fighting knife on his hip.

"Very good, Senhor. I was in the army many years. Now I am in the reservist unit. I was injured. I miss it. I love my work at the abbey, but I still miss it."

"I understand, brother. The Marine Corps life was a hard one, but I miss it every day. I'm like a bull that's been put out to pasture. I love my life, though. I see my grandkids, I have a beautiful bride. Now I'm here. Life is good." Raphael smiled at this. Hans tilted his head back and to the side. "You're awfully quiet back there, Dr. Maguire. You okay?"

The doctor next to him, Rachel Gordon, was leaning on her inner arm, exhausted from the two day trip. Australia to Brazil was a brutal itinerary. She'd nodded off about five minutes into the drive from the airport. Quinn was tired as well, but wired. He was also downright terrified.

"Please, call me Quinn. We're going to be working closely, and from what I remember of St. Clare's, it's not a formal place."

"Roger that. And you can call me Hans. I'm sure they'll be thrilled to see you again after all these years. At least some of the staff and sisters must have been working here sixteen years ago. It must be strange being back after all these years."

"You have no bloody idea, brother."

Quinn felt ready to lose his lunch. The place hadn't changed much, but in another way, reality had shifted. He was fresh out of medical school when he came here last time. Twenty-eight, on the last leg of a divorce, and ready to dive into missionary work.

Since then he'd been to Angola in Africa, Honduras during a hurricane cleanup, and then Thailand. He'd left this place emotionally destroyed. Angela had refused to see him. Refused to listen. He'd loved her so much. She'd loved him too. He knew this. She'd been two years younger, but a devout Catholic. And she'd had his baby. Well, he was relatively sure she'd had his baby. Who else could have sired the lass? The timing was certainly right, but as of right now, the only person that knew for certain was in her grave this eight years past.

Genoveva. She'd named the child after his mother Genevieve. That had to be the case. She'd just used the Portuguese derivative of the name. He'd watched the video over and over again. Freezing it on shots of the girl. She had his eyes, his dimples that he got from his father. The broad shoulders that came from the Maguire side of his family. *Stop it.*

He had to stop it. If she wasn't his, it would be like losing Angela all over again. Losing a child that he'd never known he had. *Please, be mine.* He was the devoted pediatrician who'd never had his own children. He thought he'd never have them. He hadn't been involved with anyone in five years. The last woman hadn't wanted kids. It was a sore spot that had festered between them over a three year period. She'd been the one to end it.

Just like his ex-wife, she'd moved on to greener pastures before actually ending it with him. Hedging her bets, so to speak. Getting another man on deck before she'd given him his walking papers. It didn't matter. He hadn't actually loved the last one. He'd just been lonely. She was smart and beautiful. A pharmaceutical representative who was a master at engineering a favorable outcome with her long legs and polished looks.

He was past all of that now. All that mattered was finding out if Genoveva was actually his daughter. If she was, then the next step was to convince her that he was worthy enough to step into the role that he'd been ignorant of. To be a parent, although she was nearly grown. He could give her a good life back in Ireland. But would it be enough? Would she even want him as her father?

They pulled onto the dirt path, shrouded by tangled vines and lush forest. Like being swallowed, the dirt of the city disappeared. He heard the man in the front, the American, whistle through his teeth. "Wow." That's all he said. Quinn looked up, the sun peeking through the canopy. The trees still fresh and damp from the last rain. Birds and insects fluttering and humming around them. It really was breathtaking. In a small way, he felt like he was coming home.

* * *

Doolin, Co. Clare, Ireland

Michael O'Brien had learned to just stand back and wait for instructions when it came to packing up the car. He was the muscles of the operation, Branna the brains. He knew this. She was the most practical of packers. Three children in carseats in his SUV, she pointed to the final empty spot where he put the box of freshly baked items from his mother's house, and three jars of Branna's homemade gooseberry preserves. One for each apartment, and an extra just for Seany, because the fiend ate the stuff right out of the jar.

"That's it, baby. Let's roll!" She smiled and he just couldn't start driving before he kissed her. He pulled her by the waist, and she looked up at him. She was a wee thing, the top of her head coming to the center of his chest. He leaned down. "Give me your mouth, darlin." She met him half way as he kissed her. He cupped the back of her head with his other palm, deepening the kiss. She moaned against his mouth. When he broke the kiss, she let out a sigh.

"Didn't you get enough last night?" She knew him. It was never enough.

"Those damn apartments are filled to capacity. I won't be getting my share of you with these little fiends crammed in the guest room with us," he said,

She giggled. "Getting more than your share is how we got these three fiends."

"True enough." He let her go, and she gave the carseats one last check before getting in the passenger seat. "Off to Dublin!" she said. Her twins said in unison, "Dublin!"

"Can I sleep with Uncle Tadgh?" Brian loved his uncle. Branna had to laugh. In all of her imaginings, having twins speak to her with the full force of the local brogue wasn't even on the radar five years ago. She'd been burying her mother, swearing she'd never fall in love or have children. She gave Brian an indulgent look.

'Honey, we are staying upstairs at your Uncle Patrick's flat. Uncle Tadgh has a wife he sleeps with. Uncle Seany will be on the pull out sofa. Maybe you can sleep with him or Uncle Patrick? Uncle Patrick might be lonely."

"Do ye think he'd like that?" Brian was so sweet.

"I don't know, but you can ask." She traded looks with Michael. The family had all agreed to take turns making visits or inviting Patrick for dinner on his days off. Going home to an empty apartment every night was hard for a man in his place. She understood Caitlyn. She'd done her own bit of running when she was grieving. She'd fled her own country, moved to Ireland on a whim. But she hadn't had a husband at home. She hadn't had anyone. Caitlyn had a husband and parents and sisters. It was their duty to take care of him until Caitlyn found her way back. And she would. Caitlyn was a wonderful woman and a devoted wife. But pain changed you, and sometimes you just had to bug out. She'd be back, and she and Patrick would figure things out. They had to. None of them were perfect, but O'Briens worked things out with their mates. Always.

* * *

Pearson St. Garda Station, Dublin

Patrick jumped up from his little cubicle in the headquarters of the Dublin Garda. He'd been going over a map of the city districts, memorizing specifics for the armed response team. Mapping out alternate routes to major targets, in case emergency vehicles couldn't get through the more traveled roads. He was going to be late if he didn't leave now. He was supposed to meet his sister-in-law, Branna, and Josh and Seany, the dynamic duo. Michael had stayed back at the flat with the three small children, giving them all a nap. Michael had pulled a twenty-four hour shift yesterday at the Shannon Coast Guard station. So, it wasn't a hardship to let Branna go out without him. Michael sent him a selfie from the apartment that had him laughing out loud. He had the smallest child, Ian, fast asleep on his chest. Brian and Halley were curled on either side of him. *We're in your bed in case one of them pisses. And I drank your last beer.*

Now Patrick was headed to Grogans for a quick supper. He had to work until ten, then he'd have two days to spend with his brother and his family. He skirted Trinity College, trying not to think about all the times he'd met his brother Liam for a meal. As he cut through Parliament Square, he wondered why in the hell anyone, including himself, owned a car in this city. Truth be told, they'd only kept the car because they liked driving to the west coast whenever they felt like it. They'd also assumed that they'd eventually need a car when they had a child. He shook that thought off as he approached the Molly Malone statue. Native Dubliners renamed such landmarks, giving them witty nicknames instead. Molly had been given several. *The tart with the cart. The trollop with the scallop. The flirt with the skirt.* And Patrick's personal favorite, *The dolly with the trolley.* The sculptor brought it on himself, really. Molly's bosoms were half out of her bodice.

As he rounded the corner, he groaned. The place was bloody packed with locals and tourists alike. Branna was waving with Seany and Josh next to her. "Don't worry, Patrick. I'm all over it. I just called Leo's and they're frying up four fish and chips as we speak. They'll be done when we get there."

"That's quite a walk, lass. And it's take-away only," Patrick said.

She just smiled and waved a hand. "We'll eat on the benches by Dublin Castle. It's warm for this time of year. I know a good spot. It's hidden in the gardens. We'll have a proper picnic."

They started walking toward the castle, and Seany slung his arm around his sister-in-law. "I've missed you. I'm glad you're here."

"I'm glad, too. We've missed you. Just to warn you, you might have a sleeping buddy on that pull-out tonight. Brian has boundary issues."

Josh laughed and Seany gave him a sideways glance. "Ye think that's funny, do ye? Maybe I'll bring them upstairs. You've got two beds in that room."

Josh smiled and winked at Branna. He was such a good guy. She didn't get to see him as much as she'd like to, but he'd really blossomed since he'd moved to Ireland. He'd been through so much. He and Charlie had a rough childhood. Children should be loved and treasured. The O'Brien's knew this instinctively. And although Josh was hardly a child, they'd brought him into the family with a loving embrace. Unconditionally, just like they'd done to her.

Patrick started telling them about Caitlyn's Christmas gift when he stopped. They were in an alley, cutting over to the road where Leo had his fish and chip stand, when Patrick froze and shushed everyone. "I heard something. Like an animal." He was looking further into the dark recesses of the narrow street. It was lined with brick buildings. More specifically, the rear of the buildings. There were back exits to apartment flats with dumpsters, bike racks full of bicycles, dark windows with an occasional light on in someone's apartment. No people, though. It was just past dark and the city was humming with activity. But not this alley. This alley seemed to be in its own hushed universe. It was almost eerie. Like when the birds stopped singing right before a tornado.

They looked around and then everyone heard it. A muffled mewling sound. Patrick was at the recycle bin in a flash. "Do you think it's a kitten?" Branna said. Josh and Seany lifted the lid off and their eyes shot to Patrick as he made a sound like all the air had been sucked out of his lungs. They all looked inside the bin and Branna choked on a sob. "Call an ambulance!" she yelled.

Patrick was lifting the small child out of the bin before anyone else could take action. "Oh, God. No. Jesus, Seany. He's so little! And he's cold! He's freezing!" Seany went into paramedic mode as Josh called emergency services. Branna was huddled around Patrick, sobbing. "Oh, God. Patrick. Who would do this?" Every protective instinct had kicked in with her, and with the men. Josh was calling 999 and trying to stay calm so he could speak.

Seany's voice was kind, but commanding. "Branna, love. I need to check him. Please." She backed up and he removed his coat, swaddling the child. The cord was cut, but a good three inches was still there. It was a baby boy, probably just hours old. He mewed like a little kitten, but he was weak. They all knew enough about babies to see that he was weak and probably premature. "His tongue is dry. Jesus, he's dehydrated. He's had no fluids. He's probably never had fluids!" Seany's voice was raising in panic. The child was wiggling. That was a good sign. Seany wrapped him snuggly, trying to bring up his body temperature. Thank God the day had been warm.

"Should we move to a bigger street?" Patrick asked as he took the child back in his arms, while Seany took over the call with emergency services.

"No, stay right here. They're going to take about fifteen minutes. They can pull right up if we keep this alley clear."

"Fifteen minutes!" Patrick was shaking, holding the child so gently. Branna was crying.

Seany said, "God dammit. If only I had some saline or even a fucking bottle! His mouth is so dry that his tongue is sticking to his mouth."

Before the three men knew what was happening, Branna was moving, shedding her winter coat. "I can do it! I can give him fluids!" Seany didn't understand at first, but then it dawned on him what she meant.

They lowered the child to her. She was leaning against Patrick now, a soft barrier from the dirty brick of the building. She was sitting on Josh's coat. When she put the child to her breast, he made a weak little sound, trying to turn his head. "Come on little man. You can do it." Tears dripped off her nose. She touched her nipple to his cheek and leaned him into her. She'd done this hundreds of times with her three children. Ian was still nursing so she had milk. She could do this. "Please, little buddy. Take what you need."

She felt, more than heard, the sobs behind her. Patrick was crying. She looked up and realized that they all were tearing up. That's when it happened. The child started rooting. She laughed on a sob. "That's it, buddy. Don't be shy." She felt the heavy, prickling sensation move down her chest and breast as her milk let down. When he tasted the drop that trickled into his mouth, he became more urgent. Grunting and determined. "You're so strong, little man. You're going to be okay. Just take what you need." As he finally latched weakly to her breast, she felt the first swallow. "He's drinking. I can feel him." She whispered the words, not wanting to startle him.

Patrick was crying in her hair. "Thank you, sister. Oh, God. Thank God you were here." Then Josh took her coat and laid it over her and the child, blanketing them from the night air. It was the longest fifteen minutes of their lives, but the ambulance came. And Tadgh and Sal were right behind them. This wasn't just a medical emergency. It was a crime scene. Patrick couldn't take his hand off the child. The small child that survived the first hours of his life desperately alone. *I can't leave him,* he thought. And before anyone could argue, he climbed into the ambulance like he was supposed to be there.

* * *

MANAUS, Brazil

Mary heard the grumble of Raphael's Jeep and was out the door in an instant. Hans was climbing out of the passenger seat, unfolding those long legs like a giant, powerful cat. Then she was in his arms and off the ground. He was a full foot taller than her and probably had a hundred pounds on her, but when he purred in her ear, he was more like a hungry kitten than a giant cat. "I missed you, Doc. Jesus. You smell good."

She kissed him hard, cupping his head with her hands. Then she heard giggles and a cough. She turned her head, and Reverend Mother Faith was standing silently, brow raised. Cristiano and a few of the smaller children were giggling. Hans put her down reluctantly. "Sorry about that Ma'am." Hans said with as much dignity as he could muster, but the side of his mouth was curved up. A sign that he wasn't the least bit sorry. "Sgt. Maj. Hans Falk, retired. You must be the abbess." He put his hand out in formal greeting.

The abbess took it, her own grin surfacing. "You may call me Reverend Mother Faith. It's good to have you, and your wife has been invaluable at the hospital. Please, leave your bags to Paolo and come join us for lunch. Gabriela has made her feijoada especially for our new guests." Then her eyes traveled to the other two doctors. "Dr. Gordon, you must be exhausted. We will of course understand if you head for your cot in lieu of lunch. Dr. Maguire, it is good to see you again. So many years have passed, but you look much the same, my boy."

Quinn looked at the Reverend Mother and almost started tearing up. Her face was so kind. She knew, of course. Knew why he hadn't been back, and why he now returned. He dropped his bag and walked to her, and she wrapped him in a hug. Like a mother. "We've missed you, lad. God has brought you home to us."

They went through many introductions, then made their way to the cantina. The smells were the same. Bean and pork stew, cheese bread, ripe fruit, and the sweet smell of sweaty children, giggling and nudging each other. There was a beautiful, fair-haired teacher helping some of the smaller children wash their hands before eating.

Quinn's heart pounded in his chest as he searched the faces for Genoveva. Then he saw her. She had a small child clinging to her leg, and another that was curled into her, holding her hand. She was like a big sister. He wanted to cry. Partly because she'd grown up in an orphanage, losing her mother at a young age. Partly because she seemed to fit in perfectly here. Like the eldest sister with all of her young charges. Growing up faster than most kids had to.

She was magnificent. Taller than the other children. Broad shoulders and smartly cut hair. Smooth, tanned skin, neither the shade of his or of Angela's, but somewhere in between. Unique and beautiful. But the eyes were his. A luminous green that almost glowed against her darker features. He turned as he felt a hand on his shoulder.

"Come now, lad. Best not to rush it. I know it's difficult, but it is better to do this right. Wouldn't you agree?" The abbess's voice was calm and soothing, but she was giving a command. He knew this.

A shudder went through him. "You're right. I know, I'm sorry. It's just…she's quite something isn't she? I can see bits of Angela, but I see myself as well. Maybe it's wishful thinking." He smiled sadly. "We'll wait, just to be sure. So, what has Gabriela cooked up for lunch? I'm famished."

The abbess laughed. "You always did have a good appetite. Come, lad. I want to hear all about Africa."

* * *

MARY LED Hans down the path that led to the cluster of bungalows that Seamus had shown her. Seamus rarely used it, especially when he had patients that were nearing their due dates. Which was almost always the case. Liam had used it, she knew. And it was in this small cottage that the love had blossomed between him and the American doctor, Izzy.

"So, is there a good reason I didn't offload my luggage in the men's dorm?" Hans was tired, cranky, and wanted a shower.

"Well, if you really want to stay in the men's wing in that tiny cot, feel free to turn around, but I think you're going to like this much better." She grinned over her shoulder as the path opened up. She motioned with her head to the enclosed house. Modest looking, but private.

A huge grin surfaced on her husband's face. "Is that just for us?"

"Yes, it is. And it's air conditioned."

Hans let out a whoop, running up the stairs like a man half his age. He dropped his bag on the front porch and ran back down. Mary was confused, digging for the key to give him. She handed it to him, and he took it in one swoop at the same time as he slung her over his shoulder like a Viking raider. She laughed as her head bobbed up and down, him taking the steps two at a time. "I need a shower, Doc. Then you and I are going to get something straight between us."

"That joke wasn't funny the first time you told it, Hans." But even as she said it, she was laughing. God, she'd missed him. He pulled their bags in after he'd deposited her on the bed. When he got that look like he was going to eat her alive, she put up a hand. "Hold that thought, dear. Some rituals must be observed." Hans raised a brow. Then she went about the inspection that Seamus had instructed her about. Bug, snake and spider patrol. After she finished, she looked at him. "Did any of that sink in?"

"No ma'am. Now come over here." He crooked his finger, beckoning her, and she went.

CHAPTER 9

NATIONAL MATERNITY HOSPITAL, DUBLIN 2, DUBLIN, IRELAND

Patrick ended the call to his superior, Sergeant Rahn. He respected the man, but he'd been worried that he would pull Patrick from guard duty. Tadgh and his partner Sal were handling the investigation, and the child wasn't in any known danger. All he needed now was time and attention. The doctors and nurses could do that.

Their fear that the child had been dangerously premature was incorrect. The doctor in the neonatal unit estimated the boy to have been between thirty-five and thirty-six weeks. Early, and he was small, just over five pounds. This could have to do with the mother smoking during the pregnancy, more than when the child had been born. *The mother.* Like she deserved to be called anything but a devil. Abortion was illegal in Ireland, and many disagreed with that. Women had to go to England or put the child up for adoption, or find a doctor to do an illegal termination. There were some countries that had safe haven baby boxes, where someone could leave a child anonymously, but Ireland hadn't passed such a law. All that aside, the politics didn't matter when it came to dropping a newborn into a recycling bin. It was murder, plain and simple. Or in this case, attempted murder.

To leave a newborn without a stitch of clothing in the middle of winter…the thought made his stomach roll. He went back to the large glass window where the NICU patients were lined up in their clear plastic bassinets. So many children that had, for one reason or another, had a rough start to their lives. But the other children were probably loved, cherished, and wanted. They probably had parents that had gone home to get a few hours of sleep, or down to the cafeteria for a snack.

He looked at the small bundle named simply, Baby Boy Doe. He'd been suffering from severe dehydration and hypothermia, but the lid on the recycle bin had insulated him to a degree. Small favors. He hadn't suffered any long term effects from the cold. Luckily, it had been an uncommonly warm day in Dublin today. Considering tomorrow was New Year's Eve, it could have been snowing. Patrick waved stupidly at the child. It wasn't as if the kid could really see him. He'd started to cry, though, and it was the only thing he could think of to do. The shift nurses were so sweet to all of the babies, but there were three of them for twelve children. Feedings, changes, vitals, medication, recording all these things in their medical charts. One of the nurses looked up and saw that he was back. She smiled, pointing to a side door where they could meet and talk.

"Hello Officer. I see you're still here. Our Baby Boy Doe is lucky to have such a fierce protector." She was flirting with him, but not in a serious way. She was friendly, probably a couple of years older than him. "I'll tell you what. We've got a parent room with rockers right through that door. If you're going to stay, I think the lad could use some cuddles. Would you like to feed him?" Patrick rubbed his head nervously. He was so small and fragile.

"Are ye sure it's all right? I mean, I've fed my nieces and nephews before, but he's such a wee thing."

"He's made of tough stuff. His swallow reflex is spot on. I think if we hook a syringe up to your finger, that might be a good way to make him feel like he's at a breast. The flow will be slower, so he won't choke. I'd have to give you a proper scrubbing, but if you're willing, I think it would do him some good to be held. The poor lamb. How could someone do such a thing? He'd likely been in that bin for hours given the shape he was in. He's a miracle."

"I'll do it then, if you think it's okay. Listen," he said, wondering how much information he could get out of her. "My cousin is investigating this, but I was the first responder and I'll be assisting on this case. Could you tell me how the blood work came back? Were there any drugs in his system?"

She looked at him sideways, like she wasn't sure if she should tell him. "Well, since you're the only one here to take up for the boy, I suppose I can tell you. No, he didn't have any drugs in his system. Sometimes it takes a while, if there was use earlier in the pregnancy, to see if he's suffered any damage. Things like developmental delays. But he's clean as far as we can tell, and he's a fighter. He's underweight, and he's been through a lot today. By the looks of that remaining cord we trimmed and other indicators, I think he was born very early this morning. He'll likely need to stay several weeks with us so we can monitor him. He's got a bit of a rattle, probably from the cold air, and we don't want him getting pneumonia. Meanwhile, the social workers can get to work trying to find a placement for him." She smiled warmly at the child. "He's a beautiful boy. Someone is bound to take him, don't you think? But for now, why don't we just get him fed. Come, and let's get you cleaned up." She pointed the way, smiling at him the way that women did when they were wondering how far to push the flirting. He'd have to flash the gold band when she had him scrubbing in.

After a thorough washing and removing his badge and other pokies, Patrick sat in a rocker. He couldn't believe how nervous he was. After all, it wasn't like the kid knew him. He didn't likely know anything other than his fear receptors and survival instincts weren't firing off as much. He was still crying when the nurse brought him in. He was swaddled in a little blue blanket and had some sort of stocking style hat on. Like the newborn pictures up on his mother's wall. All the grandchildren making the wall of fame in their turn. How sad that this child knew nothing of family.

As if she read his mind, the nurse said, "Every child deserves to be loved and held. He'd thank you for it if he could. Now don't mind the crying. Babies do that. This one is still trying to figure it all out." She put the child gently in Patrick's arms and he began to rock. "It's all right, lad. Cry all you want." But he didn't. He stopped, beginning to grunt and root.

"Look at that. He knows you're going to feed him. He trusts you. That's a sight to see, isn't it? He must know, somewhere deep down, that you're his hero." Patrick just smiled, taking in the baby's small face. He pursed his lips, eyes trying to focus, but not quite there. "He'll start to really see everyone in about a month. For now, he goes on instinct and probably smell. You were the first to hold him. He likely senses that. And your wife was first to feed him, I hear."

He shook his head, his throat tightening. "No, my sister-in-law. We were all headed to Leo's for a bit of supper. They're visiting from County Clare. She has her own children, so she was able to feed him. And thank God for it. He was pretty bad off when we found him, and she gave him some comfort, I think." Patrick couldn't take his eyes off the child.

"Do you have any children? Are you married?"

"Aye, I'm married. She's...well she's on a mission with the church. She's a teacher. She went to Brazil for two months. We lost a child. She's had three miscarriages, actually, but the last one was the worst. She was eighteen weeks. It happened a couple of months ago." He didn't meet her eyes, choosing instead to watch the small, warm bundle in his arms.

The nurse gasped, putting her hand over her mouth. "Oh dear, I am so sorry. This must surely be too much for you. I shouldn't have suggested it. I can feed him. I'm so sorry."

Patrick waved her off. "No, not at all. It's not your fault or his. It just is. It doesn't keep me from reaching for my nieces and nephews. It's a bit of comfort, actually, having other children to love." He shook himself, "Anyway, I'm not sure what will happen with everything, but I do miss her. I can't tell her about this, though. It would really upset her. To see someone so ungrateful for a child that they'd discard him like rubbish. I can't even conceive of it, even after all I've seen with four years in the Garda. I can't conceive of it. She has such a pure heart. I can't tell her about this."

"Perhaps she's stronger than you think. A young woman doing missionary work in South America doesn't sound so fragile to me." But she left it at that. As they talked, she hooked up the feeding syringe to Patrick's shirt, hooking it to the shoulder band of his uniform where his walkie microphone would normally attach. It had a small, flexible tube running down that she taped to his freshly trimmed and scrubbed pinky finger. She un-cinched the tubing as she showed him how to offer his pinky to the baby. When the formula hit his tongue, he started to move his head, searching for the source. Then finally he latched onto Patrick's finger.

Patrick laughed, looking up at the nurse. "I think he likes it." She just smiled, smoothing a finger over the child's forearm. "Though he be wee, he be mighty," she said. Then she left them alone in the quiet room and went to check on the other children.

Tadgh and Sal walked down the hallway of the neonatal unit, following the stern looking nurse. "You can only have a few minutes. These children are under heavy security and careful medical supervision. Some of them are very sick." She stopped at the window. "Now stay put. I'll get the doctor."

Sal gave Tadgh a sideways look. "She's kind of scary."

Tadgh laughed. He could only imagine how protective his Aunt Sorcha would be over her charges. A younger nurse waved and held up a finger. A few moments later, she emerged from the door. "Which one is yours?"

"None of them, ma'am. We're the detectives investigating the baby boy that was brought in. My cousins and brother-in-law found him. I'm sorry. I'm forgetting my manners. This is Detective Rahim Salib and I'm Detective Tadgh O'Brien." He showed his credentials that were slung around his neck with his badge, as did Sal.

"So, you must be a relative to our resident officer." Tadgh gave her a questioning look. "Officer Patrick O'Brien. He hasn't left the lad since he came in."

"Is he still here?" Tadgh asked. He'd sent for a patrol officer to take

Branna, Seany, and Josh back to the flats. They'd all been a mess. Branna had been inconsolable when they'd taken the child from her. She'd fed him. He was critically dehydrated when they found him, and she'd given of her body to keep him warm and hydrated until an ambulance could arrive. Tadgh shook his head, remembering her tear stained face. *Oh God, who would do this? How could someone do this to their child!*

"Could we see him, do you think?" Tadgh's voice was hoarse. The nurse nodded. "I'll fetch him. It's better if you don't go any further. Some of these children are immune compromised."

Patrick sang to the little boy as he drifted off to sleep. He'd had his fill, and was apparently content to lie warm and satisfied in Patrick's arms. He sang softly, an Irish lullaby his father used to sing to Seany. He'd probably sung it to all of them.

He looked up to find the nurse watching him, tears welling in her eyes. He shouldn't have told her about the miscarriages. It had just come out. "Your cousin and his partner are here to see you. I'll take him and put him down for a nap. Thank you, Officer O'Brien."

She leaned down to take the child, and he had the insane instinct to not let him go. But he did let her take him. It wasn't his child. He knew that. It was just that he was so peaceful. His eyes were that hazy blue that all newborns had. No distinct color showing yet. But his hair was fair. A soft, feathery dusting of fair hair covering his small head.

When he exited the side door of the secured part of the unit, he almost had to laugh. Sal and Tadgh all but had their noses pressed to the glass. They were waving and cooing at the babies. When they saw him, Tadgh's knowing eyes told him that he understood. That he hurt for him. That he'd do everything he could to see that the baby boy got justice.

"How are you, brother?" Tadgh said gently.

"I'm sad. Sad and angry. Tell me you have something." Patrick's voice was harsh.

"We're going door to door. It's all over the news. We'll find her. Or them, I suppose. The father could have done this."

"I'll castrate the fucker if it was his father who did this!" Patrick snapped.

"Aye, I'll sharpen the knife for you." Sal said, equally disgusted. He looked over at the nurse behind the window, putting the child back into its bassinet.

"Easy, now. First we need to find the mother. I've been calling all of the hospitals, looking for a woman who might be receiving medical care after giving birth. Someone claiming to have had a miscarriage. Or someone who was in labor and left before the child was born. We're checking the apartments and the surrounding alleys. Next will be abandoned buildings where rough sleepers tend to gather."

"Okay, well keep me posted." Patrick said. "I'm glad it's you on this. I know you two will give it your best."

The doctor who had treated the boy came down the hall toward them. He had a woman with him. She was in a skirt and blouse, hospital credentials around her neck. A social worker, by the looks of it. "Hello again, officers. I'd like to introduce you to Melanie Allen. She's our liaison social worker with the Department of Children and Youth Affairs. She's put in a care order for the child, and she'll be monitoring his case until you can either find next of kin or she can place him in a suitable home."

Patrick took the woman's measure. She was about forty, attractive, and had intelligent eyes. It was a good sign. "Surely you won't give the child back to someone who tried to kill him?"

"Abandonment is not attempted murder, Officer. We'll just have to get the entire picture."

"Well, they didn't leave him on a church pew or at a hospital, did they? They dumped him in the bin!" Patrick's voice was raising. Tadgh put an arm on him.

"We understand you're just doing your job, Miss Allen. I am the senior investigating officer. Officer O'Brien is one of the people that found the child, so you can understand why he's upset." He handed her a business card. Sal did the same and introduced himself.

"I do understand." She gave Patrick a compassionate look. "I've seen this sort of thing before, but I can't say I ever get used to it. I promise you this, he won't be put anywhere or with anyone that would do him harm. If he's not reunited with kin, I will find a good home for him. There are plenty of people in this county that would love and cherish a baby boy. We just can't do anything until we know for certain that no one is going to claim him."

The thought of it soured his stomach. He looked over at the inconceivably small baby, now sleeping soundly in his bassinet. Smaller, even, than his niece Halley had been when she was born. He had monitors taped to his feet and an IV for fluids. Patrick didn't want to leave the hospital, but he knew he had to. This wasn't his child. *Don't get attached. He's bound to have kin out there somewhere. He isn't yours to keep.* He knew this deep down. He just felt responsible for him. He'd been the one to find him. Michael called regularly, but hadn't left Branna. She'd been devastated by the whole thing. That' s how she was. She kept her head together in a crisis. It was in the aftermath that she let herself feel. Sean Jr. and Josh had gone to work, trying to stay busy, but they'd both called a couple of times as well. It had hit everyone very deeply. Crimes involving children usually did. *God, Caitlyn. I miss you. I wish you were waiting at home for me.*

* * *

St. Clare's Charity Mission, Manaus, Brazil

Caitlyn fanned herself with a child's primer while looking out over her classroom. She'd decided to put Zantina right into the classroom setting. According to Sister Maria, she'd had no formal schooling. She couldn't read or write. But these children were kind. They all had their own stories. They wouldn't tease her. Actually, they'd all seemed to be quite fascinated by her. She was a pretty child. Painfully thin, but even in the last few days, Caitlyn had watched the color return to her cheeks. She had intelligent eyes and a quiet way. Like a child who was used to solitude. So, she was right where she needed to be. And although she was working at a pre-school level academically, she seemed to love being in school.

Caitlyn felt a tug on her long skirt and looked down. Little Estela was handing her something. She took it, smiling at the sweet child who always seemed to be underfoot, but never in the way. She was like the water shifting over the sand, always coming back again. Caitlyn looked at the small gift. A homemade fan that she'd made by taking a piece of paper and folding pleats into it. "Oh, my. How beautiful." She'd colored the fan with virtually every color of crayon she'd had access to. "It's so colorful. I was just wishing I had a fan to keep me cool." The girl preened under the praise, her large, brown eyes so innocent and beautiful. Caitlyn bent down and kissed the top of her head.

She smelled so good. She smelled the way that little girls did when they'd been running around in the garden. Like fresh air and sunshine and something almost like a baby's head. She was only three, after all. The first thing Liam had asked her, last time they spoke, was how his little Estela was. He'd told her about the jaguar attack, and the thought of it made her want to scoop the girl close to her and never let her go.

"Now, let's try to raise our hand before we get up next time. Okay?" She walked the child back to her desk. "Did you know, Estela, that I am family with Dr. O'Brien?" Estela's eyes widened.

"The médico? You are his sister?"

"Well, yes. He is my husband's brother. I spoke with him on the computer. He told me he misses you something fierce." Then remembering the other children, she said, "He misses all of you. As does Dr. Collier. We have a bit of free time before lunch. I think it would be very nice if you'd all make cards with pictures for them. I can put them in the post when I go to town. Now remember, make your letters all the same size and very clear so they can read them. And if you need any help with your English, just raise your hand."

As she began to stand, Estela pulled on her arm. She bent down and the girl whispered. "Did the médico really ask over me?"

"About. Did he ask *about* you. And yes, he really did," she whispered back.

Caitlyn's heart swelled as she saw the joy overcome the child's face. It was the easiest thing in the world to love a child, but children like

Estela, who'd never known a parent's love, understood the value more than most.

* * *

HANS WAS SETTLING IN NICELY. He'd met with Raphael the morning after his arrival, when they could sit quietly and Raphael could brief him properly. His English was excellent, which was good. Hans spoke a little Spanish, but no Portuguese. They had a map stretched out, on the table, that covered the entire region. Which was perfect for Hans, because maps put things in perspective. To the east of the mission, there were tributaries that fed into the Amazon River. The closest one led up a smaller river to the indigenous tribe that they served. They were also part of a vaccine trial for Zika.

Tomorrow, he and Raphael would serve as escorts into the Manaus slum. Dr. Gordon and Mary would open the mobile clinic in some parking lot on the eastern side of the city. Sister Catherine, the resident midwife, would go as well, leaving Dr. O'Keefe, Dr. Maguire, and the regular hospital staff to hold down the fort. The next day Dr. Maguire, Mary, Dr. Rinalto, and Dr. Gordon would be escorted east, stopping first at a village nearby, then to the tribal village up the river about 10 miles.

The dangers of the drug trafficking, for now, had subsided, the active trafficker having fled to Columbia after Izzy and Raphael had been assaulted and kidnapped. The only dangers now were of the natural world. He was to meet with Paolo and Sister Agatha later today to discuss the security for the grounds, and to become more acquainted with the indigenous wildlife that posed a threat to the residents of St. Clare's.

As the meeting came to an end, Raphael pulled up a duffle bag from the floor. He unzipped it and started lining up fighting knives, flex cuffs, and impact weapons. Hans could not carry a firearm in Brazil, but Raphael assured him that when they were out in the bush, there would be two pistols, not one, handy for use. Hans fingered the sheathed blades, feeling the balance and fit in his large hands. He settled on a military style fighting knife that was similar to the Marine Corps K-Bar.

Raphael grunted his approval. Then he looked at his watch. "I told Genoveva and Dr. Seamus I'd work out with them. Would you like to join us?"

Hans laughed. "Given the amount of cheese bread I've consumed in a twelve hour period, I'd say it's mandatory that I join you. That Gabriela is a genius in the kitchen."

* * *

HANS GROANED as he picked himself up off the ground. Mary and Caitlyn were laughing from the sidelines. "Raphael, are you sure you aren't a reincarnated Marine Corps Drill Instructor?"

Genoveva smiled at this. She was sweating already, even though they'd only been going for about fifteen minutes. Seamus was still groaning on the ground. "Call a doctor," he moaned, laughing at the same time.

Hans looked over at the two older boys who'd been playing soccer, or football as they called it. They were watching intently. He gestured to the boys and asked Raphael, "Any reason those two can't join in?" He saw Genoveva stiffen. He narrowed his eyes and looked between her and the boys. "Any issues I need to know about?" It took Genoveva a moment to realize that the question had been directed to her.

Mary interjected. "Hans, a minute?" He stepped to the side and Mary spoke a few words to him in private. "I think she has a history with some of the older kids. Specifically Emilio. You know how boys are. Just make this her choice. If it's going to alienate her, then she'll pull back and stop these little sessions. You have to let her decide whether to let them in. This has been a sort of safe space for her, I think." Hans nodded, understanding that being fifteen was the pits. Then they approached Genoveva who was standing with Raphael and Seamus.

"Sweetheart have you had any problems with these boys?" She just shrugged. He thought he understood. Boys this age could be little dickheads. He'd been one, and he'd also raised one. Erik was a right little shit at this age. "I'll tell you what, Genoveva. My experience has been that bullies can't be avoided. They can, however, be confronted. I can tell they want to join in, and I think it would be good for them. No one is going to let them give you a hard time. If they do, then you let me know. But from what I see, you can take care of yourself. If you had a mind to, you could eat their lunch. How about we try to put our differences aside? If it doesn't work, then they will leave and you will stay. I can always work with them separately."

Mary didn't interfere. She knew he was right. She gave Genoveva a smile and a nod. "You're tough, kid. I think you can handle it now. Maybe not before, when you were younger, but now," she waved a hand. "You can handle them. And maybe they've grown up a little as well. So, are you ready to forgive and forget?"

Genoveva straightened her back, taking a deep breath. "Yes, Doc Mary. I can handle them. Let them…" she paused, like she was trying to remember something. Then she leaned into the words. "Let them do their worst."

Hans cracked off a laugh. "Now I see the resemblance. You've been hanging out with Izzy."

Genoveva gave him a sideways grin. Then she raised her fist to bump Seamus, "Strong is the new skinny."

Seamus shook with suppressed laughter. "That's my girl."

Hans laughed as well. "Well, then. This is your show, honey. You want to do the honors and invite them to join us?"

Genoveva's eyes widened, then she looked at Seamus. He gave an almost imperceptible nod. She put her shoulders back and walked.

Henrico straightened, surprised to see Genoveva walking straight toward them. She met both their eyes, which she never did. His stomach flipped. She stood in front of them, arms folded, stance wide…like she was measuring them and deciding whose ass to kick first. His belly did a double flip. Emilio stiffened beside him. "Would you like to join us for the workout?"

You could have knocked them both over with a feather. Henrico was no dummy. "Yes, I would like that." He looked at Emilio who was more hesitant. He almost said something, but Genoveva spoke first. "Only if you think you can behave yourselves. It's very difficult, though. I wouldn't blame you if you were too scared to do it."

Henrico's adoration of this girl doubled as he watched her smoothly handle Emilio. He loved him like a brother, but he'd never understood why he was such a jerk to Genoveva. The sad truth was that Emilio wasn't very smart. He struggled in school. He was better with his hands, which was its own sort of intelligence. He was athletic. He'd also had a very hard life. It had given him anger issues. Henrico was a small boy when Emilio had come to them. He remembered the day, however. It was burned in his brain. Someone had beaten him horribly. Right now, he was intimidated by the girl in front of him. Normally he masked that by being mean, but somehow Emilio knew this was a test. He'd been invited into the inner sanctum of hard core athletes. Adults that had closed ranks around Genoveva and related to her through punishing workouts.

It had started with Doc Izzy, and Henrico had watched Genoveva thrive under her care. Henrico looked over, into the shrewd eyes of that blonde military man. The one that looked like men he'd seen in the history books. Hard men with swords and shields, sacking villages in Europe. This was definitely a test. One he would rise to, but he didn't know about Emilio. The kid was kind of messed up. It was hard for him to trust a life boat. Emilio stood suddenly, and Genoveva stood her ground. His English was labored. "Yes. I would like to do this."

Caitlyn watched the whole drama unfold, and had to quell the urge to throw her arms up and cheer for sweet Genoveva. And the boys. Puberty was awful. Like waking up everyday in an unruly body, on the verge of losing your mind. Good for Hans. These boys needed a strong male figure in their lives. Someone to harness that testosterone and teach them what being a man was really about. She wanted to cry as she watched them walk slowly over and join the group.

Quinn did everything but glue his feet to the grass as he watched the exchange between his daughter...his possible daughter...and the two boys. He'd caught the drift of what was going on, and he couldn't take his eyes off of Genoveva. According to Izzy, she was naturally shy and introverted. Thankfully, she'd had some strong females to learn from and model their behavior. He envied them, though. He wanted to be in her life. He wanted to teach her. He wanted to be her hero, even though that was archaic thinking. Right now, he wanted to protect her from teenage boys who spelled trouble in every way possible. His inner papa bear was roaring to get out. He felt the presence before he saw it.

"She's blossoming into quite a young woman, isn't she?" He looked into the wise and soulful eyes of the abbess. "It's difficult to sit on the sidelines, but I promise it won't be forever. Tomorrow, we'll line the children up for cheek swabs. Checking them for strep. It's a good enough excuse to get her in the clinic without singling her out."

Quinn smiled, meeting her eyes. "That's downright deceitful, Reverend Mother. What would Father José say?"

She gave a chuff. "Father José retired to the south. Father Pietro is our visiting priest now. And he's as wise as he is devout. These young priests learn more quickly not to get in my way."

Quinn laughed. "I missed you, Reverend Mother. I really missed this place."

"I'm glad to hear it. I thought we'd lost you for good." She remembered Liam's words. *I feel like we're not done, you and I.* She knew Liam would be back, and his beautiful, brave wife. "This place has a sort of pull on one's soul, does it not?"

"Yes. It does," said Quinn. And he moved backward, into the hospital where his work awaited him.

Caitlyn walked back to the school, glancing toward the play yard where her students were enjoying a few moments with no rain. Sister Maria was watching over them, content to let the older children do their own thing. Right now, the sister was lecturing one of the middle grade boys about taking turns with goalie duties. Caitlyn glanced over to the new swing-set and slide, just in time to see Estela walk into the path of a swinging child. Her head was down, inspecting something in her hand, and Cristiano's momentum was too great to stop. She yelled as she ran toward the child.

Cristiano's face showed panic as he tried to stop himself mid-air. He had thick glasses, and his peripheral vision wasn't good. He'd seen her too late. He dug a foot in as he swept the ground, trying to stop himself. He launched off the swing, crashing head first into the side of Estela. They both went down just as she reached them.

Estela screamed, wailing as she held her elbow. Cristiano was frantic. "I try to stop! I sorry, Senhora! I try to stop." He was fumbling on the ground, looking for his glasses. Caitlyn knelt down and picked the girl up. "Now, now. Let's see, darlin'. Let me see your booboo." As she left the ground, Caitlyn groaned. Cristiano's glasses were under her in three pieces. Now he was crying. She pulled him to her, hugging him with her free arm.

Sister Maria was there in a flash. Caitlyn's voice was soothing. "It's all right, lad. It was an accident. I know you tried to stop. There, there. Everyone is okay. Let's just go see Dr. Maguire and let him have a look. Sister Maria, could you watch the other children and hand me those glasses?"

They walked into the hospital and both children were sniffling. Tear stained faces and grass stained clothing. Dr. Maguire looked up. "Oh, my. I see we've had some sort of collision. Slide?" he looked at Caitlyn.

"Swing, I'm afraid. The lad's glasses are broken. He's got a small cut where they dug in. She's got at least one scrape. I think it's all okay, but I thought we should clean them and let you take a look." Estela gripped her tighter around the neck. "Maybe you should take him first."

She went to the chair in the exam room and sat down, Estela coiled around her like a baby monkey. "There, there. I think you're okay." The elbow wasn't broken. Caitlyn had broken her elbow as a child, and there was no way Estela would be holding on this tight if that joint was broken. "You've just got to watch where you're goin', lass. Ye scared poor Cristiano half to death. Now, can I see what was in your hand? What was so interesting that you weren't paying attention?"

Estela leaned her head back, meeting Caitlyn's gaze. The poor thing had tears and dirt on her face. She put her thumb in her mouth, but Caitlyn gently pulled it out. "That's not clean enough to eat, pretty girl. You must wash up. Now, let's see the other hand. That's it."

She looked at the rock in the child's hand. It had bits of quartz in it, and it was shaped almost like a heart. "Coração," the girl said.

"It's a heart. Can you say heart, Estela?"

"Heart." She emphasized the *H* dramatically, wanting to get it right.

"You are so smart. Very good. Now, can you tell me where you are hurt? Ouchees?" The girl's face was pitiful. She showed Caitlyn her elbow. "Oh, my. I think you need a bandage for that one. Any other ouchees?" The girl pulled her shirt up to show her side. A small pink mark where Cristiano had made contact, but no broken skin. "I think Cristiano got the worst of that one. Now, I'm no doctor, but when I was little, my mammy used to kiss my ouchees and make them better. Would you like a kiss?" Estela nodded, a little smile forming. Caitlyn kissed her arm, just beside the scraped area. Then she kissed her finger, and put it to the girl's side. Estela smiled, her tears sparkling. Then she pointed to the other elbow, which didn't have a mark on it. Caitlyn's heart squeezed. "Oh yes, we mustn't forget the other one." She kissed her other elbow. Estela pointed to her forehead, and Caitlyn heard Quinn give a little laugh. She gave him a look like, *Can you believe this kid?* "Okay, one more and then Dr. Quinn can clean you up." She kissed the child on her head, and Estela nestled into Caitlyn's chest, wrapping her arms around her neck again.

CHAPTER 10

DUBLIN 2, DUBLIN, IRELAND

Patrick used to love New Year's Eve. That was, until he moved to the city. Yes, there was plenty of partying to do, but it wasn't the same as home. When he and his brothers were younger, they'd sneak to the Cliffs of Moher, under dark of night, to an area on the coast path which didn't have any gates or security. It had been thrilling to have the cold, rushing wind hit their faces. The blackness of the cliff's edge adding some fright to the experience. They would pass a flask around and talk about what they had planned for the next year. Brigid had demanded to come with them the year she and Michael had turned twenty, offended that they'd never included her. She was a pushy hen. Aidan had gone off to war, and the need to close ranks among the siblings had been strong.

When he was older, and had begun seeing Caitlyn, he'd taken her to the same spot. By then, they'd all begun their own traditions. Brigid was married. Michael was with Fiona. Liam was starting university. The moon had been full that night, lighting up the water in an endless landscape of yellow and black. The stars shone bright. Such a clear sky for western Ireland. Like it had been made just for them. That's when he'd first told Caitlyn that he loved her. Her green eyes sparkled. *Well, it's about time ye came out with it,* she'd said with a come hither smile. He'd taken her on the blanket, ignoring the cold winter wind. She'd been desperate for him, rolling until she was on top. Her hair was a silvery tangle in the moonlight as she threw her head back, coming in waves like the sea below them. Crashing against him as she cried out to the night sky. It was one of those perfect moments that burned itself into his memory. The stars bright behind her as she rose above him and took her pleasure.

Now he was sitting on his balcony, looking at a shitty, dirty little alley. A glass of Kilbeggen in his fist. God, he felt so alone. His apartment was full right now, but he felt alone. Separate from everyone because he was missing his mate. He missed his sweet Caitlyn. What time was it in Brazil? He took out his phone and checked the time zone that he'd set for South America. So he'd always know what time of day it was in Brazil.

The other problem he was having right now was the thought of that little baby in the hospital. Completely alone for the coming year. His nieces and nephews would never know what it was like to not get a kiss and a hug and a big meal on New Years. They'd always have a safe place to rest their head. Thank God for it.

He heard the sliding door open and looked up. It was Branna. She smiled with a hopeful look, like she really wanted to come out, but didn't want to intrude. "Come, hen. Sit with me a while."

She did. "The kids are passed out. All three of them." She looked at him, wanting to say something. He cocked his head.

"I was thinking about the baby. He's all alone. I mean, I know he has the nurses, but I'm sure the other kids have family coming in and out. Do you think maybe…"

Patrick was off his feet in a flash. "Aye, I do." Half way through the living room, he stopped. Now everyone was staring. "Oh, shit. The kids. You can't leave everyone. I'm sorry. It's okay, I can go alone."

Michael stood. "You want to go see the baby at the hospital, I take it?" He looked between them. "They'll never let the kids into that wing of the hospital. You two go. I'll stay back."

Seany was working, but Tadgh and Charlie were there. So was Josh, who stood and said, "Why don't you all go. I can watch three kids sleep. I haven't had anything to drink."

Charlie shook her head. "I don't want you to be alone."

"I'm a big boy. And I have the cat to keep me company." As if on cue, Duncan hopped on the arm of the couch, roaring with gusto. Josh ran a hand over his smooth, silky fur. "See, no worries. Duncan and I will take watch." The cat regularly wandered up and down the fire escape, checking on the residents of both apartments.

Josh went to his sister. Smoothing a palm over her dark, wavy tresses, he smiled sadly. "Go and see him. You'll fall in love. I guarantee it. He shouldn't be alone." Then he spoke in an exaggerated Irish accent. "Don't worry yerself. It'll be grand altogether."

Michael's laughter cracked through the room. "Christ, hellcat. Ye've been giving him lessons haven't you?"

* * *

PATRICK AND TADGH led the way through the maternity hospital to the neonatal unit. It was on a very secure floor and it was past visiting hours, but they showed their police credentials and were given a pass. As they approached the glass encased nursery, Branna looked through the window. A little sob escaped her and Michael closed in, putting a protective arm around her. "You did an amazing thing, Branna. Ye gave the boy comfort and sustenance during the most horrible moment of his short life. I'm proud that you're my wife."

She leaned into him, seeking comfort. "Look at him. Oh, Patrick. He looks really good. He's small, but compared to when we found him, he already looks so much better!"

"He does," Patrick said, smiling at the boy through the glass. One of the nurses waved at them, coming out to speak with them. She was the nurse that had let Patrick feed the baby.

"Nurse Siobhán! Working the holiday, I see." Patrick was ecstatic that he knew the nurse on duty. He really wanted them to all be able to go in and visit with the child.

"Yes, I'm tragically single. Hard to believe, I know." She put her hands up as if to stop their protests. "So, I take the holiday shift and let the attached nurses get a bit of fun. You've got quite a crowd with you." She set her eyes on the two women. "Which one of you was with the boy and fed him?"

Charlie pointed to Branna. "She has the wonder breasts, mine are decorative." Tadgh nudged her as they all giggled. The nurse laughed too, but then she set her eyes on Branna.

"It was a wonderful thing you did. We all think so. He wasn't just dehydrated. He was close to dying from exposure and going into shock. Ye gave him something warm and beautiful to cling to. You gave him a mother's touch. It matters. Babies come into the world not knowing which way is up." The woman was tearing up and so was Branna. She hugged her. "Now, I suppose you're all here to ring in the new year with the lad? It's nice. Most of the kids have had visitors today. Holidays, we let extended family in the parent room. So, I think you all qualify. Come in and let's get you all scrubbed and fresh. He'll be happy to see you."

After they'd all sanitized themselves and taken a seat, the nurse brought the baby into the room. She instinctively went to Patrick. He had a gown over his shirt, and he took the child without question. When he spoke, the baby started to wiggle. "Happy New Year, lad."

Branna covered her mouth, tearing up. "I think he knows your voice." Patrick smiled at that. "Aye, we go way back. I've known him all his life." The group laughed. "Now, let's go see wee Branna. You're more familiar with her than most, although you might not remember it."

He went over to Branna and let her take the baby, and he watched his brother melt. Michael knelt next to her in the rocker. "He's a beautiful boy. Jesus, he's as small as Halley was." Branna wiped a tear off her nose, nodding, unable to speak.

Tadgh and Charlie knelt on the other side. "Now you have to share. No hogging the baby." Charlie's eyes were sparkling. Her fingers twitching, wanting her turn to hold him. "He's small, but he's a fighter. I can tell. Josh had that same determined look."

The nurse watched them all silently, then said. "Josh and your brother Seany have both been by as well. Earlier today. I think this little man has bewitched the whole O'Brien family." And he had.

Michael laughed. "If Brigid and mam get ahold of him, he's done for."

* * *

Manaus, Brazil

Caitlyn sat in front of the abbess's desk, a cup of tea in her hand. They'd been talking for about twenty minutes. Caitlyn had told her all about her family and in-laws, about her work, and about her brave, wonderful husband. She'd avoided any real hot button topics.

Reverend Mother Faith leaned back in her chair, assessing the young woman in front of her. "You've got a way with the children. Truly, Sister Maria is very impressed with how you've dealt with the multi-grade classroom, and how you've been acclimating Zantina. She's already seeing the younger children improve with their English. Miraculous considering you've only been here a little over a week."

Caitlyn shrugged. "They're bright children. They love to learn. It makes my job much easier. Sister Maria gave them a strong foundation."

"How does your husband feel about your abrupt departure? Does he support you coming to Brazil?" And there it was.

"My husband supports me. He didn't like it, but I'm not the sort to be ruled over, and he has accepted the situation."

"Still, it must be difficult for him during the holidays. Especially given your loss."

"Losses. And yes, I'm sure it has been. I won't pretend the guilt hasn't been weighing on me. But we've been in touch regularly. We're in a good place. A better place than when I left."

"Why is that? Was he angry?"

"We both were." Caitlyn didn't expand, but Reverend Mother Faith had learned that silence often made people talk more than questions. She just sat still, waiting.

"He'd seen a urologist," Caitlyn finally said. "Looking into a vasectomy. I know that's against the church's teachings, but he was trying to do it for me. He changed his mind. Rather, the doctor changed his mind."

"You said losses. As in more than one. Did you lose another pregnancy, Mrs. O'Brien?" Her voice was much softer and kinder now.

"Three. I had three miscarriages. The last one was...difficult. I lost a lot of blood. I had to stay in the hospital. I was further along, and we chose to cremate the remains and keep the ashes. At least until we find a place to sprinkle them."

"I'm so sorry, lass. I only knew about the one. I'll remember you in my evening prayers. All three of you. Your husband must have been very frightened. I can see why he would consider such drastic measures."

"He'd be giving up any chance to have biological children. I couldn't let him do it. I wouldn't let him do it." Caitlyn wiped a tear away.

"There are many ways to be a mother. The loss of a child is the most devastating pain there is, I know, but there are other ways."

"I am aware of that. I am also aware that you can't really understand, Reverend Mother, what it feels like to lose a child. What it feels like to feel your own babe move inside you. So, you'll pardon me if I..."

The abbess's voice was different. It held an edge. "I get very tired of people making assumptions about my life." Then she stood abruptly. "That's all for today. I'll see you next Friday?"

Caitlyn stood, surprised at the abruptness with which she'd dismissed her. She started to apologize, but the abbess just waved her off. "I have some time open on Tuesday. I'll see you then instead."

Caitlyn nodded. "Tuesday it is. Oh, and if it's okay with you, I'd like to go into the villages on Sunday. The children don't have lessons and I'd like to meet the neighboring children and the ones from the indigenous tribe. I want to see if there are any smaller children getting overlooked. And...well I suppose I'm curious."

The abbess had reined in her emotions. She gave Caitlyn a crooked smile. "Aye, I suppose you would be. It's one of those things that one needs to experience for themselves. If it's all right with the doctors and Raphael, I don't have a problem with it."

Caitlyn walked through the garden to the back door of the hospital. She was supposed to go over her blood work with Seamus. She smiled as she saw the lines of children lined up to get a strep check. She supposed that the dorm-style living would be difficult when trying to contain sickness. The kids slept four to a room. Two sets of bunkbeds and two chests of drawers to share. They had one small shared armoire for hanging dresses and rain slickers and lining up their shoes.

Right now, Genoveva was holding Estela and the doctor swabbed her throat. Estela gagged and shook her head, not liking it at all. But then Dr. Quinn handed her an ice lolly out of the cooler and all was forgiven.

One of the local nurses was sealing each swab with a label. She almost looked away when she watched him do something odd. He did the strep test, then for some reason did a second swab on Genoveva. He swabbed her inner cheek, then put the sample apart from the other children. She watched as Genoveva left, and just for a moment, something like sadness came over Dr. Maguire's face. So sad that it almost stole her breath. Something was wrong. She saw it plain as day. And she was going to find out what it was.

She walked down the hall to Seamus's neck of the family clinic. She could hear the new surgeon, Dr. Giles Clayton, getting settled and talking to his anesthesiologist about how nice the updated equipment was. He was older, practically a pensioner, and had been here several years ago for a two week commitment. She was happy to hear that they'd signed on for three months, but she found herself wishing Izzy was here instead. Knowing she'd been responsible for getting the O.R. up and running again.

She refocused her attention on finding Seamus. She found him giving instructions in Portuguese to a very pregnant local woman. Caitlyn's heart squeezed. She stood back, waiting. When the woman left, Seamus turned his attention to her. "Well, she looks ready to pop."

He smiled, "More than ready. She's the reason I stayed. We induce her next week. I need to control the situation since she's high risk. I want Antonio here in case she needs a c-section. I can do it, but I want him there as a wing man, just to be safe. This is her first child and probably her last."

Caitlyn didn't pry, because it wasn't her business and he probably wouldn't tell her anything anyway. "You said my blood work was in?"

"Yes, come sit in my office." He put a hand out to show her to the patient chair. "Well, the good news is that you aren't pregnant." She couldn't help but feel a little sad, and he read her reaction. "That's a good thing, Caitlyn. You need to give your body a break. And when we are home, away from malaria and dengue fever and Zika virus, you can start fresh. If you'd been pregnant, I'd have likely sent you back to Ireland on the next flight, and then where would Sister Maria be?"

She knew he was right. She took a breath, nodding. "Yes, you're right. So what did you learn besides that I'm not going home?" She liked Seamus. He was a character. Funny and sweet and just sarcastic enough to keep up with Doc Mary. Right now, he was serious and professional.

"Your hormone levels are good. The old saying is that the cure for infertility is pregnancy. Those hormone shots gave you a jump start. Now you're doing it on your own. How do you feel? You said you haven't menstruated. You probably should have by now."

"I feel fine. The only thing strange is…" She stopped, feeling a little shy. Seamus didn't push, he just waited. She finally continued. "My breasts are still sore, like when I first found out I was pregnant and they started to change."

"Have you had any milk? It's possible, considering you were pregnant three times in as many years."

"No, nothing leaking. Just not like they were before."

Seamus nodded, "Well, likely it will subside. I can have Mary check you, maybe set up a mammogram?"

"No, I don't think I need that. Maybe I can have Mary take a look. She's seen all of this already." She grinned at him as she swept her hand up and down her body.

He laughed and nodded. "Aye, well she's an exceptional doctor. I trust her judgment. I will set it up for later this week. Now, as for the issue with your cervix, it's not an insurmountable problem. It just takes caution, planning, and a small surgery. It also takes some self discipline. Light duty or even bed rest, and unfortunately it sometimes involves sexual abstinence after the first trimester. Let me explain the two options we have, and then we'll put the matter to rest until we are back home and ready to talk to your husband. Then you can relax and enjoy your time here. And you can let your body and your heart heal. That's important Caitlyn. The quest to have a child can become all consuming. You can't paper over the loss with another pregnancy. I hope you know that you can talk to me and to Mary, and it goes without saying that the abbess is available." He put a palm over the top of her hand. "You aren't alone, lass." She gave him a tearful smile. She was afraid of hope. She couldn't lose another child. It would kill her.

After discussing some options for the next pregnancy, if there was a next one, Caitlyn felt lighter somehow. Before she left, she remembered something she wanted to talk to him about. "Seamus, about the strep tests they are doing on the kids." Seamus perked up, waiting. "I know they are swabbing the tonsils, but is there any reason for a second test where they swab the cheek?"

Seamus crinkled his brow. "I don't know? They're swabbing the kids twice?"

She shook her head. "From what I saw, only Genoveva." Something passed over Seamus's face. Then he shuttered the response.

"I don't know. Could be a test for older kids. I'll look into it. Not to worry. There's surely a logical reason why they're doing it."

"Don't say I asked. It was more curiosity. I like the girl, and I want to make sure she's okay. Dr. Quinn just looked..." She shrugged. "Sad, I guess is the word. Sad and anxious. It didn't make any sense because he just got here. He doesn't really know the kids."

"Don't worry about our Genoveva. She's healthy as a horse. We'll take care of her. She's in good hands. I'm sure it was nothing." But he knew. Or at least he thought he did. It wasn't his place to spread the news around that Izzy had uncovered, but it was obvious. The why of the extra swab. DNA. Genoveva's father had come for her.

After Caitlyn left, he sat for a moment, thinking about the beautiful young woman he'd just counseled. She was every young lad's dream. Silvery blonde hair with streaks of honey, fair skin, a dusting of freckles. Smart, spirited green eyes. But there was a heartbreaking sadness in those eyes as well. Three babies lost. *Jesus,* he thought. She wasn't much older than his own daughters. And her poor husband had to be mad with grief. She'd left abruptly, after such a traumatic loss. If he was anything like his brother Liam, Patrick O'Brien wouldn't have liked letting her go one bit. Especially after sitting in that ambulance afraid she was going to bleed to death. If he was anything like Liam, he liked his women strong minded as well. A blessing and a curse. But Patrick couldn't be his concern. Patrick wasn't his patient. Caitlyn was. As of now she was his patient, and she was in charge.

He exhaled, suddenly tired. Suddenly missing his girls. He had a week left, and he'd depart. Live back in Ireland with a fresh start, a new town, and a new job according to his e-mail this morning. He hadn't told anyone yet, but he'd gotten the job. Apparently the gleaming letters of recommendation from Liam, the abbess, and Mary had worked, along with Sorcha O'Brien, a woman who'd never met him, pulling some strings. The clincher had been his old partner driving up and hand delivering his reference to the chief at the Galway hospital. His partner had an in-your-face, cocksure personality. He'd likely told the bloke that if he didn't hire Seamus, he was a stupid, fecking eejit. In those exact words. His brand of candor worked for him, thankfully. He stood, heading to the area of the hospital where they were swabbing the kids. He'd thought it was an odd thing to do. No one was sick. Now he knew why.

As he walked into the room, Quinn and Pedro, the lab technician, were cleaning up and organizing the samples in trays. Quinn met his eyes. "How are ye Dr. O'Keefe? Is your patient going to hold until the surgery?"

"Aye, her cervix hasn't dilated and no Braxton Hicks. She'll hold. And ye need to call me Seamus."

Quinn smiled, "Sorry, it's habit. It's a little more formal at my workplace. And don't worry about the baby. I've got a lot of experience with newborns. As long as everything goes well, we should be able to keep the child with the mother. I know you're probably anxious to go home and..." He stopped. "Is everything alright, Seamus?"

Seamus shook himself. He'd been staring at the man like an idiot. Pedro was gone now. This was his chance. "I'm sorry, Quinn. It's just your eyes." Quinn raised a brow, backed up just a hint. "Don't worry, I don't fancy you." Seamus laughed. "What I mean is," he gave him a direct look. "You're the one. The green eyes should have given you away immediately. I've been distracted, but I see it now. You're her father." Quinn stiffened. "Don't worry, I won't say anything. But seriously, mate. You aren't going to need that swab. Ye've seen the child. Jesus. The coloring is different, but the resemblance is there." Seamus watched a tremor go through the man, and he swallowed hard. His eyes, so much like his daughter's, were pained. Seamus misunderstood. "Ye do want the girl? Or else why the hell would you..."

"Of course I want her! Are ye mad? God, the thought of all that I've missed. You've got daughters, Seamus. You know what I've missed! The thought of it threatens to buckle my feckin' knees! If she's not mine, it will kill me!"

Seamus put a hand on his arm. "I'm sorry. I'm just protective of her. She hasn't had it easy. And I'll keep my mouth shut. How long until you know?"

"I'm mailing the test today. I was waiting until the holiday was done. Sister Agatha is driving me to a place where I can overnight it to Dublin. I have a colleague in genetics. He'll do it immediately. He already has my sample. I think I should know in the next week or two."

Seamus gave him another pat. "I hope you get the result that you want. For both of your sakes. She's a special girl. If she's yours, you just hit the jackpot." Quinn stifled a sob, swallowing it down. Seamus's eyes were understanding. "Best get that to the post, while you've got a vehicle. I'll see you at lunch."

CHAPTER 11

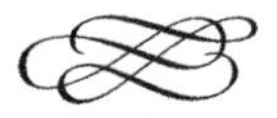

MEANWHILE ... IN PHOENIX, ARIZONA

Liam's teeth were going to be little nubs by the end of this quarter. He drove home from the hospital tired, frustrated, and grinding his molars. He missed Izzy. His attending physician was a plonker. The Chief Resident was an arse licker. He hated this whole thing. When they'd moved to America, he knew that the medical board was going to insist on additional training. He wasn't licensed to practice in America. He just hadn't thought about how bad it was going to be starting from scratch and going back to being a resident. He had more hands on infectious disease experience than the entire group of residents combined. More internal medicine experience as well. He'd wager that his attending hadn't seen as much as he had. The fucker had never been out of the state other than to posh medical conferences in San Francisco and Chicago. And the rotter was the fact that half the training wasn't even in medicine. Sensitivity training. Feckin' hours and hours of sensitivity training. Americans really needed to lighten up.

The traffic was horrid right now. He just wanted to be there when Izzy woke. Maybe even crawl in next to her, all warm and sweet smelling under the blanket. Pretend that they had slept like normal couples. She'd arrived at her new hospital, hopeful and starry eyed.

When she'd realized that her boss wasn't actually her boss, and that the dickhead below him was her direct supervisor, it all made sense. It's why they hadn't promoted internally. No one wanted to work for this Dr. Dickhead. He'd immediately surmised she was a threat. She had a lot of experience that was out of the norm for someone her age. He'd stuck her on night shift, away from the prying eyes of the hospital gentry. Another damnable arse licker. Every hospital had them. The doctors that sucked up to the higher ups. Rigged the schedule to make sure they could attend all of the charity events. Shook all the right hands.

He internally chastised himself. He wasn't going to do this. They'd agreed to move here and follow Izzy's career. For now, she was willing to gut out the bad hours. Especially if it meant she ran the show on her team. She was so tired, though. She was a child of the light. Graveyard shift was sucking the life out of her.

He pulled into their shared parking lot where they rented an apartment in an adobe style building. All palm trees and sand and big rocks. It was hot. Even for winter. It just wasn't natural. Where the hell was the rain? There was wind, of course. All that meant is that your fecking car was coated in sand and had to be washed once a week. He wanted some feckin' rain. Was that too much to ask? He wanted to feel it on his face. Sunshine was great, but he felt like a dried up sandal. His body wasn't used to this desert heat. He put the screen over his windshield, so the inside of his car didn't bake. He grabbed his bag, and the bagel he'd bought for Izzy, and went into the building. As he cracked the door open to the apartment, it was silent. Like the whole place had gone to sleep along with the woman. He put the bag down on their little secondhand table and put his head through the bedroom doorway.

There she was. Christ, she was beautiful. Her hair was getting longer every day. Caramel waves all over the pillow. One toned arm over her forehead. She was in a tank top. And he knew if he looked, she'd have some simple cotton panties on and nothing else. Suddenly he wanted to do more than cuddle, his cock thickening.

He started at her ankle, since she had one cute little foot slung out of the covers. He kissed it lightly as he gently lifted it to his mouth. She stirred, stretching and squeaking like a little kitten. His mouth was hot, leaving warm, wet kisses along her calf. "Good morning." She purred.

"It's four o'clock," he said with a nip on the soft flesh behind her knee.

"It's morning for me. Don't you have something better you could be doing with that mouth? Uhh!" She arched up just as he cupped his mouth over her panties, going right to the heart of her. She moaned.

"I brought you breakfast, but first," he crooned, "I'll need my snack." Then she sighed as he slid her panties down her long legs.

* * *

Izzy took a bite of her toasted green chili bagel with veggie cream cheese. He knew exactly what she liked for breakfast. He gave her a devilish smile, his hair coming out of his pony tail and brushing his cheek. "Are you enjoying your breakfast?" His look was steamy.

"Yes. It's delicious. Did you enjoy your snack?" She licked some cream cheese off her finger.

Liam watched her pink tongue make an appearance and he almost whimpered. He had her down on the rug in a matter of seconds. "FFFUUUCK!" He moaned as he slid into her. He'd meant to wait, but he couldn't. "We don't do this enough. Not nearly enough." She was resplendent under him, taking his thrusts and glides. She was so wet from coming against his mouth. Still so wet and tight.

"Don't wait. I want to see it." She thrust her hips up, meeting his strokes. Her eyes were hungry. She pulled his ass in tight to her. "Liam, let go."

He cocked a leg and let her have it full force, and she started to climax right along with him. This was perfect. Fuck everything else. Forget the traffic, the long hours, the asshole bosses. This was perfect. This was enough.

Back at the table, he joined her for a cup of coffee. They were both half dressed, spent from loving each other, and Liam was grinning like the cat that got the canary. She smoothed his hair back. "I miss you. How was work?"

He kissed her hand. "I miss you too, love. It won't be forever."

Their wedding was planned. One month and they'd be in her parent's apple orchard, the blooms starting, his family and hers mingling before and after the nuptials. Music and her father's apple cider fresh out of the barrel. The apricot schnapps right out of the still. He couldn't wait. They'd get one night of a honeymoon and have to drive back up to Phoenix, but they'd be married.

He loved her family. Her paternal grandfather, father, and brother partnered to run the orchard. Apples on one parcel of land, apricots on the other. Her maternal grandfather was a rancher, and lived not too far from her parents. So, they were well stocked with steak and spuds for dinner, just how he liked it. He couldn't wait to put Cora on one of the ponies. It was going to be grand altogether. A day he'd never imagined. He leaned forward and kissed Izzy properly. "I can't wait to be your husband." She smiled under his mouth, but it didn't go unnoticed that he'd never answered her question.

* * *

Doolin, Co. Clare, Ireland

Sorcha dried the last dish, placing the old, chipped platter into the cupboard. She turned to the breakfast area, smiling at the sight of her mother-in-law. A wave of affection rolled up her body, from her chest to her throat. Aoife O'Brien was as beautiful as a white rose. The roses that had a hint of blush pink, just at the center. Her hair was a combination of pure white and silver, still as smooth and silky as a girl's. Her cheeks were pink on her fair skin. Her brow was bent in concentration.

Before her was an old seamstress dress form from the fifties, draped with the object of her attention. She was working diligently on Izzy's wedding dress. She'd let Izzy pick from her many vintage dresses. Izzy was taller and bustier than the other women in the family and had laughed at the prospect of there being a dress in her closet of beautiful garments that would actually fit her. But she didn't know Aoife. Not all were family dresses. Some, she'd picked up here and there when major estates were liquidated. She only picked the finest. No staining or tears. They had to be professionally preserved. The dress Izzy had chosen was lovely. She'd loved it at first sight, saying little prayers out loud that made them all laugh. *Please fit in the boobs and ass, please fit in the boobs and ass.*

It was an ivory, slip-style dress from the 1940s, accentuating her bust and smooth stomach. Not flaring until it got to her hips, then elegantly draping as it traveled down to just above the ankle. There was a simple cluster of pearls applied in the center and just below the breasts. The straps were wide, but had a band on each side, inches below her collar bone, that gathered the flat silk, puckering it to accentuate as is dipped below to the neckline.

It was, of course, stunning on Izzy. Her pale, olive tones had deepened in Brazil. Her bouncy curls lengthened, showing the caramel and butterscotch highlights of her warm, brown hair. Her figure was curvy and fit. Liam was going to drop to his knees at the sight of her. Because the dress fit, but Izzy was a bit tall for it, they'd decided to shorten the dress. Oh, Izzy had protested at first, but Aoife had won out in the end. They'd shorten it just a bit, to stop at the lower part of the shin, and it would look as if it had always been that length. The bolero that went with it was beautiful, of course, but Aoife forbade her to wear it. *No woman with such a smooth, toned back and arms should ever cover up,* she'd said.

Now Aoife was carefully putting the finishing touches on the hem and tightening up the pearls that were the only adornment. Another son marrying. Soon it would be Seany. Her last baby. "She is a lovely lass, isn't she." Sorcha's words were a statement, not a question. "She's going to make him very happy."

Aoife smiled as she pulled the needle up, stopping as the thread resisted, then starting again. "She's perfect, as they all have been. As you and Katie were." She smiled at the thought. "They'll all be happy, Sorcha. Even Seany will find his way."

"How did you know I was thinking about him?" Her mother-in-law just shrugged a shoulder. "He'll be the last, and the most difficult to let go. He's young, yet. You've still got time with him. Maeve was my baby. Still at home with me when you and Sean and Katie and William were running around having your grand adventures."

Sorcha laughed. "We were quite a quartet, weren't we?"

She nodded. "Aye, you were. It reminds me of Patrick and Tadgh and their women, crammed in those little flats trying to make their mark on the world. Sharing meals and running up and down the fire escape to see each other. Soon they'll be pushing prams and watching each other's children."

Sorcha's face grew pained. Aoife saw this and stopped, meeting her eyes. "Don't you worry, love. It will happen for Patrick and Caitlyn, just as it did for the others. If not one way, then another. Could you even doubt it?" Her voice raised in a distinctly western lilt as she flicked her fingers, banishing any doubt. Like the idea was preposterous that everything would be anything less than fine. "Look at the ripple effect that's happened in this family. Finding Branna was as improbable as finding a hen with teeth. Yet, Michael found her. And look at all that's happened since. Aidan met Alanna through Branna, then Izzy came along. Now Patrick has found a child. A newborn, for God's sake."

Sorcha put a hand up, "Don't say it. Don't even think it. Someone will come for the child. It won't do any good to let our mind wander to that possibility. Caitlyn is in Brazil, and someone will claim him." She gave a nod, as if it were final. As if there was absolutely no reason at all to believe that God himself had sent that fair-haired child in the hospital to save the day. To make Caitlyn and Patrick parents. She couldn't entertain the thought for a minute. Because she couldn't watch her son lose another child.

* * *

Rio Puraquequara, Manaus, Brazil

Caitlyn's smile was so big, she thought her face would split. The mist from the rain was mild as they made their way north up the river, leaving the larger Amazon and tributary near the mission, headed toward the indigenous village that imbedded itself within the rainforest. It was so beautiful, so green. And coming from Ireland, that was saying something. The greens were brighter with a waxy shine. Large flat leaves and a palette of color speckled throughout. Birds and flowers enhancing the effect. There were vines so thick, it was like another tree had wrapped around the trunks. As the rain subsided, the birds began to sing and the insects swirled.

The river was high and clipped along, until they were soon coming to a small, roughly made dock. Some young boys waved and smiled, yelling behind them that the médicos had arrived. They had a full staff today, as the new doctors needed to be oriented. Quinn, Mary, Antonio, and the Australian infectious disease specialist, Rachel Gordon, who had taken Liam's place. Sister Agatha's video had ensured that recruitment was booming. Raphael docked the boat, having become the new captain. Paolo only came on occasion now, as his duties were never ending at the mission.

Caitlyn watched as Hans jumped to the dock, catching the lines and tying them off. He took Mary's hand and said, "My Queen," and helped her to the dock, which made everyone snicker. Hans and Raphael had done a trial run, checking for obstructions, problems up river, and to get Hans acquainted with the area. After the trouble with Izzy, Raphael had been hired as full time security for the mission. He went on all of the excursions. Hans was a self-appointed personal body guard for his wife, and she suspected, for her as well. Patrick had immediately contacted Hans once she'd arrived, and given him marching orders to keep an eye on his unpredictable spouse.

Now they were here, traveling a worn path that led to the village. As the elders approached, introductions were made. The young men were immediately sizing Hans up, as warriors did. The doctors set up under one of the common, open shelters. As soon as they introduced Caitlyn, and told the women that she was a teacher at St. Clare's, she became the center of their focus. Beautiful dark eyed children approached her, smiling shyly. They touched her hair and seemed particularly fascinated with her face. She heard the mothers whisper.

Esmeralda. The little ones ran hands over her face. She wasn't sure how to react, so she just stayed still and let them get used to her. Raphael appeared at her side. She heard him give a little laugh.

"Raphael, I seem to be a bit of a distraction. Can you translate?" She talked out of the corner of her mouth, still smiling.

"They like you. I think it's the blonde hair and the green eyes. They're calling you Esmeralda. It means emerald, like the jewel."

"So, why aren't they over there looking at Hans and Quinn like a zoo attraction?"

Raphael laughed. "Well, Senhora, you're a little less intimidating. Look at them." She turned and had to laugh. Quinn and Hans had at least a foot on the men that were helping them. "And you're much prettier."

Caitlyn smiled, running a hand over a toddlers soft hair. "Esmeralda, eh?" All the children giggled. She was completely in love.

* * *

Two hours of exams, minor stitches, and well-child checks went smoothly. Dr. Gordon was pleased to see that every child had current vaccination cards on file with St. Clare's. Doc Mary noted that there were two pregnant women. One about six months along, and one that looked close to her time. They were not Seamus's patients, per se. The women of this village usually gave birth at home. But she checked the women anyway. She noticed Caitlyn, and it broke her heart. Caitlyn watched the women out of the corner of her eye, sadness coming over her as she looked at their rounded bellies.

Caitlyn was playing with the children, helping them bring baskets of dried and fresh fruit and nuts, steamed fish, and some sort of corn and bean stew to the common area. The villagers wanted them to stay for lunch, which they graciously accepted. Mary and Rachel were gathered around the cooking fire, and Caitlyn suspected they were inspecting the cooking methods to avoid anyone getting sick. Antonio joined them and Caitlyn smiled when she saw the toddler girl in his arms. "She's beautiful, isn't she?"

Antonio kissed the child's temple. "They love when we bring the clinic. We're a novelty, I suppose." He gestured with his chin, "You've got some admirers." Caitlyn didn't look, blushing. It hadn't gone unnoticed that some of the young men from the tribe were eyeing her. "None of them managed to win Izzy's hand, so they've set their sights on Esmeralda."

She gave him a chiding look. "And did ye tell them that I'm happily married?"

Antonio laughed, "Of course not. Where's the fun in that?"

She cocked a brow at him. "Well then, perhaps we'll circulate a rumor that you're looking for a nice Brazilian girl to settle down with. I see a few of them are quite smitten."

He gave her a crooked smile. "Touché. Maybe we should offer up Quinn. They seem to like your coloring and you two could be brother and sister. They likely think Hans is your father." He was right. Blonde hair and green eyes weren't that common of a combination, yet there were three of them here today. Caitlyn smiled at the little girl as she reached out to take a lock of Caitlyn's hair. A woman that was stirring the stew said something that Caitlyn couldn't understand. Antonio obviously understood her well enough. "She wants to know how many children you have at home." Caitlyn stiffened. She saw Mary stop what she was doing and give her a discreet glance. Antonio sensed something was wrong, but he was just the messenger.

Caitlyn smoothed her hands over her front, instinctively. "I don't have any children. Not yet."

Antonio suddenly looked like he didn't want to be the interpreter anymore. He said something in Portuguese. *Esposa.* "I just told them you were a wife, but not yet a mother." The women persisted. The oldest of the group, probably a grandmother or even a great grandmother, gesturing to Caitlyn. Antonio listened and said, "I'm sorry, I'm not following her. She's speaking a more traditional dialect. Perhaps…" But Raphael was behind him.

"She said she sees a mother's pain in your face," Raphael said softly. Mary cursed under her breath. Caitlyn swallowed hard, then gave a sad smile.

"Tell her she sees a lot. I've lost my children. My body..." She paused, thinking of the right words. "My body fails me." Her eyes started to tear as Raphael translated, then she turned to walk away, needing a moment. Antonio said, "Caitlyn, I'm sorry."

Mary started to walk toward her, but the old woman stopped her. Raphael said, "She says she'd like you to walk with her. To come with her and her daughter." Without waiting for an answer the woman came to her, taking her hand as her daughter followed. Mary started to interfere, but Caitlyn was beyond caring. She waved her off. "I'm okay. It's okay." She noticed that Raphael said something to Antonio and Hans, and then began following behind the women. Probably a good idea considering the language barrier. It wasn't like these two women were a threat. She followed them, almost in a trance. Like a child being led by the hand. Honestly she couldn't believe she'd just dropped that bomb in front of the medical team. Mary knew, of course, as did Hans, but outside of Reverend Mother Faith and Seamus, no one else had known about the events leading up to her departure from Ireland.

They took her down a narrow path that seemed to lead straight into the forest. The air was damp and fresh smelling, and she could hear more water ahead. The path opened up to a rope bridge, the boards lined across the small branch of the river and leading back into the forest. She held on to the ropes to either side of her, feeling Raphael's steady presence behind her. It swayed with the motion of their steps, but it was sturdy. She wasn't afraid. She didn't feel anything. A hum of nothingness had rolled over her body when she'd spoken the words. *I lost my children. My body fails me.* The fresh stab of grief had almost short circuited something. Like her body wasn't able to cry one more tear or release one more sob. Even if she somehow managed to have a child, it would never replace the three she'd lost. She heard the old woman speak to Raphael, and he translated as best he could.

This is the wishing bridge. It leads to our sacred mother spring. The mother of all mothers and of the earth itself. All the women of my village come to this spring. It is a holy place. Think of what you most wish. Think of your heart's desire as you walk the bridge to the spring.

That's what did it. Those were the words that thawed her frozen soul. She thought, *I just want to be a mother. I want Patrick to hold his child. His living child.* She thought of her dream. The one on her beloved home shoreline on the outskirts of The Burren. Patrick standing by the water with their two children. That's what she wanted.

As they covered the length of the bridge, the tears came down her cheeks. Raphael finally came from behind and saw her. "Senhora, you don't have to do this. This is too much. I didn't know. I'm so sorry, my sister. Let me take you back." But the old woman was having none of it. She pointed to his feet, and the command was clear. He was to stay put. This was woman's work.

She walked between the women now, and she heard the rumble of water and felt the fresh, mineral rich moisture in the air. It was thick, settling on her skin. The goosebumps sprung out on her flesh, the sound of the water pulling on her no less than her own beloved Atlantic shore. So she followed.

CHAPTER 12

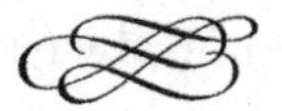

DUBLIN, IRELAND

The holidays had been hectic. The offices that held the Special Detective Unit of the Dublin Garda headquarters was buzzing again, everyone back to work in full force. Tadgh and Sal sat at their desks that were pushed together so they could face each other. They did this at every start of a shift. They went over what they knew and what new information might have come in. They'd worked through the holiday, even though they had spent some time at home with their families. The perks of working and living in the same city.

They interviewed residents and landlords of the nearby buildings where the baby had been found. Seany had just left their office on his way to work, wanting to know if there were any leads. It had taken a toll on all of them that had been there that night. Seany assessing the child's health, Branna kicking into full mother bear mode. Josh, being horrified that this sort of thing happened, even though he was from a big city. And Patrick…Jesus. After all that he'd lost, to find a child that had been tossed away and left to die. A beautiful baby boy. Tadgh had watched as he passed the little bundle to Charlie. He and Charlie were talking about having a baby. She had a demanding job, but good benefits. And if it became too much, then they'd manage without her working. Or his boss, D.C. Sullivan, would poach her from the FBI and hire her in a heartbeat.

He was currently looking at a map of Dublin, and specifically the area around the castle and Christchurch. They'd checked areas where rough sleepers congregated, nosing around as best they could to find out if anyone had heard about a pregnant woman having trouble. His instincts were going haywire. Many times, these cases were indigent people or drug addicts, but not always. Sometimes it was a young person. A teenager that hid a pregnancy and panicked. He couldn't assume that he knew the socio-economic background of the mother.

Tadgh was lost in his thoughts when their phone rang. Then he heard Sal's tone and knew something was up. He watched his partner write down an address and he looked at the pad. A Trinity College dormitory, which was odd. The dorms were usually vacant during break. The kids were just starting to trickle back. Most wouldn't be back for another week. Sal was on his feet, grabbing his coat.

"We've got a deceased female, Botany Bay student apartments. The officer on the scene said the house-keeping staff found her."

"Jesus, the poor lass. And another big case on top of the baby? Christ, this city is going to be the death of me."

Sal shook his head. "Not another case. It could be related to our case. If it's not, they've got another detective team ready to take it. The thing is, the paramedics on the scene said she may have hemorrhaged to death or died of sepsis. They aren't sure, but it looks like she's recently given birth. They've called the coroner." Tadgh froze in his tracks. This was it. He knew it in his bones. This was Baby Boy Doe's mother.

* * *

TADGH'S COFFEE was souring in his stomach. The smell was enough to have him heading for the toilet to lose his breakfast. It appeared that the young woman had been dead for several days. The heat had been down low, so decomp wasn't overwhelming, but death and blood had a distinct odor, no matter how old it was. It hung in the air like a fog.

She'd also been sick in a bin next to the bed. The custodians found her, after noticing an odor in the hall. All of the students should have been gone for the holiday, and they'd assumed it was garbage or a dead rodent. Jesus, the poor girl. The fair hair and a grayish blue pallor was like a death shroud over her once youthful face.

The paramedics lifted her to the gurney. The district coroner giving them instructions about which morgue to take her to for the autopsy. He turned to Tadgh and Sal. "I think it's definitely a possibility that this is your missing mother. She's given birth, there's no doubt, and there's been excessive internal bleeding that isn't that uncommon, but usually remedied in a hospital. I suspect she's died of complications and unsanitary birthing conditions. I don't think she gave birth here. No bloody towels, no afterbirth. I think she was brought here or made her way here on her own. If she'd have given birth in a hospital, this wouldn't have happened."

The coroner left with the body, shaking his head. Twenty years on the job and it never got any easier. He mumbled that sentiment on departure. The first responding Garda officer approached them. "I've contacted the resident advisor, the dean of the school, and campus security. I've also got the name and contact information for her two roommates."

"Thank you, brother. Good work and outstanding job securing the scene. I'm sorry you had to walk into this today." The young officer couldn't have been more than twenty-two. Not much older than the young co-ed that was just taken to the morgue. He just looked at the blood soaked cot.

"It's a shame. She died alone over the holidays. I hope she didn't do it. She probably did, but I hope it wasn't her." His eyes glanced to the pictures of the young woman with her friends. One picture of her with her parents. Another of her getting an award. There were athletic medals for field hockey.

The next step was to notify the parents. Tadgh looked down at her pertinent information. Her purse had all they needed to know. She was from a small town in Sligo. A west coast girl. They had to drive there right now and notify the parents in person. The evidence team would process the room. He looked at the picture again. Fair hair, just like the baby that was currently being cared for in the neonatal unit just a few minutes away. Why in the hell hadn't she gone to the hospital? Did this sweet looking girl actually dump her baby and leave it to die? And where was the father? Sal's eyes held the same questions. He was a father of two, with another child on the way. "I can go alone, if you want to..."

"We go together. I'm not letting you run this fucking gauntlet without me. We've got our best team here and this officer," he patted the Garda officer on the back, "is going to make sure no other assholes get in here and contaminate the scene."

"Absolutely, detective. Consider it sealed."

* * *

PATRICK WAS WORKING an armed security detail for the prime minister when he got the call from Tadgh. It had taken two hours for him to be able to call back. When he had, Tadgh and his partner were almost at their destination in Co. Sligo. They'd driven from one coast to another to deliver some truly terrible news. While he'd been watching politicians maneuver through the hand-picked crowd and press corps, the coroner had been ordering DNA from the child he'd visited yesterday at the hospital. They thought they'd found the mother, and she was dead.

The impulse to get to the boy was strong, but he was still at work. He was done with his security assignment, but he couldn't break for tea for another hour. They had a follow-up brief in five minutes.

As he went through the motions of his job, he had trouble keeping his mind off of a small apartment not more than a fifteen minute walk from his own. A twenty-one year old young girl who died alone. Parents who were finding out that their child was dead, and that they could very well have a living grandchild sitting in the neonatal unit without a mother. His heart was heavy. Like a lead ball in his chest. She had to be the mother. Abandoned babies didn't happen often in Dublin and the pieces fit. The odd part was how far the baby had been dumped from where she'd ended up. He hoped it was her baby. The thought that there was a second child lying dead somewhere was more than he could handle right now.

He rubbed his forehead. He missed Caitlyn. Not that he would ever tell her about any of this, but he still missed her. He wanted to go home and crawl in bed with her. Smell her hair and feel her hands on him. A visceral comfort that he wasn't going to get. Not for another month or so. How was he going to make it through this without her?

He finally exited the meeting, hungry and sad and with an aching head. He looked up to see Charlie standing in the hallway, waiting for him. She knew, and she wasn't going to leave him to stew in the news. He walked into her arms. "Thank you, sister," was all he said. Then they left for the hospital.

The unit was well staffed today. They arrived to find four nurses working, which was good to see. Charlie suppressed a smile as she watched Patrick making little faces through the glass at the child with no name and no mother. It was enough to rip your guts out. She also noticed the moony glances of the nursing staff. There really was nothing sexier that a hot man with a baby. They knew the drill, and they let him in and let him scrub up without a word of argument. She stayed back, giving him some time with the child. She thought of her men. Josh had come home after finding that baby and had been so quiet. It was his way. He'd learned to stifle his emotions. She drew it out of him in her well practiced way, Seany bearing witness. His tears had been silent. Seany had choked his down as well. Branna and Michael processed it together in private, and they stayed up in Patrick's apartment and clung to their children. This had marked them all, even the family back in Doolin. Because when one hurt, they all did. It was one of the miraculous things about this family.

Patrick looked down at the child in his arms. Still so small. He'd put on a little weight, but he didn't like the bottle. His first introduction to food had been at his worst moments. It had been soft words and a warm breast from a woman who knew what it was to love a child. And in the wake of that experience, he instinctively knew he was being ripped off with this silicone nipple. "I hear ye, little man, but you must eat. Ye need this. Go on now, don't be so bloody-minded." He nestled the boy closer, the way he'd seen his sister do, and he held the bottle steady. He tried to get eye contact and was rewarded with a small hand over his. If he'd been a weeping man, this would have completely broken him. He might never have this with his own child.

The head nurse that he'd become so familiar with was watching. She smoothed a hand over his head. "You're so good for him. He's always better after a visit." The child wiggled at her voice. "I wish I had some real milk for you, lad. We need a team of wet nurses on staff, I think. That's how they'd have done it in the old days. They'd have found a young mother with plenty to spare and let her feed you."

Branna had actually offered. So had Brigid. But it was against hospital policy and all sorts of stupid government health codes. Fucking politicians. He looked down at the boy. "I'm sorry, lad. I'm sorry for it all." Of course he couldn't understand. He didn't realize that his mother was most likely laid out in the morgue. He didn't know who had done this terrible thing to him. All he knew was that his basic needs were met, and that sometimes a lonely man who smelled like the winter air and aftershave would come and hold him for a while.

* * *

Knockmina, Co. Sligo, Ireland

Tadgh's heart was a thick lump in his gullet. This was hands down the worst part of police work. He was having all sorts of flashbacks of the day that his Uncle Sean and Officer Sullivan (now his current boss) had come to the door to tell his mother that William O'Brien had died of his wounds at the scene of a motorcycle crash.

He sat in this modest sitting room with its dated furniture, the smell of damp from a leaking roof that had been patched more than once. These were good people. Older than the average parents of a twenty-one year old. His tea had gone cold. He'd taken it to be nice, but he couldn't stomach anything right now. Sal was in similar shape.

The woman in front of him was at the end of her rope. There was a hospital bed where the dining room should be. Her husband's new bedroom, because she needed access to him during the day.

He had a debilitating disease that Tadgh had only read about. Huntington's disease was a slow, horrible decline over years. The person's body and mind deteriorating over time, leaving the family to take care of someone who barely knew them. They could even be violent at the end, due to the brain deterioration. According to Mrs. Walsh, they weren't anywhere near the finish line. He could possibly live for years. They had a health worker come in twice a week, but Tadgh could tell that taking care of this man was killing her slowly as well. She looked exhausted, even before he'd darkened her door and ruined her last shred of happiness. Sal sat next to her, patting her back.

"We tried for so long to have children. Finally, we knew it wasn't going to happen. When the social worker called us and told us about Kasey, we were overjoyed. We fostered her for six months, and adopted her on her second birthday. We were a lot older than the other parents, but she was a good girl and we had a wonderful life with her." She glanced over at her husband, who was sitting up in bed, eating some biscuits. "She didn't want to leave us. She was afraid I couldn't handle him. But she received a scholarship to study at Trinity. We both wanted her to go. He was more lucid then. We arranged for the home care and insisted that she take this opportunity. She wanted to study public policy. The politics of public health. She was so smart, our Kasey. She said she wanted to help with public awareness about Huntington's. That the government needed to fund more research and do more to support the families. When her father was diagnosed, it was the first time I thanked God that she wasn't our biological child. It's passed on through the genes, you see."

She put a hand over her mouth, stifling a sob. Like she'd given this little lesson on the history of her family only so that she didn't have to think about why they were sitting in her living room. "I can't believe this is happening. I can't believe she's gone. How could she be pregnant and we not know?"

"When was the last time you saw her, Mrs. Walsh?"

She thought for a moment. "She hasn't come home for a visit in a while. She was an intern in one of the Government buildings. It's why she said she had to stay over the holiday. It wasn't like her to stay away for so long, but she said she was taking classes, as well as doing her work with the internship. She couldn't visit. Was that a lie?"

Tadgh shook his head. "No ma'am. They've retrieved her records from the school. She was an intern and taking several classes. It seemed she was trying to graduate early." Probably because she had a baby coming. Had she panicked at the moment of the birth? She'd hidden the pregnancy. She was a bigger girl. Taller than some women her age, probably about 5'7" and a little stocky from the photos that he'd scene. Athletic, not petite. With big clothing and controlling her weight, she could have kept it a secret. She was pretty and had a youthful face. A nice smile. This was awful. The whole bloody thing was horribly tragic.

"They're doing DNA on the child that was found. We should know by tomorrow if they rush it."

The woman stiffened. "That is not her child. She'd never have done such a thing. She might have kept this from me, but she would not murder her own child. She was a good girl." His face was compassionate but she persisted. "I know my daughter. She didn't do this."

"You could be right. It may not have been her. Do you have any idea who the father could be? Was she seeing anyone?"

"She never said she was. Said she was too busy. Good God. Is it possible he left them both to die? Why wasn't she in a hospital!" Her voice raised and she stifled another sob.

"I don't know. But I promise you, Mrs. Walsh. I won't stop until I find out the truth. And if this goes the way we think it will, you have a grandson."

She met his eyes, trying to make him understand. "That child may be all we have left of her. Our parents are dead. My sister lives in India with her own family. Her husband's work took him there thirty years ago. We have no one here." She glanced over at her husband. "I can barely take care of him. It's all I can do to get through the day. How am I going to take care of a baby?"

* * *

TADGH WALKED into the apartment and dropped his keys on the counter. As he peeled his coat off, he wished to God that his wife was home. Duncan roared at him, and he stroked his loyal friend gently with his palm. Then he saw her. She came out of the bedroom in a pair of shorts and a t-shirt. She'd come home to wait for him. He crossed the room in three strides, pulling her to him. She knew what he needed. She knew him body and soul. Her legs were around his waist in one smooth motion. "I need you."

"I know. You have me," she whispered. He took her down on the bed after kicking their bedroom door shut. Josh was in Galway with Tadgh's mother, Katie, for a couple of days, but it was habit. He peeled her shorts off. No panties. Perfect. She had her shirt over her head a second later. He didn't even take his shoes off. He freed himself, pinning her arms over her head with one hand. He took a nipple in his mouth, touching her between her legs. It didn't take long to get her where he needed her. Her body responded with an arch and a moan. "I'm sorry, I can't wait." He thrust into her, fusing their hips tightly together. This is what he needed. He needed something beautiful. He needed to stop thinking. He needed his Charlie.

She held him after. His silky hair across her breast, his hard breathing finally settling. "I love you, Tadgh. I love you so much. I wish I could make all of this disappear for you."

He raised his head and gave her a deep, heartbreaking kiss. "You did. For a little while you did. Thank you, mo ghrá. Thank you for knowing what I needed."

* * *

TADGH ENDED the call with his partner, staring at the table top where Charlie had set the flatware and napkins for dinner. She was turning the steaks in her favorite cast iron skillet when she lowered the heat and turned to him. "What's the news?"

"She's the mother. They managed to get the test pushed to the top of the pile, since it was such an important case. The chief of genetics at St. James did the test personally. The lad's DNA is a match. She's definitely the mother, as we suspected."

"What else did he say?" Charlie could tell by the half of the conversation she'd heard that there was more.

"We're waiting on the toxicology, but initial findings have her dying from complications of child birth. She gave birth somewhere else, and was taken to her apartment, or made her way there. The coroner doesn't seem to think she'd have been in any shape to get from the castle area, where the child was found, to her flat unassisted. Not that it is necessarily what happened. She may not have been the one that dumped the child. The cord cutting had been an amateur job, according to the nurse at the maternity hospital. She either did it herself, or someone other than a doctor did it. All we know about the father is that he was a caucasian male. Not much to go on. I'll talk to the roommates tonight. One is headed here from Cork, the other from Tipperary. They both went home for the holiday. I think we'll learn more from them. I have a hard time believing that at least one of them didn't know she was pregnant. Apparently this is the third year that they lived together, so they must be close. I think they are the key to this. They both apparently have alibis. They were with their families in their home towns during the birth. Apparently they are both distraught."

"They'll know something. You don't live that closely for three years and not share confidences. Have they searched the apartment thoroughly?" Tadgh nodded absently. "Tadgh, is it possible she kept a journal? Even on her computer?" His brows raised at that. "There was no hard copy of a journal, but you're right. She may have kept a journal on her computer. We found a cord, but no laptop, which was odd." He thought for the tenth time in an hour, where the hell was that girl's laptop?

* * *

PATRICK JUMPED in the Garda car, riding shotgun with another officer. There was a disturbance in one of the dodgier parts of Dublin. Sheriff Street had the worst of the gang and drug activity, and the graffiti boasted warnings to police and snitches. Even the Garda didn't like going to Sheriff Street, but duty called and his unit was armed, unlike most Garda officers. He'd picked up some overtime shifts to try and help the time go by faster, and to save money. He and Caitlyn wanted out of the city.

The problem on Sheriff Street today was serious. Some local shitbirds were setting fires in dumpsters and one pulled a knife on an officer. The officer hit him with his expandable baton, breaking his arm, and that's when the larger clash started. The ambulances were advised not to go in until they'd secured the scene and put out the fires. He hoped like hell that Seany wasn't in the middle of it.

The car was parked alongside a few more that were waiting. That's when the armed emergency response unit got in formation and went in. It was chaos. The lead officers started shooting bean bags into the center mass of several rioters, knocking them to the ground. The relief of the pinned officers was palpable. They started tasering whoever they could reach first. That's when the first wave of fireman burst onto the scene.

The dumpster fire was getting big. It had already caused two windows from a bottom floor apartment to bust out, and the window treatments caught fire. If they didn't get a handle on this, the whole apartment would burn. Patrick heard his name and turned, but realized the fireman coming alongside them wasn't talking to him. He looked forward and recognized his brother instantly. A good five inches taller than any of the other men, he had his axe in front of him like he was dancing with a cane. Some of the rioters were trying to stop the guys on the hose. Either that, or they were trying to get ahold of the hose themselves. When Seany had to dodge a rock being thrown at him, he popped the piece of shit right in the jaw with the butt of his axe handle. Fucking Seany. Leave it to him to find a way to get in on the fighting. His little brother was going to be the death of him.

* * *

GROGAN'S WAS full of cops and firemen. They'd all but chased the tourists out with their cut lips, smoke blackened faces, and edgy stares. Patrick took a long draw on his lager, smiling as one of the officers was giving a play-by-play of Seany popping someone in the jaw.

"Then, he perks up with some kind of O'Brien super hearing, runs into the back door of the building, into the apartment that has fire blowing through the window, and comes back out with this twenty something year old honey with her fecking pug. Meanwhile, his brother over here has some asshole on the ground with his boot on his chest while he sprays another guy down with pepper spray. Two at once, I'm not shitting you. These County Clare boys are something to see." Seany wiggled his eyebrows at Patrick. What a night. No major injuries on either side, twelve arrests, and one rescued honey with her pug. All in all, it had been a banner fucking day.

"Hey, Junior. Tell us why the hell you are playing with firehoses instead of joining the Garda like the real men?" Seany smiled as he reached in his pocket, pulling out a slip of paper. "The blonde's phone number." All of the firemen let out a whoop as Seany tucked it back into his pocket and took another sip.

Patrick felt someone come up beside him, and stiffened at the voice. "You O'Brien boys must just be bred to be heroes. How are you, Patrick?" Patrick didn't even turn. "Good evening, Detective Morrison."

"So formal? What happened to Brittney?"

Patrick couldn't stand this bitch. She'd done a number on Tadgh, and she had no problem cheating on her new husband with other officers. "Go away, Brittney."

"No reason to be rude. You just look lonely sitting here by yourself. I heard the wife took an extended vacation without you." She put her arm on his bicep and he jumped up like someone had zapped him with a taser.

"Don't ever do that again. I don't know why you are the way that you are, but I don't screw around on my wife. Even if I was single, which I'm not, I don't do sloppy seconds."

She reared back like he'd slapped her, but he didn't give a shit. "Go home to your husband, Brittney. Stay away from me, my cousin, and my brothers. We aren't interested."

Her brow went up, then her eyes traveled to Seany. Seany was watching the exchange and barked out a laugh. "Don't even think about it sweetheart. You aren't my type." At that, she swung around and marched out of the pub. She passed Tadgh and Charlie in the doorway, and Charlie all but hissed at her as a final fuck you.

Tadgh shook his head. "I don't want to know. Now, who's buying? I heard O'Briens were getting free drinks tonight."

"I'll get you something. Lager? Charlie, love, what about you?" Patrick asked.

"Actually, I'm staying, he isn't. He has interviews. I'll have whatever you're having. Just one, so make it cold." He started to go up to the bar and she yelled, "And a fish and chips basket!"

Patrick laughed, "Jesus, where do you put it? I can't fathom your appetite." He put in the order and came back with a drink for Charlie.

Tadgh kissed her on the forehead. "I don't know how late I'll be. Can you walk her home?" he asked. When she gave him a sideway stare, he amended, "I mean, I know my wife is a bad-ass FBI agent who can take care of herself, so maybe she can walk you home and protect you."

Patrick laughed. "Of course she is. I could use the company." He winked at Charlie who's mouth was turned up in a smile.

Tadgh left, and Patrick asked, "Is he interviewing the girl's roommates?"

Charlie took a sip. "Yes. He's working so hard on this case. He thinks they will shed some light on the identity of the father. I hope so. This whole case is awful. Notifying the parents really took it out of him." She told him about the situation the mother was dealing with.

"Jesus. Huntington's is a nasty disease. That poor woman." He rubbed his eyes, scrubbing the thoughts away. "How in the hell will she take care of the baby as well?"

"I don't think she can. I mean, some say they can't, because they don't want to. This woman just has nothing left to give. It's so sad. It's like life has ganged up on this woman with the sole purpose of breaking her heart. Jesus, what a thing to open the door to."

Patrick sipped his beer slowly, occasionally stealing a chip from Charlie. She was a beautiful, strong woman. She'd had her own heartaches. So had Tadgh. "You really are perfect for him, Charlie. You do know that, don't you?"

Her eyes lightened and she smiled. "Yeah, I think I do. I wasn't sure I'd ever marry or have kids. Now, I can't imagine living my life without him. And Josh has come so far." Her throat restricted. "You've all been so wonderful. He needed you. Maybe even more than I did. It's not always blood that ties people together. I watch him and Seany and I swear they are starting to look alike." She laughed, even though her eyes were teary.

"He's one of us now. Don't doubt it for a minute," Patrick said. His family had enough love to light up the whole world. And she was right. Blood didn't always matter. He stole another chip and thought about that little baby in the hospital. The fear of hoping nearly choked him.

CHAPTER 13

GARDA HEADQUARTERS, SPECIAL DETECTIVE UNIT, DUBLIN

Sal watched through the one-way glass as Tadgh interviewed the first roommate. The other had just arrived and was in a waiting area. They wanted to keep them separate. The girls had solid alibis, but young people lied for each other. Misplaced loyalty even when the situation was dire. The girl, Simone O'Rourke, was from Tipperary County. A sprite of a girl with blonde hair and brown eyes. Tadgh handed her another tissue, then began. They'd interview them separately, then together. He let Tadgh do the initial interviews because the bastard was handsome in a way that disarmed people. He was genuine and compassionate when he needed to be, but he was no pussy. He could tower over a suspect and have the asshole shitting his britches with fear. He was versatile like that.

Tadgh looked across the table and had the impulse to hug the poor girl sitting in front of him. She was twenty-one years old and probably had never experienced anything so ugly. This was going to be hard, but he needed answers.

After interviewing both of the young women, they put them together in the same room. The sobbing ensued, as they'd expected. They let the girls reunite because this was an awful situation, and after having interviewed them both, it was obvious that they'd loved Kasey Walsh like a sister. They both had known she was pregnant, but didn't realize that she'd been so far along. The girl hadn't told anyone else, and she hadn't gone in for her regular prenatal visits, which was odd. With the doctor-patient confidentiality, there didn't seem to be a good reason for her to not seek medical care. Regardless, they were both adamant that they wouldn't have left her if they'd known she was so close to her due date. The one frustrating consistency was that they both didn't seem to know the name of the father. He suspected that they were both holding out. Obviously they'd spoken before the interviews.

The second girl, Katrina Boyle, was sniffling as she said, "She would never have done such an awful thing. You have to believe us. She was scared at first, but then she started talking about the baby like a real person, making plans for the future. Picking names."

Simone added, "I have a cousin in England. I offered to take the ferry with her…you know…in case she wanted to end the pregnancy. She said no. She was upset and scared, but she wanted the child. I know she did! You have to find out what happened, because you can bet your ass that she'd have never left that baby to die!"

Tadgh sat back in his chair. Softly, he said, "Then you need to tell me everything. I don't believe for one moment that you don't know who the father is. I know she probably told you to keep her secret, but she's dead and that baby has no one. You need to tell me everything, because Kasey can't tell me. If she didn't do this then someone else did. That someone most likely left them both to die. Why was she so secretive? Why no doctor visits? If she was going to keep this child, then explain to me why the hell she didn't go to the hospital!" He was raising his voice just enough to get their attention. Hoping they'd feed off his anger.

The girls looked at each other, then Katrina broke first. Simone just shut her eyes and listened. "We don't know who he was. Normally she told us everything, but she wouldn't tell us that. I believe he was married. That's the only reason I can think of that she'd behave the way she did."

"Could it have been a professor?" Tadgh asked.

Simone shook her head. "No, I think it was someone from her internship. She was only taking two classes besides that, and the professors were women." She exhaled, feeling relief at finally getting it out. "I think he was someone important. Perhaps in the Oireachtas."

The legislature. Jesus, Tadgh thought to himself.

She continued, "It was little things. Like she watched the news more often, like she was looking for someone. She took extra care with her looks when she'd go to work. The only reason I noticed the pregnancy was because her eating habits changed dramatically. At first she actually lost weight. Then the baggy clothes started. She came out of the bath when she thought no one was home. She was in a towel...and that's when I noticed the bump." The girl was wiping tears away now. "I confronted her, of course, but she was so tight-lipped about it. She was adamant that no one know. I made her tell Katrina. We needed to keep an eye on her. I mean, someone needed to know in case she needed medical attention. She went to the doctor once, at about twenty weeks. She left the city to do it. Other than that, it's the last time I know of that she saw a doctor."

Katrina said, "That's all we know. He was older and she said she loved him. That he was a good man that wanted the best for the people. A real servant, is how she described him. It's why we think he was a politician. She worked so much, it had to be someone in the legislature or another intern or something. It's just, I felt like he was older. I don't know how old, but more mature. He took an interest in her and the work she was doing with Huntington's. We tried to get her to open up. I knew it was a bad business altogether. He didn't want the pregnancy getting out. She was crying one night, saying he'd tried to get her to go to England and get an abortion. She was devastated."

Tadgh wanted to walk out the door and run in the other direction. He looked at Sal, who'd let him lead the discussion up until now. Jesus. What the hell had they gotten themselves into? They'd both been in the good graces of the Lord Mayor of Dublin as well as the Prime Minister. After thwarting a terrorist attack, they'd been the golden boys. But to take on the Irish legislature and to out a politician who'd seduced a young intern? Some *public servant* who had tried to ship her across the sea to get an abortion. Fucking crikey. This was a powder keg.

"Is it possible that she kept a journal? Even on her laptop?" Sal broke the silence.

"Her laptop was in the shop. She spilled a bottle of water on it, and she was so upset. She can't afford another one. She's tight for money, and a new one is a bit dear. So, she took it to a local shop to try and save it or at least retrieve her data. I'll need a minute to find the shop, but if you give me a minute on my phone app, I can find it. I want to help."

"That would be very helpful, thank you." Sal leaned in to Tadgh. "If it's where I think it is, she'll have had a work ticket stub. Something to identify her as the owner of the laptop. We need to check the room again or look in the bagged evidence."

They finished with some follow-up questions, and as the girls stood to leave, Katrina asked, "What was the baby? She wanted to be surprised about the gender, but I think she really wanted a little girl." The girl choked on a sob at the thought of her friend.

Tadgh swallowed hard, thinking about the tiny child in the hospital. The incredibly small baby boy that Charlie had held on New Year's Eve. "She had a boy. He's very small, but he's a fighter."

Simone shook her head. "Her poor mother. Christ, what a mess. Kasey's mother has it hard enough with her Da bein' sick. What in the hell is she going to do with a baby to care for?"

Tadgh's sentiments exactly. He suddenly didn't give a shit who the father was, or his important position in the government. He just wanted justice for Kasey and that little baby. For Mrs. Walsh and her very sick husband who couldn't fully grasp what had happened. "We'll make sure he's taken care of. I promise you. Kasey's son is safe."

* * *

St. Clare's Charity Mission, Manaus, Brazil

Reverend Mother Faith was worried as she looked across her desk at her new teacher. They'd ended the last session a bit tensely, and she was sorry for it. She just had an Achilles heel when it came to those kind of comments, and she'd been short with the girl.

"How was your trip into the bush? Was it all you'd imagined?"

Caitlyn smiled numbly. Like it was automatic, but there were no feelings of joy behind it. "It was grand altogether, Reverend Mother. I feel very lucky that I was able to go. Thank you for allowing it."

"Not at all. I'm sure you were quite the attraction. The female doctors usually are, especially blondes. I heard you earned a nickname already." The corner of her mouth was turned up.

"Yes, Esmeralda. For my eyes, apparently. The children were very sweet, and the women were…interested. Very interested. They don't have a lot of social boundaries."

"Aye, that's very true. If they're curious about something, they ask. They're also a little more free with their nudity." Caitlyn barked out a laugh.

"Yes, most were clothed, but they definitely aren't shy. They took me to the spring."

The reverend mother's eyes sharpened. "Did they now?"

"Yes, they'd asked me about children and I probably revealed more than I should have. It just kind of came out of my mouth before I thought better of it. They took me over the bridge to the spring and they sort of…cleansed me, for lack of a better word. I know it's probably a load of bullocks, but I didn't want to be rude. I don't hold any hope for it helping me."

"Did you know, Caitlyn, that the Jesuits used to have a mission near that village?" This seemed a non sequitur, but Caitlyn shook her head. "Yes, they did. And if you look in the archives, they mention that very spring. They noticed that the young women bathed in it. When they inquired, they learned that women who wanted to conceive would go there. Also women who were having trouble with their milk. Others would go with their mates to couple in the pool beneath the falls, hoping to bless the union with a child. According to these records, there was no infertility in the four tribes that used it. There were more tribes back then. Now there is only the one. Of course, being from the church, they assumed that the spring was a holy well. They named it St. Anne's Holy Well. St. Anne, as I'm sure you know, was the mother of the Blessed Virgin. She was healed of her infertility and brought forth the mother of Christ from her womb."

Caitlyn's eyes were bright with suppressed emotion. "It's an interesting theory. I've given up on such things. I tried to go to the holy wells in Ireland. It didn't bring anything but disappointment."

"Yet despite this fact, did you find yourself wishing as you crossed that bridge? What is it, dear girl, that you want most of all?"

"I want to be a mother. I want Patrick to hold his child in his arms. A living, breathing child. I know that I should just feel fortunate to have found love, but I want it so badly, Reverend Mother. Our roots are deep in Ireland. The Nagles and O'Briens have been in Doolin for centuries. I just want what they've all had. I want a family."

The reverend mother stood suddenly. "Let's take a walk, love. Get a bit of fresh air, shall we? It's a grand, soft day."

The abbess walked slowly along the path to the river, keeping in pace with Caitlyn like a woman half her age. The trees were damp with the rain that had only stopped about an hour before. The scent of fresh greenery and moss permeated the air.

"I'm thinking about what you said, my dear. I do understand the Irish way of things. It's all about roots and family trees. Family crests and old bloodlines. But I've learned a few things in my absence from that home that I love so much. I've spent over thirty years in this place. Thirty-one as the abbess. It's taught me some things about love and family. Take a look up at the forest. In Ireland, ye might see the rowan trees or a blackthorn. Perhaps a mighty oak. Strong branches and deep roots." Then she waved her hand above her. "But here in this lush, dense forest, things are different. It's not the branches so much as the vines."

She pointed, and Caitlyn watched, listening. "It's a beautiful tangle of vines, all coming from here and there. They may not belong to the same plant and they may not have started growing up the same tree, but see how they reach out for the other. Tangling and entwining themselves around each other, so you can barely tell where each of them started. You can barely see where one plant starts and the other stops. But there's a beauty and strength to this miraculous system. Sometimes, the ties that bind us together are like those vines. The origin might be different, but they end up together nonetheless."

Caitlyn thought about that. "I understand."

"No, I don't think you do. But I hope that when your time is done at St. Clare's, and you are ready to leave us, perhaps you will understand."

* * *

SEAMUS SMILED as he looked down at the woman in the hospital bed. His last catch before he left, so to speak. Mary came beside him. "They look good. Don't worry. Antonio's on call if we need him, but it went off like a hitch. They're both fine. You can go home, Seamus."

He was packed, and Paolo waited in the vehicle to take him to the airport. He turned to Mary. "It was a good run. I have a feeling I'll be back. Until then, I'll see you on the west coast Dr. Falk."

He turned to find Antonio in the doorway. Antonio's eyes were intense. He was going to miss him. He pulled him in for another hug, thumping him on the back. "Goodbye for now, brother."

"It appears I'm going to need to come to Ireland. I have so many important people there now."

"Or you can go home to that vineyard your family owns, and invite me for a holiday."

Mary piped up at that. "Really? A vineyard, eh? Maybe we'll all need a holiday in Italy. I love a good Chianti."

Antonio laughed. "Well, you'll like our wine. My family is another matter. Once I get home, I'll invite you all for the harvest. How does that sound?"

They walked outside, away from the hospital that Seamus had worked in for almost four months. He turned and looked at the old stone building. "I'm going to miss this place." Then he turned to find the children lined up next to their new teacher. Caitlyn smiled, her eyes misting. He hugged her and whispered, "Until we meet again, Esmeralda."

He kissed all of the smaller children on the top of the head, then hugged the bigger children. Genoveva was the hardest. He held her as she cried. "Keep up with your training, my beautiful, strong lass. Maybe Dr. Quinn would step in and take my place." He looked past her to where Quinn was standing, giving him a nod. *Take care of her,* his eyes said, *and bring her home.*

He shook hands with Hans. "Take care of my boys. They're proper little shits when they want to be, but they're good lads."

Hans laughed. "Don't worry. They are in good hands." As he said it, Raphael grunted his approval.

Seamus cupped a hand behind Raphael's head and brought their foreheads together. "My brother. Always my brother." The emotion was thick in his voice. They'd been through a lot together. "Kiss those sons and that lovely wife of yours for me." And then it was done. He got in the vehicle, and Paolo drove them away from St. Clare's.

* * *

HENRICO AND EMILIO grunted as Genoveva jumped up from the ground and gave the next instructions. Emilio said in Portuguese, "These burpees. They are some sort of torture! Why so many of these cursed burpees?"

Genoveva snapped, "English, or I didn't hear it. You need to practice if you are ever going to improve. Just like the burpees. You must practice. You whine like an old woman." Emilio needed no translation. He understood English better than he spoke it. Henrico nudged him and they started again.

Hans took a sip of water as he looked at Quinn. "You can't be ashamed to stop and take a drink and a breath. These teenagers are going to be the death of me."

Quinn shook his head. "I'm going to have to agree with the lad.

Burpees are some sort of devilry. Who the hell comes up with these things?" He was bent over, feeling like those last few cheese breads were going to make an appearance on the lawn. He watched Genoveva in awe. She was powerful. Both in her body and how she handled the boys. He'd spoken to Izzy last evening, and once she'd told him more, he realized what an achievement this was for the lass. She'd been shy. She'd let the other children bully her. Now, her chin was up. Her eyes sparked with challenge.

"She's kind of a badass. If she were in America, I'd have already recruited her," Hans said proudly. He watched the two boys and saw that there was a strength in them as well. They were different, but seemed to move as one unit. Like twins. They were only a few months apart. He noticed that they both needed new clothes. Their shorts were rags, and the pants that he'd seen them in were about two inches too short. "Hey, what do you think about taking the older kids into town? I think they could use some new threads." Quinn cocked his head. "You know, clothes. The boys are outgrowing their clothes. Maybe Caitlyn and Mary could come and help the girls?"

Quinn liked the idea of taking them shopping. "We could make a day of it. Take them for lunch. I don't think they get out much, and they are getting older. They need to learn a little about the city. I'll speak with the abbess."

After the work out, they sent the kids to shower. Hans went to look for Caitlyn, and Quinn went to find the abbess. When Hans walked into the classroom, Caitlyn was working at her desk and the children were all gone to tea. All except Estela, who seemed to follow Caitlyn like a shadow. The child was adorable. The sight of her hit him right in the feels, every damn time. Big, soulful brown eyes. Cute little smile with straight, white baby teeth. She was on a stool, writing her letters on the old school chalkboard. "Hello, baby girl! You look awfully pretty today!" Estela smiled, and flicked back her yellow scarf. It was tied to her head like a gypsy. He patted her head. "What's with the new scarf?"

"Sister Maria is giving it to me. It is my new hair. I like the yellow hair." Her eyes traveled to Caitlyn and he understood. Caitlyn gave him a small, knowing smile. "Well, it's just lovely. But I have to say, I love your pretty brown hair. Look at Doc Mary. Her hair is as dark as yours. I'm blonde like Mrs. O'Brien. We can all be different, right?"

Estela didn't look convinced, and she gave the scarf a flick over her shoulder, like it was real hair. Caitlyn said, "Oh yes, I agree. My husband has darker hair with a little bit of red in it. It is just like Estela's when the sun hits her's just right. I love his hair. I wouldn't want him to change it. I hope our children get his brown hair."

Estela's eyes were big and inquisitive. "Do he have the brown eyes too?" she asked in the best English she could muster.

"No, he has blue and green eyes. He's very handsome. I'll have to show you a picture." Then she looked at Hans who was smiling at the exchange. "Did ye need something Hans?" When he told her about the planned excursion, her face lit up. "That's a grand idea. Let me check with Sister Maria to see if there are any other children who need clothing. The smaller ones are easy. I can just make a list of sizes. Tomorrow, I suppose?"

Hans nodded. "Yes, tomorrow if they can spare you. I figured late morning and lunchtime would be a safer time to go and show them around. We've got four kids. That's about all we can handle with the adults. We'll already need both vehicles. Raphael will drive one and I'll drive the other."

"Well, I think the new girl Zantina could use a few things and Rosalis needs new shoes. I'll put a full list together and we can take care of it all tomorrow. We just need a budget from Sister Agatha. I think she handles the bookkeeping."

"Okay, then. I'll see you at supper. Oh, and Caitlyn...have you spoken to Patrick?"

Caitlyn straightened at that. "Yes, but not since last week. I was going to call tonight. Is something wrong?"

"No, no. Not at all. I just spoke to Alanna and she said that he'd had some rough nights on duty. I just thought maybe he'd like to hear from you. I know I'm meddling like an old dad, but sometimes men need their women when they've seen too much of the ugly side. Do you understand?" He couldn't tell her. Wouldn't tell her without betraying Patrick's wishes. The whole family knew about the baby that Patrick, Branna, and the boys had rescued from certain death. An abandoned newborn baby. *Jesus.*

"I understand. Working in a big city can take it out of a person. I'll make sure to call him. Thank you Hans, for being an old dad." She grinned a crooked grin at him and he went on his way. "Now, Miss Estela. Let's get you cleaned up before dinner. I have to go see Sister Agatha." She spoke English to the child, wanting to help her with her comprehension. She put her hand out and the little girl folded her hand in hers.

She looked up at her, "Do your husband really have hair like mine?"

Caitlyn smiled, "*Does*, not do. *Does* he have hair like yours? Well, his is much shorter and a little bit lighter, but yes. His mammy has red hair. So he got some of the brown from his family with just a little bit of red for good luck. Just like yours when you've been in the sun."

Caitlyn didn't say a word as the child pulled the yellow scarf off of her head and tucked it under her arm, but she couldn't hide her smile.

* * *

CAITLYN WAS sorry when the computer rang and rang with no answer. She left a message, told him she loved him, but he hadn't been home. He could have picked up a night shift, or simply gone home to see his parents. She suddenly missed him very much.

Sister Agatha came into the library quietly. "I'm sorry, I can come back."

"Not at all, Sister. I was finished." She liked Sister Agatha. She was small and quiet, except when she sang. She had a pretty voice. She watched the small figure come into the room with an envelope in her hand.

"I've got the list for you and some funds from the orphanage's clothing fund. We take donations, of course, but often the items are rags. It would be nice for them to get some new things. The boys have shot up a few inches in as many months. Genoveva was the tallest for a while, but now the two older boys have passed her. They'll be able to give most of their clothes to Luca and some of the other boys." She showed her the list. "There's a budget for each child. I'm afraid the little girl Zantina came with nothing. Rosalis is small for her age, but the clothes are still large for her. We have a few of the younger kids that have shared, but she really needs everything. There's a second hand clothing store that carries clean, gently worn children's clothes. You can start there. Down the road, just a couple of blocks, is the Amazonas Shopping Center. It's a large mall. Just take care that the clothes aren't too..." She blushed.

"You want them to be age appropriate for teenagers living next to a nunnery?" Caitlyn said with a brow cocked. The sister laughed. "It's okay, sister. I've seen the clothing in some parts of Brazil. Genoveva will be dressed like a sweet little fifteen year old."

"But perhaps a new dress." Both of the women jumped at the voice behind them. Sister Agatha had her hand over her heart. "Forgive me, Reverend Mother. Ye startled me."

"I can see that. Now, about the shopping excursion." The abbess handed another envelope to Caitlyn. "I want you to take them somewhere for lunch. Have them order their own food. They need to learn to speak up and use their manners in public. As for the clothing, I have just spoken to Father Pietro. Apparently St. Fransisco's, the Catholic secondary school, has a dance planned for next week. Unfortunately, their gymnasium has flooded. They will not have it ready by the time the annual winter dance happens. Since St. Clare's is on high ground, they've asked if they can use our garden for the dance. They'll bring in tents and our older children will be invited to attend. They will also use the monies allotted for this event to make a donation to St. Clare's. My intention is to complete the two married housing units within six months time. We could use the funds. So, I've agreed to host the dance."

Caitlyn clapped her hands, fumbling with both envelopes. "That's a grand idea, Reverend Mother. A real teenage experience for them. So, can I assume the extra funds are for a party dress?" Caitlyn loved shopping and playing fashion advisor.

"And trousers and ties for the lads. Emilio will likely have a stroke on the spot, but I insist he follow the other school's dress code. And I'll talk to Hans and Raphael about getting them both a haircut." She exhaled. "They're growing up on me. I'll have to admit, it hurts my heart a bit at the thought of them leaving me someday. But I suppose all parents go through this, don't they?"

Caitlyn saw sadness and distance in the abbess's eyes. Like she was somewhere very far away. The reverend mother seemed to wake, looking at Sister Agatha. "Now, my annual vigil will begin at midnight. I won't see you tomorrow. If you could please give Sister Maria some assistance in the school, I would appreciate it. I think this field trip is important for the older children. A taste of the outside world, under tight supervision of course." She looked at Caitlyn. "Tell Genoveva the dress is not optional. I'll bid you both goodnight."

As she left, Caitlyn looked at Agatha and asked, "What sort of vigil starts at midnight and goes all day?"

Sister Agatha just smiled. "Have fun tomorrow. I can't wait to see the children's faces when they get their new clothes. There's enough money for all of the children who have particular needs, and there's some wiggle room if you find something for the other children. Don't feel like you have to get them all something. The children who aren't on that list got new things this past summer. They know how the rotation works, and they'll likely get some nice hand-me-downs."

Caitlyn's throat was suddenly tight. She'd grown up in such privilege. Not decadence, but a comfortable middle class household where she never had to wonder when she was going to get a new pair of shoes, or pants that fit. She missed her sisters. They'd loved getting all of her hand-me-downs. She wondered what they were up to now. Her sweet, beautiful sisters. Mary, the fun loving girl with lots of admirers, and Madeline, equally beautiful, but more of an introvert. One of those girls that was too smart, too quiet and serious, too bewitching for the average boy her age. At twenty, she'd only had a few dates. She seemed to be content with that. Letting Mary, always the more flirtatious, outshine her in social gatherings. They were close. Neither wanted to be anything other than what they were. She hoped they always felt that way.

"I'll use it wisely. I promise you," she finally said to Sister Agatha. "I know these funds are precious." And as the petite sister left her, she tucked her laptop under her arm and went to the small cot that waited for her.

CHAPTER 14

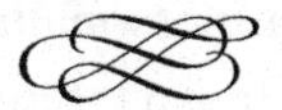

DUBLIN, IRELAND

Patrick sat in the patrol car, willing the computer repair shop to open early. Tadgh and Sal would be here any minute, but he hated waiting. They'd called him last night, when they'd found the work stub for her laptop in the top drawer of her desk. Water damage was tricky on a laptop, according to his brother-in-law, but not always fatal. If anyone could get the data off of her laptop, Finn could. They had a court order to seize the laptop as evidence, and he was here to make sure that it happened. Tadgh and Sal could take care of themselves, but this was personal. A prickling happened at the base of his skull, and he turned in his seat. A very large man in business attire was walking down the street. He watched him try the door, find it locked, and stand aside, waiting. When he noticed the Garda patrol car, he turned his back to Patrick. The shop clerk came a minute later, flipping the sign a few minutes early and letting the man in. *Shit. Where are you Tadgh?* He looked at his phone. Should he text Tadgh? He wasn't technically supposed to be here.

"Fuck it." He got out of the vehicle and walked toward the shop. He'd just make small talk, ask some random question about hard drives or some shit. He could fake this. Something about that asshole in the starched collar didn't sit right, and he'd learned to trust his sixth sense when it came to his work.

Patrick eased the swinging door open, just as he heard, "But she was dropping it off as a favor to my employer. He needs it immediately. He cannot wait until she returns and he doesn't have the claim check."

The shop employee smiled indulgently. "I'm sorry. No stub, no pick up. Unless she comes in personally with the stub or ID, I can't release the laptop. Besides, it isn't finished. I have it drying, but I haven't even started the data retrieval." That's when the man noticed they weren't alone. He'd started to lean in, menace rolling off him. The clerk shot Patrick a look, and the man straightened, looking behind him.

"I'll return at a later time. Thank you."

The man was headed toward the door just as Tadgh and Sal entered. Tadgh took out his credentials. "We have a court order for the laptop of Kasey Walsh. Can you please..." Then he noticed the look on the clerk's face. He looked at Patrick.

The clerk answered, "A court order? But that man just said..." Patrick was out the door in a flash. He heard Tadgh behind him, yelling for Sal to secure the computer. Patrick ran for two blocks, looking in the bustling morning crowd for any sign of the big man from the shop. Far ahead, he watched as the man got into a cab, and he was gone. "Feckin' bastard!" Patrick growled.

Tadgh was winded. "Did you get a number?"

"No, it was too far. It was an NRC Taxi, though. I saw the logo." Tadgh nodded and started dialing his headquarters.

He was surprised when Sullivan answered. "Janet is sick with the flu, what is it?"

"I need NRC Taxi to pull a fare from Stephen Street Lower. Big bastard, caucasion, brown hair, black dress coat and trousers, early forties, clean shaven."

"I'll put one of the men on it. You okay? Ye sound out of breath."

"Yes, we're all fine. Just call me when you get a drop off. I doubt he'd use a credit card."

Tadgh ended the call, looking hard down the road. Like if he willed it, the taxi would do a u-turn wherever it was and return the man to them. They walked back slowly, both needing a minute to let the adrenalin spike fade to a simmer. When they re-entered the shop, Sal was bagging the computer.

"I hope it helps. She was a nice girl. Did someone kill her? Jesus, was she still pregnant?"

They all looked at him, brows raised. "What? She was trying to hide it, but I know that waddle. I have three older sisters who have been pumping out kids every year for the last six years. Ye get fairly good at seeing it. Did someone kill her?"

Sal said, "We can't talk about any of that. It's an open case. Just please don't talk to anyone. If that man comes back in, you need to stall him and act like you are going to help him, try to get some ID. Then you will call this number immediately." It was the phone extension at his desk, but it forwarded phone calls right to his cell. "Do you have cameras in the store?" The man pointed to one camera that was shrouded under a dome on the ceiling above him. "Great, and we'll have someone watching the place after you close, in case he comes back and tries to take it after hours."

They left together, walking toward Patrick's patrol car. "We're parked about two blocks down," Tadgh said.

"Get in, I'll drop you at the car." They did as he asked, and he continued. "I want in on this case."

"Not going to happen, brother. Sorry. Sullivan's orders," Tadgh said plainly.

"Why the fuck not? I was the first on the scene. I was on duty. That makes this my case as much as anyone's."

"You're not on the patrol unit or special detectives. You're needed elsewhere. Where are you supposed to be right now?" Patrick ground his teeth. "Right. I know this is emotional for you, but you're too close to it. Let us work this case." Tadgh's phone went off and he answered, "O'Brien, what do you have?" He put it on speaker. Big mistake. Detective Miller, affectionately known as Detective Hairy Ass by Tadgh's beloved wife, said gruffly, "The cab driver said he didn't use a card. He dropped the man off across from the Leinster House."

"Did he now? Thank you, Detective Miller. Just leave the man's contact information on my desk." He hadn't even ended the call when the vehicle took a random turn. He looked at Patrick who was single minded. "Patrick, turn this bloody car around and take us to our own vehicle."

"You can bite my arse, brother. We're down the feckin' street from the place."

"Yes, we are. And you're in uniform, driving a marked feckin' car, you jackass! You need to stop and think." Patrick was forced to stop for the traffic light. "Patrick, you need to trust me. I bleed for that child just as you do. You have to step back and trust us."

Patrick closed his eyes for a moment, then let out a breath. He changed the direction and headed back to the computer shop, toward their detective's vehicle. "I'm sorry. I just can't explain it. I need to know. I need to protect him. I want that fucker's head on a spike. Whoever left him to die, I need some justice for him".

Sal broke the tension and put a solid palm on his shoulder. "And you shall have it. I swear it. We won't stop until we find out what happened to both of them."

* * *

PATRICK SMILED as he walked into the parent room of the neo-natal unit. Josh and Seany were taking turns feeding the little boy they'd found. His heart clenched in his chest so hard that it almost buckled his knees. *He's supposed to be ours.* The boy was fussing up a storm, thrashing his head around and refusing the bottle. The nurses, who'd obviously been charmed into expanding the visitor list, were swooning at the sight of the two devilishly handsome young men taking turns with the baby. "He doesn't like being held like that. You're doin' it wrong." Patrick put his arms out in a silent demand. When Seany handed him over, the boy melted into the nook of his arm as

Patrick cradled the tiny body to his. "There, now." The boy immediately started to suckle the bottle.

Seany huffed. "That's exactly how I was doing it! Do I smell or something?" The nurses in charge came between them.

"No, lad. You smell downright heavenly. You just don't smell like him." She palmed the soft head and looked at Patrick. "He's like a wee duckling that's imprinted on you. He's never so content as when you hold him."

"Well, that's not going to help us. We need some baby time with our little changeling," Josh said, taking the baby's tiny hand between his finger and thumb.

"Well, try holding him a little higher on your chest, let him mold to you. He doesn't have a mammy to feed him. He needs to feel the connection to someone when he eats."

Patrick looked down at him and swore that as the child gulped, he saw gratitude. Relief. Like he'd been waiting for him to show up and make everything better. When he looked out the glass window of the door, he saw an older woman approach. He heard the nurse whisper to the other, "It's the granny. The mam of the lost mother."

Patrick felt like tucking the boy into himself like a rugby ball, and running as fast as he could. But another part of him was flooded with tenderness. This woman came to see the only tie she had to her daughter. So when she came into the room after a thorough scrubbing, Seany helped her into the rocking chair and Patrick handed her his precious cargo. "Well, lad. Here is your Gran."

* * *

PATRICK HAD STAYED LONGER than the other two. The nurses had to enforce rules for how many visitors could be in the area at once. He'd introduced all of them, of course, and the woman's capacity for tears seemed like a deep ocean. Her daughter's child had been saved, and she took comfort in that one thing. She said that she hoped that her daughter was watching from heaven. That she knew how her son had come to be in this place, and surrounded by strangers who loved him.

Patrick couldn't offer her anything else. No explanation of how this tragedy had unfurled. Who had separated them, and then left them both to die? After this time with the woman who held this parentless child, he found himself knowing, or at least praying, that her daughter had not been the one to cast this beautiful, frail life aside.

Now he walked. The way that Dublin was laid out, he usually left his car in his normal rented car park and had an easier time making it on foot to his home. As much as he longed for sleep, the emptiness of that place they shared together was an ever present fog that blanketed his every step. Even in his sleep, he longed for his Caitlyn. What was she doing? Was she content? Did she miss him?

When he got home, he went straight to his laptop, hoping to have an email or something from her. When he saw a video message was waiting, his heart jumped in his chest. *I miss you so much. I love you, Patrick. I really want to talk. I want to hear about your days and your nights. I want to feel like I'm there with you.*

She did miss him. Thank God. He called her back, knowing he wouldn't likely catch her at her computer. She had very limited internet. So he left her an email, coordinating a time for them to talk. He looked over at the little fake tree in their living room, and knew he had to take the decorations down. It was so odd to do that sort of thing without her. Before he started, he took the beautiful bouzouki in his hands, and rested it on his knee. Then he began to play.

* * *

TADGH WAS EXHAUSTED. He'd been up all day and half the night. He looked over at Sal, who was checking his messages. The interior of the car smelled like coffee and cigarettes. Detective Miller wasn't supposed to smoke in the car, but he did it anyway. Leaving behind the lingering stench for the rest of the detectives on the other shifts to endure. They were parked in an alley behind the computer repair shop. The night shift was short regular patrol officers, so they'd decided to stake the place out on their own. They hadn't found the man by the time they'd arrived at the Senate building. They'd checked the whole area, including the parts of the building that were semi-open to the public. Tadgh just had a feeling that their tall friend that had come in looking for Kasey's laptop was going to show and try to do a snatch and grab. So, for three hours they'd watched.

"Did I mention how much I hate stake-outs? It's like bad American tele. Take out, cold coffee, needing to have a piss, but having to hold it." Sal was cranky when he went without sleep.

"Go behind the dumpster. All the drunks do it. Look, over by that massage parlor. I'm pretty sure that one gives a happy ending, so if someone comes out the back door, best stow the beast before you identify yourself."

"Very funny." Sal gave him a crooked grin. "I do have to go, though. I can refill the coffee around the corner. Don't kick anybody's ass while I'm gone, eh?" He gathered the trash like a good boy and headed down the street. They had phones and a set of radios on a closed station. He watched his partner turn the corner toward the all night coffee shop, and put his attention down the alley to the back door of the shop. The front door was on a main drag. No way would he break in through there, but they had a camera rolling that faced the front door just in case. Tadgh pulled up the camera feed from the nanny cam he'd placed strategically, and the front of the building was clear. That's when he heard it. A car humming down the east alley, out of his visual. It stopped, and he prickled to awareness as he heard a car door close.

It took a moment, but he saw the man. He was hard to miss. Dressed all in dark clothing, but the build was the same. He had a crow bar in his hand, headed for the back door. "Bingo, mother fucker." The slang he picked up from his FBI agent wife. She'd be so proud. He grabbed his radio. "Sal, do you copy. I have a visual." Nothing. "Sal, drop your wanker and get the fuck back here! I have a visual!" he hissed.

Sal was drying off his hands when he heard the squelching. "Shit!" He left the men's room to get away from whatever lead pipes were blocking his radio signal. He emerged from the water closet just as the clerk said, "Two Lattes with an extra shot for Sal?" Just as Tadgh came over the radio with *Sal, drop your wanker and get the fuck back here!* The brows raised from a couple sitting across from each other, having a cup of tea, and the clerk who just smiled and shrugged. Then he was out the door in a flash.

Sal rounded the corner to see the door of the computer shop open, and Tadgh going fist to cuffs with the big bastard who they'd been looking for. By the time he closed in on them, Tadgh landed a kidney punch and brought the guy's nose down on his knee. Crunch. The man moaned and slumped as he fell at Sal's feet. "Didn't I tell you not to kick anybody's ass while I was gone?"

Tadgh wiped the blood from his lip with a grin. "I didn't even touch his ass."

The man stirred, like he was ready for round two. Sal put a foot on his shoulder. "Think twice, my friend. He's as mean as he is pretty. You got off easy."

* * *

Manaus, Brazil

"What better time than when the two best virtues -- innocent joy and the boundless desire for love -- were the only motives in life?"

Leo Tolstoy

Mary walked toward the two vehicles and toward her smiling husband. "What? He's small. We'll squeeze him in." Next to her was Cristiano. He was as sweet a boy that had ever drawn breath. Small for his age with straight, white teeth and disarming, kind, dark eyes. His hair was a bit shaggy, coming over his glasses. His taped glasses, hence the invitation to join them in town. "There's an optical shop in town. He needs new glasses. I want to check the script to see if he needs an adjustment. You just do your thing and he and I will do ours. Isn't that right, lad?" Cristiano just nodded eagerly. Overwhelmed at the thought of hanging with the big kids today.

Hans said, "We stay together. It's not a problem. We have all day. Are you ready to hit the town, buddy?"

Cristiano's face lit up. "Buddy. Yes. I am ready, buddy!" His English was very good. He was a very gifted student, and although they weren't supposed to have favorites, he was Mary's favorite on any day of the week.

Quinn and Raphael got in the front seat of one car while Henrico and Emilio got in the back. Rosalis and Cristiano got in the back of the other vehicle with Hans and Mary. When Genoveva approached, she expected to cram into the back with the two smaller children, but then she heard Henrico yell. She looked up and he motioned for her to get in the Jeep with them. Then quick as lightning, Caitlyn was squeezing into the last seat of the other car. Genoveva was dumbstruck. She wasn't sure how to feel about the invite from Henrico. They never invited her to do anything. She didn't trust it.

Raphael watched as Quinn tensed, looking behind him at the close quarters where his potential female offspring was about to get cozy, and thigh to thigh with one of the hormonal teenage boys in the back. Raphael laughed at the look on his face. "This is why I'm glad I have two sons and not daughters," he said under his breath.

He knew. Quinn saw it in his eyes. "Aye, well better to be within striking distance I suppose. I suspect she can handle herself, though."

Raphael nodded. "Yes, she is tough. Like a female warrior. But she's soft in other ways. Be careful, my friend." There was a warning in Raphael's voice that both chaffed and impressed Quinn.

Quinn had expected Henrico to just move over, but instead, he hopped out of the open top to let Genoveva sit in the middle. Great... Now she'd be thigh to thigh with a boy on each side. The look on her face would have been amusing if he'd been anyone other than the potential baby daddy. *Shit. I'm not ready for this.* Henrico was a sweet kid and had never been anything but a gentleman to Genoveva, but Quinn was ready to yank him by the collar and threaten him just for wanting to sit next to Genoveva.

As they pulled out of the dirt driveway of the mission, Genoveva handed Raphael her iPod. A gift that she'd received from Izzy. It was all of their favorite music, and although second hand, it was a precious commodity for an orphan. The wind kicked up with the top off the Jeep, and suddenly the teenagers couldn't contain the excitement. They never got to go out like this.

Henrico smiled at both of them and raised his arms above his head. "Liberdade!" Raphael laughed as the other two joined him. "Liberdade!" A small taste of freedom in an otherwise sheltered life. Imagine Dragons was blaring out of the Jeep stereo and suddenly Genoveva wasn't uncomfortable anymore. Who gave a crap what these boys thought of her? She was going to enjoy this day. She sang and swayed her head. *I was lightning before the thunder thunder thunder... feel the thunder.*

Her hair flew around her, wisps of it hitting the boys in the face, but she didn't care or didn't notice. She smiled at Quinn, and she had no idea what it did to him to see her joy. To be young again and so full of life. He exchanged glances with Raphael who said, "You're in big trouble, médico."

* * *

HANS FELT a warmth infuse his heart as he watched Mary with the optometrist, fitting little Cristiano with new glasses. He'd often thought about what it would have been like to raise Erik and Alanna with Mary. She'd have been a wonderful mother. She was a spectacular grandmother to Alanna's two children. He turned to keep an eye on his other charges, who were waiting patiently for them to finish. The day had started chaotically. Traffic, and the pursuit of two parking spots that were near each other, being the big challenge. This optometry shop opened before the retail stores, so they'd come here first. Caitlyn and Genoveva were keeping the other three kids busy, quizzing them on their English.

The optometrist didn't speak English, so Raphael was translating for both of them. "His eyes haven't improved or worsened. He just needs entirely new glasses because these will not fit any of the current frames they offer. Apparently he gives the reverend mother a discount for the sisters and children."

The man brought a tray out for them to look at. "Jesus, so much for style points." She gave Hans a sideways glance and saw the cringe. The glasses were awful. The bottom of the food chain in eyewear. She looked at Cristiano who hadn't said one word of complaint. He really was a handsome kid. She said to Raphael, "Ask him if he has some non-discounted frames that will fit his old lenses. Something a little more stylish?"

"Amen to that. Those are worse than boot camp glasses. We called them BCGs, birth control glasses, because they'd never get…"

"We understand the metaphor, Hans," she chided. Raphael was grinning at the exchange. Then he interpreted.

The man shrugged and began collecting a few of the different options around the shop. He brought them for inspection. "Doc Mary, the abbess won't like it if we spend too much. The other ones are okay." Cristiano was such a good, agreeable lad.

"Don't worry about that. I've got excellent negotiating skills." Mary took a pair off the tray. "Now, this is more like it." She slid them on his nose. When she did, she noticed the other kids had closed in behind her.

"You look older, Cristiano. I like them," Genoveva said. Then she nudged the boys with her elbows.

"Yes, very nice. You look good, little brother." Henrico's voice was sincere.

"All the girls will want to…" Emilio paused thinking of the word. "Dance. They will want to dance with you. It's good. You listen to the médico." Everyone laughed, but Cristiano was like a new man.

"I like them, but the cost." Mary gave the optometrist a look that said, *Are you really going to make me take those off him?*

"Ask him how much to put the old lenses in these frames." Raphael asked and then translated the amount for her from real to euros. Eight hundred Brazilian real was about two hundred euros. Hans whistled. "And how much for the discounted ones with new lenses?"

Raphael asked and then said, "Six hundred Real which is about…"

Mary waved him off. "I got it. About 50 euro less. Tell him we need these old lenses put in these frames for the same price. And he'll need some cleaning papers as well." She said it so matter of factly, that

Raphael was almost afraid for the man if he told her no. Her brow was cocked, and Raphael had learned a thing or two over the years about women when their brow was cocked. The optometrist was no dummy. He saw it too. He looked at Raphael as he explained. Then he looked back at Mary. Hans folded his arms in front of him as the man looked him over.

"I find in these situations, it is best to just submit." Raphael laughed and translated for Hans.

The man grinned and said in Portuguese. "She reminds me of my older sister. A bit scary. Tell her okay. Six hundred and I'll buff some of the small scratches off the old lenses. If you can give me an hour?"

"Perfeito!" Mary clapped her hands together. "Now, everyone keep an eye on the lad. We can't have him walking into walls without his glasses. Come on big guy. Let's go get some clothes to go with those new spectacles."

The first shop they went to was a children's second hand store. The kids didn't even blink at the thought of used clothing. They were used to living on a tight budget. Caitlyn took Rosalis into the dressing room to try a few things on while she started browsing for the other children. She found items for several of the smaller kids, including an adorable seersucker dress for Estela that had a watermelon slice across the top and neckline. It was adorable, and she seemed to remember a photo of herself at age three or four with the same sort of dress.

There were no adult clothes, and the three teenagers were well past children's sizes. After going back and picking up Cristiano's new glasses, they walked into the main shopping mall, Caitlyn led them into a trendy but tasteful shop for younger clients. Hans and Quinn took the boys over to try on shirts and trousers. Emilio was horrified at the thought of wearing a tie. "Reverend Mother Faith's orders, sorry boys. The dress code for the dance is a button down and a tie." The boys groaned.

Hans said, "Don't worry. We'll get you some new shorts and jeans and some t-shirts without holes in them. When we're done, everyone is getting a haircut." The boys looked at Hans and hoped he was kidding. Then they looked at his hair. A buzz cut just like Raphael's. Emilio ran a hand through his hair protectively.

Caitlyn could tell that Genoveva was ready to have a full on panic attack. "I'm okay. I don't need clothes. I don't need to go to the dance."

"But you love to dance. This is supposed to be fun, darlin'. Relax and enjoy it. You're beautiful, Genoveva. Let's just try a few things on."

Genoveva was wringing her hands. She looked over at the boys as the big man Hans shoved them into a dressing room. Then she felt Caitlyn take her hands. "Sweetheart, don't be nervous. Let's pretend Izzy was here. What would she say to make you feel better?" Mary stood by with Rosalis, watching.

Genoveva thought about it. "She'd say *Suck it up, buttercup. Get your ass in the dressing room.*" Caitlyn and Mary both barked out a laugh at the same time. Rosalis clapped a hand over her mouth. Caitlyn said, "Exactly right. Now, grab some dresses and get your bum in the dressing room!"

Quinn watched out of the corner of his eye as Caitlyn handled Genoveva. God, he hated the world. He hated that such a magnificent girl felt so awkward about her body. How could she not, when everything on the tele and in magazines and billboards told young girls that thin was the only way to be pretty?

He turned as the two boys emerged from the changing rooms. Jesus, to be sixteen again would be hell. They both looked miserable. Caitlyn had put Genoveva into a dressing room and appeared next to him. "Clip-on ties and white shirts? Oh, no no. Boys, come here." Caitlyn took over like she was on the fashion channel. She plucked one pale blue shirt and one gray shirt off the rack. Then she ran her hand over the ties. The real ties. She handed the gray shirt and a black neck tie with skull and crossbones all over them to Emilio. He smiled and went back into the dressing room. She looked at Hans. "You can teach him to tie that tie after you've taught him how to shave those chin whiskers."

Hans put his hands up. "Yes ma'am."

The blue shirt needed a little more finesse. She held up two ties for Henrico's inspection. One was slate blue with red foxes all over it. The other was navy blue with a nautical star chart pattern. Henrico chose the nautical one. Then she handed him a web belt and a pair of suspenders. He raised a brow.

"Just trust me. And switch out the black pants for khakis." Quinn helped him find a pair of khakis in his size. "Deck shoes for him in cognac. Black loafers for Emilio, and don't forget dress socks." She swooped back to the girls side before anyone could say another word.

Quinn looked at Hans. "I think I need her to pick out my clothes. My nursing staff keeps telling me I wear old fart ties."

Caitlyn knocked on the door to the dressing room. "Sweetie, I am passing under some shoes for you. Then I need you to come out, okay? Let us see you."

Genoveva's voice was dripping with the same misery she saw on the boys' faces, but this was worse. Izzy had talked to Caitlyn, during one of their video chats, about Genoveva's body image issues. "Come on darling girl. Let's see those long legs and strong shoulders." Then Rosalis joined in, coaxing her in Portuguese to come out and show them.

The first dress was fuchsia and halter style. When she walked out, Caitlyn's eyes bugged out. She put her hand over her mouth. The girl was so shy, pulling on the hem. It came to her knee and the color was fantastic with her bronze skin, but she looked a little too good. Caitlyn heard a choking noise behind her and turned to see if Quinn was still breathing. Mary broke the silence. "Wow." She looked the girl up and down. "Genoveva, lass...You are beautiful. I mean," she looked around for confirmation. "Am I right?"

Quinn broke the spell. "Yes, lovely, but I don't think the reverend mother is going to approve that dress. It's a little bit too..."

Hans filled in, "Va va voom?"

"Exactly. I mean, don't get me wrong. It's gorgeous altogether, but..."

Caitlyn smiled as she watched Genoveva look in the mirror and finally see what they all saw. She was tall and solid, but she was also curvy and beautiful. Way too curvy to wear a halter dress back to the nunnery. Caitlyn hadn't chosen the dress for that reason. She'd chosen the dress because it was going to look great on her, and Genoveva needed a confidence booster. If she hadn't been convinced, she only needed to watch the two teenage boys emerge out of the dressing room. They swaggered actually, right up until the moment they saw her. Both of them froze, and the shock on their faces was a tangible thing. Shock and a flash of appreciation. Caitlyn watched the girl kick her chin up just as Quinn and Hans jumped in front of the boys. "Let's get those ties done. You guys look great," Hans said. Raphael and Mary were laughing on the sidelines.

Caitlyn walked to Genoveva and put her hands on her shoulders, meeting her eyes in the mirror. "It's gorgeous, but it might make the abbess drop into a dead faint. Let's try another one." Once she'd ripped the band-aid off, it started being fun. The boys had settled into chairs as Rosalis and Genoveva started the fashion catwalk. Cristiano was too young for the dance, so he tried on hats with Hans and Raphael, trying to pick some snazzy fedoras to go with their new clothes. They were probably going over budget, they knew, but Hans and Mary had already decided to kick in whatever they were lacking. Emilio surprised Raphael by saying, "Luca, he's back at the orfanato. It wasn't his turn for new clothes. He usually gets my old ones but he doesn't have anything nice enough for the dance. Do you think we could get him something too? Maybe I could put something back." Raphael translated for Hans.

Hans's throat tightened. This boy had almost nothing. He loved his new clothes. But he was willing to do without for the sake of his brother. "Don't you worry. You give me his sizes and I'll pick something."

The boy squirmed and looked over his shoulder. "Tell him thank you, but could Senhora O'Brien pick them?"

Raphael barked out a laugh and Hans didn't need a translation. He messed up the boys hair. "Wise guy, huh?"

Cristiano rode on Hans's back as they plopped down for the final dress. Caitlyn had known the right dress from the moment they'd walked in the store. She'd staged this whole thing for Genoveva and Rosalis to learn how to choose. How to celebrate their beauty. When

Genoveva came out of the little dressing room, everyone gasped. The dress was a pale green. It had small periwinkle and fuchsia flowers and darker green foliage. It came right to her knee in front, then graduated down in the back to mid calf. The sleeves were down to her elbows, but the shoulder cutouts gave it a whimsical, flirtatious look while revealing nothing. She was stunning. The light green set off her eyes in a burst of green ice. She looked over and Mary winked at her. "Crushed it."

Then she saw Quinn, and his face took her aback. Tears. Tears and pain. He ducked his head and walked out of the store. She looked at Mary who shrugged. "That's the one, Genoveva. And the shoes are perfect. Low sandals with a chunky heel, since you'll be on grass. They won't sink into the ground. Mary, if you'll help them pick out a few more everyday items, I'm going to go..."

"Go ahead, lass. I'm not sure what's going on, but something's wrong." Mary gathered all of the kids as Genoveva retreated back into the changing room with a big smile on her face.

She found Quinn around the corner, tucked into a small alley and away from the foot traffic. He was a large man. Almost Patrick's size with broad shoulders and long legs. He was also blonde, which made him easy to find. He was leaning against the building, jaw tight, tears ready to escape his lashes. He was shaking with the effort of keeping something in. "Quinn, what is it? Please, dear Quinn. What's happened?"

He closed his eyes, letting one tear escape. "She's almost grown. I missed it. Oh, God." He put a fist to his forehead. "I missed it all. She's grown. I missed everything."

Caitlyn pulled his hand down. "Quinn, Jesus. Let me help you. Who is she? Genoveva? Open your eyes and look at me." It was a command, and it was only when he obeyed that she saw it. When he opened those dazzling green eyes. His lashes were light, hers were dark, but it was there if you looked. She was taller than most of the kids, taller than many adults in Brazil. Her hair and skin were lighter. But the eyes never lied.

"Oh my God. You're her father, aren't you?"

"I didn't know. I swear it." He croaked the words. "I didn't know until Izzy and Liam came to me. I still don't know for sure. The DNA should be back any day."

That's why he'd swabbed her cheek. Obviously Seamus had kept it quiet. "I don't believe that for a minute. You do know. You know she's yours as surely as you know that sun is going to set tonight." She watched a shudder go through him. "But I won't say anything. I'm so sorry, Quinn. I'm sorry for both of you. But you're here now, and she needs a home. You haven't missed it all. You've lost a lot, but you haven't lost it all. Now, get it together. They're all distracted, but you need to collect yourself before we go back in there."

Quinn shook himself and ran his fingers through his hair. "She's quite something, isn't she?"

"She is a miracle. And she's kind of a bad-ass." Quinn laughed at that, and so did she. "Now, what do you say we take your daughter to lunch?" He came off the wall and put an arm out. Caitlyn took it. "And Quinn, maybe we need to have me sit in the back of Raphael's Jeep on the way home."

"That is a feckin' brilliant plan, Mrs. O'Brien. Absolutely brilliant."

They joined the group as Mary helped select the final items for the older children. Caitlyn laughed at the two boys, one in a sharp looking black fedora, the other in a more casual linen one with a pale blue hat band. They were going to look so handsome the night of the dance. She inspected the other items and was pleased to see that Genoveva had picked some color in her selections. There was, of course, a fresh pair of track pants, some new trainers, and two t-shirts, but the t-shirts could be worn with her new jeans as well. The boys kept it simple. Cargo shorts and graphic t-shirts and a hoodie each. She took a few minutes to help the boys choose something for Luca. Henrico was insistent that their brother get a hat as well, so they opted for a stylish driving cap. She'd created a monster.

Mary, ever the negotiator, managed to secure a 10% discount, bringing them in at just under budget. Raphael and Hans took the packages from both stores to the parking garage, while everyone else walked the expansive shopping mall, looking for some lunch. As they walked through the building, Quinn smiled at all of their faces. He leaned in to ask Mary, "Do ye think they've ever been to a big shopping center like this?"

"Likely not. I think the sisters clothe them in mostly donations. With Sister Agatha's promotion video, the cash has been coming in from around the world. Before that I think they were in danger of losing their funding. I shudder to think where these kids would have gone." She stopped and looked at Quinn, "Are ye alright, Quinn? You're as white as a ghost."

Caitlyn came to the rescue. "He's Irish, Mary. We come from pasty bog people. Plus he's hungry."

"Aye, I'm feeling a bit peckish as well. I don't like skipping meals. Just ask my husband. I get downright testy." She stopped, noticing that the boys were distracted by some sort of display. The sign was in Portuguese. "Henrico, love. What's this about?"

"It is a…" He conversed with Geonoveva and she gave him the English. "It's a job fair? Could we go see?"

"Of course." After all, these boys were getting older. They'd age out of the orfanato and need gainful employment. "Let's all go have a look. I'll text Hans and tell him to meet us here."

They walked around, looking at the tables. There were oil companies that didn't seem to want to bother with two young teenagers, and other companies that wanted experience or degrees. The boys took pamphlets from logging companies, which made Mary and Quinn exchange glances. Dangerous work, but it paid well enough. They stopped as Genoveva's attention drifted to a recruiting table for the Brazilian Navy. Caitlyn had to grab Quinn's arm before he launched himself at the table. "Easy, big guy. She's only fifteen. They'll give her a sticker and a key chain and send her on her way."

Quinn eyeballed the men, looking at the pamphlets. Males had to register at eighteen, but many became exempt or disqualified for one reason or another. Males and females could volunteer, however, at age seventeen. He exhaled, because by hook or by crook, his daughter would be safe in Ireland before she was anywhere near that age. Hans and Raphael came into the job fair area, and Quinn noticed Raphael's eyes were narrowed in on the boys. Then he walked with purpose. Hans noticed it too. What the hell were they looking at?

"Oh, shit. Hell no." Quinn muttered as he formed a perfect triangulation, approaching the booth from all sides.

"What is it, Quinn?" Mary said.

"The gem mines."

"I don't understand." She looked at Caitlyn who just shrugged. As they followed, Raphael became as agitated as she'd ever seen him. "Genoveva, what is he saying?"

"It's the mines. He say they aren't getting these boys. They'll be..." She listened, trying to make out how to explain. "They won't be slaves in some gem mine so they can destroy the forest."

Quinn interrupted, "Let's go, boys."

The men working the recruiting booth said something to the boys, and Hans had to grab Raphael by the shoulders. "Easy, brother. We're leaving."

That's when Emilio started to argue. Quinn, Hans, and Raphael took the two boys aside, sitting on some benches away from the fair. "It is good pay. I need a job. They say they will train me, feed me, put me in a nice house." Emilio was arguing his case, passionately, which was new for him. "I need a job. I have nowhere to go!"

His voice caught and Raphael knelt in front of him. "We will find another way. This is not the answer. Look at me, Emilio." When the boy met his eyes, he wanted to curse. He wasn't convinced. "These mines promise everything, but there are some bad people running these mines. They keep you dependent, pay almost nothing, work you to death. It's dangerous because of their greed!" He took the pamphlet from Emilio's hand. "This is full of lies, my boy. You have to trust me." He looked at Henrico. "Tell him! Your father died in these mines. Tell him!"

That's when Hans got involved. Up until this point, Quinn had been translating. "Tell him that the military will train him, feed him, and house him. And they won't make him a slave. They'll make him a man of honor."

Raphael translated. Emilio shook his head. "You know who my

father was. You know what he did. He almost killed you and Doc Izzy. They would never take me!"

Hans said, "Don't be so sure. You are not your father. I will help you. We all will. Just get this mining business behind you. You have to trust me. Do you trust me?" Emilio wiped a tear away and nodded. "Okay, big man. Let's go get some lunch."

* * *

McDonald's, for pity's sake. Of all the places in the city they could choose, they'd ended up here. But teenagers were teenagers, and this was a rare treat. Hans grinned at Mary. "McDonald's is a thing. You can't fight it. Besides, it's not like any of these local places are going to beat Gabriela's cooking. Just order something beefy and cheesy with a side of crack fries and you won't go wrong."

Quinn was all in. "No complaints here. I love a good Big Mac."

Mary smiled, "You're a shame to your blood line, lad." They all lined up for the big order, with Caitlyn and Rosalis saving some seats at a big table.

The mood had swung back to festive as they filled their bellies. Mary nudged Caitlyn who was eating a Happy Meal. "Don't judge me. The toy is good. I can put it in my classroom."

"Dr. Gordon is going to be so jealous. I have it on good authority that she's a double quarter pounder with cheese connoisseur." Mary said.

"Well then, we buy her two and take them with us. She can reheat them back to their original glory." Hans accentuated that with a large bite of his own double. He looked over at the five kids sharing a table. "It was a good day, wasn't it?" He smiled at Raphael. "Don't worry about him, brother. We'll help him find his path."

Raphael gave a half grin, popping some fries into his mouth. "Sim, Senhor. We will protect him, even if it's from himself."

* * *

"WHAT IS HELL? Hell is oneself.
Hell is alone, the other figures in it
Merely projections. There is nothing to escape from
And nothing to escape to. One is always alone."
— T.S. Eliot

The mood was more sedate as they pulled into St. Clare's. Genoveva looked up at the canopied jungle that shrouded them on all sides. The vehicles were full of shopping bags, and the three boys had all gotten haircuts from the barber in the mall. As she looked around her home, it seemed smaller somehow. But in the dimming light of evening, the smell of Gabriela working on dinner, the soothing sounds of the forest around them, she felt peaceful. It had been a good day, but she was glad she didn't live in the city. She saw the trash and the concrete buildings and the nightclubs, and wondered how anyone slept with all of the chaos around them.

She was in the back of Raphael's Jeep, but next to her were Caitlyn and Rosalis. All the boys were in the other car. She didn't know why they'd switched, but it hardly mattered. They were home now, and she was excited to show the other children their new purchases. She'd keep her dress to herself, however. She wasn't sure how she felt about actually trying to look pretty. She'd never be like Izzy or Mrs. O'Brien with her long blonde hair. Not even like Doc Mary or Dr. Gordon. She didn't feel like she fit in with these pretty, smart, worldly women. She wasn't European or Brazilian, but a strange mix of both that left her feeling separate and unremarkable.

Caitlyn nudged Genoveva out of her thoughts. "Time to unload. I think you should give Estela her new dress."

"Why? You chose it for her. It should be you." Genoveva didn't know why adults made everything so complicated.

"Yes, well." Caitlyn didn't know how to explain. The child was getting attached to her. And admittedly, she felt the same. But the abbess had rules about the missionary workers adopting out of the orfanato. Not that she was thinking of adopting. Of course not. She and Patrick were going to have their own child. Seamus said he could help her.

Even as she said it, she took the little watermelon dress out of the bag. The dress was pink seersucker and perfect for the girl's beautiful dark hair and bronze skin. "Well, I suppose we could both give it to her. Maybe a little later. I want to see the abbess and give her the change back. We didn't spend all of the money because lunch was so cheap."

As she left the kids to divide up the bags and carry them into the dormitories, she wandered toward the stone structure of the abbey, where the sisters lived and ministered to the people in the area, cared for children, worked in the hospital, and even helped Paolo keep the grounds. She could hear them singing in the evening prayers. She thought about Reverend Mother Faith. She'd talked about sitting vigil in her private chapel. She'd started at midnight and said she'd be tied up all day. Caitlyn walked into the abbey and Sister Agatha and Sister Catherine, the resident midwife, were discussing something. She caught just a bit of it before they saw her.

"But I don't understand why we can't just go check on her. She's got the heart issues now. Surely she should at least..." Sister Agatha looked up to see Caitlyn approaching and held her tongue.

"How was the shopping?" Sister Catherine was keeping a deliberately light tone.

"It was a grand day altogether. The children really enjoyed themselves. We all did." She handed the envelope to Sister Agatha. "That's leftover from what the reverend mother gave us. Is she available?"

"I'm afraid she won't be until tomorrow sometime." Caitlyn started to put the pieces of the conversation together. Not so much an argument, but two worried women sorting out what to do.

"Has anyone checked on her since midnight?" Caitlyn asked.

"It's her wish not to be disturbed. She's in mindful prayer." Agatha said.

"Aye, I understand, but she's also seventy years old. Has she had anything to eat or drink?" She knew the answer by the look on Catherine's face. "Catherine, you're a nurse, for God's sake!" At that, Sister Agatha crossed herself. She exhaled in a burst of breath. "I'm sorry sister, but I can't understand this."

"Reverend Mother is very private about this time of the year. We can't interfere. She's given us strict orders."

"Well, she didn't give me any strict orders. I'm not particularly good at following them anyway." She brushed past both of them, which sent them into a tizzy. Caitlyn walked into her office waving them off. "I'll tell her you tried to stop me. I'll take the heat. I just want to look in on her."

Caitlyn opened the door before she could chicken out. She knew grown men who were afraid of this woman. The chapel was dim, several candles burning. At first she didn't see her, then she heard the soft, raspy prayers. Latin, which Caitlyn was rusty in from Catholic schools. The abbess hadn't even heard her come in. She approached carefully. How had the woman held her bladder this long? How could she go without drink or food? Unless she'd been restricting her fluids in anticipation of this. Jesus, this was lunacy. She approached and the old nun was on the floor in front of the altar. She was on her knees, crouched over her knees to the point of her forehead touching them. She looked so small, even though she was as tall as Caitlyn with a slim, straight back. She held something in her palms, and she rocked, praying and silently weeping.

"Oh, God. Reverend Mother." The woman barely registered her voice. She was almost in a trance. But deep prayer could be like that. Hours of this, and she was probably barely conscious.

She put a hand on her back as she knelt down beside her. Then she saw it. A photo. She pressed it to her head, her weak sobs breaking Caitlyn's heart.

"Abbess, please. I'm worried about you. Let's take a wee break. I beg you." Caitlyn's own eyes were tearing, because she was starting to understand. This vigil was about someone she'd lost. Probably a long time ago.

As if the spell was broken by her touch, the abbess tried to sit up. She slumped in Caitlyn's arms. "I can't go. I must finish. I must give them their full day."

Caitlyn looked up to see Catherine in the door. "Bring Mary. I want to get some vitals. She's a bit out of sorts."

Mary appeared a few minutes later. "Reverend Mother, your pulse is a bit low and erratic. Let's get you to the lav."

"I told you I wasn't to be disturbed." She was looking at the sisters.

"It's my fault. They didn't disobey you. I wouldn't listen." She noticed that the picture was tight to the abbess's chest now, and she couldn't see it.

Doc Mary said, "Your health comes first. If you take a lav break, drink some water, and let me get some vitals on you, I will bring you back in here. If not, you're going to have to come to the hospital."

The abbess straightened in a wave of righteous indignation. "I'm fine altogether. If going to the water closet will make everyone happy, then fine, but I am in charge. This is my private day. Mine. You'll all be leaving and I don't want to see you again until breakfast."

One private trip to the bathroom, on threat of violence if anyone tried to assist her, the reverend mother emerged with a clean face and a tight jaw. Doc Mary asked her to sit while she took her blood pressure. "I'm going to have to insist you at least take a bottle of water back in with you."

The abbess took the bottle from her and walked back into the chapel without a backward glance.

* * *

CAITLYN SAT on Genoveva's bed while Estela rifled through the shopping bag. A pack of ruffled socks, new shoes, and her secondhand watermelon dress were plucked from the bag with exuberance. Estela threw her arms around Caitlyn's neck. "I like the pink color! I like my pink dress."

Caitlyn laughed. "I'm glad, love. Would ye like help trying it on? Ye can leave your shorts on." She helped the child pull her t-shirt over her head. That's when she saw it. A hairline scar and healed suture marks. Genoveva saw what she was looking at.

"Her heart. But she's okay now. She's all better now," she said. She understood the defensive tone. No doubt the reason the child hadn't been adopted was due to a prior medical condition. The little girl ran a hand over her scar. "I had a broken heart, but Dr. Antonio found a médico to fix it. I'm all better."

"You're perfect, sweet girl. Absolutely perfect." She slid the dress over her head, then kissed her hair. "You're both perfect." She gave Genoveva a smile. "You're a good big sister, Genoveva. I'm a big sister, too. I know what I'm talking about."

This seemed to please the girl. Then she looked down at Estela who was smoothing her hand over her new dress. "You look good enough to eat! Did you know that I had that same dress when I was your age?"

Estela's eyes grew big. "Like my pink dress?"

"Yes, and I loved it. I didn't want to take it off. I was put out because my mammy wouldn't let me sleep in it."

They took time putting the other items away. Rosalis joined them with her own bags and they went about using their one shared closet and dresser to put the things away. As Caitlyn left them, she heard Estela say in her thickly accented English. "I'm going to sleep in the dress. I'm never going to take it off."

CHAPTER 15

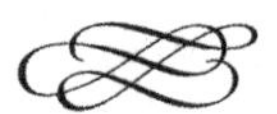

DUBLIN, IRELAND

The bastard sitting in the interrogation room was feeling the effects of his tango with Detective O'Brien. Sullivan had followed protocol and made sure he was examined and cleaned up by a paramedic. He'd live. The problem was that he'd called someone. A boss, probably, and according to the government ID that was in his wallet, he had connections. Some sort of security in the Senate building. All that aside, breaking and entering into a private business was against the law no matter who your boss was. Jesus, why hadn't he retired last year? After that case with the thwarted bombing, he and his detectives were the golden boys of the hour. He could have gone out on top. Now this feckin' mess was going to bite him in his aging, fat ass. He thought about Sean O'Brien. Kicked back in some village house with a pretty wife and grandkids around him. Plenty of time to fish. *Shit.* Why the bloody hell hadn't he retired?

Sal was across from him. The suspect was smug, with a cocksure grin that made Sullivan want to pound him. And by the body language Sal was throwing off, he felt the same. The man said, "You have no right to hold me. I was merely walking by that open door when your officer assaulted me."

They'd been holding a piece of information back, for dramatic effect. Time to use it, because soon the guy would have a lawyer.

"Really? That's terrible. You'll be so relieved to know that we caught that assault on tape." The man's face twitched involuntarily, then went blank again. "That's right. We had cameras from two angles as well as some good footage of you coming into the shop earlier that day. God bless modern technology. Tell me, friend. What is it on Kasey Walsh's computer that's worth going to prison for?"

* * *

FINN WORKED SILENTLY as Tadgh and his Uncle Sean stood aside, trying not to hover. "Thanks for getting up here so quickly. I just didn't trust anyone else."

"Not at all. Yer Uncle drives like one of those American NASCAR nutters."

Sean grinned, giving a shrug. "Your Auntie covers her eyes when we're in a hurry. She wasn't complaining, since I let her come."

Finn laughed sharply, "Hah! As if you could stop her."

"True. She's held out long enough. She's been trying to stay put, but she's been dying to come see Patrick and get a peek at that babe ye've all been caring for."

Before Tadgh could reply, he heard some arguing outside in the main offices. He left them and followed the voices.

"If you're not an attorney, I don't have to let you see him, Senator. Come back with legal representation and we'll let them in to see him."

"Do you know who you're talking to?"

"Aye, I do. Do you know what your man was caught doing? Do you know he assaulted one of my officers? "

"So you say. I haven't heard his side of the story."

"And you won't until you hire a lawyer for him. This is an ongoing investigation. So if you'll excuse me."

Tadgh watched from a distance, letting his boss handle the man who'd shown up demanding to see Kendall Shoney. He'd caught the man's name, Jacob Blakesley, one of the few Independent Party senators. Which meant he leaned whichever way the wind blew. He was one of the younger senators, in his late thirties. He had an English father, an Irish mother, and a French wife that had ties to the Socialist party. They were all over the place politically, and Tadgh had never cared for the shifty bastard.

As the man took his leave, he turned around to come face to face with Tadgh. He took in the dried blood on Tadgh's mouth and sneered. "So, can I assume it will be your ass in the sling when it's time to see the judge."

Tadgh leaned in so slightly, that only a weaker man might have tweaked to the aggression. "Let's get something clear, Senator Blakesly. I'll do my job. Whichever shitbird ends up in the sling will completely depend on what he's been up to. Now, I'm going to go home, take a hot shower, see my wife, and when I've had a good night's rest, I'll be crawling through the halls of the Senate like a feckin' blood hound. Tráthnóna maith, oireachtas."

The man gave him an appraising look. He said cooly, "Good night to you, Detective. Rest assured you'll have our complete cooperation."

Tadgh's Uncle Sean approached from behind. All he said was, "He got in." The senator's ears pricked, his brows twitched. *Wouldn't you like to know.* Tadgh turned and walked away, blocking the thoughts from his mind about whether or not this prestigious senator was the father of Baby Boy Doe.

* * *

Sorcha looked down at the small child in her arms and wanted to weep. Of all of her grandchildren and the babies she'd delivered, she couldn't ever remember any of them being this small. The twins had been small, but this little lad was barely five and a half pounds. The nurses had spoken to her, nurse to nurse, about not only the low birth weight, but his failure to gain weight. In the weeks they'd had him, he'd only gained five ounces. It wasn't enough. "If we could move a cot in here for your son, the lad would weigh a stone by now."

Sorcha smiled at that. "Some babies just don't take to the bottle."

"Aye, your son started feeding him with a drip system attached to his finger mostly, but now he'll take a bottle from him too. I've never seen anything like it. It's sad. His first real meal was at the breast, wasn't it? He knows the difference."

Branna. Sweet, dear Branna had fed the lad in a cold, dark alley. Given him his first taste of love and comfort. Even in her sixties, there was a phantom ache that came over her breasts when she heard a newborn cry. The need to offer warmth and succor.

"Patrick has a warm heart. He was always such a good boy. I have five sons, you know. And one daughter. He was smack in the middle, and never a bit of trouble unless someone was messing with one of his siblings. He's had a hard time, he and Caitlyn."

The nurse knelt down, smoothing a hand over the small, downy head. "Yes, he told me." She shook her head. "To lose three. The poor lass. Is she a good sort, then?"

Sorcha smiled. "Oh yes. She's like watching the sun come up when she walks in the room. Each loss, though…." Sorcha shut her eyes. "Each one has taken a piece of her." Then she looked down at the child, afraid to speak anymore.

"Do you think, maybe," The nurse started, but stopped. "Aye, well. No use going down that road is there? They've not found the da."

Sorcha exhaled. "Right. Not yet. They'll find him. My boys will find him, whether he wants to be found or not."

* * *

PATRICK WOKE to the smell of pure heaven. He'd been living on fruit and prepackaged muffins from Tesco in the morning. Right now, the smell of sizzling rashers was permeating the early morning fog of fatigue. He'd been working extra hours, keeping busy, banking extra money while Caitlyn was away. He stretched in bed, wriggling in the pajama bottoms that he'd only worn twice. There was just something about sleeping bare assed with your mother in the guest room that seemed wrong. He shuffled toward the kitchen, sliding a worn undershirt over his chest.

"Morning, Mam. It smells gorgeous altogether." He kissed his mother's soft cheek and headed for the kettle.

"There's tea in the pot. What time do you have to work?" Sorcha slid a plate of eggs and rashers in front of him.

"Half seven. There's some sort of protest in front of the legislature building today. Some pro-euthanasia group. Who the hell knows. They're probably harmless, but you know how those protests can go. Brings out the nutters."

"Oh, I am well aware. Be careful, lad. It's bad enough that your brother is throwing punches and running into burning buildings." She grinned.

"Aye, well. The fervor of a new convert. He likes the action. And the building had a twenty-five year old blonde with C-cups."

Sorcha cuffed him behind the ear. "Deliver me from sons."

Patrick finished his meal and started walking to work. He called Tadgh, who must be in the office by now. Sal answered the phone. He said, "He's headed to the Senate building."

"For the protests? I didn't know they were bringing detectives in for that."

Sal paused, weighing his answer. "No, not for the protests."

"Something has happened with the case." Not a question, but Sal answered.

"Yes. I'll have him fill you in when we know more."

"Sal, quit pissing about. What's happened?"

"The man from the computer shop...we have him. He tried to break into the computer shop last night. He fought with Tadgh. Unfortunately he's connected, because he works for some senator. His bond hearing is at eight. That's why I'm not with Tadgh. I have to go to court and try to stop the judge from granting bond. We don't want him taking off."

"How connected is he? Do you think he's the father?"

"Could be, or he's working security for the father. He's the equivalent of a personal body guard for Senator Jacob Blakesly. Some slick talking Independent. Finn is going through the files in her laptop. There are a few that have password protection, so he's trying to work around her security. Look, that's all I've got. I need to go. Tadgh will fill you in later."

Before they ended the call, Patrick said, "Sal, thanks for telling me. I won't do anything stupid."

* * *

TADGH COMMANDEERED an empty office for the purpose of interviewing. He didn't really speak to the politicians. When you got that high up in the government, you were expert level at telling half truths and covering your ass. He started with the circle of low level staff and interns. Specifically anyone who had daily dealings with Kasey Walsh. They all had the same story. Kasey stopped coming into the office three months ago. Probably because she was showing too much to hide her condition in business attire. She was working remotely. From home or somewhere else in the city, and exclusively for Senator Blakesly.

Sal showed up at about eleven, having lost a pissing match with the high-priced defense attorney. They were releasing Kendall Shoney within the hour. "You can't fight city hall, apparently. But I put a tail on him. Oh, and your cousin is standing by for that protest outside. He looks like he wants to choke someone."

"I don't doubt it. He called me right after he spoke with you."

"I have good news. Finn has gained access to those secure files. He's waiting for us when we get done here."

Just as the next intern was due to come in and speak with them, Senator Blakesly barged into the office. Apparently he'd been in a meeting all morning, and hadn't known about Tadgh's interviewing. The man put a hand on the young male intern. "You don't have to talk to them, David. Go back to work."

Tadgh stood abruptly. "Excuse me, but you have no authority here. He's going to talk to me here or down at the Garda headquarters. And before you start throwing your weight around, why don't we get the Prime Minister on the phone? I have his private number. Do you?"

That gave the man pause. "Just don't go harassing my people. They have work to do."

"Aye, so do we. Now, if you'll excuse us." He looked through the doorway and the young man he was supposed to interview, David Shaunessy, was gone.

* * *

FINN PRINTED ALL the information from the files off of another hard drive that he'd saved the contents of Kasey's laptop on. Sal and Tadgh read through everything. After that, he began downloading everything from her phone. She didn't have a habit of keeping her texts. She cleaned them out regularly, which was odd. Maybe not so odd if you were sleeping with a married man, however.

"These are all related to some sort of legislature for medical research funding. Apparently she'd gone before the Senate, late in the fall. She was pushing for more research to find a cure or treatment for Huntington's. She had Blakesly's backing and it looks like they were budgeted two million euro in extra funds."

"Does it say where the research facility is in any of these papers?"

"No. It's weird. I mean it's nowhere. There's data about the promising research, a patient list that is by number instead of name to protect their privacy. It all looks legit, but what the hell do I know?" Sal was rubbing his eyes. "I've been reading up on Huntington's. It's bloody awful. I just keep thinking about that poor woman in Sligo. What she's got ahead of her with her husband is nasty stuff."

"I've got something, boys. It's in her iPad. The one she lent the roommate for her holiday trip. She's got a lot of her stuff backed up on a cloud. There are other files in here that weren't in her laptop. They were likely deleted off the device, but the cloud saved it to her iPad document file. It may have been on her phone as well, but since they didn't find it at the scene, the iPad may have some items or pictures we haven't seen yet. I'll need a little while to transfer everything, but I can retrieve it." Sal and Tadgh turned to Finn, just as someone appeared in the door.

"Hello Janet. Good to see you back." Officer Janet Tomblin ran the front desk for the special detectives unit.

"Ye've got a young man here to see you. He seems a bit hesitant, so I left him with the boss. Didn't want him running off on you. His name is Dave Shaunessy." They were both out the door before she said another word.

He was sitting nervously across from Sullivan when Tadgh and Sal entered his office. "I've just been getting to know our young friend. Please detectives, let me introduce you to Mr. Shaunessy. I think you'll find him more than willing to be interviewed. You can use my office."

The young man couldn't have been more than twenty-two. "I'm sorry about before. About buggering off on you like that. It's just, I didn't want to..." He looked around, almost paranoid.

"You didn't want the senator to know you were speaking with us?" Tadgh offered.

"Yes, I suppose that's it. It's just, I don't know anything for sure. But she was such a nice girl. Pretty and smart. Jesus, what a waste. I didn't even know she was dead! They've been keeping it quiet, the heartless bastards."

"Actually, we've been keeping it quiet. There's more to this than you may know. When is the last time you saw Kasey?"

The man closed his eyes. "Boxing day. She called me."

They both sat up straighter. "You saw her the week before she died."

He nodded. "I was going on holiday with my family. We went to the Caribbean for New Years. I didn't get back until January 5th."

"She was already gone. I'm sorry. Was she your friend?" Tadgh asked gently. "Or were you more?"

The man gave a bitter laugh. "I wish. I would have jumped at the chance. I'm not the one that got her pregnant, if that's what you're asking. It's horrible to even think about. She was due in a few weeks. How the hell could someone kill a woman that was so pregnant? I mean to kill any woman is awful, but one that was pregnant?"

"So you knew," Sal said.

"Yes, she called me when she didn't know who else to turn to. She'd found something out that was going to ruffle a lot of feathers in the government. She didn't trust anyone but me."

"Not even Blakesly? He's the father, I assume." Tadgh said matter of factly.

"She never said, but I believe so. Why else would she hide out? But she didn't trust him even though, for some reason, she still cared for the piece of shit. It was something to do with the funding that supposedly went to medical research."

"What do you mean supposedly?" Sal asked.

"I mean she found the facility, if you could call it that. She couldn't figure out why the hell there was no disclosed location, or why she couldn't go there and interview for her final paper. Somehow she found the location, though. She was afraid to go alone, so I went with her."

"And what did you find?" Sal asked.

"Nothing. The address is an empty building. It's a front. I don't know where the money went, but it didn't go to a research team. The building is rented by a pharmaceutical company, but it was empty."

"Do you have the address?"

He wrote it down for them and then put the pen down, staring at what he'd written. "Did this get her killed?"

It was Tadgh who answered him. "We don't know. It's looking like she died of complications from childbirth."

His head snapped up. "What? Childbirth? But she wasn't due yet. You mean she had the child? Where is it? Is it alive?"

Tadgh said, "We can't give you any information other than the child is alive. The details are not public and honestly, I don't think you really want to know. Before you leave, would you mind giving our evidence techs a sample of your DNA? It's just a swab of the cheek."

"Of course not. Whatever you need. Do you need me to take you to the address we checked out? I want to help. She was a good lass. Jesus Christ, to think she died alone and left her wee baby." He squeezed his eyes shut. "Whatever you need. I will do whatever I have to for her."

"Can we find you at the Senate building?" Tadgh asked.

"No. I just officially quit. My internship was over at the holiday break, just like hers. I was hired part time, but they can shove that job up their ass. I won't spend one more day in that fecking building."

They shook hands with the young man. As he left, Tadgh said, "Did you tell anyone else about this empty building you found? And do you know if she told anyone?"

"I haven't told anyone. I don't know about her. Listen, I didn't know her long. Six months was it. She was a good sort, though. She actually seemed happy about the baby. A lot of girls her age would have been on a plane straight to England with that kind of news. Whatever happened, I hope you know that. She was one in a million."

* * *

FINN STOOD WHEN THEY RETURNED. "You need to see this. You remember, her phone was missing, but she'd taken some pictures of empty rooms that I accessed on her iPad. Looks like an old office area or facility. The light fixtures aren't something you'd see in a private home. There's also something saved in her notes. Not a document, but the notepad of her iPad, that I think was originally on her iPhone. An address that may match up with the photos. Here's the other thing I found. She saved a digital recording. One of her talking to a man. She dumped the file into her audio, so no one would think to look there. Listen to this."

"I don't understand this. I did some research on this drug. There's no protocol for Huntington's. It's a drug they use in Switzerland for end of life. It's a euthanasia drug. You told me this money was being used for research. For a clinical trial. You said you understood. You know how important this is to me!"

"Calm down, love. There's obviously been a mistake. You've gotten ahold of the wrong file. I've been to the lab. It's undisclosed because they are doing other work involving animal testing and they don't want the activists showing up. Whatever you think you know, you're misinformed."

The recording ended after a secretary came into the room and said, *Senator Blakesly, your three o'clock appointment is here.*

Finn asked, "Jesus, are we sure this death was of natural causes? This stinks like something way more sinister." He was pale. He wasn't used to such ugly dealings. Working on Eve's murder had taken a lot out of him, but he was one of the top contractors when the Garda needed computer expertise.

"I think so, but it doesn't explain who dumped that child. Everything I've heard tells me that she didn't do it." Tadgh rubbed his temples. "This isn't enough. We need to sit on this and get a warrant to search that building. The address matches the one that David Shaunessy just gave us."

"Hold up, I've got a voicemail," Sal said. "It's the coroner's office." He pushed the speaker phone.

"Detective Salib and Detective O'Brien, I'm going to need you both to come in for a full briefing. This case just got more complicated. It's looking to me like her labor was induced. I'll explain more when you get here."

* * *

TADGH WALKED into his apartment to find Charlie switching out the laundry in the kitchen. "Hello, love." He wrapped her in his arms. "Jesus, what a day."

She pulled him down for a kiss. "Are you done for the day? You've been at this for nine hours"

"I'm afraid not. Just home for a cup of tea and some leftovers. We're waiting on paperwork to enter an empty building. It comes back to some landlord who lives down south in Waterford. They signed a waiver so we don't need a warrant. It's a nasty business, Charlie. I just came from the coroner."

"I thought the cause of death was internal bleeding from childbirth? Although, it sounds fishy. Women don't just die in childbirth like that very often. Not anymore."

"Aye, the issue isn't what killed her. It's why. She had traces of ether in her toxicology report. She also had Pitocin in her system. It's a drug that is similar to hormones in a female that are released during childbirth. It induces labor. As far as the coroner can tell, she was knocked out with the ether and put into labor. Her inner arm has a small site that looks like someone ran an IV or gave her an injection. She'd likely not have woken up until the baby was either coming out or gone already. He doesn't know if she pushed the child out, the child came out on its own, or if someone tried to get it out of her when she was unconscious. Regardless, she was left drugged with no medical care and was bleeding internally. She also didn't pass all of the placenta. If she'd been taken to the hospital, she would have lived, but…" Tadgh shrugged. "I don't know Charlie. I think she may have stumbled onto some shady dealings with this senator. I also think he may be the father."

"Yeah, well someone dumped that newborn across town. How far is this mysterious empty building from the area where they found the baby?"

"Jesus, I see where you're going with this." Tadgh's phone rang and he answered it. It was his partner. He ended the call. "Paperwork is done. Can you do me favor? Can you snoop around on the Internet to see if Senator Blakesly has any ties to Defta Pharmaceuticals? That's who was renting the building."

Charlie wrote the name down. "Whatever you need."

Someone knocked and Tadgh went to the door. It was Patrick in uniform. "I've been assigned as the armed escort for a building search. Ready when you are, brother." His smirk said it all.

"I'm not even going to argue," Tadgh said. "We need to pick Sal up in twenty minutes. Come in and eat something before we head out."

Patrick came in, kissed Charlie on the cheek, and watched as Tadgh started to make them both a hang sandwich with some leftover ham. "Tell me everything, Tadgh. I want to hear it all."

* * *

THEY DROVE west to a building complex off the R810, about a four minute drive from the area where the baby had been found. It was quiet and dark. No cars, not even a sign identifying what business was housed in the structure. They parked, grabbed their torches, and proceeded to the back door of the building. A property manager, that the owner used, had left the keys with Sal right before they picked him up.

The door creaked as they entered it. The back entrance led into a stairwell that went up a half flight to the main floor. As they made their way through the first of the rooms, it was obvious that the place had not been occupied for a while. The pharmaceutical company was leasing the whole building, but nothing was here. When Tadgh walked into a room close to the north side of the building, a feeling of dread washed over him. He smelled disinfectant. He opened the door to the room and the corner had a perfectly cleaned area. Noticeably cleaner than the rest of the building. Like someone had scrubbed something up.

"I need a processing team down here. Call Sullivan," Tadgh said to Sal.

Patrick was shaking, he was so angry. "This is an old building, there might be a chute to the incinerator. We need to check the large bin out back as well. The one we passed coming in."

In the end, it was as simple as that. The landlord didn't arrange trash pick-up. That was the responsibility of the occupants that were renting the building. It was empty and unused, so there was no trash pick-up. That obviously hadn't occurred to the person that had brought Kasey here.

The medical waste was sealed in a garbage bag along with a lot of towels and a sheet. Among the items, they found Kasey's phone. Everything was bagged. Despite the clean up, there were traces of blood in the seams of the flooring.

The local judge was contacted, the bond of the bodyguard was revoked, and other officers were sent to the home of the regional branch manager for Defta Pharmaceuticals.

Tadgh and Sal worked until two o'clock in the morning, but it was worth it. The moment the big Pharm dickhead flipped was a thing of beauty.

He said she'd be fine. I got him the drugs. That's all I did. I gave his secu-

rity man the drugs and gave him a key to the building. This is not on me. I wasn't even there! Tadgh went over the table at him before Sal pulled him back. This piece of shit was using tax money to fund a euthanasia drug, instead of doing research on Huntington's. The senator was no doubt getting a huge kickback. He was also supporting the right-to-die movement, and trying to get assisted suicide laws relaxed in the Republic. What a piece of shit. He was hoping to make money off the end-of-life drug when he managed to push the bill through.

Next was the bodyguard. After you got one accomplice to flip, it usually came pretty easily to the next one. Even with his lawyer present, he didn't stand a chance.

"Ye've got one opportunity to do the right thing, here. Do you really think that the senator is going to keep paying your legal bills now that it's all out?" Tadgh motioned to the suit next to him. "It's every man for himself, Kendall. I am offering you a life preserver. He's going to say that it was all you. You're the one that picked up the drugs and the key. Your prints are likely all over that bloody building. I bet he made sure you're the one who transported her as well. Your personal vehicle, right? Not his. Why do you think that is?"

Sal interrupted. "I don't know. Maybe we have this wrong, Tadgh. He could be the father of that baby. He saw her everyday. Maybe she wasn't shagging the senator. The people certainly love him. Maybe it's old Kendall here that got her pregnant."

The man's face was chalk white. That's what did it. "That's a load of shite. The kid isn't mine! I am not going down for this. No feckin' way." He waved off his attorney, who was trying to shut him up.

"Fuck you. You're working for him, not me. Consider yourself dismissed." Tadgh opened the door as the lawyer walked out. "I guess ye'll be needing that public defender after all."

"Listen, I want a deal. I want a deal and protection."

"You're not getting shit. You dumped a newborn in a goddamn recycle bin." Tadgh's face was murderous.

"He wanted me to smother it or throw it in the river. I couldn't do it! I put it in that bin hoping someone might find it! I lied to him, because I couldn't do it."

Tadgh slammed a hand down on the table. "Ye should have taken him to a hospital! You should have taken them both to the hospital!"

The man's hands were over his face. "You don't know what these people are like! They own this fucking city!"

"Don't give me any of your bullshit. You either get a lawyer in here or you start talkin'. I will see what I can do with leniency, but that girl died. He's going to make it seem like that was your doing."

The man stared down at the tape recorder that was going. "She wasn't supposed to die. He knocked her out so that they could get the baby out and away from her. He said he wasn't trying to kill her. When I met him at the girl's dorm, she was alive. She was coming around. He told her that she'd been in the hospital. That he'd found her collapsed. That the baby had been stillborn. She was weak, but she was alive. She wouldn't quit crying. I left them there with her and she was still pretty out of it, but she was alive. I thought he just wanted to get rid of the baby. I didn't know they were going to let her die."

"Wait, who's they? Who else was with you?"

"The pharmaceutical salesman. He used to be some sort of medic. He delivered the baby, and he's the one that transported her. I took the baby and met them later. Did it die? Jesus Christ, I thought someone would find it!" They didn't correct him. No one needed to know where that baby was. They left that poor woman half out of her head on medication, and overcome with grief, with no phone and no medical attention. Whether it was due to negligence or done deliberately because she was sniffing around their shady dealings, they didn't know. But they were sure as hell going to find out.

CHAPTER 16

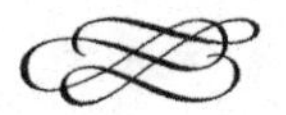

MANAUS, BRAZIL

The next couple of days went quickly. Caitlyn taught every morning during the week, and continued to meet with the abbess. The abbess was sharp of mind, and Caitlyn admired her, but they ended up at odds quite often, the Reverend Mother pushing her to share how she was feeling and talk about the miscarriages. *Have you named your child? Have you spoken to your husband this week? Have you prayed over the matter?* Last afternoon, she'd snapped at the abbess. Accusing her of isolating herself in this remote place. Telling her again, much to her shame, that there was no way she could understand. She'd snapped back at Caitlyn. *You have no idea, Mrs. O'Brien, the depth of my understanding. Do you think this habit shrouds me from the pain and despair of this world?* Caitlyn's tears had been bitter, her jaw set with anger and resentment, unwilling to yield at the time.

Caitlyn felt guilty about it in the aftermath, but they always ended up back in the same place. Last night she finally broke. *You tell me to pray? While God fills this orphanage with unwanted children, some of them abandoned, yet he denies me? Gives me the heart of a mother, but a body that fails me!"*

She looked over the grounds of St. Clare's and felt a longing for her mother that was so deep. Her mother wouldn't push her. She'd just open a pint of ice cream, hand her a spoon, and listen. Even so, she knew that although Reverend Mother Faith deliberately triggered those difficult emotions, that she did so out of love. Out of the desire to help her. She watched the sun peek through the canopy and knew that she was meant to be in this exact spot, no matter how trying these weeks would be.

* * *

PAOLO WORKED on the gardens for the upcoming dance. The children went to school. The doctors went back and forth with the mobile units and the hospital. It was a surprise when a villager from the east came running onto the grounds from the small road that bridged the village with St. Clare's. "Fogo! Fogo!" Behind him was a more traditionally dressed young man who was out of breath and covered with soot. Antonio got to them first.

"Onde?" he asked.

When the man answered, the others were coming in fast behind Antonio. "A fire in the native village down river. It caught from the controlled burning nearby. The wind took it, he says."

It was uncommonly windy today. Paolo and Raphael started calling out to everyone who was listening. *Get the trauma kits, all men on deck!* Within seconds, Hans and Quinn were gathering anything they could get their hands on. Fire extinguishers, buckets, and tools were gathered while Mary, Antonio and Rachel were grabbing as much gear as they could from the hospital. Sister Catherine was calling the fire house closest to the tributary. Dr. Clayton and the anesthesiologist were to stay at the hospital in case of another emergency, and to prep the surgical unit for incoming wounded.

The rest started cramming into vehicles. Some headed to the boat, others to the illegal access road that had been cut by drug dealers several months ago. They weren't sure how far south the fire had advanced and needed to go in from both sides.

As Caitlyn made an appearance next to Mary, Hans said, "Oh, no. I know I can't stop her, but you need to stay back. Essential staff only. I'm not taking you into a fucking forest fire."

The nuns who were present cleared their throats. Then Sister Agatha was next to her. "We are essential. She's good with the little ones and I'm not letting those poor people think the church has abandoned them. We are not staying back."

"Right on, Sister." Caitlyn gave Hans a pointed look. "You better be prepared to drag me out and tie me to a tree! I'm going. All help is good help. Now get your ass in gear!"

There was no way Sister Agatha had permission for this, but Hans didn't have time to argue. They loaded the vehicles, including Antonio's Land Rover and the mobile unit, and headed out.

Quinn drove the mobile unit to the riverside village and up to the boat dock. "Can I get this thing down the access road?"

Raphael shook his head. "No médico.. It's too wide. It will get stuck. We need to leave it and bring the patients down river if there are any wounded." Paolo, Sister Agatha, and Rachel took the boat. Raphael insisted that Antonio leave one vehicle at the boat dock as well, so he left his Land Rover. They piled in the Jeep and the abbey's old Land Cruiser and headed into the forest.

Caitlyn's head was spinning. Within fifteen minutes, their whole world had flipped into chaos. All she could think about were those children. The children of the forest who had no need for her spelling lessons or English, and needed only a sense of family and tribe. Those beautiful, engaging children with their mothers running around after them. The two pregnant women... She closed her eyes as a wave of panic went through her. The forest was so dense. It was the wet season, but vines still burned. Houses made of wood and thatch still burned. Mary squeezed her hand. "You're in it now, Caitlyn. Keep your wits. Do as Raphael and Hans say."

Raphael's knuckles were white on the steering wheel. This fucking road almost killed him once, but he needed to get to the village. They were so isolated. Fire spread fast in this dense forest, even during the wetter season. He prayed, and it must have been out loud because

Quinn put his hand on his shoulder. The smoke was getting dense as they got closer and closer to the end of the road.

The two drivers hit the brakes almost at the same time as the noise reached their ears. Screaming. The men were out in a flash. They'd sent all but one bucket with Paolo, since he was approaching from the river. Hans and Raphael had fire extinguishers and Quinn and Antonio had trauma kits. Before he could order them to stay put, Hans watched Mary and Caitlyn jump out of the vehicle with more supplies. The flames had reached the buildings, the main shelter was burning with an unholy roar. There were men on the other side bringing bucket after bucket to dowse the flames. Caitlyn saw the women running with children down the path to the waterfall.

"They're headed toward the spring. It's over a branch of the river. It's a good place to go!" she shouted over the burning trees and shouts of panic. Then one scream reached above the rest. They all looked in horror at the small, burning, stick house. The roof was completely consumed, as was the only door. The old woman, which they knew to be one of the tribal mothers, was standing outside of it, hitting the front door with a blanket, yelling for help.

"Oh, God. Someone's in there!" Mary screamed, running to keep up with Hans. He blasted the front door with the extinguisher as Caitlyn and Mary pulled the old woman back. The other men in the village turned their attention to the house as well, dousing it with all the water that they had to hand. Quinn was through the door first.

Quinn looked through the dense smoke, barely able to keep his eyes open. He had his shirt over his mouth, coughing as he searched. It was a small building, on stilts that raised it a few steps up from the ground. The roof was threatening to come in. He noticed the flames had crept down one wall, and roof debris had landed on the bedding and rugs, little fires having dotted the entire one room house. Then Hans and Antonio were behind him. He heard the moan, and that's when he saw it. A charred blanket with a figure huddled under it. Hans put out a small flame on the rug and pulled it up off the floor, shrouding the figure on the bed and smothered the burning remains of the blanket. "Be careful. I'll take the head and you two get on either side of her!" Quinn joined Antonio and Hans with fits of coughing as Raphael appeared through the door to take the feet.

Caitlyn watched in horror from the north and west sides of the village. The flames were spreading. Then she saw the four men go into the burning house and emerge with a limp figure. At first she couldn't tell, but then she saw the blue wrap that the woman had been wearing that first day she'd visited. The woman had been so beautiful. Her long hair and full, round body. She'd been quickly approaching her due date. "No!" The woman was burned on her forearms and chest. Her thick, black hair was seared and gone, but it seemed to have protected her scalp for the most part. Her face was pink and blistered, but most of the damage was to her arms and the top of her hands and her chest.

The old woman in her arms was wailing. Caitlyn yelled over the chaos. "Get her to the bridge! The waterfall will be safe. I saw the others head that way!" Then they were running as fast as they could. She wanted to stay and help the doctors, but too many people trying to carry the woman wasn't what they needed. They needed everyone safe so they could assess her injuries. They were cut off from the mobile unit and the main river. She vaguely heard Mary shouting from behind her.

"Female, early twenties. Late in her third trimester of pregnancy. Second and third degree burns to hands, arms, and chest. Pulse is in the basement. Breathing is shallow and labored!" Then they were all at the wishing bridge and Caitlyn's knees were shaking as she guided the old woman over the wooden slats that were tethered together with rope. *Please, God. Please spare her daughter and the baby. Please, if you're listening, save them both.*

IT SEEMED like only seconds passed before the fire was at the bridge. They'd made it to the other side of the small branch of the river, but the smoke was fierce. They gathered in close to the waterfall, the mist causing a protective shroud over them all. The two male doctors huddled over the burned woman. Mary assessed the older woman and two other women that were suffering from smoke inhalation and minor burns, while Antonio and Quinn figured out what the hell they were going to do. The pregnant woman was barely conscious, as she called out for her mother. Raphael did what he could, helping Caitlyn keep the other women and children calm. The few men from the village had already left to travel to the mouth of the small river, where it joined the main river. Their hope was to guide the floating clinic to them.

They could hear the firefighters now. They'd arrived in a boat and were fighting the fire with hoses that pulled water from the river. The problem with deforestation was that it threw off the natural order of things. Flash floods, droughts in certain areas, not enough fire fighters to control the blazes that got out of control.

Quinn came to Mary and she knew by his face that she wasn't going to like what he had to say. "She's in labor. The trauma must have kicked it off, or maybe it had already started. I don't know, but she seems close. I think I can tell when the contractions are happening. Mary, she's bad. I don't think she'll survive the birth. I'm not sure either of them will. Her lungs are damaged and the burns are bad."

The woman called to her mother, who sobbed at her side. Mary and Quinn went back to where Antonio was trying to field treat her burns. "We need to get her to the city, but the baby is coming! She needs a burn unit. This is more than we can treat! She needs oxygen!" He was choked with emotion. All of their faces were smoke blackened, but he and Quinn had taken the worst of it. They needed the oxygen on that damn mobile clinic which was currently floating on the other side of this fire. They hadn't been willing to risk taking the small tanks into the fire. Their tanks weren't air, they were pure, flammable oxygen.

Antonio ran an IV in the woman's ankle, since it wasn't burned. Miraculously, her face had been spared the worst of it. Some heat flash and second degree blistering. Her arms and chest had suffered because she'd been sleeping topless. She succumbed to the smoke before she could wake herself and get out.

Her throat was raw as she tried to speak, a death rattle in her chest. She spoke a dialect to her mother, and Mary watched as Raphael put a hand over his mouth, fighting tears. "What? What did she say?" Antonio asked.

"She said to take the child. She wants her mother to save the baby." The sob from behind them was a swallowed, painful, garble of misery. Mary turned to meet Caitlyn's eyes. This was going to break all of their hearts. The tribal mother sharpened up at her words and spoke to Raphael. "She says to get her daughter into the water. The spring will protect them both.

"I can't put her in water with these burns. It's not sterile! No fucking way!" Antonio was half out of his head, because a small part of him knew it didn't matter. This woman could very well die anyway.

Quinn and Mary closed in on him, putting comforting hands on each shoulder. "Antonio, you've done all you could. Give her something for the pain and let's try to save her child."

He shuddered with grief. "This birth will kill her."

"The lack of it might kill them both. If she dies before this child comes..." As if on cue, the woman seized up and they watched the muscles of her belly tighten. She was on a clean palette, and her legs, belly, and hips were smooth and youthful. "Wait. We can keep her upper body out. She can squat. I've seen midwives deliver this way. Hans, Raphael, come here!"

She used a second sterile bit of sheeting to form a long band. "It's going to hurt, but if we sling this under her arms and suspend her above the water." Mary didn't know if this spring was real, but Ireland was full of Holy wells and springs. She would take all the help she could get. She was a scientist, but she was also a cradle Catholic. She'd seen miracles happen before. She was going to give both the woman and the child a chance at the miraculous.

As she started to work, they all understood. Hans and Raphael would hold the sling on either side with a log, standing in the water. Antonio would cradle her head and take some of her weight off of her shoulders. Mary and Quinn would deliver the child as the woman squatted. The worst of the burns were chest and forearms, so the morphine would have to be generous. Caitlyn got in front and was instructed to bag the woman if her breathing was too shallow. Then it began. As soon as the woman's lower body touched the water, her body seized and her eyes cleared. "Oh, God. She's pushing!" Mary had tears rolling down her cheeks.

"You got this Doc. I love you. You're a God damn superhero. You got this!" Hans was fighting his own tears, willing all of the badassery and bravery that had put medals on his chest to pour into his wife. Caitlyn was sobbing, but ready to aid if she needed to. She was mid-calf in the spring as well. Mary and Quinn were on their knees in the water, in front of this straining woman.

They heard it first, then they felt the women around them. All the women of the village praying to whatever God was going to come to the aid of this woman and her baby. Children around their knees of various ages, swaying with their mothers. The hum of the prayers surrounding them took on a tangible presence. Mary swore that the water warmed around her. This woman before her met the eyes of her own mother. The moment she looked into her aging mother's face, clarity overcame the pain, as if she'd tethered herself to her mother's soul. She pushed again. The gravity was on their side in this position. "She's crowning. Jesus! We might do this!" Then she heard Raphael's prayers in his first language, and Hans joined him in English, then Antonio. *Hail Mary, full of grace. The Lord is with thee. Blessed art thou among women and blessed is the fruit of thy womb Jesus.*

She heard Caitlyn as well, and then a hitch in her breath. She looked as Caitlyn stumbled and put her hand to her chest. The wet stains forming where her nipples should be. She looked confused and in discomfort. Mary shook herself and refocused on the woman in front of her. "Again. Push again." The woman didn't need to know English. The surge of tension came over her as the next contraction started. She pushed with everything she had, her scream shattering the canopy of the jungle. The child's head slipped out, followed by the shoulders, and then it was done. "Lay her down again!"

As they cut the cord and delivered the placenta, Quinn examined the newborn. "Looks good. Now where's the feckin' boat!" That's when he looked up into the stunned faces of Sister Agatha and Dr. Rachel Gordon. The sister crossed herself. Rachel barked. "The fire's almost out, but the men are all tied up! We need help holding the boat while we load them. I need all the muscle we've got!" All of the men went. There was a step down to the river, but the banks were steep. Nowhere close to tie the boat off. Quinn handed the child to Caitlyn. "You know how to do this?" She nodded. She was still in the water, numb and stunned by what had just happened. Ignoring the ache in her chest.

Mary readied the woman, using the dismantled sling to cover her. Rachel returned. "It's taking all of the men to hold the boat steady. We'll have to move them ourselves." They started to lift her when the other women circled. Between six of them, they kept her steady as they slowly made their way to the place where the wishing bridge used to be. It had burned on one side, falling loose to the river, tethered on the other side and sloshing in the moving water.

Caitlyn walked slowly with the precious baby in her arms. She heard the whispers behind her. *Esmeralda.* Had they all seen what had happened to her? She felt the dampness as her breasts leaked into her shirt. The old woman walked beside her, quietly praying. As they approached, she was stunned at the scene. Men holding ropes on either side. Two tribesmen had made it across the river. They all held the boat in place. It was tied to a tree, but that wouldn't keep it steady. The river was flowing and Paolo had driven it upriver in reverse. It's why it had taken so long. Paolo and Antonio were on the boat, ready to receive Talia.

That was her name. The strongest woman on the planet. The mother of the child Caitlyn held. Then they took the baby from Caitlyn. She helped as they brought the grandmother aboard. There was no sign of the baby's father. Likely, he was still fighting the fire. He probably didn't even know his baby was born and his wife was wounded. How fast everything had gone to shit. Their village was gone.

As they all boarded, some having to stand, Caitlyn looked over and realized that Antonio was holding the baby, weeping. It was swaddled and crying in the mewling, kitten-like way of a fresh newborn. A good sign. "I didn't see," he said. "What is it?"

"It's a girl," Mary croaked as she adjusted the oxygen mask on her patient.

Hans knew better than to touch his wife right now. She was in doctor mode, and it was the only thing keeping her upright. He'd hold her later. They'd likely both break down like a couple of sissies. But he'd learned that getting stress out was a whole lot better than keeping it in.

Damn. What a scene. The woman she treated should be dead. But it had something to do with female strength and prayer. Something had happened in that spring. Something tangible and almost supernatural. They'd all felt it. He'd watched the strength pour into the wounded woman, and watched a transformation happen before his eyes with a young woman who had emerald green eyes and no children of her own. Caitlyn O'Brien had spontaneously lactated in the mist of that holy waterfall that sprung from somewhere deep in the earth.

He looked at Mary, then at her. Mary nodded. The girl had her arms over her chest, her eyes shut, and she rocked. The child cried out and Caitlyn was trying to shut it out. That's when the granny of the group stood up like she'd been born on a ship, and started to speak.

She spoke with her eyes first on Raphael, and then on her daughter. He took the hint and began doing what he did best. He translated.

Our Mother Earth has saved my daughter and granddaughter. She has given us many gifts. She has given us strength, healing, and this woman to take the place of Talia until she is strong again. Our mother earth gave milk to the childless Esmeralda.

The last part almost killed Raphael to say, but the matriarch of this tribe was not to be trifled with. She would be obeyed and she would be heard. Caitlyn flinched and then looked up to make sure she heard them correctly.

The old woman went to Antonio and took the child. Then she knelt like a woman half her age in front of Caitlyn. As Raphael translated, tears pooled in Caitlyn's eyes. "The mother earth has given you a gift. To deny the child is to deny the gift. She has healed you. Made you a mother. You will leave this place and have your own child. Please, Esmeralda. Would you deny this to a child who needs her mother, but cannot have her?" Caitlyn looked to the woman lying on the stretcher. Their eyes met. The nod took all of the energy she could muster. The birth had almost killed her. Somehow, Caitlyn knew she would live. She would live to raise this child. She opened her arms.

Mary said, "Caitlyn. This is too much to ask. You can say no. We'll be to the dock in fifteen minutes." As if to weigh in on the matter, the child let out a squall.

"Give me the child. I will feed him for my sister Talia." That's when Sister Agatha came next to her. Caitlyn looked up into the tear stained faces of her fellow missionaries. Antonio prayed in Italian, his hand on the mother's ankle as she labored to live. Then she looked back at the novice Sister Agatha. The youngest at the abbey and a petite, Irish woman that had a warrior's heart.

"The Lord is with you in this place, Caitlyn. And he is well pleased."

* * *

IT TOOK several minutes of trying, but nature took over. Her breasts were heavy. It was the same heaviness she'd told Seamus about, but the discomfort was tenfold. The child rooted, as she'd seen her nieces and nephews do so many times, and the slow dripping started. The overwhelming heartache was almost too much to bear, until she looked at Talia. She was barely hanging on. Her mother was at her side now, giving her soothing words in an unfamiliar tongue. Mary helped her, and finally the child latched. The more she rooted, the more the milk came.

"Oh, Caitlyn." Mary's voice broke. "You are the most selfless woman I've ever known." Caitlyn gave her a weak smile and Mary touched her face. "If I'd born a daughter of my own, I would wish her to be just like you. Strong and beautiful and so giving."

Caitlyn's tears came slowly, but she knew this was right. How could she deny these two women? Her body had kicked in, right when she was needed. Maybe it was the gift of the mysterious spring and Mother Earth, as the tribal mother believed, or of St. Anne and the Blessed Mother of her own Catholic faith. Or maybe, just maybe, it was a parting gift from her own son. The one she'd lost. What she couldn't give him, she must give freely to this little baby girl in her arms. Just until they could get to a hospital. Just until someone else could take over. She looked down at the small, fleshy child with tufts of dark hair and mauve lips. Such deep trust bred from instinct. Such fulfillment. She might never feed her own child, but she could feed this one.

CHAPTER 17

NATIONAL MATERNITY HOSPITAL, DUBLIN, IRELAND

Patrick sat and rocked the little child with no name. The child with no mother, and now with no father. After the arrest of the pharmaceutical sales manager, the story started to leak out. The press was sniffing around, asking about a dead girl at Trinity. Soon they'd link her to the baby. They'd put the pieces together as the trial dates were set. Apparently that piece of shit senator hadn't had the stomach for it. He'd hanged himself in his office for the cleaning staff to find. His poor wife played the grieving widow, and maybe she was. But she also knew of the affair. Of the child that had been the result of a young, lonely girl and a greedy, selfish politician. The social worker was on her way. The baby was almost strong enough to go home, but he had no home to go to.

The nurse across from Patrick was like an old friend. Maybe a sister. "I'll speak on your behalf. If you want him, I'll stand up in court for you. Have you spoken to your wife?" she asked.

He hadn't. Dammit, why was it so hard? It wasn't about him giving up on the idea of having their own children, if that's what she really wanted. It was about this little child in his arms. About a cold, lonely night and a weak cry that had rooted itself in his memory. It was about watching him get stronger, having the child be genuinely happier the moment Patrick picked him up. "No one has even named him."

"No one legally can except next of kin. His grandmother just couldn't. She couldn't let herself name him. It implies a bond and an obligation that she's just not capable of. She can't take him. She knows that. I think you've got a good chance, Patrick. You've just got to give yourself permission to want it."

A sob escaped Patrick's throat. "I'm afraid. For the first time in my life I'm afraid for myself and not someone else. I'm afraid to hope that he could be mine."

She knelt in front of him. "You listen to me, Patrick O'Brien. God put you in that alley to claim this boy. To be his salvation."

He knew that. He felt it instantly, like the wheels of destiny had begun turning with one small cry in the night. "I need to call Brazil. How much time before he's ready to be released?"

"I can stretch it a week. I will stretch it a week."

He nodded, saying nothing else. Just looking down into those hazy blue eyes and pursed, rosey lips. *I'll fight for you, lad. I'll make her listen. I'll bring her home to you.*

He stirred as he heard the clipping of high heels come down the hall. Not a nurse. His stomach flipped. He handed the baby to the nurse and went to meet with her.

* * *

Manaus, Brazil

Caitlyn rocked in the chair that they'd brought into the hospital nursery. The little child in her arms was apparently not done with her yet. The last day or so had been a blur. After getting the mother and child to St. Clare's along with two others that had minor burns and smoke inhalation, they had transported Talia by ambulance to the large private hospital where Antonio was employed as a surgeon. Dr. Clayton had treated the people that had sustained minor burns, and they'd been kept overnight.

Antonio had insisted that Talia go to the private hospital, even if he had to pay the bills himself. Caitlyn remembered his words, and they'd been so sad. A reflection of the lonely, beautiful man who drifted in and out of St. Clare's. *I'll sell that oversized villa of mine and move into the dormitory here if I have to. She deserves nothing but the best medicine. She's a miracle.*

They'd all been marked by the events. Not just the devastation of the fire, but of the indescribable and unexplainable strength that the young woman possessed. She'd willed her dying body not only to save her child, but to live long enough to raise her. She was alive, against all odds, and was receiving treatment at a renowned burn unit that used the unorthodox treatment of fish skin on burn patients to regenerate the skin cells. Sterile tilapia skins, to be specific, to aid in resisting disease, relieving pain, and providing collagen to the healing skin. It was going to be a long recovery, but she would live.

Raphael's friends from the Brazilian army, along with the Red Cross, set up a temporary camp for the villagers. Tents, clean bedding, food and a mobile water purifier. They would rebuild. After the miraculous events, they would never leave the spring. Raphael had taken Henrico and Emilio with him, as well as Hans. Together with some of the men from the village, they'd fixed and repositioned the bridge to the spring.

The baby nursed as she rocked, and she thought about her husband at home. How on earth would she ever tell this tale? Talia's husband had come down by canoe, frantic to get to her. His name was Renan, and his mother stayed with the baby at St. Clare's, the sisters making a bed for her in the abbey. Before Raphael drove him to the hospital, he came to Caitlyn. She held his daughter out to him, and he fell to his knees and wept as he took her. It had been a devastating, private moment between them. Then he left to be with his wife, but before he did, he asked Raphael to translate. Raphael's smile was sad. "He said, they named his daughter Esmeralda."

Caitlyn taught morning classes, but the heaviness in her chest was compounded when Sister Catherine came to the classroom holding the crying child. So she went, and did what she could to soothe the girl. Now she rocked as the child suckled, and she barely heard Reverend Mother Faith come into the room.

She sat in the chair next to her, taking care not to disturb the child at Caitlyn's breast. Her smile was small, a sort of distance in her eyes. "She's a miracle, our wee Esmeralda."

"Yes, I suppose she is. It seems like it's all been a dream."

The abbess said, "Yes, memories are like that sometimes. So much so that you start to doubt you lived them." She exhaled, watching the child. With a voice that sounded very far away, she said, "I used to love nursing. It was one of the many joys in my life as a woman." Caitlyn stopped rocking, but she stayed quiet. She thought of the deep mourning she'd witnessed in that little chapel. The abbess slumped in prayer, clutching an old photo.

The abbess looked at her. "Ask me how long I've been a sister."

Caitlyn cleared her throat. "How long have you been a sister?"

"Almost forty-one years. Now, ask me how old I am."

"How..."

"I turn seventy-one next month."

Caitlyn cocked her head. "You didn't take orders until you were thirty years old?"

"That's right, my dear. I lived an entire life in those thirty years. I went to university, although that wasn't common in my day. I studied psychology. I met my husband."

Caitlyn's head snapped up, meeting her eye. "But, you're a nun. How is that possible unless..."

"Unless I'm a widow. That's right my dear." She began to rock in her own chair, looking off in a distant place in her past. "I have loved. I loved so deeply that I never thought I'd be parted from him. His name was Peter." Her voice broke. "I tell you about this because I thought I knew how to help you, but it's all a lie. In this, I cannot. I loved my Peter. So much that I named our son for him. The two loves of my life, and in one instant, I lost them both. I can't help you learn to live with your losses because I never managed to get over mine." She gasped as though she'd been struck, putting a hand on her heart. "I lost them, you see, and I never thought I'd walk on two feet again."

Caitlyn was frozen into helplessness as she listened. "I was a family psychologist. Very busy. Very focused. It was hard, back then, for a woman to go back to work after having a baby. Most of the time we managed it all. My mother helped. She'd watch our little Peter until we got done with work. One evening, I had a patient in crisis. I was late picking my son up, so my husband went. It was a terrible night. Wind and rain coming off the coast. I told him that he needed to pick the boy up. That he had to pitch in because my work was just as important as his. I needed another hour to write up my session notes. I absently told him I loved him. You know, in that automatic way that people do when they see each other every day. I did love him, but when I said it, it wasn't with any particular passion behind it. It was habit. I hung up the phone and it was the last time I ever heard his voice. A car coming the other way slid head on into our little car. Ye know how narrow the roads are. No room for error and a ghastly night of slanted rain and sleet. My two loves died on that road. My husband first. Our son died on the way to the hospital. He was twenty-two months old. He had twelve teeth, he liked teddy bears, and he had my blue eyes. I never saw them alive again. My last warm kiss was over their breakfast. Everything was just gone." She straightened, wiping the tears from her eyes

Caitlyn asked, "So you joined the church?"

"Not at first. I could barely get out of bed. Could barely wash myself. My mother dressed me like a child for their funeral. It was all a blur, really." She looked at Caitlyn. "I became a sister because I wanted to die. I thought about dying every waking moment. About seeing them again and having my pain be over. I longed for it with every breath. Then one day my Aunt Maggie came to my home. Others knew her as Sister Margaret. I hadn't been off the sofa in days. Hadn't eaten anything. Hadn't answered the phone. She ordered me into the bath and warmed up some bread and soup that she'd brought from the abbey. Then she took my hand and said, *You're not going to die from this, and you're not going to live as you were. That's over, and I'm so very sorry for it. But I can show you another way to live, to honor those you lost. A way to use your gifts."*

"It wasn't easy. I resisted living. I railed against the very idea of living out a full life without them." She paused, swallowing hard as tears fell into her lap.

"So I take one day. I let myself have just one day every year on the anniversary of their death. The other three-hundred and sixty-four days, I live my life in service to God, to these children, and to the sisters under my care. But one day, I remember. I remember the love. I remember the feel and smell of the only man I ever loved." Her voice cracked. "I remember the soft feel of my son's head against my lips. I remember the feel of him at my breast." She reached over and touched the soft cap of hair on the newborn's head "I remember the love and the loss and the guilt. I ask them to forgive me for not dying with them. I ask God to forgive me for the times I wanted to die." She straightened her back. "Then the day ends, and I walk out of that chapel ready to live another year."

Caitlyn's tears were rolling down her cheeks. Her heart was breaking as she looked at this frail, elderly nun. The only thing about her that spoke of her strength was her uncommonly straight back. Very uncommon for a woman her age, but it spoke of control, of someone who was used to being in command. And the eyes…her intelligent, steely blue eyes. Even as they filled with tears and despair, they were warrior eyes. "Oh, Reverend Mother." Her voice caught, and she swallowed her emotion, wanting to be strong for her the way that she, as the long standing abbess, had been strong for so many years, and so many people. This vulnerability was a gift. A glimpse into the woman that went beyond the habit that she wore like armor.

She took her hand, wishing that she could easily detach the child in her arms for a moment and take the old woman in her arms. She thought, maybe, that she needed it. When was the last time anyone had just held her and let her take comfort from them?

"Reverend Mother, I'm so sorry. That seems such a weak and silly response, but I can't even put into words what I want to say. It's a loss that would have indeed killed most women. A loss that most of us wouldn't dare even consider, or it would cripple us with fear. You're the strongest woman I've ever met. And considering the women in my life, that is sayin' something."

The abbess just smiled a sad smile and wiped one tear from her pale, thin cheek. "It feels a bit like the story of Ruth and Naomi. One old, one young, and the shared grief like a tether, keeping them together and moving forward."

Caitlyn had always liked that story from the bible. So sad, but it spoke of devotion and the strength of women who kept living even in the midst of great sorrow and an uncertain future. She thought of Katie and Sorcha. Like sisters. They didn't always agree, but they never abandoned each other. She squeezed the abbess's hand. "I'm glad you told me. And the only comfort I can offer you is my presence with you. And even after I leave, I will feel as though we are connected, you and I. And I'll know that if we have need of each other, the connection will not diminish with time."

Faith smiled at that. "You're a strong lass, Caitlyn O'Brien. It seems the way of it with these O'Brien mates. Women of substance, all of them, I'd wager."

Caitlyn wiped her nose on a cloth she had at hand. "I wish I had half their strength. I feel very weak. I left my husband to grieve alone. I abandoned him. I'm selfish."

The abbess gave a very uncharacteristic snort. "No, child. You came to find a purpose that went beyond being an incubator. You found a way to keep moving. Your husband is on his own path, and the two shall merge again. I know this in my heart or I'd have sent you packing back to Ireland. Sometimes running is a survival instinct. If you aren't sinking into the bottle, or some other destructive direction, but pursuing something that will ultimately bring you out of your grief, then no one should naysay the effort. You're surviving. You are healing. And sometimes it takes a change of scenery to do that. It's what Liam did. It's what I did. What I'm still doing. And when you're ready, you get back to things and move forward."

The abbess was quiet for a time, reining in her emotions. She got a curious look on her face. "I've kept it in for so long, I never thought I'd tell anyone."

"Then why tell me?" Caitlyn asked gently.

"Because I couldn't help you as Reverend Mother Faith. Not really. But perhaps I could help you the way that you helped Talia. Sometimes it's the bond between women that keeps you putting one foot in front of the other."

Caitlyn thought of her family at home. Her mother and sisters. All of the beautiful, strong women in the O'Brien family. From the youngest to the oldest. Sweet Cora and lovely, sensitive Alanna. Of Branna's stormy eyes and Aoife's perfect cup of tea in the middle of a crisis. Of Brigid's cheeky grin and sharp wit. Of Sorcha, with her warm embrace and motherly scent. "I think you're right. I'd be lost without the women in my life. I wish you could meet them all. It's quite a tribe."

"Perhaps I will some day. When I'm old." She gave Caitlyn her own cheeky grin.

"Was that a joke, Reverend Mother?"

She gave a subtle shrug. "Aye, I might have been south of the equator for the last thirty odd years, but I didn't lose my Irish wit." Caitlyn began burping the baby on her shoulder, just as Quinn gave a knock. "You've got visitors from the school. Is it okay?"

"Send them in, lad, and walk me to my office, would you? I believe we have a message waiting for you."

Quinn treated the abbess like fine china. Caitlyn said, "Reverend Mother, are we still set for tea tomorrow? I think I'd like to talk some more."

The abbess nodded, "Quid pro quo, is it?"

Caitlyn shook her head, "No, just two women supporting each other. You're allowed to take some of your own medicine."

The shrewd blue eyes warmed, "All right, then. Let's make it two o'clock instead of four. The children from the other school start arriving in the early evening."

They passed Genoveva on the way through the door. Next to her was Estela. Caitlyn smiled broadly. "Hello there, girls. What brings you out of class? Does Sister Maria know ye've gone?"

Genoveva said, "Yes. She asked me to bring her to the nursery. She had an accident." Estela was sucking her thumb again, a sure sign that something was amiss. She also spoke in Portuguese, something she reverted to under stress.

"English, please," Caitlyn chided.

"I am a baby. I need the fralda!"

Genoveva blushed. "I don't think she knows the word. She says she needs a diaper."

Caitlyn raised a brow. The child was almost four, but regressions happened. She still slept in a pull-up nappy, but she never had accidents during the day. "A nappy? I don't think that's necessary. Estela dear, you can change in your room and get some clean knickers."

Then she saw the wistful look in the child's eyes as she watched Caitlyn cuddle the baby in her arms. "I'm a baby. I need the fralda," she said again.

Caitlyn gave Genoveva an understanding look and noticed Quinn was in the doorway listening to the exchange. "I'll tell you what, Estela. You go with Genoveva and change into your watermelon dress. That's a big girl dress that you must wear big girl panties with. When you come back, would you like to rock in the chair with me? You can sit right here on my lap and let me hold you a while. It's nice to be held, isn't it?" The girl nodded with her thumb back in her mouth. "Go on now. Get changed, and I'll be waiting."

As they left, Quinn shook his head. "She is adorable. I can't believe she hasn't been adopted."

"I know, it seems impossible. Sister Maria says it's because of her heart defect."

"I saw her charts. She's fine. That defect was fixed. She's as healthy as any child here." Caitlyn exhaled, suddenly tired and weary. "Are you sure you don't want to go take a nap?" Quinn asked.

"No, not at all. I promised some rocking chair time to Estela. Are you ready for this little lass?"

"Oh yes, absolutely." He took the baby from her and looked down at the little bundle. "She's beautiful. I wish I had a baby picture of Genoveva."

"Is that what your message was about?" she said hopefully. Quinn's smile told her the answer. "Oh, Quinn. She's yours, isn't she?"

His eyes misted. "Yes, she's mine for certain. She's my daughter." He looked down at the baby and laughed. "I have a daughter."

Caitlyn stood and hugged him. "It's grand altogether. You'll be a wonderful da. Truly, Quinn."

"I hope so. I just need to think about how to tell her. I have to choose the right time."

"You'll know when it's right. And she'll be happy. I know she will be. She's a good girl."

Quinn left with the baby just as the girls were making their way back down the hall. "Well, now. That was fast." Caitlyn sat again and patted her lap. Estela didn't need to be asked twice. She crawled in her lap, and as Caitlyn began to rock, the girl sighed, melting into her. The thumb went back into the mouth, but Caitlyn didn't have the heart to argue with her about it. She'd won on the diaper, at least.

She felt the girl tangle her fingers in her hair and felt an overwhelming sense of rightness. She pulled her closer. Nursing Esmeralda had never felt like this. She knew that Esmeralda had a mother. What she did for the child, she also did for Talia. But this, in this moment, felt indulgent in a way that had everything to do with wanting her own daughter, and about Estela not having a mother to rock her to sleep. She smelled the sweet scent of childhood in her hair. Sunshine and grass and children's shampoo. She couldn't keep the drowsiness at bay anymore than the smile that teased her mouth. And within a few rocks, they were both asleep.

* * *

THE DAY WAS CLOUDY, so the men showed up early from St. Fransisco's to start assembling the tent. Paolo supervised, making sure the garden wasn't ripped up in the process. The smaller children were devastated at the news that only children fourteen and up were invited to join the dance.

The principal of the school was a bit pushy, but she'd met her match with Reverend Mother Faith. She'd taken one look at Cristiano and said. "My house, my rules. We'll push that down to twelve for the children that are hosting."

Mary had ordered Hans to drive her back to the store to get her boy some new clothes to go with his awesome glasses.

Now the children were dressing, and although it hadn't rained, it was inevitable. Caitlyn helped the girls get ready, even doing Estela's hair and putting her in her big girl dress and shoes, promising her that they'd have their own dance inside the classroom. The dance was in two hours, and everyone was so excited. A real dance. The first one for these children.

Caitlyn looked down the drive that led into St. Clare's from the city. A large truck with two men pulled up, but it wasn't the men from this morning who had set up the tent. A prickling sensation burned at her neck. The men got out of the vehicle and started looking around. That's when she saw who they were searching for, and recognition struck. Emilio approached them and she ran to the hospital. She looked around for Paolo and Raphael. Where the hell were they? She didn't want those men from the mines trying to sink their talons into Emilio. He was a hard boy to break through to. He struggled with his English and also his math skills, but he was a good boy. She sprang the door open to the hospital, and Mary was startled. "Get Quinn."

"He went with Hans. What's amiss?" Caitlyn ran to the lab. "Pedro, please. I need help."

Pedro rarely poked his head out of the lab, but he came without question. She, Mary, and Pedro were a united front with Rachel Gordon hot on their heels. She stopped at the place where the men were talking to Emilio. "Pedro, I need you to translate."

"There won't be any need for a translator." They all turned to the abbess's voice. Her Portuguese was flawless. They didn't move. No way were they leaving her alone. They didn't know these men. Obviously when they'd talked to Emilio at the mall, he'd told them where he lived. The abbess's tone was commanding, almost sharp. Pedro interpreted under his breath to the women. Rachel could speak Portuguese, but Mary and Caitlyn were in the dark.

Reverend Mother Faith looked at Emilio. "Who are these men?"

"They are from the mines. They've offered me work."

"Aye, Raphael told me about this, and that you were warned against it. So, why are they here?"

One of the men said, "Forgive us for stopping by unannounced. We brought some paperwork, just to give the boy information. He's almost a man. What will he do when he leaves this place? We can offer him a living."

Quinn and Hans pulled up just in time. Just as Raphael and Paolo came running up from the riverside. "Reinforcements," Caitlyn whispered under her breath.

The man put his hands up. "Please, we meant no harm. The boy should make his own choice. We can offer him what you cannot. A roof over his head and food in his belly. Good wages. When he turns of age, can you say the same? He has no family. Where will he go?" Raphael watched Emilio shrink into himself. They knew exactly how to get to the kid.

Raphael had menace rolling off of him. "I lost a cousin to your slavery ring. He was worked half to death in barely human living conditions. Buried alive in some hellish hole in the earth. All for what? For gems? You strip our land and kill our young men for some rich woman's jewelry? Get out! You can't have him! He has a family here. We are his family."

When Pedro finished the interpretation, Hans stepped up. "You're damn right, we are."

The abbess broke the tension. "You have been warned. If you return you are considered trespassers and I will call the police."

Hans put a hand on Emilio, who was stoic through the whole exchange. It was so hard to be seventeen. On the cusp of manhood without the juice to run your own show. "We'll talk later, big man. You have a dance to get ready for. Easy, boy. Breathe." Hans pulled the boy to him, cupping his unruly hair and hugging him. "Come on. I promised to teach you to shave, didn't I? Get that furry brother of yours and lets go foam up." He messed up the boy's hair and got a crooked smile. But the worry in the boy's eyes made him look ancient.

"Way to rally, team. Caitlyn, you did good grabbing Pedro. He's bilingual. And Mary because she's kind of scary when she's pissed." Hans winked at his wife. He clapped his hands together. "It's almost dance time, people. Lighten up!" But as he walked toward the school, he exchanged glances with Raphael. This issue would be revisited.

* * *

Dublin, Ireland

Patrick stared into nothingness, exhausted from a poor night's sleep. It was his day off, and he'd shuffled around the apartment, feeling lost and empty as he went about household chores. He didn't realize how much Caitlyn did until everything was left to him. She worked as well, and from now on, he was going to pitch in more at home.

Now he sat in the dining area of Tadgh and Charlie's apartment trying to be social. Being one apartment above them, they often shared meals, like being in the same house and occupying two floors. Charlie was a great cook, but she liked her three food groups. Meat, cheese, and bacon. Tonight it was Josh and Seany's turn. Seany had to cook at the fire station sometimes, so he knew his way around the kitchen. Josh loved anything to do with the ocean. Growing up in Cleveland, Ohio with only a freshwater lake nearby, the boy was obsessed with the ocean. Lighthouses, boats, wildlife, coastal lore, and pretty much everything else that was great about living on the coast in Ireland. Tonight's menu was cockles and razor clams in a beurre blanc, rocket salad, and pan seared plaice, which was in the flounder family. Seany was laughing as Charlie negotiated a way to get some sort of pig or cow meat into the meal. Josh said, "I'll crumble some pancetta over it."

"Now you're talking." Charlie sat next to Patrick at the table and he sharpened up, giving her a weak smile. "Not buying it, brother. What gives?"

Tadgh was coming out of the bedroom, drying his hair after a shower. Patrick said, "Christ, would you put some pants on."

Tadgh gave his cousin a crooked grin. "Charlie likes my chili pepper boxers." He leaned down and kissed his wife on the mouth. "Now, what's happening here. You're a bit off tonight, brother. Let's have it."

He sat next to Patrick whose face was pensive. "I need to talk to Caitlyn. I've been putting it off."

"About the baby? Patrick, you have to know she will fall in love with that little guy." Charlie said.

"It's not that easy. He'll be released in a week. I spoke to the social worker. She's in my corner, but I can't take custody of him if I'm single and working. With her out of the country, they consider me a single parent. And honestly, I don't have the time to take off. I've used up all my sick time from when Caitlyn lost the baby and my remaining leave was going to be for Liam's wedding. I have a few days to spare, but not enough. Caitlyn isn't due back for a while yet."

"She'd come back if she knew how important this was. What is the real issue, Patrick? Are ye afraid she won't want to adopt?" Tadgh asked.

"Maybe," he shrugged. "I mean, she feels guilty. She shouldn't but she does. She gets going on about our two ancient bloodlines, family trees and all that. You know how it's been. I don't want her to think I'm giving up on her. It's just when it comes to that baby, I feel like…" He shut his eyes tightly.

"Ye feel like he's yours." Tadgh's face was knowing and so kind. He looked over at Josh who's eyes burned with emotion. Tadgh had been ready to adopt him at seventeen rather than leave Charlie's only brother with an abusive father. "Aye, I understand. It's not always about blood, is it? It's a deep knowing in your belly."

Patrick smiled, his face easing a bit because Tadgh understood. They all did. Seany and Josh had been there from the beginning. Seany said, "So go to Brazil. Surely the social worker can work something out until you go and explain things to Caitlyn. Some things shouldn't be handled over the phone."

Tadgh nodded, "Yes, I agree. You need to get on a plane, brother."

"That's the problem. If we aren't both here and ready to take him in a week, then he goes to another foster family. They'll get priority to adopt. I think Kasey's mother would have some say, but there are no guarantees. I could lose him if the people who step up want to adopt him."

"That's not going to happen." Charlie said simply. Then she reached her hand over and put it on top of Patrick's. She looked at Tadgh. He was confused at first, but then he understood. His nod was slight, and it was only for her. He started to tear up. She said, "We'll step up. We'll offer to foster the baby until you come home. I'll take leave from the FBI. I will not let you lose him."

Josh interrupted. "I'll sleep on the sofa bed in your apartment and give the baby my room until you get back. They'll want him to have a room, right? He can have mine." The pride on Charlie's face made her glow.

Seany broke the tension with, "What? You don't want to spoon in my double bed?"

"No thanks. Your legs are too hairy," Josh shot back.

Charlie smiled and said, "We gotchu, Patrick. No matter how long it takes. And I'll bet the Garda will pull some strings to give you some extra time off."

"You'd do this for me? You'd take a leave of absence and care for him?" Patrick's tears were silent, but they flowed out of the corner of his eyes. He looked at Tadgh for confirmation. He thought about Christmas Eve, when Brigid and Branna had offered to be surrogates and carry a baby for Caitlyn. It seemed impossible for one man to have such a family. Giving and loyal to the extreme. He was humbled by it. "I don't know what to say."

"You don't have to say anything. We've got you covered. As long as it takes, Patrick. We'll keep the lad as long as it takes." Tadgh stood and hugged him, thumping his back. "Is this a little weird with no pants? It got weird, didn't it?" Tadgh asked, as his face was muffled into Patrick's shoulder, hiding his smile.

Patrick cracked off a laugh, pulling away. "I'll call the social worker in the morning. We should all have a sit down. And I'll send a message to Caitlyn."

"I don't know. I think a big romantic gesture might be in order. I wouldn't tell her. I'd show up with your heart in your hand and convince her O'Brien style." Charlie wiggled her brows.

Tadgh laughed. "Absolutely. Don't give her a chance to think about it. Contact Hans and clear it with the abbess. Liam said she's a tough cookie. But I would absolutely make plans to surprise her. You'll need time to get your visa in order and sort out some leave at work. You can see the boy is settled and get an initial court appearance."

Patrick knew he was right. He had to plan this. He also had to get the social worker and family court on board with this unorthodox plan. He could not lose this chance with the child. And once Caitlyn saw him, he'd never have a better mother. This was meant to be. He knew it down to his marrow.

CHAPTER 18

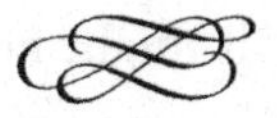

ST. CLARE'S CHARITY MISSION, MANAUS, BRAZIL

To be yourself in a world that is constantly trying to make you something else is the greatest accomplishment—Ralph Waldo Emerson

Genoveva hadn't watched much television in her life. They didn't really have it here. She'd seen movies on occasion, however. When she pictured school dances, this wasn't the vibe she got from those imaginings. Weren't people supposed to dance at school dances? She looked around at the awkward factions, broken up by age and by school. The St. Francisco's kids were keeping their distance. She leaned over to Rosalis, within ear shot of the boys she'd made a tentative peace with. "What's the problem? Do they think they'll catch something? Do they think they'll get orphanitis? Like if they say hello their parents will leave them here?" Henrico and Emilio were stifling laughs under their breath. She looked at the staff, hoping for some divine intervention from Sister Maria or even Reverend Mother Faith, but they seemed just as uncomfortable. What the hell was this music? Brazilian granny music?

She looked over at the little play area for the small children. They all had so desperately wanted to come out and participate or at least watch from the swings, but it was starting to rain. Now she wished they'd been allowed. At least they were fun. She took a deep breath, smelling the hundred tons of bug spray that Paolo had treated the area with this morning. Underneath it was the fresh, sharp scent of rain and green forest. It didn't smell like this in the city. She wondered what these kids thought of it.

"That's it. Let's just go dance." The boys' eyes bugged out, but Rosalis was totally on board. It might not be what Genoveva listened to, but all Brazilian music had a good rhythm, even the stuff that was decades old. *What would Izzy do? What would Izzy do?* She knew. Izzy would dance. She'd dance like no one was watching.

Genoveva took Rosalis's hand and Cristiano's elbow, dragging them both out into the middle of the dance floor. The school had set up a tent, and the grass was soft under her low sandals. She loved how her dress flowed in the breeze. She'd worn a dress, for God's sake, and she didn't get dressed up for nothing. They started slowly at first, then loosened up a little. She watched out of the corner of her eye. The St. Fransisco kids were swaying, but they watched. They giggled. She wanted to hiss at them, but she kept dancing, glaring at those three cowardice brothers of hers. Brothers by proximity, not blood. They wanted to dance. She could see it. They just needed a little nudge, but she was too busy nudging herself. This was painful.

Quinn leaned over to the reverend mother and said, "You couldn't pay me to be this age again. It's brutal to be a teenager."

She smiled, "Aye, I vaguely remember it. We can't interfere, though. You know that. They've got to learn to maneuver these things on their own."

The song ended and the girls and Cristiano walked off the dance floor, retreating to their side of the tent. Genoveva walked over to Raphael who was rifling through the music the other school had provided. He shook his head as he put a ten year old Brittney Spears song on the top of the pile. Genoveva pointed and said. "Don't do it!"

He laughed. "Well, we've got speakers. Maybe we need some fresh material?"

Genoveva shrugged. "I don't know. No one seems to want to dance."

"It doesn't matter what they want. If you want to dance, then do it." She looked back at him and saw him rigging the speakers to a laptop. Caitlyn's laptop. "Izzy helped her with the playlist. You want to choose?"

Genoveva's face lit up. "Just make it count."

When the music started, the snappy percussion was so familiar. From their workouts and dancing in the yard with Izzy. She gave a tomboyish whoop and started reaching for her classmates. "Get out there. Now. This is our house and our dance. Forget the others." She pinned Emilio and Henrico with a hard stare, then flipped around skipping to the music. Sia's *The Greatest* started blaring out of the speakers.

Suddenly she didn't care who was dancing and who was watching. She loved this song. Her hips were going, her arms strong and high. Her movements not quite sexy, she didn't do girly and sexy. She did powerful. She did it her way. Suddenly they were all with her. Cristiano, Rosalis, Luca, Henrico, even Emilio. She laughed and then she sang, swinging her head around with the music.

Don't give, I won't give up, Don't give up, no no no. I'm free to be the greatest here tonight, the greatest, the greatest, the greatest alive... Oh, oh, I've got stamina. I've got stamina.

Motion caught Genoveva's eye and she looked over at the St. Francisco's kids. Their faces had changed. They seemed fascinated, like they'd never heard this strange music before. *Yeah, well get used to it. Keep up or stand aside,* as Izzy would say. She met Henrico's eyes and he was smiling. Emilio, on the other hand, was swept away. Dancing, spinning, holding his fedora like a boss while he did some funky move with his feet. Holy cow. Who knew the boy had those kind of moves. Suddenly she was laughing. One of those rare, big laughs that came from being swept up in the moment. And they danced. Henrico thumbing his suspenders, wiggling his brows to the beat of the music. This was the best night of their lives.

The song was ending, and suddenly Genoveva was afraid the spell would be broken, but Raphael knew how to keep it going. Imagine Dragons poured out of the stereo. *Thunder, feel the thunder.*

She looked over at the school house and saw the small kids all crammed on the porch. Well over a dozen kids that were excluded from the only dance they might ever attend. She clapped her hands to get the other's attention. "Let's go get them. We make our own rules tonight." They ran before anyone knew what was happening. Each grabbing a small child, the rest urged to follow. The principal of the other school was sputtering, but in this case, the mob ruled.

I was lightning before the thunder.

As if God had decided to join the party, the rain went from a drizzle to a downpour, thunder rolling off the river. Genoveva kissed Estela who she'd propped on her hip, and she ran out of the tent, her family of beloved misfits following her. This group of unique, beautiful children that lived between two worlds. Sandwiched between the tribal areas and the big city, they were like the woodland sprites, protected by the forest and the sisters who cared for them. Like the halflings in mythology. Part human, part Fae. Always set apart, as if touched by God.

They pranced in the rain, wild and free. At first the other school children looked at them like they were insane. The school principal shouting above the music to stay under the tent. But sometimes you couldn't fight peer pressure. Soon all of the children had abandoned the safety and dryness of the shelter for the cool, pouring rain.

Quinn and Caitlyn stood beside Antonio and the abbess, watching the coup unfold. Quinn's heart was in his throat, caught between pride and sadness. And the overwhelming urge to throw blinders on every male in attendance. His daughter was stunning. She had no idea how pretty she was. She didn't dance to impress or entice. She danced because it was fun. She was an athlete, and she was impressive to watch. He felt tenderness for his co-workers who seemed to genuinely love Genoveva. Antonio was off today, but wouldn't have missed this for the world. Hans and Mary had stayed back to watch the baby, Esmeralda. Rachel and Giles covered the hospital, but the rest were watching in fascination as Genoveva helped the orphans of St. Clare hijack the St. Fransisco's dance like seasoned pirates.

The reverend mother leaned into Quinn. "Do you know what her name means, Quinn?" He shook his head, not taking his eyes off his daughter dancing like a pagan princess in the rain. "Leader of the tribe," she said softly. She laughed as she watched them run out into the rain. "Ah, I do love a good mutiny."

"That's her Irish coming out, isn't it?" He said finally, the paternal pride unhidden in his voice.

"Without a doubt. Mayhem is what we do best."

Quinn laughed and put his arm around her, then another around Caitlyn. "Irish women are a force of nature. You should meet her grandmother." Then they all laughed.

Antonio was stunned at first, then came to a conclusion based on what he knew of Genoveva's parentage. "This is a night of revelations, to be sure." Then they all looked back out at the wet, giggling, happy children who were no longer separated by class or geography. Joined as brothers and sisters in teenage high adventure and rebellion. *Well done, Genoveva. Well done,* the abbess thought to herself.

The principal of St. Fransisco's approached with a resigned look on her face. She said in Portuguese, "I expect they'll talk about this dance for years to come. Your children…." She searched for the right words, so as not to offend. "They're quite something, aren't they?"

The reverend mother answered, "Aye, they are indeed. It reminds me of the passage in the book of Isaiah. *Behold, I have refined you, but not as silver; I have tried you in the furnace of affliction.* Only by knowing great pain and adversity can we show our greatest strength, and taste the sweetness of innocent joy."

CHAPTER 19

DUBLIN, IRELAND

Sergeant Rahn sat across from the Chief Superintendent for their district and ground his jaw. Patrick was beside him. "Please, I ask you to reconsider. Officer O'Brien is a decorated member of my unit. He has a family matter which is very important. I would not ask for just anyone. Surely we can extend some leave to him?"

Chief Superintendent Kennedy had the look of a man who loved lording over his subordinates. Patrick could tell the guy was a dick from the first time he'd met him. "If Officer O'Brien thinks his family name is going to get him some special treatment, he's mistaken. If he wants to chase after his wife, he's going to have to skip his brother's wedding. Even then, you're asking for an additional week of leave. Where do you think this is going to come from? He's already used up several sick days this quarter."

"My wife almost bled to death losing our child." Patrick was done groveling to this prick. His boss, however, put a hand on his shoulder, giving him a silent plea to shut his gob. Patrick eased back, biting his tongue.

"His sick leave was completely legitimate. Other than that, he's never taken a sick day. He has an exemplary attendance record. The unusual circumstances have to do with..."

"I could give a shite why he wants the leave. We don't have it to give him. If we do it for him, then we are setting a precedent." A knock came at the door and Kennedy barked, "Come in!"

It was Officer Tomblin from headquarters, where Tadgh and Sal worked. "Excuse me, Sir. I have a bit of paperwork here from headquarters. It's regarding the leave you denied." Kennedy's face blanched. She savored the next words. "It's from Commissioner Byrne." She handed it to the Chief Superintendent, then gave Patrick a wink. "If you don't need me to stay, I'll get back to..." He waved her off impatiently.

The man's forehead had a juicy vein running through it, and Patrick swore it was starting to pulse. "It appears the entirety of the Dublin Garda and some of the Shannon division has formed a donation pool for Officer O'Brien. He's had thirty-two days of leave that's been donated...including by the goddamn commissioner himself."

Patrick wasn't sure he understood. "Donated?"

Sergeant Rahn said, "Yes. It's been done before. During emergencies or times of great need. An officer can donate a leave day to another officer. It appears, Officer O'Brien, that you have a lot of friends."

Patrick left the office of his boss's, boss's, boss with a grin as wide as the River Liffey. "Jaysus, I don't know how to thank you."

His boss turned his kind, dark eyes to him. "I can't take credit for it. It was your cousin's idea. I just tossed a day of leave into the pot. I was fairly certain that the Chief Superintendent was going to be a tosser about the whole thing, so I didn't tip my hand, lest he try to thwart your cousin's efforts."

"He really is a dickhead, isn't he? Well, despite all of that, I appear to be in the clear. I don't expect to need the whole thirty-two days. I promise you I'll be back to work..." His boss stopped and threw a hand up.

"You're talking about bringing your wife home from Brazil, adopting a newborn, and trying to relocate all in one month. That's putting aside your brother's wedding in a few weeks. You'll be lucky to have it all done in thirty days. Don't push it. You've been given this gift because you deserve it. Take it and be glad."

"I want you to know, I'm not trying to leave your unit because I don't love it."

Sergeant Rahn smiled, "You can do the same work there as you can do here. And you can commute from your home town. You're lucky to have that option. Dublin is a wonderful city, but I've been to the west coast on holiday several times. I understand the appeal. You're going to need your family. It is time to go home, my brother."

If it wasn't for his male pride, he'd be tearing the fuck up right now. "Jaysus. I hope my new boss in Shannon is even half the man you are, Sergeant. Truly."

He smiled. "Yes, well perhaps I should be looking in that area. Your boss is one year from retirement."

Patrick slapped him on the back. "Absolutely, Sergeant. Anything you need, you've got it. I've got kin from Kerry to Donegal." As they walked off the elevator into their own part of the building, Tadgh and Sal were waiting. Tadgh opened his arms and Patrick picked him off his feet like a grizzly bear. "I love you, brother."

"Just go get our girl. There's a little boy that's dying to meet her."

"Aye, I think we may just pull this off. You ready for that court date in the morning?" Patrick asked.

"I'm ready. I'll even wear a tie."

* * *

Circuit Family Court, Arran Quay, Dublin

Patrick sat outside the courtroom, ringing his hands and tapping one foot. Charlie put a hand over his. "Don't worry. We've got this."

"Maybe I should have more character witnesses. Did your boss send that letter for you? Is all the paperwork in order? I should have hired a lawyer. Dammit. Maybe..."

"Stop it. You don't have to worry. We, ummm, kind of called in the calvary." Charlie said with a nervous grin. Patrick looked up and thought he was seeing things. "Uncle Nolan?" He hadn't seen his uncle in months. His Aunt Maeve's husband was a solicitor in England. Patrick's mouth dropped as he saw the line fall in behind him. His breath stuttered. Aidan in his Army uniform with Alanna dressed in business attire. Next was Seany in uniform with Josh in a coat and tie, his mother, his father, Michael, Branna. Jesus, the line just kept going. D.C. Sullivan was next, probably here to vouch for Tadgh. Sal and Tadgh were with him. Next were Brigid and Finn. He couldn't stop the tears when Granny Aoife and Grandda David appeared, bringing up the rear, as well as Granny Edith and Grandda Michael. He refocused on his Uncle.

"I can't believe you came all the way from England to be a character witness. Is Auntie with you?"

"No, she and the boys are back home, and I didn't come to be a character witness. I'm still licensed to practice in the Republic, not just the U.K. You remember that I went to law school in Ireland. Family court isn't my specialty, but I'm free of charge and one of my colleagues spent the last forty-eight hours drilling me on everything I need to know to help you. He helped me assemble the case file. Am I hired?" He directed that to Tadgh and Charlie as much as Patrick.

Patrick barked out a laugh. "Oh, aye. You're hired."

* * *

WHEN THEY WERE UP on the docket, the judge's brows raised as she saw the huge crowd of people pile into the closed session. Then she looked down at the file. Everyone was seated, patiently waiting as she continued to leaf through the case file. She exhaled, "Well, this is refreshing. I should have put you on first thing this morning. I'm hungry, and I have a feeling this is going to take a while. Mr. Carrington, why don't you start by explaining to me why we have one couple interested in fostering, while another wants to adopt. I'm a bit sketchy on the details. Then I'd like to hear from the social worker who signed the original care order."

Patrick watched in awe as his Uncle Nolan flipped into lawyer mode. He laid everything out, starting with the night that Patrick and the others had found the baby. The judge stopped him. "Wait, I read about this. Is this the child whose mother was found deceased at Trinity?"

"Yes, your honor. If you look in the case file, you'll see the reason the rest of the case has been kept out of the press. The father of the child was confirmed through DNA."

The judge read for a minute, then began rubbing her forehead. "St. Michael defend us. What a bloody business. I see here that the next of kin is waving custody rights? Is there a reason they haven't appeared here today?"

When Nolan explained, the judge's face drew down. "Huntington's is a nasty business altogether." She refocused on the paper. "I'd like to hear from the social services representative." The social worker who had taken on the case from the beginning stood. "Explain to me why you are willing to give temporary custody to Tadgh and Charlotte O'Brien, but have endorsed a," she looked down at the paper, "Patrick and Caitlyn O'Brien for adoption."

"Your honor, the potential adoptive mother is currently serving on a mission in Brazil through the church. We need time to get both parents back in the home before assessing for adoption. Officer O'Brien has plans to fly to Brazil in three days to meet with his wife and tell her everything."

The judge looked at Patrick and took her glasses off. "You mean to tell me, Officer O'Brien, that your wife has no idea about the child or your plans to adopt him? Why should I even entertain this? You found that boy weeks ago and never even mentioned it to your wife. I find that very odd."

Patrick cleared his throat. "If it is okay, your honor, I would like to explain." He checked with his Uncle who nodded. She waved impatiently, urging him to speak freely. "My wife went to Brazil after she lost our third child. The last miscarriage was very difficult. She was eighteen weeks along. To be honest, it broke us both. She went to Brazil to teach at an orphanage. She's the best woman I've ever known. I didn't tell her at first because, well, it was such an ugly business. I didn't think of adoption at first because I thought the baby would be claimed. That he'd have someone out there to love him. I didn't dare hope for it. But to tell her, after losing three children, that someone discarded a beautiful newborn baby boy in the bin like trash?" He shook his head. "It would have broken her heart. Our last child was a boy." He choked on the words, putting his fist up to his mouth for a moment. "Forgive me." He swallowed. "But now, I feel like God put me in that alley. All four of us. We were meant to save him and to claim him for our own. I know that when my wife comes home and holds him in her arms, she'll feel the same. I just need to go to her. Some things..." He paused, looking intensely at the judge. "Some conversations you just have to have in person."

"I'm sorry for your losses, Officer. It's a noble thing that you're doing. I hope you're right. I hope she wants him, because this is bound for more heartache otherwise. Now, Tadgh and Charlotte O'Brien, please stand."

They stood and she looked around the room. "You two are willing to keep this in the family so to speak. Foster the boy until Patrick brings his wife back to Ireland. Is that true?"

Charlie spoke, "Yes, your honor, for as long as it takes." Tadgh squeezed her hand. "I've included a letter from my supervisor at the FBI. I am taking a leave of absence in order to care for the child."

"The FBI ? Well, now. We've got quite a crowd here." She shook her head, looking at a sheet of paper. "Garda, Reserve Garda, fire services, Royal Irish Regiment, U.S. FBI, Irish Coast Guard, midwife, social worker, a letter from two doctors, one of them prior U.S. Navy, did I miss anything? You O'Briens are like the bloody Avengers now aren't ye?" She put the list down.

She continued, "Here's the onion. There's a possibility that Mrs. Caitlyn O'Brien will not want this situation. She's lost three children, but they can't be replaced by that lad in the hospital. What happens if she doesn't want this adoption? There are other families ready and willing to take him off the adoption wait lists. People we could place him with now. What if she says no?" she said with her hands spread out.

Tadgh spoke then. "Then we'll take him." Charlie's eyes teared up and she nodded. Then Branna and Michael stood from behind them. "And if they can't take him, we will take him." Branna's eyes were bright with tears. Sorcha and Sean stood next to them, then Brigid and Finn. "We'll take him." Then Alanna and Aidan, "We'll take him." Soon everyone was standing, and Patrick could have sworn he saw some tears forming in the judge's eyes.

"Well, it seems this young lad with no name is destined to be an O'Brien. Petition granted. Tadgh and Charlotte O'Brien will take temporary custody of Baby Boy Doe until the next court date twenty-one days from today. I expect the maternal grandmother of the child to be here to officially waive her rights to the child. Our clerk will help you, Mr. Carrington, with that subpoena. Officer O'Brien, you've got three weeks to get your wife to court." She slammed the gavel down and the room was filled with whoops and cheers. Tadgh grabbed Patrick, who was openly crying now. "Let's go get our boy."

* * *

St. Clare's Charity Mission, Manaus, Brazil

In the aftermath of the dance, the school house was buzzing with social chatter. Caitlyn smiled at Sister Maria, not envying her the task of keeping teenagers and pre-teens on task. Esmeralda's family was taking her home today. They'd arranged for a wet nurse in the village. A woman who'd been weaning her toddler that agreed to feed the child. Caitlyn was happy for the family, and sad as well. It had been nice, for a while, to feel like a real mother. To have her body work like she'd always thought it would. She fed the child, and for that experience, she was both proud and grateful.

She'd spoken to Patrick last night, and for some reason, the words had failed her. She wanted to tell him everything. All the feelings she was having. All of the adventure and the satisfaction and the bouts of longing. Everything. But some conversations were better done in person, so she'd held back. He'd seemed so happy, lighter somehow. She hadn't had the heart to dim that mood with the story about the fire. So instead, she'd told him about the dance. If she was honest, she was just a little sad that he seemed so happy without her. A fear that he'd grow accustomed to it nagged at her. She remembered with clarity what she'd said to him, in the throes of her grief and self hatred. That the church would give him an annulment if he wanted one, because she couldn't give him children. Man, how she wished she could take that parting shot back. The thought of it made her blood pressure spike.

Hans came into the classroom and waved as he went through the room and into Maria's class. He took the older children out for physical education at this time. "Have a good workout Hans!" she said with a wave. She really liked Alanna's father, and he was perfect for Mary. Proof positive that it was never too late to find true love.

* * *

GENOVEVA PERKED up as she saw Hans walk into the room. She began putting her books away, as did Henrico and Emilio. Time to work out. They all left the school house and she was surprised when Raphael wasn't there with the music. "What's up, boss?" Henrico always called Hans boss.

"Well, we've got a little run planned." They all moaned. "Listen, strength is good, but so is endurance. It's not a race. The slowest runner sets the pace and you stay together. Raphael is at the finish line, which is a mile and a half." He waved a walkee-talkee at them. "I'll tell him to start timing you. We will start doing this twice a week. You'll run to the neighboring village. You know where. He'll stop the timer when you reach the Jeep. Then you'll cool off by walking back. Three miles total. Within a month, I'll bet you that you'll be able to run both ways. For now, we take it easy. It's hot today. Raphael will give you water before you head back this way."

"Where's Dr. Maguire?" Genoveva asked. Hans's heart squeezed. The child didn't know who Quinn was, but seemed to be genuinely fond of him. He hoped she responded to the news in the way he thought she would, but you never knew with teenagers.

"Quinn has a patient that came in from the city. A sick child. He can't play today."

Genoveva laughed. "Are you sure he's not dirt bagging it?"

Hans barked out a laugh. "I think you mean sand bagging. And yes, I'm sure. He wanted to come. The patient walked in unexpectedly ten minutes ago. I am not running because I'm an old man and my knees are creaky."

Henrico slapped him on the back, "You are very old. You'll need the cane pretty soon." Hans put him in a headlock and he squealed with laughter.

"Not that old, smart ass." Emilio covered his mouth, laughing. "Okay, line up. Who's the slowest runner?" Genoveva smacked the boys both in turn when they pointed at her.

"We'll see, won't we?"

"This is not a race. Do you hear me? Stay together. If you show up separated, it's fifty burpees on the other end." That was all they needed to hear. Fifty burpees was a death sentence. So they were off, keeping a steady pace side by side.

* * *

Dublin, Ireland

Patrick watched with a lump in his throat as his family crooned to the baby. Brigid had him now. "Ye've got to name him. What the hell are we to call him?"

"I won't name him without Caitlyn. We have to do this together." That's when Seany interrupted.

"Oh, we've named him." He gave Josh a sideways glance. Everyone turned to him. "Haven't we, brother?"

Josh smiled mischievously. "Yes we have. You can change it later, but he's Carlos until I hear otherwise." Tadgh caught on first, cracking off a laugh. Charlie pointed, "You are not naming him after that baby on *The Hangover!"*

"Oh yes we are. He's Carlos. He likes it. It makes him feel edgy and worldly."

Patrick was shaking his head, and Brigid was clutching the baby closer, looking for any signs that Carlos was an appropriate name. "Call him lad, call him Carlos, call him Eleanor. I just don't want to hear one more person call him Baby Boy Doe."

"What about Doe-boy. Get it, like doughboy? I think the lad has put on a stone since we found him." Seany was leaning in, trying to take the baby from Brigid, but she wasn't having it. She snapped. "Ye'll call him no such thing. Now get away. Ye've had him for weeks, and we have to leave in an hour." She motioned for Charlie and Branna to follow her. Soon the three of them, and Alanna right behind, were all piling in Tadgh's bedroom and locking the door.

Brigid put the child on the bed and laid down next to him. He wiggled and gurgled. "He's so beautiful." Brigid's eyes were misting. "It makes me ready to have another." Charlie sprawled out on the other side.

"I think my ovaries are kicking into overtime." Charlie said.

Brigid looked at Branna and snorted. "She'll be knocked up by May Day." They all giggled.

Branna was bouncing from foot to foot. "I need in. I want some too! Don't make me spoon you, Brigid!"

Charlie and Brigid scooted in and Branna spooned Brigid and Alanna took Charlie. They rested their chins on their sisters' sides and played with the baby. He didn't know where to look. They heard the door jiggle and then open. Brigid said, "Cora! How did you..."

"Ye think I have that many uncles and can't pick a lock?" She gave her mother a look that said...*Duh*. Then she saw the pile-up of women surrounding the baby. "Hey, I want in! Ye can't be hogging Carlos behind locked doors. I have rights!" That's when all of the women broke into hysterics.

* * *

PATRICK LOOKED at the nursery that, up until two days ago, had been Josh's room. Josh was sleeping on his sofa bed until he left for Brazil. The family had really come together. Sorcha came beside him, as did his father. "I'm proud of you son. So proud that I could burst from it." Sorcha hugged her son, kissing his head just behind his ear.

"I love you, Ma." Then he turned to his father. "And I love you, Da. I hope to God I can be half the father you've been."

"This is going to happen. I know it. He's already in our hearts. We won't give him up without a fight. No matter what it takes, this family sticks together. Now, are ye ready to leave? You've had your shots and rushed a visa?"

"Aye, I'm ready. I leave tomorrow evening. I'll be back with her by the court date. I swear it." He didn't feel as confident as he sounded. Caitlyn was as close to a saint as he'd ever met, but she'd been pretty damned clear she didn't want to explore alternatives to having their own blooded child. *God, give me strength. Help me convince her. And help me live with it if I can't.*

* * *

CHARLIE'S HEART hurt as she looked at their easy chair and saw Patrick asleep with…nope. She wasn't going to call him Carlos. With the lad. Their lad. Because he'd been universally claimed by the entire O'Brien clan. Damn. That scene in the courtroom had been a heartbreaker. Mainly because it had to have given Josh the same flashbacks that it gave her. She looked over at her brother. He noticed her staring and cocked his head. "Are you okay, Josh?"

"Sure, why wouldn't I be?" Josh's tone was light, but he knew what she was worried about. He shrugged. "Our court date wasn't quite the love fest this one was, but I'm not quite as adorable."

She walked over and rubbed his hair off his face. "You are every bit as adorable."

"True." He grinned. "Look at it this way. The result was the same. Tadgh was the only O'Brien there, but this was a package deal. They all took me into their hearts without question. Carlos and I are lucky boys." She smacked him. Josh looked over at the baby cradled on Patrick's chest. "He'll be a good dad. He had a good example. They're all good dads. Tadgh is ready when you are. You're going to be amazing parents."

Charlie smiled. "Maybe in a couple of years."

"You mean maybe when I'm strong enough financially and mentally to move out on my own?" Charlie started to argue. "Come on sis. You have baby fever so badly, you're practically sweating from it. I'll be fine. I can go anywhere. I can take on-line classes. I can move in with Granny Katie. She's offered about a million times. I can work at the ferry full time. Don't worry about me. As long as I keep up with classes, my student visa is valid. Hopefully my citizenship gets approved forever. If it doesn't..."

Charlie threw a hand up. "Don't even go there."

He laughed. "What if you get transferred in a few years?"

"I won't go. I'll quit and take a job with the Garda." Josh's brows went up. "I won't take him or you away from Ireland. This is our home. I mean, shit. You saw that scene in the courtroom. No job is worth leaving this. I don't know how Aidan and Liam do it."

"Aidan does it out of duty. Liam is doing it because Izzy is hot as hell." Charlie's jaw dropped and she gave him a little shove. "What? Have you seen her in jeans? Curves aaaaall day long. He was done for!"

Seany spoke from behind them. "Amen to that," he said appreciatively. Charlie narrowed her eyes at both of them. "Pigs. You two are total pigs."

"No. We're just young and virile. It's a thing." He gave Josh a fist bump and she snorted, pulling them both in for a hug. They were pigs, but they were her boys. Her brothers. Seany had taken Josh into his inner circle without hesitation, despite an almost three year age difference. "Well get your young, virile asses in the kitchen and help me do the dishes."

"They're already done." Seany said. "Ye think my mother and granny would be physically capable of leaving for home before ridding you of a sink-load of dishes?"

"Alright then. Help me get this one up to bed. He has a big day tomorrow. Transcontinental flight and all that." She nudged Patrick.

"Wake up, big guy. It's time for bed." Patrick woke instantly, tightening the palm on the baby's back. "Do you want to take him downstairs tonight?" She knew he didn't want to be parted from him.

He rubbed his eyes with the other hand, then stood with the child "No, he needs to get comfortable with you. Ye need to bond with him. You might have him for two weeks or more. I'll get my turn." He kissed the boy on the head and handed him to Charlie. He looked at Seany. "You two coming up?" They both did, leaving Charlie alone with the baby. Tadgh had been called into work.

They walked up the fire escape and entered through Patrick's window. "We need to talk. The three of us, without Charlie here. We need to make a plan. You two can't afford this place on your own. Caitlyn and I could barely afford it, and I have four years with the department. I think I'm going to get that transfer. Shannon has a major airport, and they need more men." He watched a look pass between them. "Ye've already got a plan, haven't you?"

Seany ran a hand through his hair. "Aye. I put in for a transfer as well. I'm waiting to hear back."

"Where?"

"Three potentials. Donegal, Ennis, and Galway."

"Donegal? All the way up north? Are ye sure?"

"It's along the west coast. I could live near Granny's people. Galway, we could be closer to Katie and to home. Ennis, too. Don't get me wrong. I like Dublin. It's just a bit too fast for me. Too many people. With you and Caitlyn gone, and Charlie and Tadgh thinking of buying out of the city, it makes sense. Liam's gone. Josh and I have talked about it. We want to go west."

Patrick looked in Josh's eyes and saw that he agreed. "I'm with him. I can work at the ferry or find something else to do while I take classes. I'll take them on-line until I get settled somewhere. There are community colleges in Galway, Ennis, and County Mayo. I've researched this. We aren't going off half-cocked. Charlie and Tadgh need to worry about themselves, and feel free to start a family if they want to. I'm ready to leave the nest, so to speak. I've been taking care of myself for a long time. My parents weren't real hands on, if you catch my meaning. Unless you count fists. Then Pops was really hands on. After Charlie left, I learned to get by on my own. We can do this. Stop worrying about us. We'll be okay."

He exhaled. "I know. I know you will be. And you're together. That will help you sell it to Charlie. After this business with Eve and now the lad, I think we're all ready for some wholesome, hometown living." As Patrick went by the urn they kept in the living room, he stopped and kissed his fingers, touching it. Then he realized he wasn't alone. "Sorry. It's just…something I do."

"It's okay, brother. You don't have to apologize. And Carlos isn't going to replace him. Will you scatter them, do you think?"

He nodded. "Not without her. We'll name him and scatter him. Then we'll start living again," he said. Hoping to God it was true.

CHAPTER 20

MANAUS, BRAZIL

"I'm going to tell her today." Quinn was finishing off an early breakfast. Caitlyn and Mary sat across from him. The children were in morning prayer, and would join them shortly. "Tonight. I'm going to meet her in the abbess's office. Izzy made a video for her. I think it will help, but I have to admit, I am nervous as hell. What if she doesn't want to leave and tells me to bugger off? What if she hates me for breaking her mother's heart?"

Mary reached across the table. "Quinn, you will deal with her however it goes down. She's a bright lass. She'll understand. She's got a good heart. I think she's going to be thrilled. Then again, what the hell do I know. I haven't got any kids, and teenagers can be unpredictable."

"She's going to love you, Quinn. It might take an adjustment period, but surely every orphan dreams of someone coming to claim then. They dream of being wanted."

He looked around him, as if he was picturing the wide expanse of the mission. "This place is a good home. Ye hear all the horror stories about children being taken into care, getting abused. People doing it for the money. But she has been loved here, hasn't she?"

Caitlyn thought of little Estela. They were like real sisters. She loved Genoveva. It was going to be hard for her to say goodbye. "She is loved. They'll miss her, but they'll be glad to see that she's cared for in the long term. It's time, Quinn. We're all here for you."

The kids started piling in. It was Saturday, and they didn't have school. Hans and Raphael came in behind them. "Workout starts at ten. Get ready for a smack down. You're running again!" Hans bellowed.

The children ate with gusto, as they always did. The three oldest children left to do their run. Hans and Raphael were helping the two oldest boys get into shape to qualify for the military. She remembered the scene with those men from the mines. They'd seemed like predators. It had to be even worse for the girls. What would girls like Rosalis and Genoveva do if they had nowhere to go. What type of predators would target them? She couldn't bear to think of it.

She looked over at Estela sitting at a table with several other small kids. She shouldn't have favorites, but little Estela just did something to her heart. She loved the sisters at the abbey, but she hated the idea of Estela spending her life here. She'd been born here, and because of a thin scar on her chest, she might never get adopted. That rule of the Reverend Mother's was wrong. Not letting the people who came to St. Clare's as missionaries adopt any of the children was just wrong. Why shouldn't they be able to take a child into their home? Why did they have to wait for someone to walk in off the street? It rarely happened. Sometimes a child would be adopted through an agency or a distant family member would eventually track the child down and claim them, but it was rare. Reverend Mother Faith was in her office this morning, and Caitlyn was going to go have a chat with her. Her heart raced at the idea. Afterall, she'd all but attacked Patrick for suggesting they look into adoption. Patrick had been so supportive, so open to discussing alternatives, putting her health ahead of the desire for a biological child. She'd been so consumed with grief and guilt that she'd outright refused to discuss it.

Was that why God had brought her here? To show her another way to be a mother? Her throat was tight with emotion. She thought of that little urn in their apartment. Of Patrick being home alone, left to grieve alone. She had to talk to the abbess, and then she was going to call her husband. Maybe, if she approached it just right, she could get him to come to her. Surely he'd fall just as head-over-heels with Estela as she had. Liam had adored the child. Had he been married at the time, maybe he'd have taken her. All but for that stupid rule. She stood, resolve washing over her, and she began the short walk to meet with the reverend mother.

* * *

QUINN WATCHED as the three teenagers began to run toward the village. Hans was on the other end, armed with water bottles and a walkee-talkee. Usually Raphael helped him, but Raphael had been sent off the property on some errand. He was going to tell Genoveva who he was tonight. The thought of it made his heart race. His beautiful daughter with a quiet strength and guileless way, was going to find out the truth about her parentage, and hopefully agree to love him and accept him as a permanent part of her life. Fear almost choked him. The thought of her anger or outright rejection of the idea of coming home to Ireland with him. He watched her shove one of the boys as he laughed. Henrico had it bad. He'd noticed immediately what had eluded everyone else. Emilio was different. He didn't smile or flirt, but there was something in the way he watched Genoveva... Quinn shook himself. He watched them disappear into the forest, a smoothly worn dirt road leading from the abbey to the eastern village.

Tomorrow they would go back up the smaller river, to help with the construction of the new settlement. The tribal leaders had agreed unanimously that they'd rebuild in the same spot. They wouldn't leave the spring. Especially after what had happened the day of the fire. He had to admit, as he watched the beautiful young teacher walk with purpose to Reverend Mother Faith's office, that it had been something other worldly at work that day. To have a childless woman spontaneously lactate, to watch a woman near death deliver a healthy babe, it had all been miraculous. Talia was alive. She'd sustained the worst of the injuries, but she lived. And she'd raise her baby in the old way, among her people.

He knew why Caitlyn was headed to see the abbess. He'd confided in her about Genoveva, in a moment of deep emotional turmoil. And last night after dinner, she'd returned that confidence. She wanted Estela for her own. The beautiful, fair haired beauty who'd come to the jungle to forget her pain. The woman who'd lost three pregnancies and left her husband in Ireland to teach at St. Clare's. She wanted Estela with every fiber of her being. It was obvious every time he saw them together. A bond of love that could bring tears to a grown man's eyes. He just hoped to God it happened, and that her husband was on board. He'd always failed in love. But he saw a light in Caitlyn's eyes when she talked about her husband. A deep belonging that he envied and respected in equal measure. There was resolve in Caitlyn's eyes as she walked to the abbey.

* * *

Patrick stood at the luggage carriage, watching the varied baggage go by. He couldn't believe he was here. Thirty days. His friends and family at the Garda had given him the gift of time. The one thing he needed more than anything. He grabbed his bag off the belt, turning to come face to face with a small, fit looking man that was about his age. He held a sign that said *O'Brien.* So this was him. The fierce protector that helped guard the mission and its occupants. The one that had almost died in the jungle, alongside Izzy. He was smiling. "You must be Raphael." He put his palm out and the man shook it. "Sim, Senhor. It's good to meet you. Your wife talks of you often. I think she'll be very happy to see you."

He took Patrick's large bag and motioned for him to follow. "I hope you're right, brother. I hope you're right."

* * *

Caitlyn sat down, at the invitation of the abbess. "What brings you to me this morning? It's not our scheduled session. Not that I mind. My door is always open." Her face was calm, and her eyes flashed intelligence.

"I'd like to discuss something with you," Caitlyn said with a burst. "About your adoption rules." The abbess leaned back, brow raised as she sipped her tea.

"Oh, aye. And what in particular would you like me to clarify?"

"It's not about clarification. It's about revision." Caitlyn said with a little less gusto. Then she raised her chin, rethinking her approach. "I'd like to argue a case for changing the rules."

"Really? Well, now. I have those rules in place for a reason. Time and experience has made them necessary."

"Then maybe we can start there. Why, Reverend Mother? Can you explain to me why you don't let the visiting missionaries adopt?"

The abbess slid her tea forward, folding her hands on her desk in front of her. "Three times, earlier in my time at St. Clare's. Three different times, I had a mission worker come here, get the adoption bug, then return to their home country and cancel the arrangement. Mostly due to their spouses. They meant well, but the results were catastrophic. Henrico was one of them. The other two aged out. Henrico came here as a small lad. His mother couldn't support him. The father had died in the city when a building collapsed, leaving the mother with no means of support. She left him at age three. A little over a year later, a male doctor from Belfast came to work for three months. He fell in love with the boy. He had three daughters at home whom he loved dearly, but he'd longed for a son. Henrico was four and a half by the time the man left, just starting to attend school. The man assured me and the boy that he'd be back. He was completely convinced that his wife would be thrilled to have another child. Well, as you can imagine..."

Caitlyn's voice was small and sad. "The wife said no." The abbess nodded. "So he never came back?"

"No, he didn't. Honestly, I think Henrico was of an age where he may have forgotten. Or maybe remembered it in another way that didn't hurt so much. But I'll never forget that first six months. Every time the taxi would pull in with a new missionary, Henrico would run to the garden to see if it was his doctor coming to take him home."

Caitlyn wiped a tear from her face. "It's a terrible story. I understand why you think you must protect the children, Reverend Mother, but surely there can be a better screening process."

"The truth is, dear Caitlyn, that most of these kids will never be adopted. It breaks my heart. But many of them have been rejected by living birth parents. I will not let them go through it a second time. I won't have them auditioning every time a new missionary comes to town."

"I understand, but to deny everyone is wrong. Some people won't do what that doctor did to Henrico. Some people will take the child and love them as their own. You can't punish them or the children for the actions of a few misguided people!" Caitlyn was raising her voice.

"What is this really about, Caitlyn? Speak plainly."

"I want Estela. I want to adopt her. And I think she wants me too. I feel it."

The abbess's face softened, but Caitlyn's jaw tightened. "Cailtyn, you're grieving. After this business with the baby being born the day of the fire. After nursing Talia's child, you're emotional."

"No! I am not confused or hormonal or anything else you might come up with. Talia's baby was different. The connection to Estela was almost instant. She needs me. I can't leave here without her. I won't. You have to reconsider. I won't change my mind."

"And what of your husband?"

"He'll do whatever it takes to make a family with me. He wanted to look into adoption. I was the one that refused. The losses were too fresh."

The reverend mother narrowed her eyes. "Believe it or not, I've been considering a change to my rules. They've started the construction for the married housing. I spoke with the diocese and with Sister Maria. I have considered some revisions, as you call it. If a couple comes to do missionary work together, they can be screened for adoption. But they must both be here. Both get to know the children.

Both agree before anything is initiated. Missionaries who come on a solo venture will not be considered. I can't have a repeat of what happened with Henrico. I need both potential parents here. I won't take any chances with my children."

Caitlyn threw her hands up. "A fat load of good that does me! My husband isn't here. He's back home alone and grieving and I left him to volunteer for you! Is a little grace too much to ask? He has a job, Reverend Mother. He can't just leave. How can you do this when you know how perfect this situation is for Estela? Do you want her to live her whole life in an orfanato?"

The Reverend Mother looked at her watch and a wave of annoyance flushed Caitlyn's face.

The abbess said abruptly, "Come walk with me, lass. We'll discuss this as we take a stroll around the garden." Caitlyn stopped the caustic comment before it popped out. She was not going to give up.

As they walked out into the main garden of the mission, Caitlyn saw the children playing in the yard. Rosalis was swinging Estela and she felt the hot prick of tears in her eyes. The abbess put a hand on her shoulder. "Easy, love. It'll all be grand in the end. You'll see."

As if on cue, Caitlyn heard a vehicle coming down the road from the west. Raphael's Jeep, if she heard correctly. She watched as the ragtop drove into sight, and she could scarcely process what she was seeing. She stood there, frozen in place, wondering if her fragile mind had finally snapped. That's when Mary came along the other side of her. She started to shake. She watched as her massive, beautiful husband climbed out of the passenger seat. The tears started coming double time.

She didn't have to say it. The abbess said, "I assure you, he's real. This is not a dream, Caitlyn my dear. Now go, and greet your husband."

Patrick's breath was stolen as he looked across the expanse of green garden to his beloved Caitlyn. She was so beautiful, it hurt his soul to look at her. She wasn't moving. She looked good. Healthy. But right now, he wasn't so sure that surprising her had been such a grand idea after all. Any doubts he had vanished as she broke into a full run.

He met her half way, pulling her into his arms as she sobbed and kissed him. She kissed his forehead, his cheeks, his eyes.

"Oh, my love. How did you know? How are you here?" Then she kissed his mouth. They didn't stop until he heard some loud throat clearing, and some childish giggles. He put her down and looked around, realizing that they'd drawn quite a crowd. He looked into the face of a woman that looked like she knew how to run the show. A wise, strong face with shrewd blue eyes. He put out his hand. "You must be Reverend Mother Faith."

Quinn watched the scene unfold just as Hans called out over the radio that the three runners had begun their journey back. Hans was on his way back as well. Their times were improving, and he swelled with pride as he thought about how his daughter kept up with the two older boys. In fact, seemed in better shape in some ways. Just a couple of days ago, Hans had taught them the fireman carry. Hans carried Raphael, then the two boys had argued over who got to carry Genoveva, as the alternative was carrying Quinn who outweighed all of them by at least eighty pounds.

When it was time to switch, Genoveva had put Emilio on her shoulders and walked the fifty yards to place him back on the ground. It had been difficult, but she'd done it. It was only when Emilio started to sing at the top of his lungs that she'd become distracted. Soon they were all laughing and she barely made it to the end. She'd dumped him with a little less care than she should have, but still they laughed. It was like music to his ears. She had her mother's laugh. So shy the way she covered her mouth and turned pink with the effort. He kept watch as he thought about his Angela. Even after sixteen years, he still thought of her as his. Even in death. She'd rejected him, but he'd come to terms with it. All he could do now, to honor her, was to take care of their daughter.

* * *

GENOVEVA LAUGHED as Emilio took a big sip of water and spit it at Henrico, nailing him right in the ear canal. Henrico hopped around, wiggling and trying to get the water out of his ear. *Boys,* she thought. Hans had just driven by, intending to drive alongside them until they got back. They'd wave him on, arguing that they'd grown up traveling this road. It wasn't like they could miss a turn. They kept the pace brisk, using part of the walk back as a cool down, as Hans and Raphael had taught them. They were winded, but they'd already improved their time. At first, they'd taken a little over thirteen minutes to run the mile and a half to the village. Today they'd done it in just under eleven minutes. The goal, of course, was to run the entire three-mile loop in under twenty minutes. So, they had a lot of work to do. Genoveva had a cramp, and bent to take a couple of deep breaths. That's when she narrowed her eyes and saw something near the river bank. She called out to the boys who stopped and doubled back, wondering what the issue was.

* * *

HANS SMILED as he saw Raphael's Jeep parked in front of the hospital. "So, he's here."

Quinn smiled at him. "Aye, he is. You knew, I take it?" Hans nodded, then looked behind him. "Go, brother. I will wait for them. Go see your friend."

Hans walked over to the Jeep and Raphael was starting to unload Patrick's bag. "Hold up, my brother. Can this thing make it to the bungalow?"

Raphael gave him a look that feigned offense. "This Jeep could climb that tree."

Hans laughed. "Alright. How about a little help? Mary already packed a bag for Caitlyn while she was busy. What do you say we head over to the love nest with their gear?"

Raphael needed no explanation. "Ah, sim senhor. A good idea. They need some privacy by the looks of that kiss he got when he arrived."

"Exactly." They exchanged a purely male look and Hans retrieved Caitlyn's bag from the hospital lobby. Then they were off to drop the luggage at the little house to the west that he'd been sharing with Mary. This time, it was Patrick and Caitlyn that needed to get something straight between them.

* * *

GABRIELA DELIVERED Patrick's tray personally. She wore a smile that only another woman could understand. Reunions were bliss when you were in love. Caitlyn sat next to Patrick and told him what all of the sumptuous dishes were. She knew how much O'Brien men loved to eat. "No wonder you've stayed so long. This is pure magic. Thank you, Gabriela." Everyone had departed but Mary, and Hans came in behind a few of the children who lingered in the doorway. Patrick watched as he smoothed his hand over a small child's head. A little girl. She had warm, dark, sad eyes, and she watched them. It pulled at Patrick's heart in such a way that he felt a little twinge of pain. Then he refocused on Caitlyn. She was smiling, her eyes finally drying from all the tears she'd shed.

Hans gave Mary a nod, and she said, "After you murder that plate of food, we'll take you to your quarters."

Caitlyn's face fell a bit. She'd be on the women's side, away from him. Patrick ate and talked about the trip. Long lay overs and little sleep. "Ye know how bloody small those airplane seats are. Especially if you're our size," he said to Hans, then he noticed that Caitlyn was stealing glances at the little girl. "Caitlyn, love. Would you like to get the lass a plate and put her up to the table?"

Caitlyn straightened her back. "No, that's okay. It's not allowed. This is a staff table and she takes her meals with the children."

He narrowed his eyes, trying to read his wife's mind. "Yes, well perhaps you can let me meet all of your students in a while."

She smiled warmly. "I'd like that. But first, let's get you settled. You've had a long journey, and I'd like to just sit with you a while and talk. We've no classes today. I can give you my undivided attention." But he saw it again. A discreet glance at the small child as another older girl came and tried to take her hand and lead her away. Her thumb went into her mouth and she did the oddest thing. She looked so intently at Patrick that it unnerved him. Then she took a lock of dark, coppery hair from her shoulder and looked at it. When her eyes returned to his face she was smiling around that thumb, and he melted.

* * *

GENOVEVA SAW the old tire peeking out from a bush. They needed another tire. Luca was going to start doing the workouts with them, and they were already sharing. Paolo had promised to find one more next time he went to his sister's farm. An old tractor tire or something. This one wasn't bad, though. They could clean it up and use it in the meantime. "We can roll it home. It's too heavy to carry, I think." The boys looked at her like she'd grown a horn in the middle of her forehead.

"We can't go off the road. You know the rules." Henrico was adamant they not piss off the big Marine or Raphael, or they wouldn't trust them to be out of sight.

"We'd be doing good. It's littering the river bank and we can use it. It's only a few yards off the path. Come, now. I need help. She went ahead of them, walking with purpose. She hated litter. People lived and died by this river. She was actually helping the situation. She heard Emilio now. They were both still on the road. His voice was more urgent.

Emilio watched that stubborn woman-child march off to get that filthy tire. All kidding aside, they had rules for a reason. This wasn't some sort of fairytale land. They learned at a very young age that Brazil was uncommonly good at breeding dangerous creatures. Drug dealers aside, there was a list a mile long of bugs, spiders and snakes...

He screamed at her more urgently now, heading toward her. The river bank bushes were a particularly favorable hiding spot. "Genoveva! Watch where you are walking!" he barked in Portuguese.

She gave him a cheeky grin. "English or I didn't hear it." He saw the broad, green head coil back just as she bent to pick up the tire. "Genoveva, não!" he yelled. Henrico saw it at the same time and they were both running. Genoveva screamed as she jerked back, seeing the green viper hanging above her. The snake was quick, and she felt the fangs pierce the flesh of her forearm as she shielded her face. Then Emilio was there, smashing the snake with a stick as it slithered back into the bush. The threat wasn't over, because its tail anchored it to the tree branch. Emilio swatted at it again as Henrico pulled her away. It struck at him, just as he bashed it in the head again. Then he backed away, broadening the distance between them and the snake.

Genoveva felt them lift her, her arms around both of their necks. Her arm felt like hot lava was boiling under her skin. A white, hot pain that seemed to melt her flesh. She heard the boys talking, panic in their every word. Then she started to black out.

Emilio's heart was racing. He looked at Henrico, and his brother's tears undid him. They were halfway between the village and the hospital. He tried to remember what he'd been taught. Did he elevate the bite for swelling, or did he lower it? Venom was more dangerous than swelling. If he lowered the bite away from her heart...yes, lower it. He stopped just as she passed out. "Run, brother. You're faster. I will carry her. You must run for help!"

He tried to remember the mechanics of the fireman carry. He'd want her arm and hand down as low as possible, but he needed both shoulders. She weighed almost as much as he did. "Go! You must get the Jeep!" Then she was up on his shoulders. Her body seemed too cold. Jesus, why hadn't he paid more attention? If Hans was here, or Raphael, they'd know what to do. Or better yet, Dr. Maguire or Antonio. They were smart. They were doctors. *Jesus, please help me. Don't take her from us.* He went as fast as his fatigued legs would carry him. Better to have one carry her and the other run for help. They could get the Jeep here before he reached the hospital.

Walk, you piece of shit. You've never done anything good in your life. You need to do this one thing right. The self loathing was nothing new for him. It was an old friend. Throwbacks from all the things his father had said to him. All the things other people said about his father. His blood was tainted with bad deeds, both from his junkie mother and his violent, corrupt father. But he'd been in church just last week. He prayed every day like he was taught. Maybe God listened. Maybe he would give him this one thing. "Por favor, Deus. Ajude-me!" He gritted his teeth at the plea. *Please God. Help me.* He heard Genoveva moan, coming in and out of consciousness. Then he saw the blood drip down his bicep. She was bleeding from her nose or mouth. Something was very, very wrong.

* * *

QUINN STARTED to worry as he looked at his watch. They were taking longer than normal. Fear spiked through his chest as he imagined the mischief three unsupervised teenagers could get into. He quelled it. They were good boys. They'd never hurt Genoveva. And she was smart. They all were. They'd lived their whole lives in this forest. He exhaled, checking his watch again. He heard Hans coming out of the cantina, laughing at something someone had said. When he looked at Quinn, his face stiffened. He walked quickly. "They aren't back yet?"

"No, they're not. Five minutes past when you said they'd be. Should I be worried? Maybe we can get the Land Cruiser and head back that way." Just as he said it, he heard the shouting. Henrico's voice pierced through the din of the school yard. They looked at the mouth of the road as they saw him emerge from the forest, waving his arms. "Help! We need the médico!" Hans ran to Raphael's Jeep as he heard the engine come to life.

Quinn grabbed the boy, who collapsed from exhaustion. "What is it?"

"Genoveva! It's a snake biting her! A snake!" Mary ran up behind them.

"Jesus, get the Jeep!" No sooner had he said it than it was there. "Mary, get the anti-venom ready."

"Which one? There are like four different ones!" She was as panicked as he was.

A calm came over him and he looked at the boy. "Think, lad. What did it look like? What kind of snake?" *Please don't say a lancehead. God, please not a lancehead.* There were several deadly snakes in Brazil, but the Bothrops asper, or the *per de lance,* was by far the most catastrophic. Not only toxic, but causing fast and massive tissue damage. Untreated, the limb will rapidly become necrotic. It killed more people in this part of the world than any other snake. If it didn't kill them, it could rapidly rot a leg off. Henrico said one word. *Verde.* Then he closed his eyes, trying to think. "It was green, but the stripes were yellow. Two yellow stripe. It bit her arm. Emilio is carrying her, you must hurry. She fall over. She not awake!"

He yelled to Mary as he jumped in the Jeep. "Bothrops anti-venom. It's a forest pit viper. It's bad, Mary. Be ready. Her blood will stop clotting." Mary's face blanched as she watched the men drive into the forest. Patrick was next to her. "What can I do?"

"I need everyone. Go wake up the surgeon, Giles is his name. He took the night shift. Find Rachel. I need everyone!" She took Henrico into the hospital with her, as the boy was ready to drop from exhaustion. "Come, lad. Tell me exactly what happened." Rachel could help her with the translations if needed, but Pedro was off work today. So was Antonio, but he'd want to know. She shouted over her shoulder as Caitlyn ran for the abbey entrance. "Tell Sister Agatha to call Antonio!"

Caitlyn was stifling the urge to fly into full hysterics. *Oh, Genoveva..* "I'll tell the sisters! Patrick, the men's dorm is through that east door!" Then they all split up, hoping to God that Quinn got to Genoveva in time.

* * *

QUINN WAS REACHING full panic as they ripped down the road. "Easy, Doc. We'll get her." Hans was trying to sound calm, but Quinn felt him shaking with the adrenalin and fear next to him. That's when they saw them. "Jesus Christ!" Hans jumped out of the vehicle with the other two men right behind him. Emilio was red faced, carrying Genoveva over his shoulders.

"No, no, no!" Quinn's brain fried as he saw the blood leaking from her arm and now out of her nose. The men grabbed both kids, hoisting them into the Jeep. One rapid k-turn later, and they were headed at full speed to the hospital.

Quinn's sobs were enough to have Hans tearing up as he cradled an equally distraught Emilio against his chest. "Are you bit? Emilio? Are you bit?" The boy shook his head, then with a pitiful moan, he grabbed Genoveva's ankle, the closest limb he could get to, and put his head on her. He sobbed like the world was ending. "Por favor Deus." Hans didn't need a translation. A plea to the Almighty had its own sound. He rubbed the boy's back as they jostled in the Jeep, headed for that little hospital and his Doc Mary. *Be ready, my love. Be ready. This is going to be close.*

Quinn sobbed in her hair. There was nothing they could do. All of those old wives tales about how to field treat a snake bite would do more harm than good. They needed the anti-venom that was kept on hand in the hospital. "Please, my darling girl. I've just found you. Oh God, don't leave me. We've got a whole life together. Please, my sweet girl. Don't leave me." She was bleeding from her gums now, her body's clotting ability shutting down. Her breathing was so shallow. It wasn't unheard of to die from such a bite, but they were so close. She lived next door to a hospital, for fuck sake. He kept a hand on her pulse, which was erratic and slow. When they burst through the canopy to the yard of St. Clare's, relief washed over him as he saw the hospital staff ready with a gurney. That's when Genoveva's eyes shot open and she moaned, then she vomited as Quinn put her head to the side. Her color changed rapidly. "She's going into shock. Mary, did you find that…"

"Got it!" Dr. Clayton, Rachel and Hans lowered her down as Raphael pulled Emilio out of the van. The boy could barely walk. His legs were like rubber and he cried out, reaching for Genoveva. Raphael picked him up, running into the hospital behind the team of doctors. As he and Sister Catherine got Emilio settled in the room with Henrico, forcing fluids into them, Raphael heard the frantic shouts of the doctors. *Quinn. Oh God. Poor Quinn.* Then the abbess appeared in the doorway. Paler than usual, and tears in her eyes, she went to her boys. She went to them and their sobs grew more heavy. "Oh, my lads. You did so well. She's going to be okay. You did so well." She was crying now, and she and Sister Catherine held the boys like a mother would. It was enough to break your heart.

* * *

PATRICK WATCHED as Caitlyn ran to the smaller children. The little girl he'd seen before was beside herself. He knew almost no Portuguese. She put her arm out toward the hospital entrance. "Irmã! Minha irmã!" Caitlyn fought the urge to break down as the little girl struggled. That's when Patrick went to them and took the little Estela from Caitlyn. She grabbed on to his neck and cried.

"What is she saying?" he asked as Caitlyn's face was fixed on them both.

"She's saying sister. They're not blood, but they're...they're family. They're more than blood." He nodded as he began to soothe the child.

They took all of the kids into the cantina. Gabriela was crying as she made some quick snacks to distract the children. Then Sister Maria joined them. They all said a prayer for Genoveva who wasn't just a classmate, but a sort of sibling to everyone. Patrick said, "Those two boys may very well have saved her life."

Sister Maria nodded, "Sim, Senhor. They are good boys. Very brave. They've had hard lives, but they take care of each other."

* * *

QUINN WATCHED as Genoveva's stats dropped. Her breathing hadn't stopped, but she was on an oxygen mask. Her heart rate was erratic, but she was coming in and out of consciousness. He felt her jerk and try to sit up. "She's going to vomit!" They turned her just in time to vacate her gorge all over Rachel. This time, there was blood. Then she passed out again. "Oh, Jesus. Hang on baby. Please don't leave me! I just found you!" Quinn was rubbing her hair so affectionately that a few of the staff were taken aback.

"What's going on here?" Rachel asked, not understanding. Quinn was crying, trying to clear her mouth before putting the mask back on.

He ignored the question. "We should intubate. She's going to choke if she vomits again!"

Mary looked at Rachel and Giles, the two doctors that kept to themselves more than the Irish doctors. "She's his daughter. He just found out and she doesn't know, yet."

That's when Dr. Giles Clayton got serious. He grabbed Quinn's arm. "We will not lose her. Let the anti-venom do its job. She'll likely need more in an hour or so. And yes, we'll need to intubate. Now, you need to leave."

Quinn shook off his hand. "The fuck I will. You will have to shoot me before I leave her side."

"Doctors don't treat family members. Quinn, you need to back off."

Quinn started to tear into the guy, but Genoveva's blood pressure hit the basement. "No!"

Genoveva felt herself drifting away. She didn't want to go. She had so much to do, and she couldn't leave before she accomplished all of those things. She also couldn't bear the thought of Estela not having a big sister. But here she was, floating. She heard the doctors plainly. She wasn't doing well. Would she die? Then she heard the voice. Distant and so familiar. Her mother. *Momma.* If she left this world, would she see her mother again. She heard it again in that sweet, smooth Portuguese that she'd grown up hearing. *Not yet, my girl. Go back. Go back to your father.* Father? What father?

"She's leveling out! I think she's trying to open her eyes!" Mary yelled over the chaos. She leaned over Genoveva and said, "Welcome back, beautiful girl."

* * *

HANS HATED waiting on the sidelines more than anything else in the world. Jesus, Joseph, and Mary. Why had he left them to walk back alone? This was his doing. He should have done like he'd originally planned and stayed with them. The thing was, you sent a mixed message to young people if you tried to teach them leadership, integrity, and competency, and then hovered over them like a British nanny. He closed his eyes as the pain of the guilt washed through him. Quinn's sobs were still fresh in his mind. He knew what it was to almost lose a daughter. He knew what it was to lose a lot of things. The thought that something like this could happen to Mary almost sent him into a full panic. He had all sorts of triggers going off. But then he thought of those two boys. His two surly, mischievous boys that had probably saved Genoveva's life. Suddenly, he felt the overwhelming need to get to them.

He went down the hall to the patient rooms, looking for them. He heard the abbess's voice and went to the room to find them huddled together on an exam table. He advanced on them to pull them into the biggest man hug he could muster, but as he approached, Emilio recoiled. He actually threw his arms up to what? Protect his head? *Oh, God.* He thought Hans was angry. He thought he was going to be punished. Suddenly Hans wished he could kill that fucking father of his all over again. He knelt down, palms up. "No, big man. I'm sorry. I didn't mean to scare you. Easy, buddy." He kept up with the reassuring words as he pulled Emilio's hands away from his face. The boy was babbling in Portuguese.

"He apologizes. He didn't watch her well enough. He let her get hurt." Sister Catherine said, then she took his hand. "No, Emilio. You did well."

He shook his head, protesting. He tried in English. "I'm the oldest. I should have…"

Hans stopped him. "No, Emilio. You both saved her. This is my fault. I shouldn't have left you. I should have stayed with you. I'm so sorry. This isn't your fault. I'm so proud of you both." Henrico wiped his face, the tears flowing freely. "You both did well. Real hero stuff."

Emilio looked at his lap. "I come from bad people. I don't do anything right. I should have run faster. I was weak."

"You did as well as any of the Marines under my command. You took care of her. She will make it through this."

"I was mean to her. I was bad to her for so many years. I didn't know…" his voice quivered. "I didn't know how to be good to her. My father was so bad. He beat us. Me and my mother. He beat us and say such bad things. I'm just like him. I was mean to her! She is so good and I was mean to her!"

Hans pulled him into his arms as he leaned against the wall. "You are a good boy. And you aren't mean to her anymore. You learned because you are in a good place. You are surrounded by people who love you. We will teach you to love, Emilio. We'll teach you to love and to be a man of honor and goodness."

Emilio pushed away. "You will leave! They all leave! You come for a little time and you go! The sisters cannot teach me to be a man. They protect me! They don't show me how to protect. I will never learn these things because you all leave! I only know how to hurt! You want me to go be a soldier, but you leave and I will be here with the sisters. I can't do it!"

"Emilio, listen to me." Hans was crying now. They all were. He took the boys head in his palms. "I won't leave you. Do you hear?" He took the other hand and palmed Henrico's head, bringing them both to eye level. "I will stay until you are of age. I won't leave you." He hugged them both to his chest and they wept. When he looked up to see the response of the sisters, he saw Mary in the doorway. Her hand was over her mouth, tears filling her eyes. "I'm sorry," he mouthed, because he couldn't do it. He couldn't leave these two boys even if his life depended on it. It went against everything he stood for. Never leave a man behind. He'd led so many young men during his career, not much older than them. He'd raised a son who didn't need him anymore. They did, though. These two needed him, and he couldn't let them down. He looked at Mary, begging her to understand, and hoping to hell he hadn't just caused a major rift between them.

She shook her head. Then she knelt down beside them. "We won't leave them. I'll settle my affairs for the long term and we won't leave them until they have somewhere to go." A shudder went through him, and such deep gratitude, that he was glad he was already sitting.

Reverend Mother Faith thought she'd seen a lot of miraculous things in her day, but this was enough to bring her to her knees. Emilio was right. Being raised by a bunch of nuns was not going to teach him to be a man. Father Pietro came once a week for mass, but then he was gone. Raphael had his own family. Antonio came once or twice a month. Paolo was completely overworked. They had no steady men in their lives. But this man had come to them. This big military man with wide shoulders and eyes that had seen too much. Eyes that were looking at his wife with such adoration, it caused her throat to seize up.

This was not a man who made empty promises. He'd come here to watch over his wife, as was his nature. But he'd found a niche in their little place along the river. He'd found his calling. The older children's emotional needs were often neglected because they were able to care for themselves. The smaller children needed so much more attention. But she realized, in this moment, that God had sent her this man to guide her boys into manhood, and he would stay here until he'd done just that.

CHAPTER 21

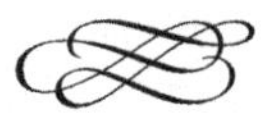

Quinn watched his daughter sleep, and he was so overcome with weariness. He'd damn near lost her. Her heart rate was steady now. Her arm was terribly swollen, but her blood was starting to clot on its own again. He'd run a kidney function panel on her, making sure the venom hadn't caused kidney damage. She'd been given another dose of the anti-venom and antibiotics. Now they waited. She was strong. He knew this. But right now she looked like a pale, sick version of the vibrant girl he'd come to know. She looked younger, somehow. Her sweet, innocent face like an angel as she slept. He got up to stretch his legs, but he didn't want to leave her. Then Mary was at the door of her room. "Go get something to drink and eat. You can bring it back. The abbess's orders."

He gave her a crooked smile. "You were wonderful Mary. Not a lot of country doctors would have handled that so well."

She laughed. "It's not that rural. We've just gotten an ATM in town." She motioned to the door. "Go on, now. Doctor's orders. Get a tray and come back. I won't leave her." He walked past her, out the door, and almost tripped over a mass of bodies on the floor. "They wouldn't leave her. And he wouldn't leave them."

He looked at the two boys laying on the floor, sleeping back to back like a set of twins in their mother's womb. Hans was asleep against the wall, his hand on Emilio's head. "They're good boys, aren't they?"

"They are. And I don't think they knew how much they loved her until they almost lost her." Quinn swallowed hard. He'd noticed the attraction on Henrico's end, but the boys were so close. Like brothers. Two sides of the same coin. It made sense that they'd fall for the same girl. "Aye, well. I'll bring them back some food as well. Does that big man of yours like anything in particular?"

"He eats big and often. Whatever you bring is fine."

Quinn stepped around the boys, seeing that Hans had cocked one eye open. His face was so tense. He'd gone over and over the scenario like a military man who was trying to figure out where his strategy had failed. The truth was that Hans was doing a lot more for these kids than he realized. It wasn't anyone's fault. Teenagers didn't always think two steps ahead. Genoveva knew all about the snakes and bugs and taking precautions. She'd just been acting like a stubborn teenager and not been paying attention. It happened. Quinn remembered the warnings from his own parents about this or that. Especially his driving. But it wasn't until the crunch of metal and the seatbelt grabbing him that he realized that they were right. He'd totaled a perfectly good car because teenagers did dumb shit and didn't listen to their parents. "Headed to the cantina. I'll bring back a tray for all of us to share."

Hans's face loosened. "Thanks, brother. Extra cheese bread. I need to eat my feelings." Quinn barked out a laugh, and then he went to get the food.

* * *

CAITLYN WAS SO TOUCHED by the gesture from Hans and Mary, that she was ready to burst into tears. They...meaning Hans...had actually put a sign on the door that said *Love Shack.* Patrick laughed as he opened the door. When they were both closed in, things got unusually awkward.

"Ye have to check the place every time you leave." She went about the task of showing him how to check for spiders, snakes, and scorpions.

She was rambling on about bullet ants when he said softly, "Caitlyn." She stopped, closing her eyes. What had happened to them? She suddenly felt so distant from him. Scared, even.

"Why are you here?" The question came out rougher than she'd meant it to. "I mean, are you here to volunteer or to deliver some sort of bad news?"

"Why do you think I'm here?" he asked, irritation creeping into his voice.

"I don't know, Patrick! You told me you couldn't take leave. And the last thing I said to you was that you could ask the church for an annulment. And you didn't tell me you were coming. If you have bad news then…" She stopped, watching the grin creep onto his face. She put a hand on her hip. "What the bloody hell is so funny!" She was stressed from the incident with Genoveva and because she didn't know what to expect from her husband. And he was laughing at her. He'd actually begun to laugh. She struck like a cobra, cuffing his ear. He grabbed her wrist and flipped her on her back, the bed squeaking.

"Christ, ye are a wee, daft harpy when you're stressed. Shut up, woman. Just shut your gob and kiss me properly." He didn't wait for her to ask, he went about convincing her just how much he'd missed her.

She put a palm up to his chest, breathless. "We need to talk."

"If it's talking you want, you'll get it." Then he kissed her again, mumbling to her all the things he'd been waiting three hours to do to her. She moaned as he nibbled her earlobe and then she was lost. He stripped her slowly, his mouth everywhere. Her nipples were so sensitive, and when he closed his mouth over them, she gasped. It had only been a couple of days since they'd taken the baby away. She'd been expressing her milk, but her breasts were full.

"Jesus, these are incredible. I think that cheese bread is making your boobs grow." He moaned as he licked his way down and buried his head between her thighs. He kneaded one breast as he spread her wide and tasted right where he wanted to be. She arched and screamed as she came, and for the first time in a long time, there was nothing on her mind but right now, feeling his mouth on her.

"Patrick, I need you. I need you inside!"

He worked his way up slowly, and it was torture. More time on her breasts, to the point where she feared she would let down her milk. Then he met her eyes. "Last time we were together, we were both a mess. I took ye hard and fast. I want this to last, mo chroí. I want you slow and deep." He slid into her so slowly, she was mad with it. Ready to roll into another orgasm. Then he started. He kissed her deep as he rolled his hips. He was thick and long and it was almost painful. He knew her body and he slowed his pace, waiting for her to get used to him again. His eyes took in her face with such love, it caused her eyes to prick with tears.

She said, "I love you. Oh, God. I missed you. I'm so glad you're here." His smile was broad and he dipped his head for another kiss. She ran her fingers up his neck and into his coppery hair as she tipped her hips, taking more of him. It was perfection. Everything about it. "Patrick," she said urgently. He knew, though. He felt it.

"Come again, hen. Let me feel it all. Ah, fuck!" He threw his head back as he drove into her climaxing body.

Patrick tried like hell to make this last, but it had been weeks. And she was so fucking beautiful. He looked down at her, breasts round and firm, nipples flushed peaks. Suddenly he wasn't close enough. He put an arm under her shoulders and pulled her up to meet him chest to chest. Her blonde tresses were wild around them and her mouth was so sweet.

"I need to come inside you. Jesus, Caitlyn!" And he let go. His breath quivered against her neck as he spilled in her. He ran his hand up and palmed her neck as he met her emerald eyes, and he knew nothing was ever going to separate them again.

He took a minute to come back to himself. Their bodies not ready to separate. He raised up on his elbows, not wanting to crush her. That's when he felt it. They were both wet from chest to navel. At first he thought maybe it was sweat, but it seemed too sticky. He raised up and got a proper look at her, and that's when he saw it. A drop of milk, like a tear coming off her nipple. He thumbed it and her eyes widened. "Caitlyn, darlin. What is this. You're lactating? My God, woman. I asked you after you came here. I asked you if you were pregnant. You said you were tested." He wasn't mad. He was baffled. And fear laced his voice. "Oh, God did you miscarry here?"

She took his face in her hands. "No, love. No to all of it. Except the milk, but no to the rest. I'm not pregnant. I just…Well, I guess I should start from the beginning. It's sort of a long story."

He rolled on his side, taking her with him. They were forehead to forehead. "Tell me, love. You've got stories, I suspect, and so do I. Why don't we start with why you're leaking milk?"

She told him. She started with her talks with Seamus, the fertility consult, her options if she were to get pregnant again. Then she told him about the village. How she'd visited, and then about the fire. She wept as she told him the story of Talia and the spring. Of the little baby Esmeralda, named for her. Patrick's face was so pained, it made the fresh tears run hot on her face. "They thought it was the spring. That their God had given me this gift and had also saved Talia and her baby. The matriarch of the tribe, she asked me to feed the child. Talia was so poorly. Burns on her arms and chest. It was pure will keeping the lass going, Patrick. She simply would not leave that child without a mother. I couldn't tell them no. I felt like…maybe it wasn't a gift from the spring, but from our son." Her throat was achy and rough. "My breasts never went back to normal. Not really. They ached at the loss of him."

Patrick's eyes misted. "You never told me that. Oh, darlin. I'm so sorry. I don't know how you came to have this happen but it's a miracle. Did the mother live?" She nodded and said, "Yes, she's still in the burn unit. They're having one of the other women serve as a wet nurse, and they took the child home. We've sent the men to help work on the village. They go out tomorrow. I suppose Quinn will stay back, but the ones who can be spared will go."

"And I'll go. I'll go and help them any way I can," Patrick said.

"I think that would be grand. We'll go after morning mass. Oh,

Patrick. It's so wonderful here. I want to show you everything. How long can you stay? How did you get this time?" He evaded the second question. "I need to be back in two weeks. No later. I have a lot to tell you. Jesus, I don't know where to start. I have to be back for a court date."

She cocked her head. "Is it from one of your arrests?"

He shook his head. Then he started at the beginning, the time before Christmas and New Years. "When you told me about what you did for the small child. That you fed her," his voice caught at the thought of Branna dropping onto the alley floor to feed a starving, dehydrated, hypothermic newborn.

"What is it, love? Please, tell me what's happened." So he did. With barely restrained emotions, he began.

CAITLYN LISTENED for close to thirty minutes, completely stunned. Patrick had a hard time getting the story out. The mother being found dead, the grandparents that were barely hanging on, the investigation. She could hardly absorb anything past imagining Seany, Josh, Branna, and Patrick being huddled in an alley, trying to save a newborn that had been thrown in the bin. A beautiful, fair haired baby boy. They clung to each other as he continued.

"He's strong. He's so bloody strong. And he likes when I feed him. He fusses with everyone else, but…"

Then she understood. "Ye've been going to the hospital to check on him? Every day?" He gave her a sheepish look.

"He's got no one. The bastard that sired him couldn't stand the bad press. He knew he was headed for prison. He hanged himself. The lad has no one."

Caitlyn put her hand over her mouth. "Oh, darlin. Is that what the court date is about? The father killing himself?"

"No, the court date is in family court. It's regarding the baby. It's why I've come. I know this is sudden, Caitlyn, but there's no help for it. I don't want him going into the system. Tadgh and Charlie took over the temporary fostering of him so that he wouldn't go to someone else." He squeezed her hand. "I know you want to have biological children, and it sounds like this Seamus has a good plan. I'm ready to do that with you. I'm ready to try again, but Caitlyn, I just can't even comprehend letting him go. I feel like he's meant to be ours." He shut his eyes. "Everyone has rallied. Everyone was at the first court date. Even Aidan flew in. Uncle Nolan represented us. The judge gave me three weeks to get you by my side in order to get custody. The next of kin, Kasey's mother, will request that we be given first chance at adopting him."

Caitlyn's heart was in her throat. Not because she didn't understand, but because she did all too well. Of course they should take the child. She choked down her sobs. *But what about Estela?* What would the abbess say if she took off in two weeks? They could never arrange a foreign adoption by then. Her heart felt like it was in a vice. *Oh Estela. I can't leave you.* Nor could she deny Patrick. How could she, when he'd been the child's savior? The whole family had rallied to make this happen. His workplace had donated all of that leave time to get him here for the sole purpose of bringing her home to be the child's mother. A newborn with no mother or father to love it. She shook herself. There was a way to do this. There had to be. People adopted siblings all the time. She'd just make the abbess understand. She'd make her listen!

"Okay, my love. We'll go back for the court date. I'm with you on this. Of course I am. He needs us."

Patrick's kiss was so hard, that if she hadn't already been horizontal, he'd have knocked her off her feet.

CHAPTER 22

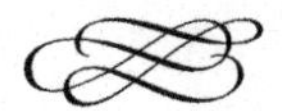

DUBLIN, IRELAND

Charlie was frantic, looking for her keys. "You're sure you can do this? Madeline and Mary are only twenty minutes away. I can call and tell them I'll be late."

"Sis, you need to calm down." Josh handed her the keys. "I've held a baby before, and I fed him in the hospital. We're old pals, me and Carlos."

She stopped and pointed at him. "Stop.Calling.Him.Carlos." Her words were clipped, but she was fighting a grin.

"It's Carlos until you name him. Sorry. Now, just go. I've got this. You can't blow this meeting off, even if you are on a leave of absence and Tadgh is tied up in court all day."

She knew he was right. Human trafficking busts couldn't simmer on low until she was available. This was a joint task force and other agents had travelled from all over Europe. "After this, I am officially on leave. I just need this one day."

"Go! Seriously, we're fine." He was patting the baby's bottom, strapped in a wrap across his chest. "Like you said, it's twenty minutes." Charlie stopped, smiled at the sight of him wearing a baby, and pulled his head down for a kiss. Then she kissed the baby on his soft head. "I love you, little man. You'll take a nap with Auntie Charlie as soon as I get home." And they would. She loved sleeping with him in the crook of her arm. He loved it too. Her hormones were raging at the thought of having her own with Tadgh. And if Caitlyn couldn't do this thing, then she would. She'd go from aunt to mom in a New York minute before she'd let him go. He was meant to be an O'Brien. They all knew it. The *how* of it didn't matter.

* * *

JOSH OPENED the door to the expectant faces of Madeline and Mary Nagle. Caitlyn's younger sisters had finally been brought into the conspiracy, on threat of death if they leaked the info to Caitlyn or her parents before Patrick had a chance to talk to her. They needed some fill-in babysitters. Everyone had jobs, and this one day, the fates had been stacked against them for having any of the O'Brien women come to the rescue. Some forty-eight hour virus had ravaged the three households. No one wanted to expose Carlos to the illness. He was still going in for well baby checks every three days, since he'd been freshly released from the NICU.

Mary bounced into the apartment, as bubbly as ever. She was a lively girl. Flirtatious and classically pretty. Madeline just approached him with a steady ease, her eyes smiling more than her mouth. His heart leapt in his chest. Her deep, grey-green eyes met his, then traveled over the baby. Her eyes shifted, looking almost pained. She smoothed a hand over his downy head and he wiggled in the wrap. She crooned. "Well, now. Ye've had your adventures, haven't you? There's a lad. You're safe now, my sweet boy." The boy cooed at her, responding to her low, silky voice. *I understand completely, Carlos,* Josh thought. She was bewitching in that subtle, quiet way. Her hair was blonde, but less honey and more ash than her sisters. Muted, comparatively, as if nature decided that a human wouldn't be able to bear the sight of her beauty if she wasn't given the more subtle coloring. But all that did was make her look more striking. While Mary was a pretty, perfect, pink rose, Madeline was a wild cornflower, blowing on a hillside. Too wild and beautiful to be owned or given.

"Thank you for coming. My sister was kind of a mess when she had to leave him. Apparently I'm too incompetent to go this alone." There was no bitterness in the words. He just smiled, and got the gift of a small smile returned from her.

"Well, then. We'll make sure you don't make a mess of things. Now, unwrap that contraption and let's have a proper look at the boy. What's his name?"

"We're calling him Carlos," he laughed at the horrified look on both their faces. "Just until they give him his own name."

"You and Seany have been watching re-runs of The Hangover, I suppose? Carlos will not do. Not at all. Carlos is the suave devil who buys you a drink on holiday in Barcelona, not the name to be giving a little Irishman. No, we'll call him Laddie. That'll do for the time being." She took him from Josh's arms and swayed as she kissed his head. "That's right, little Laddie. You'll get a new mum and it'll all be grand indeed."

* * *

CHARLIE TOOK way longer than originally planned. By the time she'd reached their building on foot, her heart was racing with a panic that was purely feminine. That pull that kept animals from abandoning their young. She rushed through the door, her words coming out in bursts. "Is he okay? I'm sorry. Agh, this smug asshole from Germany wouldn't shut the hell up! Is he okay? Where…" She stopped as she saw the scene in front of her. The baby was wiggling happily on a blanket. Mary was blowing raspberries on his belly. Madeline was folding laundry and Josh was making grilled cheese sandwiches. It was well past the time for her to be home. "I'm sorry. I faked going to the bathroom a couple of times and tried to call."

Josh shrugged. "The cell service is shitty in the apartment. You know this, Charlie. I haven't had time to check the computer. Everyone is fine. He's been really good." Mary was on her feet with the child, swaying with him up on her shoulder. She came to Charlie. "There he is. He's been fine. He took 4 oz. of formula and had the last

3 oz. of Branna's frozen milk. He's had three diaper changes, the wee fiend. Haven't you? Yes, yer a right, stinky boy just like your uncles."

To which Josh said laughing, "Hey! I resent that! I'm extremely hygienic!"

Charlie laughed as she took him in her arms. She'd worried for nothing. "It's too late for you two to drive back. I'll take the sofa bed with Tadgh and you two can rack out in my bed."

"We've already sorted it out." Madeline said. "We'll take Patrick and Caitlyn's bed. Josh will stay on the sofa and Seany will sleep in his own bed. You need your rest if you're going to be taking care of a newborn." Madeline, smoothed a hand over his head lovingly. "It's a fine thing you're doing for them. All of you," she gestured to Josh. "Caitlyn will be done for as soon as she sees our Laddie, and from what I hear, Patrick is head over heels already."

"I hope so. I really do. It's been so hard on your sister. I just want them to be happy. I'm glad they're together."

"So am I. My parents will rest easier, knowing there's the two of them now."

Josh started sliding bowls of soup and grilled cheese on the table. "Chow time. Sit, ladies. Seany should be here any minute." As soon as he said it, there was a peck on the window. "And there he is."

"Do you lot ever use the proper doorway?" Mary said as Seany climbed through the window.

"Only if it's raining. Charlie, did you ever tell them about the time you saw Patrick and Caitlyn…"

"Stop! Don't you dare share that story!" But it was too late, Mary and Madeline were intrigued. By the end of the colorful tale with Seany partially acting out the scene from the kitchen, the girls were rolling in their chairs.

"Who knew Caitlyn was such a little vixen," Mary said with appreciation.

"Yes, and I know way more about Patrick than I ever needed to," Charlie assured them.

Josh looked at Madeline, and her smile was quiet. Like she was just soaking in the light-hearted banter. She met his eyes briefly, then turned to her meal.

* * *

Manaus, Brazil

Patrick walked alongside Caitlyn, his stomach grumbling. It was dinner time, and he could hear the children laughing and running around the play yard as the path opened up to the property. He took in the sight of the estate all over again. A clearing in an otherwise dense forest and heavy canopy. Large, lush trees and tangling vines surrounding several acres of beautifully landscaped property. A stone wall surrounded them, and there were several buildings that served as an abbey, a cantina, a school, and the largest being a hospital. There were also small cottages on stilts being constructed at the south border. Married housing, from what Hans had told him. Under different circumstances, he could see himself and Caitlyn doing this together as Mary and Hans were doing.

He watched Caitlyn as she swept her eyes over the children. She was looking for someone. Then her eyes locked on that same little girl. The one that had watched them in the cantina. She was a beautiful child. He saw Caitlyn fighting some emotion. She swallowed hard, and he swore she was going to start crying. The little girl saw her and was transformed. She ran at Caitlyn arms open and ready to be gathered up. Caitlyn knelt down and scooped her up, pulling her close. Then she sniffed the girl's hair, her eyes closed. She was trying to sound happy, but he knew her too well.

"How's my Estela this evening?"

"I am well." The girl's English was stunted, like she was concentrating hard to get the words out. But she spoke it well for such a young child. "Can I see Genoveva now?"

"I'm sorry, lass. Maybe tomorrow before mass she'll be ready. Now, I'm going to show my husband to supper. Did you eat?" She nodded. "Okay, well you make sure to stay near Rosalis in the garden.

I'll see you at breakfast tomorrow. We're going to the village to work." The girl's face fell. "And maybe I'll bring you some fresh fruit?"

She smiled and ran off. Caitlyn watched her go and the tears couldn't be held back anymore. Her chin quivered with the effort. She looked at Patrick, and he saw agony and fear in her eyes. A combination he knew well. "Oh, sweetheart. You've gone and fallen in love too, haven't you?" That's when the damn broke. She wept like the world was ending, face buried in his chest. He let her get it out. All her fears. The rules about missionaries adopting, the abbess's intent to amend them for married couples that were on mission together. The fear that if she left in two weeks, the footing she'd gained with the Reverend Mother would be lost. She cried until she had the hiccups. "Calm down, love. It's all right. We will figure this out. If you're sure about this, we'll figure it out."

"But doing two adoptions. One of them foreign. Trying to do them both and all the money we'll need. Dublin is so bloody expensive and I'm not working and..."

"And, and, and. My goodness, hen. Ye've never been such a quitter. There's a way, and we'll find it. Uncle Nolan will help with the legal stuff. We have to make our court date, but we won't forget about Estela." He looked over as he saw her being pushed on the swing, "Christ, she is a beauty isn't she?" He turned to her and smiled, "I'd love a daughter." She let out a sob and it was hard for him not to break down as well. "We won't quit until we've got them both with us. I vow this to you, my sweet Caitlyn. I promise you that we will have a house full of children. As for Dublin, they've already started processing my transfer. I'm going to work out of Shannon. We're moving home, love. We're going to raise our children in Doolin. I'll commute like Michael does."

Caitlyn threw her arms around his neck. "I didn't think I could love you more. I didn't think it was possible, but I do."

He dropped a soft kiss on her mouth. "You can show me just how much later tonight. For now, I think we should go see the reverend mother. We can grab some dinner first, but I don't think we should wait on this. We'll go see her directly."

* * *

HANS WAS GRINNING WIDELY and Mary and Caitlyn were both in tears. "That's wonderful!" Mary said. "Oh, Caitlyn. I love the whole idea. The only bad part about Genoveva leaving has been the thought of separating her from Estela. They'd be near each other. In the same city!"

That's when they told them about the transfer to Shannon. "We'll have to find housing, of course. The rent is not quite so dear as Dublin, but it would be good to have three bedrooms, which will stretch our budget." That's when Patrick noticed a lightbulb go off in Mary's head. He actually saw it click on, expecting light to pour out of her ears. "What?"

"We're staying. We are extending until Emilio and Henrico age out. We've decided that we're needed here more than in Ireland. For the time being, at least. The rotation of doctors is difficult. They could use a full time family practitioner. So, we're staying." She shrugged.

Hans interrupted. "And that means our house will be sitting empty for the next year or so."

Patrick understood. "Jesus, it's perfect. It's just the right size."

"Yes, and if you can store some of our furniture to make room for yours, you can use whatever else you need. It's a perfect solution. I was planning on going home to settle everything for the long term, but if you do this, I may not need to."

"We'll pay a fair rent for the place. I'll figure out the budgeting and pay ye fair."

Mary threw her hand up. "My house is paid off. My intent was to close it up for the year, not rent it. I'm making an exception because you're like my own children and I want to take care of you. If you pay the utility bills, the house is yours. You put that money toward getting those two babies settled. Save for your own house."

Hans stopped the protests. "You aren't going to win this. We both have pensions. We don't need your money and we won't take it. And I am absolutely in love with the idea of my grandkids running around with Estela." Caitlyn choked down a sob. She grabbed both their hands. He looked intensely into her eyes, and then at Patrick. "We won't leave her. We'll take care of her like she was our own child until you come back for her."

* * *

FOR THE FIRST time in Caitlyn's experience, Reverend Mother Faith was speechless. She listened intently as Patrick laid it all out. Everything to do with the little baby waiting for them back in Dublin. The investigation, the fate of the parents, the impending court date. Then he said, "Now, all that aside, we need to discuss our options for adopting Estela." Her brows went up at that, more due to Patrick's no nonsense tone than anything. "Once we get custody of the baby, we need to know what the process involves to formerly adopt Estela and take her back to Ireland to meet her new brother."

"Listen, I realize that you've both been on these separate and rather remarkable journeys. Now that you've come together, you're trying to merge these two experiences. You each had your heart set on a child to adopt. That's a beautiful and selfless thing. But once you get back to Ireland and adopt that baby, you may feel differently. Newborns are a huge undertaking without other children in the house. You may not be so inclined to add another child into the mix."

Caitlyn said, "No, you're wrong. I've got my heart set on two adoptions, not one. So does Patrick. In our minds, we're already a family of four. I'd no sooner ask him to give up that poor baby who needs us than he would ask me to abandon Estela. This is a package deal. All you need to do is let it happen. Step in and pave the way for us. You told me once that it wasn't always about the roots and the family trees. Sometimes it's about the vines. That beautiful tangle of vines that start from separate places and reach for each other. Will ye take those words back, now? Estela is *iníon, mo chroí.* She's the daughter of my heart! You cannot ask me to leave her behind. And she'd be with Liam when he visits. He'd be her uncle. He loved that child more than life itself and so did Izzy. Estela can have a family! And she'll be near Genoveva. They can see each other regularly. I'll make sure of it!"

Patrick leaned in and put his hand over his heart. "Reverend Mother. I swear it on my own life. If you help us, I will love that beautiful little girl until I'm in my grave and beyond. We're not rich in money. I make a modest living. But I'm rich in more important things. We have a good family. A big, gorgeous, loving, crazy family that is going to fall just as in love with her as we are. So many cousins, she'll feel as at home as she does out in that play yard. Please, Reverend Mother. Please help us." She didn't say anything. "And I might add, since you know my brother, that when it comes to being stubborn, I'm half Mullen and half O'Brien."

The abbess chuffed a laugh. "Oh, aye. I'm well aware of that particular stubborn gene pool." She sighed. "Alright, then. If you are committed to this, I'll not stand in your way. As a matter of fact, I think the dioceses can intervene with the Brazilian government and smooth the way. As will our diocese in Ireland on the other end of this transition. We will do what we can to make this happen for you, and for Estela."

* * *

QUINN STIRRED as he felt motion on the hospital bed. Felt Genoveva's hand squeezing. Then she was opening her eyes. They were swollen a bit. She had a degree of edema through her whole body, but her arm was the worst. There was no necrosis at the bite location, however, which was a Godsend. No organ damage either. "Good morning, lass. We've been waiting to see those pretty eyes." Quinn smiled as Genoveva's eyes focused on him. She had a strange look on her face, like she was seeing him for the first time.

"Agua," she croaked. She watched him as he poured from the plastic pitcher and gave her water.

"We had to intubate you for a while. Your throat is likely sore. How are you feeling? Are you in pain?"

"A little, in my arm." She pulled it up and looked at it. "It was a forest snake. The green one."

"Aye, Henrico told me. They'll want to see you, when you're ready."

"How did I get here? We were...we were far away," she said, finally starting to get her brain moving.

"Emilio carried you while Henrico ran for help. He got pretty far considering how tired he was. I think you owe them your life, sweet girl."

She stared at him, processing that. She didn't know how she felt about owing them something. "I am grateful. It was difficult. I was in pain and then there was nothing. I...I heard my mother. I thought I was dying. I heard her voice."

Genoveva couldn't understand why Dr. Maguire was crying. She was nothing to him. But this didn't feel like nothing. On the contrary, it felt like something very big. She thought about hearing her mother's voice. *Not yet, my girl. Go back. Go back to your father.* That's when she really looked at Dr. Quinn Maguire. The Irish doctor with the fair hair. She looked right into his bright green eyes. "I don't understand."

Quinn's face was soft and kind. "I think you do. Deep down, I think you do. You heard your mother's voice? What did she say to you?"

Now Genoveva was crying. She couldn't stop the hot tears as they pooled in her eyes and rolled down her flushed cheeks. "Papai?"

Quinn took a better grip on her hand and brought it to his mouth for a small kiss. Genoveva felt his tears on the top of her hand. "Yes, sweet girl. I'm your da."

"How did you...I don't understand?"

"Izzy and Liam. They went through the records with the abbess. They figured it out and then they came to me. They found me in Ireland to tell me that I had a daughter." His voice cracked and he closed his eyes. "I had a fifteen year old daughter that I didn't know about, and you were at the orfanato. I didn't know. Oh, God," his sob was painful. "I didn't know, Genoveva. I'd have come for you and your mother. I would have made her listen. I'm so sorry. I never knew."

"I know. My mother told me. I had to keep the secret, but she told me you didn't know. She told me that she love you. I know she love you. She was ashamed of me, but she love me too."

"I don't doubt she loved you more than life itself. And she had her reasons, Genoveva. She wasn't ashamed of you. I think she was ashamed of what she and I did. We weren't married and she was a very devout Catholic. Not telling me I had a daughter was wrong, but she had her reasons and I wasn't blameless. I'll explain it all in time, if you care to hear it. Right now, I'm just thanking God you're alive and whole. And if you'll have me, I'd like to try and be a proper father to you. I missed so much. It wakes me up at night, thinking about all those years we missed." He put his forehead down on her hand. "But I don't want to miss anymore." She put her other hand on his head and patted him as he cried.

"I think that I'd like to have a…what you call it? Da?"

He raised his head. "Da, Papai, I don't care what you call me. Just let me stay in your life." She rewarded him with a smile and he wiped her tear stained face. "Now, let's get you fed and let those lads in to see you. They've been sleeping on the floor for about twelve hours. And this is a bit late, but Izzy recorded a message for you. Kind of a way to open up the discussion about me being your da. As it turns out, Angela did it for me." His eyes welled up again and so did hers. "And I loved her too. I'll always love her."

He turned and opened the door, and Genoveva did a double take. Emilio and Henrico were indeed sleeping on the floor outside her door. Like babies sharing a crib, they were back to back and curled into themselves with hospital blankets for bedding. He roused them and they jumped up, their hair at weird angles and marks on their faces from sleeping on their arms. It would have almost been comical if it hadn't been so touching. The sight of those two knuckleheads camping outside her hospital room hit her right in the feels, to steal a term from Izzy.

They came in with their heads down, and to her amazement, Emilio's chin started to quiver and Henrico's eyes were tearing up. She said in Portuguese, because she was tired and it was easier, "I'm okay. You got me help in time. Thank you, brothers." Then they were on either side of her bed as Quinn and Hans pulled up chairs for them before giving the three their privacy.

Emilio was so awkward, it was painful. Like he wasn't sure how to be gentle. He touched her arm lightly, and the tears were dripping off his nose. They'd all reverted to Portuguese, because it was their first language, and most natural under stress.

"I thought you were going to die," he said weakly. Then he put his head down on her and cried. She put a hand in his hair, because what could she say to that? She thought she was dead meat too? She heard her dead mother's voice? Hardly words of comfort.

She said, "I'm not going to be able to work out for a little while, so you're going to have to do my share of the burpees." The tremor was slight at first, his head still down. Then she heard his suppressed laughter. Soon they were all three laughing. The kind of laughing that happened when you were letting fear and sorrow leak out of your body. The stress response that had you in hysterics when you realized the world was not, in fact, ending. Then Emilio said with a smirk. "English, or I didn't hear it."

CHAPTER 23

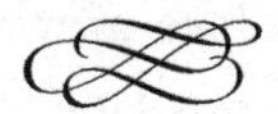

Hope smiles from the threshold of the year to come, whispering, 'It will be happier.' —
Alfred Lord Tennyson— The Outlawry, Act I Scene II

Caitlyn and Patrick talked for hours as they lay tangled in bed. Patrick had checked his messages in the library and they'd laughed until their sides split at the photos Josh and Seany and Caitlyn's sisters had taken of all of them and the baby. Then he showed her a little slide show, that he hadn't shown anyone. The pictures that only he and a NICU nurse knew about. Pictures of the baby from that first night he'd found him. Pictures of an incredibly small newborn that responded to Patrick's nurturing like no other. Pictures of him feeding him, dressing him, rocking him to sleep in the parent room. She cried as he scrolled through them. "He's so small. Oh God, to think how he came into the world. The poor lamb. Oh, Patrick. He's so beautiful. Look how content he looks when you're holding him."

Patrick blushed. Red head genes ensured you wore your feelings out in the open. "Yes, well. I'll have to admit, I'm his favorite. He always eats for me. He got used to the others, though. Charlie's good with a baby. They all are. Sean and Josh help out with him any time they can, and you know Tadgh. He loves kids."

She sharpened up at that, pointing a finger at him. "They are not naming our son Carlos after some movie hooker's child!" He'd made the mistake of telling her about the nickname the boys had given the baby.

Patrick laughed, then his face grew more serious. He shrugged. "He has no name. It was Baby Boy Doe in the hospital. Kasey's mother didn't have the heart to do it. Said if she couldn't take him, she had no right to name him. If you were in this with me, I wanted to name him together. Should we name him after her, do you think? Casey with a C?"

Caitlyn looked hard at him. "Is that really what you want?"

He didn't look at her. "No. Not really. The whole thing was so sad and violent. I just want him to have a fresh start with us."

"Good, because I haven't met him yet, but I can't think of any name I'd rather call him than Patrick. Patrick Ronan O'Brien has a good ring to it." Patrick's smile was so wide, she thought his face would crack.

He puffed his chest up. "Patrick and Estela O'Brien. It's perfect." Her face shifted, and he saw that fear again. "This has to work. We've suffered too much on the path to these two children. It has to work. We won't let any nuns or judges get in our way."

"I'd like to name the one we lost, as well. I have some ideas, but we can talk about it later. I want to put him to rest with a name that we gave him." Patrick nodded, afraid to speak for fear of breaking down. He thought about that little urn in the sitting room.

She gave him a moment, knowing he needed it. She did too. And then she said, "As for Estela, let's not tell anyone until we know for sure. I don't want anyone to be hurt, especially my parents or Liam. I think we should wait until she's on Irish soil to tell Liam."

He thought about that. "Aye, it'll be a hell of wedding gift."

Her eyes widened. "Holy hell, I completely forgot about the wedding!"

"We can't go, love. Even if I had the time. We can't take Patrick Jr. on an international flight, a month out of the NICU. I wouldn't feel safe. You know how those viruses and infections spread on airplanes."

"You're right. God, you're so right. And that might not fall in line with getting Estela home. We have to skip the wedding. I'm sorry, love."

"Yes, well I am too. He'll understand, though. He's worried for you, love. And for me, I suppose." He shrugged.

"I'm sorry I left you alone when you were grieving." Her voice was frail and her eyes were guilty.

"I'm not. I wouldn't change one thing in the aftermath. If I hadn't been in that alley..." He shook himself. "I can't even think about it. I was there with Branna and the lads right when I was needed. And if you'd never come to Brazil, you wouldn't have found Estela. We had to cross these bridges alone before we came together."

She thought about that. About the wishing bridge that led to the spring. "When I crossed that bridge to the spring, I was supposed to wish my heart's desire."

"And what did you wish?" He put a hand in her hair, getting a good look at her eyes. "What was your heart's desire?"

"I wished for you to be a father. I wished for me to be a mother. I wished for a family." Patrick's heart swelled and broke in equal measure as a tear escaped across the bridge of her nose. "But I got more than that. With Talia's baby, with Estela, I got more than I wished for. I found out that there was more than one way to be a mother. That I didn't have to carry the child in my body to give it my love."

"Yes, well maybe this will be the start of it. Two children, and then maybe more. Either by trying Seamus's treatment or adopting another child who needs us. We'll make room in our family, no matter how they come to us."

Caitlyn wiped her tears and sat up quickly. "All this baby talk is starting to give me issues. I need to pump." Patrick noticed the small wet spot on one side of her shirt. "I could have bound myself and taken medication to dry it up, but I didn't want to let go of it."

"Let go of what?"

She said sadly, "Of feeling like my body was finally working the way I wanted it to. It made me feel like a mother. That probably seems foolish. I just feel like it happened for a reason. If ye'd been there, Patrick." She shook her head. "If ye'd seen that poor, dying woman find the strength to live and deliver her child into the world in the middle of a forest fire. I'll never forget it. Not one detail. And I felt like that spring was flowing through me. Then this happened." She motioned down to the wet spot on her chest. "Right as that baby was crowning this happened. I just didn't want to stop it." She took the small, manual pump out of her bag, feeling foolish and superstitious and a little pathetic.

Then he was standing next to her. "You were meant for this." He cupped her breast so tenderly and ran a thumb over her nipple. "You can feed our son." He paused, wanting to say it right. To give her the choice. "I mean, would you feed him?"

She kissed him then, pulling his head down. "Of course I'll feed him. I'll be his mammy, won't I?"

Patrick took the pump out of her hand. Setting it aside, he slipped her shirt over her head. He drew her back under the mosquito net of their little bed. "You won't need that," he said huskily. Then he put his hand between her shoulder blades and brought her to his mouth.

She gasped and ran her fingers through his hair. "Harder." And he was more than happy to oblige.

* * *

MORNING CAME QUICKLY, and Caitlyn's heart swelled at the turnout. They went to the main river bank, and the sight of the Amazon still took her aback. This morning there were several military style boats that carried lumber and other building supplies. Along with a gas generator in case they needed power. There were familiar faces. Men who'd helped fight the fire the day it had all happened. Some of the police and firemen that were off duty showed, as well as Raphael's friends from his reserve military unit. Back at the mission, there was a large van full of parishioners from Father Pietro's ranks. Food, cloth for new clothing and linens, mattresses, all donated from people in the city and country wide. As they walked back, Patrick was smiling. "It's good, isn't it? To be a part of something like this. I see why it was so hard for Liam to leave. I'm sorry you have to cut your trip short by a couple of weeks."

"We'll be back someday. We will bring her back so that she knows where she came from. I don't want to change her. I don't want her to forget about her culture or these first four years. Her birthday is coming up. I think Sister Maria said it's in a couple of months."

"Well, hopefully she'll be celebrating with her little brother and all of her cousins by then."

"Do you really think so? I'm scared. I'm so afraid some bureaucrat will interfere on one side of the Atlantic or the other."

"I know it. I'm as sure as a man can be." He put an arm around her, giving her a playful squeeze. "We head out in an hour. Let's go see our girl and get some breakfast."

They found her in the hospital, laying next to Genoveva. She was sucking her thumb, curled up close to the best sister God could have ever given her. When she saw Patrick and Caitlyn, she smiled around her thumb. Patrick said, "Well, you two look cozy. We thought you'd like to go get some breakfast?" He put his hands out, as if to welcome the little girl. She wiggled out of the bed and climbed into his arms without hesitation. As they left, Caitlyn kissed Genoveva on her eyes. "You know, now. Your da told me that you know."

"Sim, Senhora. He told me. And I got to talk to Izzy. They let me walk to the library last night."

"Well, now. What's next? Do you know?"

She shrugged. "I will go where my father is from. I will go to Ireland. He lives in the city, but he said now that he has a daughter, we can move to the country. He said he'll get a car and a house." Caitlyn smiled. She knew all too well how expensive downtown Dublin was, and the price for owning a car you had to park was prohibitive and often not necessary. "He said no more missions. No more Africa or Brazil or anywhere else. He said I am his mission, now."

"I think that's a perfect plan. And we won't be so far. We're moving as well, but we'll live in a beautiful area. You can come and stay with me any time you like, especially when Liam and Izzy visit."

Genoveva's smile lit up the room. "I'd like that. I'll miss everyone here, but I think I'm ready to move on. I need things that they won't be able to give me in a couple of years. I know that. I'm ready to…"

"Meet your destiny?" Caitlyn said with a grin.

"Yes. *Destino.*" She played with the blanket and didn't meet Caitlyn's eye. "I'm going to miss Estela. She needs a family too. I wish we could take her. I know they wouldn't let us, but I wish we could. I could take care of her. She's going to have a hard time when I leave." The tears were big and quiet.

"Then you must pray for her. Can you do that? Pray for her and us. Because if I have my way, she won't have to do without you." She saw the transformation in the girl's face. Like it was something she'd been hoping for, but was afraid to ask.

"Sim, Senhora O'Brien. I will pray my hardest. I promise."

Patrick walked down the hall of the hospital, having left the room to give Caitlyn and Genoveva some privacy. He thought about Quinn and was so sad for him. To have missed all of those years. As he held this small girl in his arms, he was so grateful that he had most of her childhood ahead of him. She was currently staring hard at him. Specifically his hair. She ran her hands over it, then she'd steal a peek at her own. Hers was darker, but had those same auburn strands woven in that he did. Probably more from the sun than genetics. Still, he couldn't help but think back to the story Caitlyn had told him. About her wearing a yellow scarf on her head so that she could be blonde like Caitlyn. Then Caitlyn had told her that her husband's hair was darker, with bits of copper just like hers. That had, for some reason, struck a chord with the girl, and she'd taken the scarf off.

He thought about her life here. She had the sisters and Genoveva. They'd filled in with the mothering until she'd found Caitlyn. But she'd never had a father. The men of the mission came and went. She'd been particularly close to Liam. The thought of Liam's face the first time he saw her again was enough to make him weep. She was a gift that he was going to give to the entire family. "Well, would you look at that. Our hair is almost the same color. Aren't we lucky!" She had straight white teeth, still baby teeth that had not begun to fall out yet.

"Sim, Senhor. We have the same. Senhora O'Brien said so. She say she love your hair." Then she gave her own locks a sassy flick over her shoulder. *Good Lord, this kid is something else.*

"I wonder what else is alike? I like to eat. Lots. Do you like to eat?" She nodded enthusiastically. "What do you like? Squash?" She curled up her nose. "No? Well, I like ice cream, but I bet you don't. You probably hate ice cream."

She shook her head. "NO! I like the ice cream. It's my favorite. Gabriela makes the good ice cream with the cacau beans and the caju nuts and berries. I will tell her to make you some of this ice cream and you'll see. We are the same." She put her arms around his neck and he held her closer, unaware that Caitlyn had been following them. Estela was completely focused on this big man who was carrying her, and Caitlyn couldn't stop the flow of tears as they made their way to the cantina.

Once they were all settled, he said to Caitlyn, "I don't see why she has to eat over there. Can't she just come sit with us?" She smiled, because he was so not going to keep up this charade much longer.

"The other children will feel bad. Once we get word from the diocese in Brazil and from immigration in Ireland, we can feel safe telling her. We can't tell her until then."

His eyes were intense. "I don't want her alone in the garden. That fucking snake almost killed Genoveva and she's as tall as you. And Christ, that story Liam told me about the jaguar. Maybe we should just keep her inside and..." She cut him off.

"This is her home. It's all she's ever known. They keep a good eye on her. The staff and the older children. You can't wrap her in bubble wrap until we bring her home." He gave her a look that said *wanna bet?* "Heavens, love. What are you going to be like when she's a teenager?" The thought seemed to wash over him, sinking in. She pointed at him, "If you say a convent, I'll box your ears."

CHAPTER 24

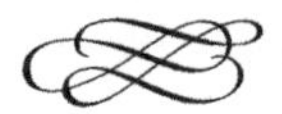

DUBLIN, IRELAND

Tadgh crept in slowly. It was way later than he'd planned on coming home. He hated these late nights, especially now that they were fostering the baby. The Baby. Carlos. Laddie. The kid was going to have an identity crisis at a month old. Patrick needed to get his ass back here and name him before one of those stuck. He smiled at the sight before him as he entered their bedroom. They had a bassinet next to the bed, and a crib in the other room. But every time Charlie tried to put him down, she couldn't do it. Right now he was nestled in the crook of her arm, snuggly monopolizing Tadgh's woman and his bed. Charlie stirred as he gently scooped him up and cradled him in his arms. He looked so peaceful. He was a good sleeper. He liked to be swaddled, unlike Tadgh's nieces and nephews who kicked out of their swaddling clothes with enthusiastic efficiency.

She smiled at him. "That looks good on you. Hot guy with baby. I like it."

He wiggled his brows and took the boy into the nursery where Josh usually slept. He gently laid him in the crib, and when he walked back to their room Charlie was standing in the doorway in a tank top and little pink panties. "Jesus, woman. You look like a vixen." And she did. Her hair was everywhere. Curls for miles. Her face got a little tight, though. He paused. "Are you okay? Did you start your period or something?" The only thing that usually got in the way of a good tussle between the sheets. Charlie was always ready.

Her words came out like a burst of gunfire. "I went off the pill." Then she gave a tense smile. "A week ago. I should have talked to you first but I don't know," She was flapping her arms now. "I just did it. I think that baby's making me shoot out an egg or something!" She didn't get any further, because all two hundred and eight pounds of Irishman tackled her, and took her down on the bed. He pulled her clothes off like a barbarian, unzipped his fly and was working into her before she even got another word out. She was so ready. No foreplay needed.

He was big and hard, and inside her with one slick glide. She moaned and he growled. "You feel fucking fantastic." He started to pump his hips, and the thought that they had nothing between them was jacking her up. No pills, no condoms, just him and her. A few deep strokes and she was going over the edge.

Tadgh could barely catch his breath. The smell of sweat and sex filled the room. His grin was uniquely male. As soon as she'd rung that bell, he'd been all over her. He'd had her four times over several hours. She was asleep now, flushed with his loving. She'd been wild as well. Demanding. He'd taken her hard and fast that first time. Then flipped her over with her ass in the air, and had her again, slow and deep. He was really going to love trying to get her pregnant. Yes, indeed.

* * *

Now a soft kiss - Aye, by that kiss, I vow an endless bliss—John Keats

Josh came awake as the sun peeked through the window blinds. "Adonis arises." He jumped and then heard a second voice. "Mary, don't tease him. You shouldn't be ogling him while he's half asleep." But as Josh met Madeline's eyes, the grin told him that she wasn't all that disapproving.

"Morning ladies." His voice was rough. They'd been up late, watching the Hangover and then Deadpool for some comic relief. The girls had taken the love seat while he and Seany had taken the easy chairs. Totally innocent evening, but the sight of Madeline headed off to bed in an NUI Galway shirt and flannel pajama bottoms had rolled on replay through his mind all night. She was a year older than him and totally out of his league. Mary was a year younger, and too cheeky for her own good.

Madeline handed him a cup of coffee, and her eyes flicked to his bare chest. "Thank you. I'll just grab the bathroom before Fabio gets in there, and then I'll make some breakfast."

"No need. We've decided to take you two lucky men out for breakfast." Madeline said smoothly. "Seany's got the morning off. Balfe's for blueberry pancakes." Seany poked his head out, "Did I hear Balfe's? Count me in." Then he darted toward the bathroom in his boxers before Josh could get to it.

Josh laughed, "Dammit, man. Don't take one of your Fabio showers. Five minutes or I'm coming in!"

"Ye can wash my feckin' back, darlin!" Seany yelled through the door, causing fresh giggles from the girls.

Mary asked, "Why do you call him Fabio? Isn't that the model on all of those old romance novels?"

Josh cocked a brow, "Haven't you seen those high school pictures?"

Madeline was laughing now. "Oh, aye. All that long hair. He was a looker."

Seany yelled from the bathroom. "I can hear you, and I'm still a looker."

She gave Josh a knowing look, "Modest, too. Isn't he?"

"You two went to school together, he said." Josh was relieved to also hear that there had never been anything romantic.

"Yes, from the time we were little. We didn't get the fancy private school like Caitlyn," she said with a grin. "He's only a few months older than me. He had all the girls swooning in their knickers, with those shit-kicker boots his oldest brother gave him and a guitar strapped on his back. He was something to see."

"Except for Madeline, here. She likes the quiet, shy types." Madeline gave her sister a look and she shrugged. "What? You do." Then she turned her attention to Josh. "How old are you? What are you studying? Yer as tight lipped as a nun."

He laughed as Madeline shook her head at her sister's bluntness. "I haven't settled on a major yet. Just community college at this point. It's all I can afford. My parents weren't the college fund type of parents." Then he looked like he wished he could retract the comment. "Anyway, I've been taking core classes and some oceanography and maritime studies classes. Seany and I were thinking of moving out of the city. I'm looking into a lighthouse keeper course."

Mary laughed, "Where on earth is that class being taught? I thought all the lighthouses were automatic, now." Madeline bristled, embarrassed at her sister's ability to be so uncouth.

"Well, they may be automatic, but I doubt they can repair and maintain themselves, Mary." She looked at Josh. "I think that would be fascinating work. So many young Irishman are getting into business, moving out of the small towns. Even out of the country. No one wants to keep sheep on the islands anymore. There are less and less fisherman to work the waters. Less willing to keep the traditions. Who'll keep those lighthouses going if someone doesn't study it?"

Josh warmed down to his toes. "Yeah, well my experience has been mixed with the local tradesmen. I get called a bloody Yank more than I'd like. It's like, at the pub everyone's good to go, but there's an inner circle with this kind of stuff that is locals only."

Madeline waved a dismissive hand. "Give it time. They'll likely call you a blow-in until you're eighty and covered with grandchildren, but they'll warm up. It's not like the city. You're hard pressed to find an Irishman in Dublin on most days, but the west coast has its own feel. Once they know you're staying for good, they'll let you in."

He shrugged, "I hope so, because I have a feeling by spring, we'll be looking for a place to live on the west coast. Seany has a transfer package in with stations in Donegal County, Ennis, and Galway. Once we sort that out, we'll know where to look for a cheap place to live and I can get a job. I was thinking about one of the ferries. I also wanted to volunteer with the lifeboats."

Mary's eyes widened. "The lifeboats? Wow, you really are goin' local. Are ye a good swimmer, then?"

"Yes, I went to State my senior year. I trained in the lake as well as the pool. Cleveland, that's where I'm from in Ohio, it's on a big lake."

Madeline said, "Well, those are all good places. No offense, but they're all three better suited to you, I think, than Dublin."

"Why do you say that? I came from a big city," he said, his head cocked in question.

"Because you just seem the sort that wouldn't mind a bit of peace and family."

Josh was shocked at how well she'd read him. He just nodded, smiling shyly. He could feel his ears turning red. Seany came out of the bathroom and he ducked out before he dropped to his knees and begged Madeline Nagle to marry him.

After two quick showers and four cups of coffee between them, they headed into the city. There was a short line to get into Balfe's, but for once, Josh was content to wait. He liked talking to the Nagle girls. Mary was lively and funny. She was smart, too. Loved to read and listen to music. She'd started at NUI in the fall as a freshman. Madeline was doubling her studies with humanities and Celtic studies. Their personalities were different, but all in all they were lovely, well spoken girls from a good family. You couldn't swing a cat in any direction in Doolin without hitting an O'Brien or a Nagle. He wondered what it would have been like to grow up like that. To grow up safe and loved, without violence. He suddenly wanted to track down Bernadette and Ronan Nagle and shake their hands. These girls were fabulous, because they'd been safe to flourish and blossom into confident adults. Looking at Madeline made his heart hurt, because she was too good for the likes of him.

"I'm going to go in and see if I can sweet talk that hostess for a quicker seat." Seany wiggled his eyebrows and the girls laughed.

"Cocky bastard," Josh said, smiling. Then he saw Madeline's laugh catch in her throat as her face changed. Dread. Plain as day on her face.

"Um, let's go in. I'm getting a chill." She went for the door when someone called her name. The hair stood up on Josh's arm, because the voice was slithery. Predatory. He turned and put himself between the girls.

"Madeline. Fancy meeting you here. I've been callin' you for weeks." He gave Josh a once over. The young man was handsome, in a skinny, emo sort of way. "Found yourself a new distraction, did you?"

Josh said, "I don't think we've met. Josh O'Brien. And you are?" The asshole ignored him. His eyes bore into Madeline's.

"A fecking Yank? Really, Mad? I thought you had better taste."

She bristled and stepped in front of Josh. "I don't owe you any explanation. Go away. Don't call me, don't even look at me. Ye hear? We had one date, and you were a complete rotter. Goodbye, Kerick."

Mary came beside her. "Is this that piece of shite that tried to…" That's when it happened. He snatched Madeline's arm, and before he could shit or go sailing, Josh had the squirmy little worm against the wall.

"What the fuck!" Seany came out the door of the restaurant in a flash.

"I got this, Seany," Josh growled. Then he leaned in. "You don't touch a woman like that. Any woman. And you don't even look at these two. Consider yourself warned. I've got so many Garda in my family, I can make every bruise look like an accident. Do you copy, asshole?"

He let the guy go and pointed down the road. "Start walking. If you call her again, I'll be at your front door." The man considered this and turned, then he had to pop shit one more time.

"Did you shag her on the first date like I did? She likes to take it in the…" He didn't finish the foul comment, because Josh clocked the mother fucker right in the jaw.

"Nice!" The people in line had been watching it go down, and a couple of girls were clapping.

"Josh! Enough! Just let him go." Madeline pulled Josh away. He was pulled out of the rage-a-thon that was stirring in his blood. Her voice just snapped him back to reality.

"Go, you piece of shit, or I'll call the guards. Every person here will say you started it. Right?" He turned to the onlookers.

One of the girls said, "Absofeckinlutely."

Another guy said, "Saw the whole thing. He assaulted the girl and took a swing at you." Seany said nothing, poised at the ready in case the fighting started up again. Then the man got off the ground, wiped his chin, looked at Madeline.

Josh took a step forward and said, "See, now you're already not following my orders. You need another reminder? Because I am itching to give you some more." The man spit blood to the side and turned, walking away.

Josh's attention immediately shifted to Madeline and he stopped short. Tears were in her eyes, but her chin was up. She was a fighter. "Jesus, Madeline. I'm sorry. That got out of hand. I'm sorry if I scared you." He was such a dick. Not only was that creep bothering her, but Josh had drawn blood on the guy in a public place.

She wiped her tears. "He deserved it. Thank you. And I didn't sleep with him."

"That doesn't matter."

"It does to me. I don't want you thinking I'd shed my knickers for the likes of him. He was in one of my classes. He took me to dinner and then tried to get too familiar with me when we got to my friend's dorm. I stayed in the city so I could go on a date with him, which was a huge mistake. One date, and he was a wanker, and I never went out with him again. He's been bothering me ever since. I have a feeling that will stop now." She growled. "He acts like we were serious, like I'm his girlfriend. Like he's set his sights on me and I don't get a say!"

"You are the only one who gets a say. Always." Josh's words gave her strength. She nodded, afraid to speak. Afraid she'd break down.

Seany said, "If it doesn't stop, you need to let us know. Tadgh has

Garda friends all over this island. And there's Da right down the road from you. We'll handle it if he bothers you again." He put an arm around Madeline and gave her shoulders a brotherly squeeze. "Now, I've charmed us a table. She likes firemen." He winked, lightening the mood. "I'm starved. Let's buy this hero a stack of pancakes."

Josh was turning red, embarrassed and flushed with adrenalin and feeling all sorts of things he shouldn't be feeling. As he walked forward, Madeline stopped him with a hand on his chest. Then she flung her arms around him. "Thank you. I'm sorry for it, but thank you." Before she drew away, she gave him the softest, sweetest kiss on his face. Just an inch or so from the corner of his mouth. Nothing overtly sexual in the act, but it was utter bliss. Her hair brushed his face, and she smelled like heaven.

His blush deepened. He walked by the other women standing in line. "I'd like a bodyguard like that one. Can ye mail order them from America, ye think?" One of them mumbled to her friend, and he couldn't help but notice his companions were smiling.

* * *

Manaus, Brazil

Patrick looked around at the small, hidden village between two rivers. People were buzzing around working, cleaning, salvaging what could be saved. He marveled at it all. He'd never felt such a quintessential sense of community. He looked over at Caitlyn and his heart overflowed with pride. She had all of the children lined up with buckets of soapy, warm water, washing out clothing that had been smoke damaged, but otherwise useful. She tended to the rinsing and another older woman helped hang them on a line to dry. This is the tribal mother he'd been told about. The work party had previously concentrated on clean up and arranging temporary housing tents until they could rebuild.

There was a mobile water purifier as well as rations from the government. Bags of rice, beans, and dried fruit to replace some of their own fresh fruit trees that had been lost. A reforestation group had started replanting around the perimeters and along the path of the fire. The government, of course, had fined the deforestation group into bankruptcy. His mission today was to start framing houses. The group worked with impressive efficiency. The posts had been dug and the pilings put in place. Now they went about making homes out of the lumber that they'd brought down river. Patrick watched Hans and Antonio, the Italian doctor that he'd met this morning, working on the other side of the camp. He wished for the hundredth time that his family was here. His da and Grandda David and his brawny brothers. He wished that everyone he loved had a chance to feel as useful and necessary as he did on this day. His mother would have loved this. His granny would've sat with the old women, sewing by hand and creating simple clothing from the bolts of muslin that had been sent.

These people wasted nothing. Not energy, not time, not food. They had so little after the fire had ripped through the village, yet they shared bowls of rice cooked into a porridge with dried berries. Some sort of pork broth with beans. It was surprisingly good, or maybe he was just hungry. The sun was low in the sky, and for the third time, he was applying sunscreen and bug repellent. Mixed with old ashes, dirt, and sweat, he knew he must look a sight. That's when he felt a hand on his shoulder.

He turned to see the old woman, holding Caitlyn's hand. Raphael was next to them, obviously there to interpret. "She says they've fixed the bridge. She wants to show you their spring. She wants to show you where the miracles happened."

Caitlyn said out of the corner of her mouth, "She makes your mother look like a pushover. Best just do as she says." She smiled at the old woman who had her chin up, inviting no argument.

They walked in silence until the air became balmier and Patrick heard the rush of water. The goosebumps were all over his arms, despite the heat. Caitlyn said, "This is it. This is the wishing bridge. I'm not sure that's their name for it, but it's what I call it. It leads to the spring where everything happened."

Patrick noticed the roping was new, reinforced after the fire had damaged it. There were fresh planks at the start, as if those had been replaced. They began walking over the bridge and he gripped the ropes, looking down at the rushing river. Luckily, the rain had been minimal today. He went behind Caitlyn, watching her cross with the old woman. Once they reached the other side, the old woman stopped. She said something he didn't understand. Caitlyn shrugged. "It's a dialect. I have no idea."

The old woman swung her hand to the path, motioning for them to go ahead. Then she put her palms together, entwining her fingers. Making the two parts into one. Caitlyn's eyes bulged. Patrick cleared his throat. "Did she just tell us to," he said, letting the end of that sentence hang.

"I think that's exactly what she's saying." Caitlyn suppressed the urge to giggle. She didn't want to offend the woman, but it was a little awkward being ordered by an old woman to go mate in the water. Patrick was much more obliging. His grin was like the Chesire cat.

"Well, we don't want to be rude. Come, love. Duty calls." The look he gave her almost started another forest fire. He walked by the old woman and gave her a wink.

The mist was like a presence in the air, settling on his skin as he approached a small, beautiful waterfall that seemed to come from nowhere. Out of a rock face, as if from the belly of the earth. The forest around it was lush and impossibly green, untouched by the fire. He heard faint noises, beyond the din of the flowing water. Monkeys and insects, nature at its most primitive, barely touched by the human race.

The minerals were sharp in the air. His arousal stirred as he looked at the pool of water, graduating from a bank of moss-covered stones, into the cloudy depths. He watched her. She took her time, peeling her clothing off slowly and deliberately until she was bared to him. Then she turned and walked into the water. He was right on board, peeling off his filthy clothes with more haste and less control. Coming in behind her as she glided in the water, he cupped her body to his, and she sighed, leaning back against him. He took her to a rock surface, close to the falls. "Spread your hands out lass, brace yourself." His demand was hoarse and needy. She knew just how to get to him.

The buoyancy aiding her as her ass floated up to his hips and her back arched. He impaled her, pulling her hips to him over and over as she was bent over the rock, moaning as he took her with deep, fast thrusts. He came so hard, he saw stars, and she was right with him, until all they could do was float, languid and boneless beneath the falls.

CHAPTER 25

The abbess watched with tenderness as Patrick O'Brien pushed Estela on the swing. She felt the presence behind her. "He's good with her, isn't he?" She turned to the knowing, intelligent eyes of Doc Mary. "He's a good lad. The best God ever made. I hope you've got some pull, Reverend Mother."

Caitlyn came in behind them both. "Have you any news, Reverend Mother?" Her eyes were hopeful and wary. Afraid to hear anything but the best possible news. Luckily, the abbess was in the position to grant that very thing. "Aye, I have. I've had the diocese pushing its weight around in Brazil and Ireland to get approval." Caitlyn straightened, her eyes seeking. "Well? What's happening? Do we get to take her?"

"It's going to take about six weeks, but yes. Your uncle has been filing paperwork since yesterday. So, I don't think I'm being premature when I say yes, Caitlyn my dear. It appears you've got your wish. You'll have a daughter, if you're both sure this is..."

"We're sure! We are absolutely sure. I have to leave, you know that, but one of us can come back. We'll find a way to come back in six weeks."

"As it turns out, you won't have to. Sister Agatha will take her orders at the Dublin Abbey next month. She will travel with the child, if you can trust her to do that. She will act as her escort, then go her own way."

"A novice no more." Mary smiled as she said it.

"Yes, she's made her decision, and the church will be better for it."

Caitlyn barely heard the rest, she just watched Patrick as he played with...their daughter. She put her hand over her mouth. She croaked. "Can we tell her? Is it safe to tell her?"

"Yes, you can tell her. And later, we'll sit down and explain about why she has to travel without you. We'll tell her about the baby brother she's got waiting for her at home," she said with a smile. "For right now, just go be with your family, dear girl. Go to your husband and child." Her voice caught, and Caitlyn knew she was thinking of her own family. She took the abbess's frail, thin hands in hers and said. "When we're all together, we'll put our son to rest. The one I lost. We'll spread his ashes and give him a name. If it's okay, we've decided to call him Peter."

The abbess's clear blue eyes teared, her lined face and aging lids showing her love and her pain. "I think that's a beautiful name." She straightened her spine, pulling in her emotions as she always did. "Now go on, before you burst with the excitement of it."

Caitlyn ran to the children's play yard and Patrick met her eyes. He knew by the look on her face. She didn't have to say it. He laughed. Then he scooped her up and swung her around. Estela squealed with delight. "Me too!" she said as she lifted her arms, her face bright with joy.

He picked her up and twirled her around, much to her delight. Then Caitlyn leaned in. "Estela, love. Could ye come to the garden with us? Can you sit a while and let us tell you something?"

They went to the abbess's small, walled garden on the back side of the abbey. "This is where the médicos got married." Not a legal wedding. More a hand fasting or engagement blessing, but it had been very real to everyone in attendance.

"Is it, now? Well, then it's a nice spot for good news," Patrick said.

They sat on the bench and Caitlyn put Estela on her lap. "Estela, do you like spending time with me and Mr. O'Brien?"

She nodded without hesitation. "Yes, I love that you come to be my teacher. I like him because we are the same. We have the same hair and he likes ice cream and he makes me funny."

"That's good, baby. That's so good. You know how Genoveva has found her father. That she's to go back to Ireland?"

Her face darkened. "I don't want her to go. I want her to stay with me. She's my *irmã*."

Caitlyn looked at Patrick for courage and he nodded. "What would you think about going to Ireland too, to live with us?"

She didn't understand. Caitlyn could tell. "Sweetie, we would like you to be our..." she searched for the word. "Our *filha*. Our baby girl. We want to be your mam and da."

The girls brows raised, "You mean my *mamãe?*"

Caitlyn smiled. "Yes, darlin'. We want you to come home with us, to be a family. Forever. *Para Sempre.*"

Caitlyn knew the moment it sunk in. Estela's smile was as bright as the sun. She looked at Patrick. "Papai?" He opened his arms and she leapt out of Caitlyn's lap and into his. And their laughter traveled over the garden wall, where Doc Mary and the abbess stood weeping together.

* * *

DINNER THAT NIGHT was a private affair. Party for five set up in Genoveva's hospital room. Quinn and Patrick were glowing with happiness, and they spent the evening telling their girls about Ireland. Patrick kept the sad details of Patrick Jr.'s parentage to himself, just having Genoveva help him explain to the small child about the baby brother she'd have waiting for her. She wrinkled her forehead. Genoveva asked, "What's the matter?"

She said in Portuguese, "If they get a baby, maybe they'll forget to come back for me." Genoveva's face softened as she took the little girl in her arms. She explained the child's concern. Quinn had understood her, but Patrick and Caitlyn had not.

Patrick took her small hand, "If I have to swim the whole way, I'll come back for you." He grabbed the globe they'd been using to show her where Ireland was. "See. I'll jump in the water just there off the cliffs by my home, and I'll swim all the way to here. Then I'll swim right up the river to your door."

Estela put her hand over her mouth and giggled. "You can't swim, the fish will eat you!"

Caitlyn exchanged glances with Quinn and his smile was so warm. He was holding Genoveva's other hand. Life was so very good.

CHAPTER 26

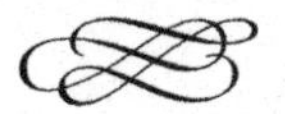

DUBLIN, IRELAND

Caitlyn couldn't even figure out what day it was. She was completely exhausted. The plane ride in economy had been like sleeping in a sardine can. Normally she liked Patrick's wide shoulders, but on an airplane, not so much. She sat in the backseat of the car now, listening to Seany talk excitedly about how well the baby was doing. Her heart was in her throat. It had almost killed her to get on the plane and leave Estela.

He parked on the curb, letting them out with their bags. Tadgh ran down to meet them, hugging Caitlyn so warmly that she started to tear up. They carried the bags into the apartment. Tadgh fidgeted nervously. "I know you're knackered. We'll understand it you want some rest first."

She smiled, realizing what it was costing Patrick not to take the steps two at a time to Charlie and Tadgh's place. "I'll do. Take me to him. I'm ready to meet our lad."

The apartment was dim, but the bedroom lights were on. Caitlyn heard the child before she saw him. He was crying. Tadgh shrugged. "He likely needs a new nappy. He's not overly fond of having a wet bum."

Patrick led Caitlyn back to the makeshift nursery, hearing Charlie cooing to the baby. "Yes, you are a stinky boy. That was impressive. Yes it was." Then she saw them just as she turned with the baby in her arms. Her eyes met Caitlyn's.

"Well, well. Guess who's here, little man." She walked to them and Caitlyn looked at the swaddled figure who was still fussing a bit. Patrick took him instantly, "Hello there. Did you miss me?" He was so natural as he curled the child into him. The baby stilled and seemed to actually look at Patrick.

Caitlyn couldn't remember ever seeing anything so beautiful. She came to them, rubbing a hand over his fair, downy head. "Oh, my. You are a dear aren't you?" Patrick's eyes held a bit of relief, like it had been an audition or something. But how could she look at this sweet, tiny little baby and not feel love in her heart. He had the cloudy blue eyes of a newborn, pale skin that was pink and healthy. He was small, to be sure, but he was perfect. She moved on instinct, taking him from her husband. She cooed at him as she took his weight in her arms. "Hello there, wee Patrick. I've been waiting to meet you."

She heard a sob, and she looked up to see Charlie crying. Not tears of sadness, but of joy. "I told him you'd love him. I told him every night. I knew it. How could you not? He's pretty perfect." She huddled with Caitlyn and kissed her on the cheek.

Caitlyn was crying now, too. She thought it was impossible that she had any more tears to spare, after the last few months that she'd had. "What you did for him, and for us, I'll never be able to repay you, Charlie. I'll never forget it." She walked over to the sofa and sat, everyone watching. She realized that the wet spot was spreading on both sides of her shirt. Charlie knelt down. "Caitlyn, is that what I think it is?"

She just nodded. "It's a very long story, and in time I'll tell you it all. Right now, I just want to look at this little lad." She kissed his soft head, rubbing her lips along it as she smelled him. He started to root on her chest and she hissed, the wet spot getting bigger.

"I think he knows. He's got a nose for the good stuff," Patrick said proudly.

"I have a bottle for him, unless..." Charlie's words drifted off.

"Best wait until we know for sure. I'd hate to let him nurse and then have something go wrong. To have him feel the loss of it, and me as well. I'll pump for now and we can get to know each other." It was difficult. The urge to nurse him was overwhelming, but she felt like they had time. Charlie handed her a bottle after warming it, and he drank greedily. It was a good sign.

"We've got a visit with the social worker in the morning. We could try letting him sleep upstairs and then bring him down early, before they get here."

Caitlyn shook her head. "No. We need to follow the rules. You've still got custody of him. I don't want to give them any reason to distrust us. And besides, I think it would be a bit much for him. We can do it gradually. I'd like to meet the social worker, if you think that's okay."

"Absolutely. She's anxious to meet you too. The court date is in two days. She wants this to work out as much as we do. I promise you, she's a good lady. She's on our side."

Tadgh interrupted. "I spoke with Kasey's mam, the lad's grandmother. She's got someone to care for her husband for the day. She wants to meet you at the courthouse an hour before the hearing. She's going to talk to the judge and ask that you and Patrick be able to adopt him outright. She wants to know that he has a stable home. One that's forever. She wants to keep the whole matter private and out of the papers."

Patrick sighed his relief. "We've got this in the bag. They'd be crazy not to let us have him." He tried to take the sleeping baby, who protested and curled into Caitlyn's breast. "I see how it is. I've been thrown over for the hot blonde with the big boobs."

Caitlyn smirked. "Is that right? Are ye going to be a mammies boy? Well, now. Wait until you meet your sister." Charlie and Tadgh froze, brows raised. "We've got a lot to tell you, I see." She looked at Patrick and said, "Should I start from the beginning or just give them CliffNotes?"

Charlie sat on the floor at her feet, eagerly awaiting the tale. "CliffNotes, my ass. Don't you dare leave one single detail out."

They talked for hours, eventually moving into the spare room where the baby cot was and Josh's bed. The two women reclined on their sides, the baby between them. Charlie played with his little feet. "I love that you named him Patrick."

"Aye, well Carlos was right out. So, I had to name him something." They giggled and the baby wiggled his small, frail legs. Caitlyn kissed his head. "I can't believe someone would do such a thing. I can't even conceive of it." Her eyes misted.

"I don't even want to tell you how often it happens. Even with the safe haven laws in America, it still happens there too. But he's okay now. He called out, and Patrick heard him. This was meant to be, Caitlyn. The court date is just a formality." Caitlyn sniffed and nodded, smiling down at the wee little man that had already stolen her heart. "So tell me about her. About Estela. I've heard some from Liam, but I want to hear it all."

Caitlyn's face brightened. "She's gorgeous altogether, and so smart. She's a happy child. Truly, no Dickens orphan tales there. It's a beautiful, magical place. The sisters have made it so. Like a little sanctuary outside of a big city. St. Clare's is like another world."

"I think I'd like to see it someday. But after the jaguar and snake stories and the huge spiders, I think...nah. I'll just watch the video." Caitlyn laughed at that.

"Oh, I know. Patrick was ready to bubble wrap the child and keep her indoors. It has all of those things, but it's got good parts as well. A wild, lush beauty that you can only read about in books. The rainforest has a rhythm to it, like nothing I've experienced. The cycles of the rain, the ebb and flow of the rivers, the bounty that grows in every acre. I hope we can go back someday, when the children are older. I don't want her to forget."

"And what about more children? Have you decided what you're going to do about that? If that's too personal, then just tell me to shut up."

"No, not at all." She looked down at the baby and smiled. "I have two beautiful children that we'll make a home with. That can be enough for now. Yes, I'd like to have the chance to experience a pregnancy that didn't break my heart. I'd like to have another child. But right now, my health is more important. I have a husband and two children that need me. I'm not in a hurry." She watched Charlie relax a bit. "And what about you?"

"I went off the pill," she said with a sideways grin. Caitlyn squealed and it startled the baby.

"Sorry, darlin. Mammy's got a big mouth. Best get used to it." She curled him closer and he settled. "I think that's wonderful, Charlie. Truly wonderful. You'll be a really good mother. And Tadgh has always had a special way with the little ones." She gave her a devilish look, "And he seems like the sort who'll have way too much fun in the making of them."

Charlie laughed, "You have no idea. I get tackled and mounted at every free moment. He's a man on a mission."

"Are ye tellin' all my secrets, woman?" Charlie's face said, *busted.* "Ye should be ashamed, talking like that in front of the lad."

"Yes, well he'll be an O'Brien soon. I'm not sure if that libido is nature or nurture, but he'll likely be trouble. Look at Josh. It rubs off!"

"Well, that's Seany's doing. They're young. As for this lad, he'll have plenty of cousins to get him in trouble. Halley on the other hand, will be beside herself at the prospect of another girl. They're a rare commodity in this family, and Estela will likely be spoiled rotten."

"It's okay. She deserves it. She's going to wrap her uncles around her little finger."

He smiled at that. "I can't wait. I really can't wait to meet her. Aunt Sorcha's going to pass out from the excitement."

Charlie said, "It's a secret. They aren't telling anyone until after the wedding. Nolan and we are the only ones who know. They're afraid someone will slip at the wedding and tell Liam."

"A wedding gift. We just want to wait until it's done. I don't want to jinx it," Caitlyn said nervously. "I want my happy ending."

* * *

Manaus, Brazil

Hans thumped Antonio with a man hug as he dismounted from his Land Rover. "Thanks for coming, brother. I just felt like you should be here. You've got a lot of history with these kids."

"I appreciate it. I wish I could come more often, honestly. I'm glad to hear that you and your lovely wife will be staying on with us. I'm sure the abbess is overjoyed."

"Well, I hope so. She and Mary have gotten pretty tight. I agreed to help out in the school a couple of hours a day, with the older kids, until they get someone new to take Caitlyn's place."

Antonio shook his head. "I hope those O'Brien men realize their good fortune. Beautiful, loyal, smart women from what I've seen."

Hans smiled at that. "Well, considering my daughter is one of those women, I'd have to agree. I love my son-in-law, or I couldn't have parted with her otherwise. They are the best people I've ever met. We'll have to bait the hook and get a couple more of them this way." Antonio laughed. "But, that's not why I called you. We've got some news to deliver to the kids tonight. We'll split them up into two age groups and handle the older kids separately."

"Is this regarding Estela leaving? I can't believe it. She was born here. I can't tell you how many times I wished I had a wife just so I could take that little girl home."

"Yes, well she is in excellent hands. I'm sure you know that. But that's only part of it. The other part involves Genoveva."

Antonio's face flared with panic. "I thought she was okay? They told me she was recovering."

"It's got nothing to do with that. It's about her father." Antonio's brows shot up. "Yep, they found him."

"So, is he a good man. Is he coming here?"

Hans looked around to make sure no one was listening. "He's already here. He's been here."

Antonio searched his mind, thinking. Then he struck on a thought. "Jesus. I can't believe I didn't see the resemblance. It's Quinn." He said something abrupt in Italian, then barked out a laugh. "All those swabs the lab processed. That was some sort of way to get her DNA? I'm assuming this wouldn't have gone as far as it has otherwise. They've confirmed the DNA." He was shaking his head. "I've only had limited days with him, but he seems to be a good man. He didn't know about the girl, I take it?"

"No, he didn't. He got on a plane within a week. He didn't hesitate. It's been a journey, no doubt. It's a betrayal I can't imagine. He missed fifteen years. But she knows now. And we don't have to worry about her aging out. This is a happy ending if I ever saw one."

Antonio's smile was sad. "It is, but I will miss her. She's a true heart. I've watched her blossom this last year. I'm so proud of her. This place will miss her." Then something occurred to him. "She'll be near Estela!"

"Yes. She won't be more than a two hour drive from her, depending on where Quinn buys a house. It's the best possible outcome, considering how close they are."

"So what is the concern today?"

Hans sighed. "Honestly, it may be nothing. It's just, those two boys are at a tough age. I just think they need some extra support when this news comes out. Sometimes they don't need to be coddled by the womenfolk. Sometimes they need some strong men around to help them work through this. Despite their erratic behavior, I think they genuinely adore that girl. They show it in different ways, but they've both noticed the blossoming too, if you catch my meaning. I just think we need to rally around them. We've got them on board for military life vs. those deathtrap mines. I just decided I couldn't leave them. Not until they age out and I know they're settled and safe. They need someone to step up and be a father figure. I'm in the position to do that, and Mary is needed here."

Antonio's eyes were intense. "You're a good man, Hans. I wish I would have had that kind of support at their age. I saw my father every day, but we never had that sort of relationship. You can count me in. I'm planning a trip home, but when those boys head off to the basic training, I'll come back. I'll stand with you when they graduate."

"Outstanding. So, just be ready for anything. Teenage boys can swing in several directions when they are hurting. We have a couple of weeks to get them acclimated to the idea. We just didn't want to spring it on them. It wouldn't be fair. I'm glad you're here. They respect you."

* * *

EMILIO WATCHED and listened with a sinking feeling washing over him. He looked to his brother, and realized that their lives were getting ready to change. It had been a while since a child at the orfanato had been adopted. He wasn't sure why. They were good kids. So many of them sweet, loving kids. Much better than him. Yet no one wanted them. He'd noticed Mrs. O'Brien's attachment to Estela, but the missionaries were usually not allowed to adopt. But that was changing apparently, and he was glad. That little girl was like an angel. He remembered so vividly when Doc Izzy had raced to save her. The day Raphael had killed the jaguar. It had scared them all half to death.

Mrs. O'Brien was a good lady. And Dr. O'Brien and Izzy would be family to Estela now. All was as it should be. But the next blow came when he watched Genoveva stand up with Dr. Maguire. He was confused at first. He thought it was about her snake bite. Afterall, Dr. Quinn was single. They'd never let him have one of the kids. Especially a teenage girl. Then Genoveva started to talk and the reality sank in. He looked hard at the man. Jesus. Those eyes. Those beautiful eyes that he'd grown up seeing everyday.

Henrico was shaking beside him. The big man, Hans, came to them and put an arm on both their shoulders. To his surprise, he didn't feel like lashing out. That was his normal response. It was ingrained in him from childhood. You get upset, you lash out. But not now. Now it was Henrico.

Henrico shook off Hans's hand and said, "No! Why now? He could have had her years ago. He could have come for her." Then Quinn was there, and he knelt down so calmly.

"I understand your anger, lad. I just want you to know, man to man. I didn't know. I never knew I had a daughter. I just found out from Doctor Collier. I didn't know or I would have come sooner."

Emilio knew he had to step in here. This is what they did, he and

Henrico. They took turns being shitheads. It was his turn to be the calm, level headed one for a change. He spoke in Portuguese, because although he was good at understanding English, he sucked at speaking it. It was like his wiring would misfire when he opened his mouth. "Easy, brother. Don't be angry. This is a good thing." Henrico snapped at him. He understood. He was torn down the middle as well. Half of him wanted to cry, and the other half wanted to smash something. Sister Catherine said it was hormones. He didn't know about that, but he knew about being an orphan. Especially one that was getting ready to get tossed out into the adult world with no prospects or money.

"This is good for her. She needs this. We can't protect her when she leaves here. Do you understand? She's almost sixteen. We can't watch over her forever. She's strong. She'll do well when she moves. She just needs this chance. Life for her in the city…you know what it is like. Especially for the young women with no family. To protect her, we have to let her go." He took him by the shoulders. "Henrico, if we love her, we have to let her go." He looked up and Genoveva was there. *Shit.* He hadn't seen her walk up. She met his eyes with confusion and tears. He'd just said way too much, but there was no taking it back. Henrico looked from him to her, and then to Quinn.

The boy said, "You have to treat her well. You have to keep your promises! You have to give her a good life! If you don't, then I'll be a man and I will come and get her! You have to be good to her!"

It was killing Quinn. The idea of harming a hair on his daughter's head or lying to her was unfathomable. But these kids hadn't had his life. They'd been abandoned, abused, or both. "I promise you, Henrico. On my life, I promise you. She will want for nothing. She'll be loved. I have a big family. We will love and protect her."

Hans pulled Henrico into his chest as he finally let go. They were all crying. A mix of misery and happiness. Miserable because Genoveva was the glue. The helper, the big sister, the dependable-to-the-end type of friend that you maybe get one of in a lifetime. She had Rosalis under her arm, comforting her, then she took Emilio's hand. Her arm was still bandaged and discolored, and he took it so gently.

As if the adults knew that this was the time to back off, they disappeared into the background. The older children made a group hug. A circle of trust and love and broken hearts. Cristiano wiped his tears under his glasses as Luca came between him and Henrico, offering what he could for comfort. All of the older children moved in, huddling. They'd always found safety in numbers, but things were changing. The older kids would move on. There wasn't a dry eye in the place.

Raphael wept silently as he watched those kids mourn the loss of each other. He wished he was a rich man. He wished he had a big house with many rooms and lots of beds. All he could do is stay. He could keep coming back every day and help the only way he knew how. Hans clapped him on the back, a blubbering mess right alongside him. "And here I was worried the boys would bust up the place. I think this might be worse."

Antonio chimed in. "Yes, well it is better than drowning your sorrows in wine and easy women."

That made the two military men laugh. "Unfortunately, that may be yet to come. They are going in the army," Hans said. "Army men excel at booze and hussies." They bantered back and forth, trying to concentrate on anything other than having their guts ripped out by these kids. Hans pulled Mary into his side, because she wasn't holding up so well. Cristiano was a soft spot for her. "We won't leave them until they're ready, baby. We'll take turns going back to see the grandkids if we need to, but one of us will always stay. Deal?"

She sniffled. "Deal."

"And if we really need a break, we'll head over to Antonio's vineyard during the harvest and smash some grapes. Take another honeymoon." She smiled and Antonio laughed, and finally the fist in their hearts eased a bit.

CHAPTER 27

PHOENIX, ARIZONA

Liam couldn't believe how fast the time had flown. It seemed like yesterday that they were boarding a flight to Phoenix. They'd found an apartment and Izzy had immediately gone to work. Liam had to suffer the indignity, over the last two months, of going back to medical school. The University of Arizona was giving him the last bit of instruction he needed to be considered worthy of practicing medicine in the United States and in Arizona. Christ, these Americans loved the three *R*s. Rules, regulations, and red tape. The fact that he was being treated like a rookie student instead of a seasoned doctor gave him the scratch. Especially when he got frowns for arguing with instructors, who had never stepped foot out of the state. And poor Izzy was exhausted. With no seniority, her hours were long and undesirable. A lot of night shifts. A lot of gunshot wounds and car wrecks. Even after three months, it was taking a toll, working in the trauma unit of a big city. But they were settling in, making time for each other no matter how much sleep they lost.

The rat race aside, he loved his life. Izzy's family was amazing. Her grandfather had demanded that he learn to ride western style, which he actually really enjoyed. He'd helped tend to the livestock, learned about the cycles of apple and apricot trees from her father. Her family loved him. Izzy's mom kept stuffing him with her roasted green chiles and would send preserves and pies and everything else back home with them when they visited. There were several generations in the area, which is what reminded him so much of his own family in County Clare

As they packed for the trip south, he watched Izzy pad around the modest apartment. They'd filled it with hand-me-down furniture, bought two used cars, and decided to live lean until they were both working. She looked so tired. She'd worked the night shift so that she could have the next three days off. Their wedding was tomorrow. His family was flying in tonight, and would stay at a hotel outside of Wilcox.

"I'll pack the car, love. Just sit and have a cup of coffee. Or take a melatonin and sleep on the way there.

She looked up at him, such tenderness in her eyes. "I really love you. You are so good to me."

He went to her, then, and kissed her softly. Any deeper and he'd be stealing some more of her energy by throwing her down on their bed. "I like taking care of you. I hate that you're working so much."

She gave him a strange look, as if deciding something. "I was thinking I would like to give you your wedding gift early. I mean...It might be a wedding gift."

"It might be? Now I'm intrigued."

She took his hand and brought him to the kitchen table. Then he watched as she took two envelopes out of her computer case. When she sat down next to him, she just took his hand. "Can I ask you something and have your promise that you will be honest with me when you answer?"

"What's this about, Izzy?"

"Are you happy in Arizona?"

He stuttered, not sure what was going on. "Of course. I love you Izzy. I want to be wherever you are. And I love your family. I love our weekends there, when we get to go. Listen, I know I complain a lot about having to take more schooling and about my instructors and all that, but I'll stop. That can't be helping your stress level. I wish I saw you more, and I'm not going to spend the time we do have complaining. I'm sorry, darlin'. Phoenix is fine. I'm happy as long as we're together. I don't care where we live."

Phoenix is fine. Not much of a ringing endorsement. She nodded, deciding something. She took the first envelope, and he recognized the fluid script of Reverend Mother Faith. "I'm not going to read the whole thing, just the part I think you need to hear." So she started reading.

Saint Clare's is not the same without you. Our current surgeon is a skilled professional, but his time here is short. I don't seem to be able to retain anyone for more than a month. Antonio has helped thus far, but has planned an extended holiday in Italy, to return home for a visit.

As for the rest of the hospital, your friend Mary Falk did wonderful work in the two months that she was here, and has actually decided to stay on for the next year with her husband.. We've been blessed with an extended commitment from an infectious disease specialist, who has overseen the Zika trials and vaccination program that Liam started. Dr. Gordon was alarmed to discover, however, that there were two more cases of breast tumors in the outer villages. One in a young mother and one in a middle-aged male. She feels certain that she is close to isolating the cause of this trend, but fears she will not find as gifted a doctor as our Liam to take up where she leaves off. She only has two months left, and fears the research will lay fallow once she is gone. So I continue to pray for God's intervention in this matter. As always, we continue to remember you in our evening prayers, and to be grateful for the time that we had you with us.

Izzy folded the paper and said, "There's more, but that's the part I thought might interest you. Now look me in the eye, Doctor O'Brien, and tell me that you are satisfied taking shit from assholes in that medical school?"

Liam stood, rubbing his beard nervously. "Izzy, we agreed to follow your career. You're a successful surgeon. I'm not going to sabotage..."

She cut him off. "I hate my job!" She looked down, shook her head, breathed a sigh of relief. "There, I said it. I don't like my job. My boss is a dickhead, I hate the hours, we never see each other. I love my family, I like Arizona, but I don't feel like I am in the right place. I tried to be an adult. Settle down and join the commuter grind. I just hate it. Between the Navy and Brazil, I'm ruined for the average Joe lifestyle. I'm not cut out for it. And I don't think that's going to change with time."

He was stunned. It never occurred to him that she felt as out of sorts as he did. She read his face and took the final leap. She shoved the other envelope at him. He opened it and his mouth stayed open for a minute afterward. It was her letter of resignation. In two weeks, she'd be free to walk.

"What are you saying Izzy. Do you want to go back to Brazil?"

She stood up and grabbed his biceps. "I think we should go back to Ireland. We can get day jobs, work a little while, save some money. But yes, I think I do want to go back to Brazil. I miss the kids and the sisters. I miss everyone. Most of all I miss the work, and so do you. You miss your work." She pulled him down for a hard kiss on the mouth, running her hands in his hair. Then she pressed his forehead to hers. "What do you say, Doc? You wanna ditch the profitable salaries, big pharmaceuticals, and high tech equipment for Goliath spiders and Gabriela's cheese bread?"

Liam's smile was her answer. "We'll start packing right after the wedding. We can shack up with family in Ireland until we get settled. The sooner the feckin' better!" Then he picked her up and swung her around. "This is the best wedding gift you could have ever given me."

* * *

Galway, Ireland

Caitlyn and Patrick walked down the hallway of the hospital, with Patrick Jr. in the baby carrier strapped to Patrick's chest. It had been a little over a week since the court date, and they'd spent that week moving out of their apartment and into Mary's house. Now, it was time to see the doctor and come up with a plan for Caitlyn. Caitlyn smiled as she walked into the OBGYN center and saw the big, brawny doctor with the dusty blue eyes, and thick, salt and pepper hair. He opened his arms and she walked into them. "Hello, mam. This must be your man, Patrick." He shook hands with Patrick and took in his face. "You resemble your brother a bit. How's Liam doing? I couldn't go to the wedding."

"Aye, well, it's tomorrow. We weren't comfortable flying that far with this little one. And we've another reason to stay back," Patrick said, smiling warmly at his wife.

Seamus cocked his head, looking at Caitlyn. She said, "Estela. We're finalizing the foreign adoption. She comes in seven days. Right after everyone gets home from the wedding."

Seamus clapped his hands together. "Bloody hell, that's great news. Liam must be over the moon."

She said, "He doesn't know and you can't tell him! We are surprising him. Once she gets here. I'm not sure how. Maybe a video conference. They won't likely be here anytime soon."

"So you haven't heard?" Seamus said. They both looked puzzled. "Izzy's wedding gift. They're moving back to Ireland. They'll be here in two weeks. Apparently the desert air wasn't agreeing with either of them. So, if you think you can sit on that little secret for a week or so, they'll get the surprise of their lives when they show up and find our wee Estela is an O'Brien."

Caitlyn's face was so excited, Patrick thought she would burst. "Oh, we can definitely wait. This is going to be priceless."

"Well, enough about them. Let's go in my office and talk about your future." He led them into an office with a small exam room.

Caitlyn sat next to Patrick as Seamus sat on one of those round, backless stools that doctors rolled around on. He put his cheaters on and said, "I've got your records from the last doctor. I told him you'd relocated. He didn't need to know you were givin' him the push. From what I see, his diagnosis is spot on. That said, his conservative approach didn't leave you a lot of options. So, that's what this is about. Your options. So tell me, Caitlyn," He looked at Patrick, "And Patrick, tell me where you're at. What's been happening? Have you been communicating about what you want? More importantly, have you been using any contraception?"

Caitlyn started. She told him about the fire. His face blanched. Then she explained what happened with Talia and what happened to her own body in the spring. He took his glasses off as she talked, rubbing the bridge of his nose. She was touched to see he was barely keeping his emotions under control. He'd been with the missionaries for over three months. "I'm sorry. I hate to unload all of this on you. I know that village means a lot to you. I just…thought you needed the backstory. I've been lactating ever since. I've been feeding Patrick Jr. since I came home. I haven't had a period. Not in nine months, since I," She swallowed, took a breath. "Since I lost Peter." Seamus's face was so kind, his blue eyes full of compassion. She continued, "I was thinking about what you told me, about the pill helping regulate things. And about the options for a cerclage before or after I conceive. I'm just thinking that with the new baby, maybe I need to take a step back for a while." She looked at Patrick, "Just for a while, until we get settled and get Estela acclimated. Then we can try. I'll go off the pill and we can try."

Seamus was looking at her so strangely. "I must say, lass. You look healthy. Your hair, your skin. You look…stronger. Ye were a bit frail when you came to us. It's good to see."

She smiled, cocking her head. He was grinning like a fool. She looked at Patrick who was narrowing his eyes. Seamus got up abruptly. "Well, before we decide anything about medication, I'd like to get a fresh blood draw. Patrick, can ye tend to the lad while I take her down to the lab? You can stay here where it's quiet. He looks content." Seamus smiled, rubbing a hand on the child's small back, where the fabric of the child carrier fit snuggly to him. "You're a lucky man."

Caitlyn came back about ten minutes later without Seamus. "He said he'd check some things in the lab and come right back. He's acting awfully strange."

They sat for a bit as the baby slept on Patrick's chest. Then Seamus came in with a computer printout. He sat, looked at them both, grinned and just shook his head. "Well, now. What did you two get up to in Brazil?" Caitlyn blushed and Patrick raised a brow.

"I can't put you on the pill, Caitlyn."

"Why not? Is something wrong?"

"Well, no. I don't think so. It depends on your point of view, I suppose. You're pregnant."

Caitlyn sat there stunned, then she looked at Patrick. "I can't be. I haven't gotten a period."

"Well, that doesn't always matter. It likely happened when you started nursing, then they took the child back to the village. You went long periods of time between pumping, I'll wager."

"And she shot out an egg and I caught it," Patrick's face was pure male pride. She gave him a sideways glance, unamused.

"You're not very far along. I'd say maybe a month or so."

Caitlyn thought about that trip with the old woman, across the wishing bridge. "The spring. The tribal mother took us to the spring and told us to…" She stopped, beginning to blush.

"Well, it's not much different than our holy wells, I suppose. Although you don't see the priest leading the couples in for a bath," he said with a smile. "I'm a doctor, but I like to believe in the miraculous. How do you feel?"

She looked at him and thought about lying. Then she just said it. "I'm scared out of my feckin'mind, Seamus. I feel afraid."

He took her hand and met both their eyes. "We are going to get through this. I have a couple of treatment plans to go over with you, and then we'll decide. I will do everything I can to help you hang on until you are full term." Caitlyn let out a little sob. "Don't cry, lass. Ye've got a fine man, here. And you're near family now. It's time to let them help you. You're going to need lots of help with your children and your household. You'll likely have periods of pelvic rest and even full bed rest. I want to meet with Sorcha and come to your home. We're going to arrange the house to limit your activity after your procedure. Do you understand? You can consider yourself on light duty for the next eight months."

Patrick squeezed her hand. "Both our mothers will be there. Sisters, brothers, grannies, and one very pushy niece. She won't lift a finger."

"That's exactly what I wanted to hear. Now, if you are ready, I need to do an exam. Then we'll get you on the schedule for an ultrasound. As for the cerclage, I went over the two options. We can wait and do the stitching at fourteen weeks, or I can place a trans-abdominal cerclage in early in the first trimester. Now, the problem with that is you're already pregnant. I can't go in vaginally. It'll have to be done surgically. Then we'll do a c-section when you come to term."

"Which is safer?" Patrick asked.

"Safer or easier? Honestly, the TAC is more invasive of a procedure. But if you want to significantly increase your chances of holding this child past thirty-five weeks, the success rate is excellent with this device. And it will stay in place. There's no reason she couldn't have more than one child if this works."

Caitlyn spoke then. "I'll do it. I'll have the TAC placed. I'll do whatever I need to do. This pregnancy wasn't planned, but I want it. I also don't want to take the risk of bleeding out when I have two other children to care for. You do what you have to Seamus. We're ready."

He smiled, "All right, I think we have our plan. Now, since I didn't say it before, I'll say it now. Congratulations. With careful planning and some prayers thrown in for good measure, you're going to be a family of five in eight months time."

The tension seemed to dissipate, and Caitlyn couldn't contain the laugh. Pure joy flooded her. "A family of five. Did ye hear that, sweet lad?" She leaned over and kissed the baby's head. "Ye've already got a sibling on the way. We're going to have a baby!"

Wilcox, Arizona

It was early spring in Arizona, a time when the cycles of nature rejuvenated. The temperature was cooler than the summer, but the sun was still warm and shining. Liam looked out over the blossomed orchard rows and smiled at the sight of both of his families. His brothers, Brigid, and Tadgh. All of the grandkids, the wives and Finn, and his grandparents on both sides. Even his cousin Daniel McPherson, the new Mullen in the family. They'd all come to the wedding. It had cost them a fortune, but he knew they wouldn't have missed it for the world. After all the shit he'd put them through, they weren't going to miss the happily ever after.

Izzy's mother had outdone herself. The orchard was beautiful. A farm to table affair among the fragrant smell of apple blossoms. And she'd had her way on the priest, despite the grumblings from Izzy's father. Now his family was tuning up their instruments, ready to start the music.

After an hour of dancing, someone yelled out, "The O'Brien set!" and he laughed as Izzy sprinted to the line of couples. Since only the O'Briens knew how to play it, they'd had to settle for a recording. Still, you didn't mess with tradition. Izzy had long since shed her heels for a pair of Toms. She was lovely in her silk, slip of a dress. It was a simple country wedding, not unlike the weddings they'd had over the years in Doolin. Family, friends, and love. The perfect trio for a happy life.

"Now, Izzy. We talked about this. You've got to behave. There are children at the party. Just watch me if you forget the steps."

She smiled up at him. "Excuse me, I really don't know what you mean. I know how to behave like a lady."

"Izzy," his tone was chiding, but she knew he loved her free spirit.

To her credit, she behaved for the first part. But she'd been too busy at work, and hadn't had enough time to learn it completely. As she started to miss steps, he tried to guide her. Telling her it was okay and to just watch Charlie beside her. Not his girl. Nope. She just started skipping down the line, grabbing people and making up the steps as she went along, making a mess of the whole thing. And no one cared a bit. They laughed and the men in his family swung her around. It was, he reflected, the most beautiful thing he'd ever seen.

As the evening went on, his heart was so full, he felt sure that it was sticking out of his chest. The only absence was Patrick and Caitlyn. They were caring for a newborn, finally out of the perilous weeks of prematurity. He was thriving and loved, and they were together. That was the most important thing. Liam's heart did a little somersault as he stood up to the microphone. Someone yelled, "Toast!" He laughed, because the apricot schnapps was catching up with his siblings. "I would love to make a toast. Charge your glasses!"

After some boisterous enthusiasm and passing around of the schnapps and apple cider, he said, "We've already spoken to Izzy's family, so I thought it was time to bring the O'Brien side in on our latest development." He winked at his wife. "Anyone who knows the two of us is likely aware of some impulsivity issues." Laughter rumbled through the group. "Izzy and I have decided that although we love Wilcox and living near the Collier family, we've not settled into the rat race of Phoenix." He watched as his mother clapped her hand over her mouth. "So, Mam, ye best get the guest room ready for an extended stay, because we're moving back to Ireland." His grin was a mile wide and the group flipped into chaos. Sorcha ran up to him and flung her arms around his neck. He picked her up like she weighed nothing. "I'm coming home, Mam. At least for a while." She kissed his face and smoothed the hair off his brow. "Then back to St. Clare's?"

"Aye, then back."

"Well, now. I can't let you have all the fun. Maybe they'll need an extra mid-wife for a month or two."

He pulled her in for another hug. "Christ, Mam. If you come to St. Clare's, you'll make me a happy man. I'd love that. Jesus, I would really love that."

"All right, but for now, let's get back to the party and spend some time with this beautiful family." She looked around the absolutely gorgeous setting. The apple trees shed petals, like large, soft snowflakes. "Ye married well, mo chrói. I think your grandda's ready to import the apple jack to Belfast." She smiled warmly. "I'm a happy woman, Liam. Another son who's settled down and found his mate."

Then Sean approached. "Are ye done monopolizing my bride? I need a dance." Liam smiled as he watched his mother's face light up. His father's eyes were so full of love and affection as he drew her to him for a dance. The love between them had been a lifelong inspiration, and his heart was full as he searched the group for his own wife.

CHAPTER 28

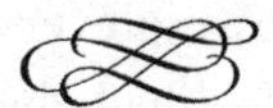

MANAUS, BRAZIL—ONE WEEK LATER

The entirety of St. Clare's was in the cantina, and the mood was solemn. They were losing two of their precious daughters today. Reverend Mother faith looked into the angelic face of their sweet Estela and wanted to weep. Wanted to hold her and never let her go. It was like the heaven's had shone down on their little home on the day the child was born. She knelt down and Estela came to her.

"Did I ever tell you about the day you were born?" The girl was sucking her thumb, not sure how to feel about this turn of luck. About leaving the only home she'd ever known for a beautiful family all her own. She shook her head. The abbess sat and tucked her in beside her. She was speaking in Portuguese, because the child was small and still learning English.

"Well, now. I was sitting in the hospital, inside of the birthing room. Your mother had been very ill. She was alone, you see, except for a sister who had to work and couldn't be with her. So I held her hand as she labored. She came to us, I think, instead of the other hospital, because she knew we'd care for you. I prayed for a miracle. I asked God to intervene, because the doctors feared they'd lose you both. I was by a window, and all of a sudden the birds stopped singing in the garden. It was so still, it startled me. Then the clouds separated and a bright beam of sunlight burst through the window of your mother's room. She reared up and pushed with everything she had, and then you were there. This little bundle crying and wiggling like a new puppy." Estela grinned at that. "When you took a breath, gaining your strength for another row, I heard the birds in the garden. They were rejoicing. Your mother's love was all over her face. We lost her, my sweet girl, but she didn't leave until she'd delivered us our miracle. Our Estela. You've been a blessing every day since then, to everyone here. And you don't have to feel bad about going away. You're in our hearts. It is time for you to go and be a miracle to a new family. A family who has hurt, and has needed you so desperately. Don't be afraid."

She looked up and realized that Genoveva was listening, her eyes conflicted and sad. She stood and took the girl in her arms. "You are my bright and shining star. You have given us such a gift the past seven years. All of us, but most especially the other children. Like a guardian. A quiet and steady leader and big sister. Now you must go, my child, and take your place with your family. They've missed too much, and our gain was their loss. It grieves me to part with you, but I prayed for it just as much. A safe place for you to land."

* * *

Shannon, Ireland

The family milled around the luggage claim area of the Shannon airport. Brigid was a live wire. "They've landed. Why can't they just open the feckin' plane door and let them out!"

"Brigid, please don't drop the f-bomb in front of Sister Agatha. She's a gentle soul." Patrick gave his sister a chiding look. They were all ready. After they'd returned two days ago, Patrick and Caitlyn had sprung the news about Estela. Sorcha almost had a seizure. Now Sean was next to him, a warm smile on his face. His father wore his happiness more quietly than Patrick's mother, but he was a man of deep feeling.

Cora squealed, "They're starting the luggage carousel. That means they're coming! Right, Da? That means they're coming!" Cora was a sweet, sensitive child. Part Finn, and part Brigid in that spunky, no-nonsense way. Finn and Brigid had talked about extending the trip to America to take the kids to Disney World. A trip Cora had been campaigning for relentlessly for about three years. But they'd been stunned when she said, "No. We must go home. Something exciting is about to happen." She hadn't been able to pinpoint what. The dream she'd had wasn't detailed. It had been an overwhelming sense of excitement. Some sort of new beginning. She didn't know what, but she was adamant that they not miss it.

Patrick was starting to bob back and forth on his feet, his father giving him an amused look like he'd done when he was a lad. The look that said, *stop fidgeting*.

Caitlyn had the baby in a pram, sound asleep. They both wanted their arms free for this. As the crowd started down the hall to the arrivals area, she saw Quinn first. "Oh my God! It's Quinn and Genoveva!" Then as they drew near, she made out the small figure of Sister Agatha. She was smiling so broadly, her eyes glistening. Between them, holding her hand and Genoveva's, was Estela. She was looking frantically, searching the crowd of faces for her new parents. She looked a little unsure of the situation. Then she locked eyes on Patrick, and she burst into a run.

"Papai!" Patrick took long strides and swooped in to pick her up. Then Caitlyn was next to him, throwing her arms around them both. Caitlyn was speaking through great, heaving sobs. "I can't believe it. Oh, God. We did it. I can't believe you're here." She pulled in Genoveva for a hug and then Quinn. "I'm so glad you traveled together. Thank you." She kissed Quinn and then threw her arms around the little, novice nun. "Thank you, Sister Agatha. Oh, thank you." Everyone was overjoyed. Caitlyn's parents and Sean and Sorcha moved in slowly, having agreed not to overwhelm the girl. Branna, Brigid, and Charlie were being restrained by their husbands, ready to bum rush the group to get their hands on the latest O'Brien niece.

Patrick turned to his mother, and her face was soaked with tears. "Estela, don't be frightened. Remember the pictures I showed you?"

Estela had her head on his shoulder, sucking her thumb. She gave Sorcha a shy smile.

"Hello, sweet girl." Sorcha brushed the tears off her chin. Sean leaned in behind her. "I'm your granny."

Estela took her measure, weighing how close she wanted to get. Then she took a small hand and reached out to touch Sorcha's auburn hair. She took the thumb out and said softly, "Granny." Sorcha kissed her hand. "Yes, and your Grandda Sean. We've been waiting to meet you." Patrick's face was trembling with the effort of not breaking down. Sean said, "Dia duit, sweet lass. Welcome home."

* * *

Doolin, Ireland

Gus O'Connor's was packed to the gills with locals, shoving the early spring tourists out and off to McDermotts by hanging a sign that said, *Private Party*. Izzy and Liam were on their way from the Dublin airport, Seany and Josh having retrieved them. "They're close. He's parking!" Everyone acted with as much nonchalance as they could, given the epic surprise they were sitting on. The whole town was there to welcome the newlyweds. Having told them that it was a "second reception" since they'd had the gall to get married in America. The doorbell jingled as Seany led the party of four. Everyone cheered as Liam and Izzy came into the pub. The music started, and the pints were pouring. There were small gift bags lined up on a table, helping them start their new household in Ireland, albeit a temporary one.

Caitlyn approached Liam, carrying her son. Liam's face melted. "He's a handsome lad, isn't he?" He looked at her, Izzy by his side, and his eyes softened. "You're a mam, Caitlyn. Ye've made us all so happy." He palmed her head and kissed it, trying to choke down his overwhelming emotions. "I'm sorry I missed you, but it seems St. Clare's was just what you needed." He kissed baby Patrick next. "It's the best present you could have given us. A new nephew." Then he touched her abdomen. "And another one on the way."

She smiled at that. Izzy said, "I told you that spring was legit.

Good for you, sister. You are actually glowing. You look radiant." They hugged and Caitlyn wiped a tear that had escaped from one eye.

"Yes, well. We've got one more present for you. It was hard to keep a secret, but I think you're going to love it." Liam cocked his head and Izzy raised a brow. They looked up as the crowd parted. She put a gentle hand on Liam's forearm. "We will actually be a family of five, deartháir," She moved aside and Patrick appeared. "I'd like you to meet our daughter."

Liam and Izzy stood completely dumfounded for about five seconds, then Izzy burst into tears. Weeping with the full force of the ugly cry. Snot and hiccups and wailing. Liam dropped down on one knee. "Oh my God," he choked out. His chin trembled and he couldn't hold back the tears. "Oh, my wee lass. Oh, my darlin' come give your Uncle Liam a hug."

She ran to him, finally satisfied that he'd been sufficiently surprised. She threw her arms around him and he fell on his bum, just clutching her and crying. Then he yanked his brother down on the floor with them, hugging and thanking him while fighting complete hysterics. It was the most emotion they'd seen from him in years. Maybe in forever. Completely undone by his happiness. "So I take it you like your present?" Patrick smiled, wiping his nose.

"Oh, aye. More than I ever dared wish for. Another O'Brien niece." He laughed, an edge of hysteria in his voice. He looked at Estela. "You're an O'Brien, my sweet. You're an O'Brien!" Then Izzy was on her knees, kissing Estela on every inch of her face. She looked up at Caitlyn who was watching the display with utter joy. "Well done, sister. Well done."

* * *

Caitlyn walked the green expanse, feeling the grass give way to pebbles. Patrick had gone ahead, giving her a minute to herself. She held the little urn in her hands, and she felt her parents' eyes on her as they watched from their back garden. They'd decided it was best for them to do this alone. Just she and Patrick and the children. It was too hard, otherwise.

It was in that moment when the sea air filled her nostrils, and she felt the small rocks under her feet, that she was overcome with a sense of déjà vu. Then she realized why. Her dream. Oh, God. There he was. Facing the water, holding the hand of a small child, and another child in the crook of his arm. This was her dream. This exact moment that had played over in her mind so many times while she slumbered. It had finally come to pass.

She felt the small weight of the urn in her hands as it rested on the small swell of her belly. Peter, the child who'd broken her heart. She couldn't take her eyes off of her husband. He was poised at the shore, their two children staring out across the sea. The children that had healed her broken heart, when she was sure she'd never be happy again. It was a fitting place to set their baby's ashes adrift. He'd dust the Irish coast, forever a part of the elements where the sea met the earth. His native land where both Patrick and Caitlyn had grown up. They'd never walk this shoreline and not think of him. She approached and Patrick turned to her. "Are you ready, love?"

She nodded. "Yes, I am. I'm ready to set him free."

EPILOGUE

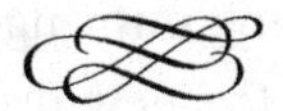

Caitlyn's house was filled to bursting with females. There were extra beds made up, cots, linens and pillows on the sofa, and bed rolls on the floor for the smaller girls. Patrick was headed out the front door when Caitlyn shoved one more thing in the diaper bag. "Caitlyn, love, that's enough. It's only one night. Go get back in that bed!"

She kissed her son again, leaning over to accommodate her swelling belly. "Are you sure you don't want to just leave him?"

Patrick looked aghast. "He is not staying with a house full of women. We've got the men waiting. You don't want him to lose all his dude points, do you?" She put her hands on her hips. "We agreed, hen. Girls sleep here, the men go to Ma and Da's. He'll be fine. It's a ten minute drive. You can't be hogging the baby all to yourself. It's Da and son night. No chicks allowed."

She gave him a crooked smile. "Just make sure he stays dry. He hates a wet bum. And if he needs me, then…"

"Goodbye, hen. We love you." Then he got on one knee. "Estela, love. Come give your da and your brother a kiss goodnight." She ran from the living room, wrapping her arms around his neck. "I love you, my sweet girl. Take care of your mammy, okay?"

Estela nodded. "I love you too, daddy." Patrick's smile lit up his face. Then with a swift kiss on her baby brother's cheek, she ran back to the mass of cousins.

Caitlyn watched as Patrick left with the baby, blowing them kisses from the doorway. Then she turned and had to laugh at the spectacle in her home. Genoveva, Halley, and Cora were on the floor with Estela, going through Disney movies for the evening viewing. Her mother and Sorcha were laying out finger foods while Granny Aiofe put the finishing touches on the new dress she'd been sewing for the baby.

A girl. Jesus and his Saints. She was having a girl. They were like unicorns in this family, but she was getting another girl. The dress Aoife was sewing was newborn sized. Impossibly small and lovely. Pink seersucker with a watermelon collar, just like Estela's second hand dress that she'd bought her in Brazil. She'd found the retro pattern in a collection of vintage Butterick patterns that had been scanned on-line. Estela was over the moon at the idea of being a big sister. At the orfanato, she'd always been the youngest.

Caitlyn was led back to the bedroom by Izzy, having been given her twenty minutes out of bed. After the cerclage had been placed, she'd been restricted the first two trimesters. Now she was in the third. The home stretch, as it were, and she was having early contractions. So Seamus had ordered her to spend the last trimester on bedrest. She got twenty minutes, four times a day. She could walk and do light housework. The housework never happened. Her parents had hired a cleaning lady as soon as she'd been put on restriction. But she could play outside with her children. She could swing Estela and carry her son for that short time, four times a day, and then she'd be ordered back to a chaise lounge or bed. The summer was in full swing, and they'd decided to do this shindig in order to cheer her up. She hated being confined.

Charlie came into the bedroom behind them, and she laughed at the sight of her noshing on a plate full of food. Charlie was six months along, her belly already protruding impressively because she was so small.

"What? I need my iron. It's for the baby," she shrugged as she took another bite. Charlie loved to eat, and right now she was walking with a plate underneath a large steak that she'd speared with a fork. She was tearing bites off of it like a barbarian. The girl liked her red meat.

Katie came in behind her. "Aye, she's feeding my first grandson. Give her all she likes." They didn't know for sure that it was a boy. They wanted to be surprised, but Katie was sure it was a boy. Charlie smiled and leaned in for a kiss on the cheek. Tadgh and Josh were at the O'Brien homestead, filled to bursting with the O'Brien men, as well as Finn, Daniel, and Quinn. Aidan and Alanna had taken the ferry from Liverpool yesterday, and Alanna was currently rocking in the chair next to Caitlyn's bed, holding Isla who had passed out from the excitement. Alanna was also expecting, only she wasn't showing yet. Davey had gone with his Da to be with the men. Caitlyn smiled at Katie. "Why have we never done this before? It's grand altogether."

They eventually all settled in the living room, women piled two at a time in the recliners and the large sectional sofa that Hans had bought to replace Mary's dainty sofa and chair. Caitlyn had her feet on her mother's lap, propped up with pillows behind her back. "Sorcha, Katie, please come and sit. Ye've done enough. The dishes can wait."

Katie and Sorcha squeezed on to the far end of the sectional, cuddled together like sisters. "It's good to have us all together, isn't it?" She palmed Izzy's head where she sat on the floor at her feet, fingering her loose curls. "All of our girls in one place."

Aoife smiled at that. "It seems like just a day ago that you two were running around in your corduroy trousers and platform shoes, pretending for all the world like you weren't head-over-heels for my William and Sean." Sorcha and Katie giggled like school girls. Aoife said wistfully, "Time goes by in a flash. Now I've got three more great grandchildren on the way." She laughed, "My goodness, how my boys chased after you. Ye didn't make it easy, but I knew. That bone deep knowing when ye find your kindred sisters or daughters. You know each other, don't you? Ye feel it just as powerfully as ye feel it when you've found your mate."

Sorcha smiled at that, her eyes misting. "Yes, Aoife. It's just like that."

Branna spoke then. "You know...you've got us all here. Maybe it's time to stop with the teasers and give it up. Won't you tell us about meeting Sean and William? I think you've made us wait long enough."

Katie and Sorcha exchanged looks. Sorcha said, "Well, now Katie. What do you say? Are they old enough to hear our secrets?"

Katie cocked her head, "I don't know. There's children about." She winked at Sorcha as the women all started with the pleading.

Brigid immediately began shoving the youngest into the bedroom, sweeties and bags of crisps and Disney blue-rays shoved at them before shutting the door. She swept her hands together at a job efficiently done. Then she gave them an expectant look. "No excuses, now. Let's have it all."

"Alright, alright. So, sister, would you like to start or shall I?" Katie said with a mischievous grin.

Sorcha gave a wry smile, "Well, let's see. It was early autumn in 1978..."

AUTHOR NOTES AND AKNOWLEDGEMENTS

I would like to first thank my readers. This book has been planned for a while. Since I wrote Shadow Guardian, actually. My vision solidified after I wrote River Angels. When Caitlyn's story came to me, it broke my heart. When I released book 4, I was surprised by the response from some of my readers. Several women reached out to me who had lost a child or multiple children due to miscarriage, and also women who struggled with infertility. Other women contacted me who had, with loving partners, chosen to adopt children. They wanted to hear Caitlyn's story, and I wanted to tell it.

My mother is one of my first readers for every book. She gets that ugly rough draft that I refuse to let anyone else read. One night on the phone, we had a talk about the child that she lost. She's given me permission to share her story. She'd been quite far along in her pregnancy, entering the third trimester, when she suffered a catastrophic placental detachment. It almost killed her, both in body and soul, to lose the baby that would have been my older brother. She was so weak, she didn't even get to see him before they took him away forever. My father did get to see him, and he walked that crucible alone.

She told me that she was very happy that I had allowed Caitlyn to be by Patrick's side to say goodbye to their son together, and it brings me to tears to even think about my twenty-three year old mother suffering such a loss. And to think about my father making arrangements for their baby, while trying to give my mother a reason to get out of bed and keep living.

So this book is for her, and for you. All of you strong, brave women who have suffered your own heartaches in the pursuit of motherhood. And it's for your partners, who stood by helplessly and suffered those losses and pains with you.

I know there were a lot of irons in the fire with this book, but I thought it was about time we checked up on everyone. Their lives are changing, and they had stories to tell you, and we needed to tie up those loose ends with the children at St. Clare's. This story was about family. Patrick and Caitlyn couldn't have done it without the enduring love and support of the O'Brien Clan and also Caitlyn's wonderful family. This was more than a romance tale, for me, and I hope you understood that while you read it. I shed a lot of tears writing this book, but as with all my tales, we'll get our happy ending.

As for the ending...well, sometimes you have to go back in order to move forward. Coming soon, we'll travel back to 1978 to see war-torn Belfast through the eyes of a twenty-three year old nursing student named Sorcha Mullen. As well as her unlikely collision with a young Garda officer and his brother, Sean and William O'Brien. The prequel ***No Borders: An O'Brien Tale*** will be released this coming winter. Along with a new novella that will remain a mystery for now. Sorry, a girl has to have some secrets.

Made in the USA
Las Vegas, NV
24 June 2023